Saving Grace

An Ecology Romance

Featuring

Ward Thomas

New Edition

S C HAMILL

Earth Angel Book Media

CONTENTS

QUOTE:

"Biological diversity is messy. It walks, it crawls, it swims, it swoops, and it buzzes. But extinction is silent, and it has no voice other than our own.

Paul Hawken

ACKNOWLEDGMENTS

Thanks, and gratitude to everyone involved who provided their encouragement and support who were also driven slightly mad by the writing of this book.

My parents Margaret and Clifford.

My children Thomas & Louise

My sister Amy & my dear brother, John.

Special thanks to the wonderfully talented singing sisters;
Catherine & Lizzy that are:

WARD THOMAS

Special thanks to Stephen Foster from

HARLAN COUNTY CAMPGROUND CABINS & KAYAKING
Of Putney, Kentucky. For his factual input, help and advice.

Special thanks also to **Robert W Causey** of Mayapple.net for the beautiful back cover photograph.

Thanks also to the good people of Harlan County whose solid hardworking character & gritty determination in life gave me the idea in the first place.
Thank you all for your time, patience & grace.

**Very, very special thanks to Maria Tamayo
for loving me.**

ONE: *The Skoolhouse*

"The marriage is over and done... its back's broken and its dead in the water Page... and what's more, I'm getting the hell outta the hock starting right now!" Eden retorted as they walked into the bar and she headed for an empty tall stool at its far corner. "Hey mister bartender," she shouted banging hard on top of the counter. "Can we get some water of life over here sir...? I'm celebrating being a single woman again. Amelia, what's your poison honey?"

"Oh, come on now, don't be saying stupid things like that," Page squawked feeling her feathers ruffled as Eden blatantly blanked her sister and waited for Amelia's reply.

"I'll be taking a big ass beer Eden, because I'm a looking for some hot girl fun tonight." She quipped in her Harlan county twang, concentrating hard into a cosmetic mirror and glossing her gills with fire-engine red lipstick and swishing her long black locks out of the way.

"Hey, have you cut your hair short to look like me Page?"

"Your hair's long Amelia... whatever do you mean?" She sniffed, completely puzzled but still looking at Eden.

"If I gave your ass a motorcycle, you'd look straight outta dykes on bikes," she grinned.

Page blatantly ignored Amelia's sarcasm and continued to look at her younger sister secretly jealous of her slim figure and natural way. "You can save your marriage Eden, it's not as if he's slept with every woman in

Kentucky.... and I don't want fighting-talk whiskey, and you shouldn't either. You know it boils your blood, and you're a roomful of angry as it is. Get me a Merlot or Pinot Grigio, if they got such a thing, in this second-rate dive," she stuffily replied looking down her nose on the room decor and its working-class folk, as if she was somewhat higher class.

"Oh... a Merlot or a Grigio.... oh, how simply divine darling? Pah! I shoulda guessed, how darn typical... you two-buck wine snob. You got champagne tastes on lemonade money," she implied shaking her head. "You got your nose so high in the air, you'd drown in a rainstorm," Eden replied in a high-faluted mocking tone, pretentiously throwing her head into the air to mimic her older sister. She flicked her hand through her long curly red locks and grabbed the barman's attention fully. "Hi honey, do me a double whiskey and water, a white, smarty-pants wine, whatever you lay your hands on," she whispered. "And a cold beer sir. But make mine a nice sweet double malt with ice, I wanna treat me really bad, and that's allowed since I ain't been out for over ten God-damn months," she confirmed loudly for her sister's benefit, charging him into action.

"Hey, angry heads, stop being so damn nasty! We're supposed to be having a good time tonight," Amelia claimed, puckering her lips and finishing off her lipstick duties.

"Halleluiah to that Em, I guess at least somebody's listening to me for once," she agreed to her friend and glaring at her sister again. "Shoot! You just don't have a clue Page, I just don't get you're stupid thinking sometimes. Now you just go ahead and stop for a second and listen to your crap. You're my older kin, and I'm supposed to look up to you and follow your lead. Learn by your example and you gotta look out for me... steer me from the bad stuff, you get it...?" She paused. "I thought we was tight... I thought we was so much closer. You ain't never got my back and hell, I told you so many times he's hit me. You were my first port of call... my one confidant. If I'd told Mom or Pop 'bout all of Kyle's crap, he'd of had him hung, drawn and castrated.

"I think you should have told them way back Eden," Amelia chipped in.

"Mom'd just kill him straight out. You're taking his side yet again, just like you always have Marks. Kyle's a whoring liar and hell, if he can hit a woman, he ain't even a man, and that goes for Mark too," she fumed.

"I'm not taking sides Eden, all I'm saying is ask yourself do you still love him and is it worth another chance. And as for watching out for you, you're a grown woman not a little girl no more," she maintained in her fake refined tone, fiddling incessantly in her bag as the barman placed the drinks in front of them.

"Right, that's it... time ladies, enough already!" Amelia interrupted. "You'd better stop this damn bitching and bickering and start getting your cracked heads together before I get back," she derided. "Cos I ain't sitting here, bored outta ma tree all the night long, listening to you two a-holes, some ways tearing strips from each other. Now you just listen to me real-good," she rasped anxiously standing up and wiggling her voluptuous chest and frowning like an angry dog left in a car. "I'm going for a cigarette and to powder my bits... and there ain't no law about that either Page Buckley... I mean all my bits, cos I'm looking for getting some lady-eeeeee action tonight, and no amount of your BS fighting is gonna stop me," she crowed, openly pulling down on her tight top and re-positioning her ridden black pencil skirt back into place as Eden watched openly smiling.

"I'm glad you pulled them things down honey, we could see clear through to the promised land and your religion," she teased.

"Oh, shut up Eden... don't make me self-conscious... I know my clothes are too small. Fact is, I'm just getting a far too fat ass for my own liking," she conceded, yanking hard at her red blouse that was leaving nothing to the imagination then frantically shaking her shoulders making her huge gold earrings smack against her cheeks. "I'm too damn chubby. Now you listen to auntie Em, baby doll," she whispered flicking her long black hair over her shoulders and leaning forward on Eden's arm. "You know I wasn't Kyle's biggest fan when you gotten hitched honey. That isn't that I'm advocating him or his ways, or any other God damn SOB man's either," she said pointing her index finger at Eden. "Cos as far as this pretty lady is concerned, all of their asses are a whole space of waste. I can get a full engine service and my suds bubbled just fine without their kind," she brassily retorted to Eden's laughter. "Oh, and as for you Page, I'm disappointed with your crabby hashing," she claimed loudly crossing her arms and leaning backwards as a few of the patrons tried to secretly zero-in on her words. "You stick with your sister's heart and her decision, whatever it may be. That's a given girl," she encouraged, slamming her stiletto heel hard against the wooden floor. "Are you hearing me...? That's just what you're supposed to do... so you just go right on down and do it girl. You're both unbelievable," she proclaimed. "It's actually incredible!" She clamped her hands tightly on her hips and swayed back on her heels. "He's got you both at each other's throats and he isn't even here? He'd be lovin' every spoonful of this badness if he knew, that's for sure," she lectured, standing head and shoulders tall and shaking her head. She looked around, clenched her jaw then leaned forward to get close between their ears, then put a hand on each of them making her big backside stick out to greet the quiet, amalgamated, and whispering heads. "Now when I get back, I want this arguing crap put to bed or I'm gone. As for you baby doll... stop actin' all hissy fit with a tail end on," she motioned to silent Eden. Page and her sister continued to look daggers at each other but sat deathly silent, as they watched Amelia animatedly walk away. Obstreperously flaunting all her wares for all and sundry. The barman disappeared and the sisters automatically cogged up another gear.

"We'll that's what it feels like to me Page, you're all for him and dead against me," she raged. "And as for do I *LOVE* him? I *HATE* him! He is not the same man any more. He's not the *good* man I married. Maybe he was never *good* to start with," she explained pulling her long red hair into place. "Perhaps it was all part of the big show he put on for everyone's benefit. Maybe he's always been bad inside," she theorized. "All I know is, he changed for the worse. He's a twisted chameleon and a leopard that'll never change its spots," she surmised sipping on her whiskey as the barman walked past again. "He's a hurtful son of a bitch that dines with the Devil. Do you know he's put a claim on the house? Our house," she badgered waiting for a reaction from her sister as Pages eyes widened. She unfolded her arms, then pulling her white blouse down over her burgeoning stomach as her eyes rolled at the startling news.

"Yeah Page, that's right... our house. The one given to us by Pape," she said waiting again for any kind of reply. "The same house Langdon Dainty's tryna get his hands on with Eminent Domain law. So, I got two evil asses tryna take away the place I made my home. The damn coal company might even be on Dainty's side too. It was their land after all. Shucks... as if they haven't done enough damage over the years. Mercy me!"

"Who the hell is Langdon Stanley Dainty, Eden?" Page asked in confusion.

"Who is Dainty? God Damn it! That question tells me exactly how much you listen to me," she decried shaking her head. "I told you all about the fat son of a bitch on the phone over two weeks ago. He wants all the houses on Coal Cut lane flattened to build the highway 1-75 link road."

"Oh erm, I was under the weather when you told me," Page inferred looking for the easiest excuse.

"Under the weather my ass. It's your house as much as it's mine. Kyle's name ain't even on the deeds, its Pape's name, and yours and mine. The crazy fool is pissing in the breeze with that but hey, that isn't the damn point. It just shows what he's capable of the low down... aargh!" She took a deep breath and sighed to calm herself sown. "He would sooner see his own son homeless just to feed his drinking and womanizing ways. He makes me so mad. So mad, that I made sure he was served with the divorce papers two weeks ago. So, as I said, the marriage is over and there's nothing you or him or anyone else can do about it. *D.I.V.O.R.C.E* just like sweet old Tammy Wynette said," she explained singing the tune of the song as her sister worked out a reply.

"Wait a minute, Eden! Just think about what you're saying, please. And think about it properly. You have little Jamie to consider here," she advised still not thinking it out thoroughly.

"What did I just tell you Page? You still haven't listened to a damn word have you? It's too late, and it's all over," she retorted narrowing her eyes as she picked up her glass and slugged hard at her whiskey. "And don't you dare bring my son into this either. Jamie's the reason I'm doing it."

9

"People change Eden, everything changes. Kyle could change. You gotta change with them and make allowances. Do you remember your vows; for better or for worse?"

"Allowances? Allowances my ass! Oh, my, oh my... you'd sure make a damn good politician Page," she said nodding and clapped her hands to mock her sister. "That statement makes about as much sense as tits on a bull!" she fumed. "You're talking crap, and you know it. And don't you dare make right what he's done or try using the Lord's words against me. I knew my vows and I understood their virtue when I said them. They we're sacred to me, and now they're nothing but tainted with him with his man-on-the-make drinking ways and beating me bad. Yes, he beat me black and blue, Page. Even when I was pregnant. Those vows mean nothing to me. You hear me, Page... nothing!" She cursed, sighing to herself and hanging her head as she paused to take a breath. "They mean nothing next to diddly squat," she raged glugging hard at her whiskey as her rant got more and more Harlan county sounding the angrier she raged.

"They didn't mean for better or worse, or for blacker or bluer, Page. For bitcher or whorer?" She asked at Pages face, toking another swig of whiskey. "Pah, what a bad joke. They are not the words I spoke. How about; in sickness from the belts... is that good... huh Page? Does that fit the bill better?" She shouted throwing a *'hate-you'* face at her sisters shocked eyes. "You know what, Page, dollars to donuts, I swear they were the vows you took with Mark. But they sure weren't mine," she snarled.

"No! Now, that's just horrible," Page protested, clearing her throat and biting her fingernails then quickly glancing around the room as if every person in the bars eyes and were attuned to Eden's voice.

"None of that is true, Eden. You're acting like a *poor-me*."

"Huh? Acting like a *poor-me*? Is that so?" Eden replied recoiling in her chair. "And I guess you'd call an Alligator a lizard you, stupid fool! You're plain deluded, Page," Eden said quietening her mouth to think. "Mmm... I'm a poor-me, huh...? Well, I bet you declare that to your holier-than-thou ass every time Mark punches you up and down the stairs."

"He's never punched me around the house, how dare you insin____"

"Insinuate? Is that the word you're looking for?" She snapped. "The next thing I know, you'll be calling me pedantic," she replied drinking the last of her whiskey and then slammed the empty glass down on the bar so hard, the whole bar-room went silent.

The bartender spun his head around to give Eden an appropriate frown as Page remained formally silent as Eden impatiently scraped her glass along the uneven bar surface to get the barman's attention. She lifted her glass in the air, smiled and then and shook it from side-to-side as he angrily approached.

"You were always top of the class at big words Page. You swallowed a God-damn dictionary when we were kids, but you're still completely useless at common sense. Useless of affairs of the heart and the good and the right. Fact is.... you should have just choked on the damn dictionary," she scolded as the barman appeared right in front of her.

"Hey mister. Yes, that's right, more whiskey. You catch on quick, unlike my dumb ass sister. Set em up again, sweet-cheeks and make mine a double-double this time. P l e a s e." The bartender reached blindly behind himself, keeping his eyes firmly trained on Eden and picked up a bottle of whiskey.

"Ok, Page. So, let me get this straight in my head, once and for all." Eden said wetting her lips and going in for the kill:

"I'm sorry... *slap*, I do... *slap*, apologize... *slap*," she goaded her sister, hitting her own wrist at the same time. "That was a poor choice of words... *slap*... stupid old me. Not when he's punching you. When he's SLAPPING your ass all over the house. Can you hear this people," she shouted, standing up and glancing around the crowded room with her finger pointing down at the bowed head of her sister? "Physical and mental marital-abuse right here! And don't you dare deny it girl. I've seen you caked with make-up to cover the bruises and hiding behind your sunglasses:

"Hi, I'm Page Buckley and I enjoy nothing more than hanging from my ceiling as a human punch-bag!" She said, mimicking her sister's snobby voice. "What bull-crap you talk. And you stay with him and you take

it? You're a damn tragic comedy of a woman, and a self-torturous fool. Do you honestly think I'm as stupid as you?"

Page did nothing but sat deathly silent and looked away as Eden impatiently waited for an answer, then angrily banged down her glass.

"If brains were leather, you wouldn't have enough to saddle a June-bug! Hell, I bet there's a tree stump in a Louisiana swamp with more brains than you," she shrilled as Page's head sank lower. "Even the kids have told me what he does to you," she explained as Page suddenly looked up. "Oh, yes. You'll look at me now, won't you? Aaron told me Mark picked him up off the floor and raised his fist to his face," she stormed. "They rang me up crying their little hearts out, Page. They we're both scared out of their wits in case Mark or you found out they'd told me. You're living a bad and sad hollow existence of denial and fear, and I am not going to end up like that Page. I refuse to end up like you. I will not! I swear on my child's life, you hear me. NEVER!" She screamed.

"Keep your voice down Eden, you're embarrassing me."

"Me embarrassing you? You, don't need any help on that score, miss posh-ass. Living a life like you, IS living a lie. You embarrass yourself just fine on your own," she snapped. "Shall I tell you what I want Page. I want to be healed. I want to be saved, in love and happy. I have been missing the rapture this whole time. I want to feel whole and loved again. That will never happen with him by my side, with him around me, or with him anywhere near. Or with you, sitting there like you know everything and trying make me paper over the cracks," she whispered as she took pages hand and the barman returned:

"Well butter my butt and call me a biscuit, thank you honey," she said to him, smiling and changing the mood. She nodded and thanked him as he put down her glass, noticing a young woman who seemed a little more interested in the situation than she should be.

"What the hell are you looking at, missy?" Eden grimaced, quizzing the dyed blonde girl who was now looking away as she waited for the barman to serve her. "Are you enjoying listening to my grief and my sad ass pain? Oh, I'm such a sorry-assed drunken single mother, aren't I? Eden asked as if that was what the young girl was thinking. "If you keep on staring at me, I'll give you something you can be sad about. Do you want some of my personal pain? I make it to order, right here. It's free too," she said lifting up her clenched fist. "I'll slap you to sleep, then slap you for sleeping," she cursed taunting the fear-faced teenage girl.

"Eden, stop it, right now! That's not fair. Leave her be and stop taking your personal baggage out on her," Page interjected, feeling her sister wasn't being fair, but feeling more than thankful she, herself was out of the firing line.

"She's looking at me like she's seen a whole world of life. The girl hasn't seen nothing yet, Page," Eden explained turning back to face the girl. "Not saying anything, huh? Has the cat got your tongue?" She questioned picking up her drink. "Stop judging me or this cat will have its claws dug in you in a second," she purred, waiting for any kind of reply. "Good. So, keep this zipped and keep that out," she motioned pointing at her own nose and mouth feeling bad about her own crass behaviour. "Sorry honey, but you don't even know your own ass from a hole in the ground yet, so just order your drink and disappear like a good little girl," Eden motioned her dismissal with quick a wave of her wrist.

"Hey, and don't you be going far with that whiskey bottle, mister bartender," she shouted across the room. "This glass right here has an empty heart to fill, so it's gonna need filling up all the time. Hey, why don't you save yourself a heck of trouble and leave the bottle right here?" She asked, winking at him as he returned and leant across the bar and close to her face. "I'll take good care of it. In fact, it's a nice place you got here mister, what's it called again?" She asked realising he was angrier than she thought and she was being a little more than a handful.

"It's Brannigans Skoolhouse and keep your voice down. There's good folk in here. I value my business and their custom. I don't want them scared away by the likes of you. Deal with your own heartaches and get over yourself. Then you can get over him," he advised as she looked wide-eyed shocked and silent. Page looked straight back at her and shrugged her shoulders out of the debacle. Eden scowled over her full glass at the pair of them.

"Are you two in this together or what…! Out to get me, huh…? I'm here to forget my troubles and have a good time. That's the whole damn reason I'm even here at all," she frowned. "To celebrate my divorce and move on. Isn't that what hanging out at the Skoolhouse is all about, mister? You two ain't my parents, you pair of dumb asses."

"Please calm down, Eden. You're embarrassing everybody in the room now. I'm very sorry sir, she's so contrary she'd float upstream," Page retorted, resorting to Eden's tactics as a few more people turned around to tune in to the commotion.

"And you're so highfaluting, you think your crap tastes like sherbet," Eden responded as Page grabbed Eden's arm.

"We're not ganging up at you. You're just getting an inferiority complex and repeating yourself. So, go easy on the fire-water or you'll be on your back and I for one am certainly not carrying you out of this place. You'll be drunker than *Cooter Brown* if you carry on like this."

"Oh, shut up about the damn whiskey, Page. You're all gurgle and no guts with the big words. You're so full of sh___! I'll inferiority complex your face in a minute," she beefed, grinding together her teeth. "You just don't get it do you Page? I'm done taking heed from you, about anything. You're wasting your breath. Kyle hit me more than one time, you hear me Page. He slapped me, kicked me and punched me! He even kicked Bailey for no good reason," she chided, taking another hard slug of her drink then banging it on the bar as the bartender turned around and watched, still in earshot of every word. "He's an out-of-work, drunken bum, who cares for nobody and nothing but himself. I wouldn't walk across the street to piss on him if he was on fire. On top of everything else, he's whoring. Getting his home comforts elsewhere. And knowing that, you tell me forgive him?" She asked looking at Page, and then the innocent barman. "He's slept with other women. I know that for a fact," she said stopping herself talking by putting her hand over her mouth and feeling her hard shell begin to crack. "Now forgive me for being just a heartache or two upset, Page, but knowing that. Well, it cuts deep and it hurts so much." She spun her seat to the bar and clasped her hands between her knees, then bowed her head. "I'm scared of him, Page. It just couldn't go on anymore. And still, he keeps coming back to the house in the middle of the damn night, drunk. I'm scared for me and my boy. Jamie is the most important person in my life." Page and the barman listened in silence as Eden's voice began to shake and falter with emotion. She let go of her hand and put the other one across her mouth, then bent lower as her head slumped forward. She bit hard on her finger then started to openly and uncontrollably weep. She sat there, feeling completely helpless, shaking and trembling as Page quickly leant over from her stool and crowded her arms around sister's shoulders as Eden tried to blatantly resist. Shaking and wriggling her body away from her sister, until finally, she gave in to Pages caring grip as her floodgates finally opened, releasing all her pent-up aggression, anger and sadness in one go.

 She continued to shake and blubber, whilst trying to hide from every open eye in the bar. She tried everything to shield her face from the room as Page stood up and threw herself tighter into her. She felt as if every face in the room had watched her literally fall apart. Then unemotively and un-embarrassed, they had just turned their backs to ignorantly resume their conversations. A couple playing pool had made eye contact with Eden, then looked at each other blankly. Feeling lost as how to compensate her, they had silently turned back to their game feeling at a loss, and powerless to the beautiful stranger's tears.

 After a second or two, Eden slowly pulled herself together. She wiped the tears from her cheeks onto her sleeve as Amelia reappeared from the toilet and looked across the room at the sad faces and Eden's waterworks. She rambitiously strode across the bar room with her usual high-heeled clicking canter to immediately address her friends' plight, as Page continued to hug her sibling and whisper in her ear:

"Oh Eden. I'm so very sorry baby. I now know exactly what you're talking about so quit making things worse. He's a pig and a rotten apple. Just forget about him and move on and that's straight out, coming from me. I love you, and I've only ever wanted the best for you. But after what you just said, to

hell with him. I now know things have gone too far to ever make it right,"
Page admitted walking behind her sister and resting her head on her
shoulder. She wrapped her arms around her waist as Eden grabbed her
sister's hands, mirroring her kin's movement and snuggling in to her tight.
 On hearing every angered word, the bartender quickly walked to the far end
of the bar and returned with a box of tissues and placed them by her side.
She unearthed her nuzzled head from her sister's chest to see him looking
helpfully down at her as Page pulled a tissue from the box and Amelia
appeared.

"Come on now honey, dry your eyes he's not worth it. None of them are,"
Page admitted.

"Now you're talking a little bit of sense at last, Page," Amelia agreed nodding
from behind her and coming to the froe. She put her arm on Eden's shoulder
to pull them all together in a group hug as Eden finally smiled and stopped
her sniffling and tears.

"Not worth it, except him. Maybe he's a good man?" Eden suggested looking
up and straight at the bartender as he pulled another tissue from the box for
her. He smiled and offered it to her, then turned around to grab four clean
glasses from behind the bar.

"You we're getting a little sorry-ass, drunken-bum yourself there for a
minute, young lady," he said as she sat back in her chair and thankfully took
the tissue from his hand.

"Thank you, sir. I, I sure was," she acquiesced. "I'm going to be pulling
myself together and stop being a damn fool," she asserted nodding her head
and gritting her teeth. He grabbed the whiskey bottle and poured into her
glass, then repeated the gesture in the other glasses. Then, he placed the
bottle down on the bar, right beside her. "Shall we make a little toast on that
then?" He asked nodding at Page and raising up his glass. They looked at
each other, then at Eden and grabbed the glasses from the bar and saluted
together. "This is on me. Compliments of the house."

"Thank you, sir. Your, so kind. So, the Skoolhouse you say," she sniffed. "I
take it she's all your own work?"

"Me, and the little lady. I sunk everything we have into this place. We're doing ok, I suppose. Sometimes it's hard when there's no money left in the working man's pocket. But that's just like everything these days isn't it? You just put on your best smile and keep on going with the head down," he explained.

"The place is neat," Amelia said casually looking around then sitting back down and crossing her legs. "Even the funky signs on the toilets are cool. There's a big red bra daubed on the ladies and a chamber pot boy on the door for the dudes. It's great. Have you seen them, Eden? There's even a plaque over the top: *'No scratchin eyes or pulling hair'* and well... would you look at the hot clientele... golly! If it's good enough for us witches, I guess it's good enough for every damn coon-hound," she grinned. "You sure got one great place that's ours for the taking, ladies," she bubbled looking at the sisters. The bartender smiled at Amelia's comment as Eden glanced over to look at the sign above the toilets. "Sounds good okay me, girls. Just, be happy and have a fine old time," he said smiling and walking away.

"Oh, he's gone sir. That damn husband will be clean out of her mind," Amelia shouted. "It's girl time for me, so let's have a little fun. We'll be a long time dead, huh?" Amelia ran her fingers through Eden's hair and across from her teared cheeks. "Hey, come on hot-lips, you can always change things around, and have me. I still got that teenage crush on you. Come here Angel face. MWAH!" Amelia grabbed Eden's head and kissed her on the cheek then moved back out of slapping distance. "You'll always be a yummy mummy to me, ain't that right Page?" Amelia smiled as Page nodded and Eden burst out laughing.

TWO: *The Lecture*

"That's totally correct sir. We are viscerally intertwined with every living thing on this shared, spinning Earth," he agreed responding to the question that was put to him by a highly interested audience member. As he continued his stage presentation he was feeling pleased with the audience's over-keen interest, as he'd been talking non-stop, for well over an hour and a half. He once again glanced at his watch and made a positive decision to ignore the time constraints he'd previously set himself. After all, the subject was far too more important for everyone.

"For arguments sake, let's say, we've already lost the cure for cancer which just might have been waiting to be found inside the animals, the plants, or the flora and the fauna that we humans, in our ignorance have already killed off in this, the sixth Holocene extinction," he explained, giving them a minute to comprehend and digest his statement. "Yes, you heard that right, the sixth extinction wave of all species of animals and plants in the history of the planet. And all the others went before us, but this one, we've found ourselves, slap bang in the middle of." The statement was met with an audible silence from the completely enraptured audience.

"For example," he paused, "Let's take the discovery of myoglobin for DNA. It has a direct link from animals: We never thought anything like that could be possible, did we?" He reasoned hearing '*PSST*' from a whispered voice from the stage behind him as he flicked his black fringe, then continued to face the riveted, pin-drop audience as he slowly walked backwards to the stage wings. "There's so many things for us to discover." '*PSST*' the curtain veiled voice whispered, as he continued. "About this incredible world of ours. Please excuse me for one moment." He fell silent to the throng of head-turning seated people as Claude, his fellow lecturer attempted to clandestinely pass him a fax from his hiding place behind the stage curtain, at the same time briefing him as unobtrusively as possible in hushed tones. He pushed his glasses into his hair to scan the document, then clenched his fists in abounding delight. He patted Claude's shoulder, beamed like a Cheshire cat and walked back to center stage.

"Animal and plant research have helped us find treatments, and antibiotics for infections. It's played a vital role in every medical advance of the last century. Dialysis, vaccination, chemotherapy and by-pass surgery. In fact, the list is endless. Almost every present-day protocol for the treatment, prevention, control and cure of disease and suffering or pain, has happened through the knowledge garnered from animals and plants. Sorry for the wee interruption there," he apologized, taking off his smart black suit coat and hanging it on the side of the lectern. "In the first half tonight, my team was presented with an emailed query from a Mr. Samisen, who I've been informed is up there in the heavens... at the back. And no, he's not masquerading as God, either," he joked pointing toward a random guessing point, as people began turning their heads. "Are you there?" He shouted, as a raised hand poked up from amidst the assembled throng, acknowledging his own presence.

"I'm happy to inform you... sir... to tell you all... that Flora, the 28-year-old pygmy hippo at Whipsnade in England has given birth." He lifted both his arms up into the air. "RESULT!" He shouted. "Mother and the baby, that they have called Harry after the new prince, are doing very well," he clucked, his hands measuring something invisible in front of him as the crowd exploded into a fervent ascension of rapturous applause. He allowed himself a moment to ponder just how big a baby hippo might be as he waited for their charged hands to cease. "Not bad for an endangered species with a mouth tumor who's being treated for stomach cancer with medicines found by us. My team in the wings have been waiting for word all day," he pointed over his shoulder and stamped his feet on the spot as if he couldn't contain his joy.

"At the end of this lecture, I was contemplating flying back to England post-haste for personal and visual confirmation of her progress. Because that's how I roll," he smiled, increasing his easy and approachable nature and attachment to the audience, who we're already eating out of his hand. "That's how much I believe and adore what I do. But thanks to the wonders of technology and after this lecture, I'm able to go backstage and view the actual birth on a webcam recording that they've sent me. And so, can you, because I'm going to make it available straight after my closing words, for the entire world to see. For me, it's all about pushing the envelope, getting things out there and making everyone more aware of the plights we face, and the successes we achieve." He slid the papers underneath his notes on the pulpit. "Sorry, where was I?" He tried to focus on his notes but realised he'd mislaid his glasses... quickly finding them wedged in his black hair. Oh, great...? I'll have to get glasses to find my glasses at this rate.... sorry...." He glanced at his papers again, just to jog his memory. "Aaah... dogs," he grinned. "Even our trusty four-legged friends live a better life because of us, but *WE* think we're so damn clever, though don't we? That nothing can touch *US*." he turned a paper on his lectern.

"In my opinion, the things yet undiscovered outweigh the things already found. God has put all this stuff on this earth for us to find and use," he paused. "Anyone know what lizard saliva is used for?" The thousand and one eyes peering at him through the darkened room started to put their arms up and mutter between themselves. "I can see the majority in here have a pretty good Idea. Lizard saliva is a staple of treating the diabetic condition and is known as Byetta. I'm not here to imbibe you with a concise or fully loaded list of everything. If I even tried, we'd be here for days on end," he coerced to swath of titters. "I'm here to heighten awareness, nothing more. So," he echoed. "To throw in a revision curve-ball... give me the five species of life us humans wouldn't exist without." He fell silent, collecting his papers in his hands and waiting for his enthralled audience to answer. "Come on people, get with the program. The one's Claude told you about earlier, hit me," he mused, lifting his hand up ready to count off his fingers and enticing them to speak. The crowd began to chant after him:

"*Ants... bats... birds... termites...* and what was the other...?" He back-combed waiting and tapping on his last curled finger. "*FROGS!*" The audience shouted in unison laughing amongst themselves, and invisibly patting themselves on the back at their own learned colloquial and authoritative knowledge, as he counted his last finger into the equation. "Well done," he smiled, mildly giving them a clap.

"The building blocks of life are here, as well as the correct solutions to repair life. And all we have to do is to find them," he declared. "But we're not going to be able to find them or achieve these cures and accomplish these medicines or miracles if we don't have the relevant systemic knowledge, and fundamental nuts and bolts anymore," he complained. "Can't bake a cake without ingredients can you," he countered. "And what have we lost so far......? Well, blow me, If I ran through a thorough A to Z list of that lot, we'd need sustenance and hotels and a change of pants!" he inferred as the audience muttered amongst themselves.

"We've lost far too many land and airborne species thus far, and that's not even touching on the oceans of the world which cover 71% of the surface of this blue planet of ours. We need to find cures for every single paradigm and disease thrown hard against us, of which there's so many and where do we start?" He assuaged falling silent and taking a long accusing look at his watch. He took a long swig of his water and a second to look at the huge audience and lecture hall cameras picking up his every inflected word and movement.

"Tuberculosis, yellow fever, smallpox, whooping cough. Meningitis, Syphilis, Sars, Measles and Leprosy, the list goes on and on. Malaria, HIV and the more recent strains of Swine-flu, Bird-flu and Ebola. All parts of an extensive and in some ways endless and still growing list, but last but not by any means least, 'CANCER'. The big C, a disease that has directly or indirectly affected every single person's life in the world and who knows maybe the answer is within our grasp, if only we could see what we are doing wrong.

Everything remains and we assume, dealt with to the best of our ability, but let me just stop myself right there," he paused to see a muffled and head-turning reaction. Using his stocky physique, he walked closer to the crowd and jumped off the stage, then casually strolled up the middle staircase of the auditorium. Creating a closer inter-personal connection with his audience, who were now watching him walk right past or through them. "There's going to be a lot more of the same, and much worse around the corner before we get to the end of this life too. Has anybody been reading some of the stuff that's hitting the front pages of the papers of late? I don't mean your medical journals or monthlies either. Your ordinary broad sheets and page three varieties. You sir.... you have......? I beg your pardon. It doesn't what?" He furrowed. "No, it doesn't sir, and it looks, by the nodding heads around me, the rest of you have too." He walked back down the steps, allowing the audience to trade words and talk amongst themselves until he thrust his agile body back up onto the stage. As he landed, he saw Claude giving him an over-exaggerated thumb's up from behind the curtain. He squirreled three hidden fingers up in front of his chest to his smiling friend and turned back around to face the audience.

"My learned friend back there in the audience, says page three's false elegance doesn't exist anymore. He also said our beautiful species and you and I won't exist anymore, if theses *SUPERBUGS* grab a hold and believe me, he won't be a million miles away from the truth if these *AMR's,* the *NDM-1,* and the New Delhi metallo-beta-lactamase grow any stronger against our antibiotics. Just go and take a look for yourselves, I beg you. I'm not going to go into any details, because I simply don't know enough about it yet. But it's got ME scared as to what we'll be leaving behind for our children and the generations that come to pass after we're dust. Those of you who don't know what we're talking about, check it out online. Go on, blow your mind to the future of life on earth. I dare you...? Sorry, I digress," he said thinking he'd gone a little too far. "So, the bottom line is every failure in our field of endeavor to eradicate these scars on our landscape and ourselves will lead to success. The odds have got to go in our favor sometime?" He looked around the silent auditorium and glanced again to the stage side.

"I believe just the same as Claude explained earlier. That the cures are out there in this world, *WE* just have to find them and that's why these things... these protected animals, plants and flora and fauna are precious commodities to the human race. We just don't know enough about them or have the technology yet. But with hard work, the knowledge will come, and when it does, we'll all be the better for it," he said returning to his lectern. "So, summing up... we need eureka moments not maybes or possibilities! What we don't need is destruction of the planet, and all its weird and wonderful amazing species," he thumped his fist hard down on the lectern and his papers fell to the floor. He bent down and fished them off the stage and replaced them on the wooden rostrum in front of him, as he realised he'd forgotten where he was and allowed himself to go off on a noticeably angry tangent, when after all, he was standing in view of a possible worldwide audience of seven million connected to the internet. "My apologies, that's erm, the work we have to do, and it's why I love my job so much," he paused again. "It's my overawing passion, but then, I'm just a man trying to make a change for the better, for both myself and my fellow man. As well as for the good of this big spinning rock. Now doesn't that make the most complete sense in the world?" He asked gulping his water. "It's time to make that difference now, is there any quick questions? Claude, could you please come and join me on stage," he spun around and threw his hands out beckoning forward his hidden colleague as the hands automatically went up in the audience.

"You sir, one... two... sixth row up," he openly counted the seating tiers. "Mathematics was never my strong point," he explained as Claude walked to his side.

"Yes, I'm John Jackson from MT freelance farming. Is there any new breakthrough's in the use of tobacco plants as biofuel? We grow a hell of a lot of tobacco in this state" he quizzed, as James looked at Claude to answer. "They 'ave an identifier, a genetically engineered way for the leaves to produce more oil, so things are looking quite promisings for the futures of that crop and also corns and sugarcane," he replied in his suave European accent. "You can contact Thomas Jeffersooon University for more details on that sir" he explained looking at James who was already pointing to another raised arm. "Yes mam, this will have to be the last, we've already overstayed our welcome" he confirmed.

"Why are you specifically here in Tennessee at the moment," she queried standing up from her seat.

"There's some incredibly important areas of research to be carried out here right now and through our sources, which I can't divulge, there seems to be some typically ordinary threats to certain nature preserves rising. The fact that these intimidations or coercions are growing stronger is why where here. To nip them in the bud, excuse my terribly lame pun," he smiled. "We're also here to continue the research work set out five years ago. Which is why I'm also going to nip this lecture in the bud too. So, thank you everybody for coming along tonight," he took a final drink of water.

"I'm James Ustinov, and could you please give a big hand to my extreme ecology representative, Mr. Claude Agarde."

Claude smiled, and took a bow beside his buddy. "Thank you, Tennessee, and thanks to you all for coming along. Thank you also, to you people watching in your homes or colleges or cinemas, and on the international website. Thank you all very much and take care." They dually bowed and waved at the crowd, as a crescendo of thunderous applause echoed around the hall and in their ears as the lights came up, and they disappeared off the stage. "Fancy a libation or two James?"

THREE: *Pool sharks*

"Now this is exactly what I'm talking about," she said with a smile. "I love being friends with friends who know how to be friends."

"What say we get a piece of the action, Eden? We can look but we can't touch and that goes for them men too," Page implied.

"Damn right, Page! I'm glad we're finally got the same blue-sky thinking. Come on now, let's get that table near the dance floor with some of those hot ladies for me and the dudes for you. Hell, I might even get lucky yet," Amelia offered grabbing her hand. "I want my donut dunked, so let's go get the funk," she whispered, trying to pull Eden off her seat to her wide-eyed giggling astonishment.

"Aaw Page....look but can't touch.... come on now. There you go talking turkey again you, big killjoy," Em frowned, grabbing her glass from the bar.

"I'm with Em on that," Eden implied.

"Yeah Page, you speak for yourself. I said *FUNK* girl, hoe-down, boogie-down, dance. I meant *DANCE* Page. Glory be.... deaf as a post and as numb as a tree," Amelia retorted. "Now will you look at what we have before us?" She asked spinning Eden's bar stool around.

"Yep Em, there's some fine-looking colts and fillies in this place. I think it's time to grab ourselves a piece of the action," she replied goaded her big sister again.

"Oh, you're incorrigible, you truly are," she said as Eden was slid off her stool by Em's gripping hand, toward the dance floor. She quickly ran back and grabbed her glass and the whiskey bottle. "That ain't getting left behind and yep, I am incorrigible, and the music's great over there," she pointed with her glass. "Let's grab that table over there quick Em," she said as they made their way to the empty table near the pool table. "Listen, thanks Em, thanks for being here. Having a friend like you is like having a sister I can't get rid of," she smiled as Amelia cajoled her into her seat.

"Wow, will you look at the butt on him playing pool, Red," Page announced giggling and sitting beside her.

"I'm incorrigible... huh.... hark at you Page?" She said narrowing her eyes and turning her head sideways. "Mmm, he must work out," she imagined. "I saw him first, sister. Hands off," she joked, secretly watching the strangers every move.

"I bet he's got no slack in his rope," Amelia added from her other side.

"No, and plenty of notches on his gun I'm guessing," Eden whispered under her breath, as they both fought to keep a straight face. The three of them settled down watching the two-dark-haired smart looking muscular men shooting pool, as she poured another copious whiskey into her glass and their prey glanced back.

"Hey Claude, I think the black-haired woman over there's got a thing for you buddy," James's inferred slamming a red ball into the pocket and focusing his eyes across the pool table straight through Amelia at Eden.

"Oh, yes James. They all do. Deja savoir... I think the red-haired beauty could have been for you. She's a little tipsy, but I can see the future and it says: Triox d'entre eux, that means they're all mine, my friend," he joked as James paused his shot and looked up at his colleague's pretentiousness, to see him flesh peddlingly flick his hair into place, as he continued his crazy French talk:

"Mine des tous les miens. Why don't you set the balls up again, I'll go get the beers and I'll invite those ravissant ladies over for a jeu? See if they can resist my cosmopolitan French charm," he carped as James looked across at

Eden, then Page, and then at Eden again.

"Oh, my God, Claude. If you loved yourself anymore, you'd be on a French postage stamp. Erm, no thanks, I'm ok. My flights pretty early in the morning and much as I'd love to stay here, I'll have to get back to Nathan's house for Abbey," he paused, eyeing Eden once more. "Erm, I think I'll just drink this one and call it a night. It's been a good day, but a very long day," he nervously replied, looking across at Eden, thinking about his daughter, Abby and searching for a million excuses as he uncomfortably pulled at his shirt collar whilst thinking about his faultless devotion to his dead wife's memory. His shoulders tightened, he blinked and turned away. He picked up the pool chalk and tried to detract his mind from his sad of heart loss and the beautiful red-haired girl that had caught his eye.

"Oh, please James. Come, let's stay a while. You're far too bashfuls," Claude inferred, as if James's needed to lighten up. "Come on now, are you a man or a mouse?" He questioned, pushing the tie he'd already loosened back into its place, and folding his arms behind his back with a winning glint in his eye. "Abby is a big girl. She'll be happy she's got you out of her hair for one night. Just one more game of pool with those ladies and then we can both call it a night."

"Claude, I know it's just a game of pool and it's no biggie, but I have my daughter with me, so it's hardly the same," he explained reaching for feeble vindication.

"Besides, there's something I haven't told you, about me. I, erm recently, well, to be honest, it still feels like yesterday," he said stumbling through his words to say what he wanted to say.

"Oh, it's okay my friend, there's no need to explain, I just didn't know," Claude replied as if he knew what James's was about to tell him. "I wasn't sure if you batted for the other side, and I must admit, working with you on and off over the last few months, you've smelled amazing," Claude explained, as James frowned like an angry badger and shook his head to himself. "I mean, considering the conditions, we work in. Up to our necks in muck and yeuchs," you always smell great afterwards. Gay men are just the same."

"What! Me gay! Are you off your rocker?"

"Well, I?"

"Oh, do shut up Claude! I've been married and I have a daughter. You actually are psychotic," he furrowed. "In fact, let me just stop you right there, before you dig yourself to bloody Australia, you crazy parisienne. I don't bat for the other side, and that's really not it, at all. In fact, you're so far off the mark, I'd be forgiven for thinking you we're a complete lunatic. And God help them ladies over there, too," he said looking at his co-workers confused face and glancing across at Eden who was secretly looking back at him.

"Listen Claude, just forget I even opened my mouth. It doesn't matter my friend. You really don't need to hear any of my personal stuff, or any of my warts and all, problems. I'm just trying to get over something. A special something, and a special someone, that's all. Someone very dear to me," he declared. "That's all you need to know. So, a pool challenge with your eye candy ladies will be absolutely fine. You never know, I might beat you at your own game," he confirmed, overly conscious he was staring at Eden yet again.

"Is it a woman? Did a lady go and break your heart into little pieces?" Claude asked as James reminiscently paused and looked at *her* whilst thinking about his deceased wife, Jane.

"She did, and she didn't. Look, can we just forget I even said anything please? She's gone forever, and out of my life. She's gone, so it's time for me to move on," he replied, realising he'd just made the biggest statement of his life. A statement he never imagined he would ever have to make.

"My friend, I'll shut up. I'll put a cast-iron zip on my stupid mouths, and you won't hear me mentions it again," Claude mimed his agreement by pulling his hand across his lips. "They can do that, though."

"What?" James's enquired, losing himself in his intermittent stare.

"Women. Gent feminine, they can..."

"Claude!"

"Sorry, I'll shut up," Claude said raising both his arms up in mock surrender

27

mode. "You set them up James and I'll get the drinks then bring the daughters to the slaughter," he announced wildly.

"Mmm, you do that. I'll make quick call to Nathan, and to work," he replied realising what he'd just said and that his fate was cast. He shot another quick glance at the three women and singled *her* out with a fixed and focused stare until she caught his eye. Once he caught her eye, she playfully smiled back, then coyly looked down.

"Just one more game Claude, and I'm holding you to that. So off with you, and go do your worst, I know you're dying to get over there you, lecherous dog." James's rigidly crossed his arms across his chest and looked over at the women as Claude eagerly rubbed his hands together then walked away.

James reached into his back pocket and realised he didn't have any change to release the pool balls and looked over at Eden as if she was the solution.

"Red, he's looking right at you, put the damn, empty whiskey bottle down," Amelia said.

"No, he isn't, he's looking at you... I'm used goods, Em. Let's put some music on the jukebox. I wonder if they got any *Ward Thomas* music on the juke box," She said to Amelia, changing the subject but feeling an instant attraction to *him*.

"I'll bet you a dollar he's looking at you. No, I'll bet you a beer."

"She's right, he is staring at you," Page agreed.

"You can't bet, me... cos I don't bet."

"Neither do I. Ok, I'm telling you he's looking at you."

"You're not selling me, cos I ain't for sale," Eden inebriatedly joked, vaguely paying attention but glancing up and throwing a smile his way again.

"Oh, you, big tease. His eyes are stuck on you now. He likes you, wave at him."

"I wasn't smiling, I was giggling. Wave? Hogwash... who wants another game of spin the bottle?" She replied, not about to be strong-armed into doing anything, as much as she wanted too.

"Oh, shut up and put the stupid bottle down. He is nice though, isn't he Em?" Page fervently claimed.

"Hey, don't tell me to shut up, I already told you earlier, you ain't my Mom."

"If I was a man-eater, I'd have to agree with her, Red," Amelia encouraged. "Not sure about the other feller coming towards us, though," she frowned, looking at Claude smiling at them madly and walking in their direction. "A guilty fox hunts his own hole"

"Speaking of drunk, we'd better get another drink. Look, this bottles nearly done honey." Eden poured the last drops of whiskey equally into their glasses. "All gone... it's all gone now," she stated, as if she was feeding a baby as she cradled the bottle in her arms.

"Oh my God, the fox is coming over Red."

"Now the other ones following the fox," Amelia whispered. "Well baby doll, a severe drought usually ends with a flood, and he's hotter than a honeymoon hotel, so good luck," she announced tapping knowingly on her friend's knee.

"That so... huh? Good, cos there's plenty of room, right here. They can get the drinks in too, cos we're all out of luck in here," she answered, pretending to be deaf to her friend's advice and looking into the empty bottle, then tapping it onto the seat in-between herself and Page.

"She's right Eden, he looks so strong, he'd make Samson look sensitive," Page added for good measure. "Eden, stop messing around you, crazy woman, they're coming," she yanked on Eden's black sequined top, as they nonchalantly looked up at the first tall dark and handsome stranger with their heads in complete sync:

"Good evening Mademoiselles, are you all having an agreeable *soiree* night?"

"Huh? *WE* beg your pardon," Eden asked, drunkenly putting the neck of the bottle to her eye and feigning holding a telescope and looking up at him. "You sound from faraway shores me hearty," she said giggling to herself, suddenly realising the drunkenness of her actions, and James getting ever so closer. She instantly lowered the bottle and soberly, yet casually placed it on the table, as if nothing had happened.

"Sorry, I said, are you enjoying your evening, my apologies ladies?"

"Stop apologizing mister funny voice. You've just got too many manners for one man. Are you French?" She growled.

"Oui. My name is Claude Agarde, I'm from Paris and that's James, from England over," he turned around to point to the pool table at the other side of the room and nearly stuck his finger in James's eye. "Oh sorry, he was over there. Sorry James's," he explained looking at his finger and his compadre stood right behind him. "Very nice to make your acquaintances ladies," Claude announced again looking directly at Amelia and grinning like it was his second favourite exercise. James politely smiled and nodded somewhat directly at his eyes intriguing choice as he pointed at the mobile phone stuck to his ear.

"Hello red fury," he cheekily mocked as her eyes slowly met his at the same time, leaving him wondering what in the Devil's name had possessed him to open his mouth in a manner comparable to Claude's at all. As he waited for Eden and his mobile to answer, she crossed her arms tightly over her chest then replied:

"Oh, red fury, am I? You ain't seen nothing yet, mister." She said hardening her brash and unforgiving steel-clad facia, despite already feeling herself breathlessly flushed with butterflies inside. "Well, what do you know sis, did you hear that, gay Paris and acquaintances. Another big word for your dictionary. Whoop whoo! He uses huge nouns and syllables, just like you," she said frowning at confused Claude and pretending to totally ignore James after his ballsy comment and his blatant cheek of speaking to her with a mobile phone jammed in his ear.

"I think you two are gonna get along just fine Clyde. Acquaintances huh," she whispered and giggled at crimson-faced Page.

"It's erm, Claude," he frowned.

"That's what I said Clyde. And you'd better be careful with her. She bitches fast and slaps hard," Eden advised looking at Amelia.

"Me and my friend we're wondering if you would like a game of pool, the winning team gets the beers. I will also get the drinks now if you would like?"

"Excuse me for interrupting," James said, putting his hand up as if he were in a school class, then recoiling at his somewhat out of touch bashful and naïve approach. Quickly realising he was faced with a razor-sharp tongue that belonged to the most beautiful woman he had ever seen. "I don't have any change Claude, does anybody a dollar?"

Eden let go of her glass to grab for her purse. She looked up at him, nodded, then looked at her sister, and then stopped moving at all.

Suddenly, and completely out of the blue, she hiccupped loudly making Page look at her with disgust as she put her hand across her mouth and James's began to grin from ear to ear.

"Oops, sorry," she said feeling somewhat more than embarrassed. "What's wrong? Are you a typical Englishman?"

"What do you mean by that?" He wondered.

"Tighter than a fiddle string... hic," she replied trying to take the spotlight away from herself and the belching accident. "I'll give you a dollar you, English oink. In fact, I'll give you more than a dollar if you don't watch your... hic... step. Excuse me, again," she repeated waking her words lose any intended bite, conveniently breaking the ice and showing a wee chink in her amour.

"Aah, *vous excuser mademoiselle.*"

"What did that lunatic... hic... say?" She asked looking at her even more embarrassed, silent sister. "Ok, yep Page, I know... sorry. I got the hippy-cups just like I used to when we were kids and I'm a total disgrace to you and the rest of the family and the whole of Tennessee. I apologize for my manners," she explained. "I'm making you fellers as welcome as a porcupine at a nudist colony. But what the hell. You won't have to suffer as much as me, because it'll probably take me all night to get rid of these damn hiccups now," she explained. "Ok, mister frog's legs. We're gonna accept your challenge and kick your ass... hic! Damn! I'll be lucky to hit a ball at this rate... hic! But we're still gonna kick your... hic... asses, anyhows."

Eden stood up, showing herself to have a slight drunken sway. "Come on now ladies, let's go Amelia." As they stood up, Eden grabbed Page's embarrassed hand for steadiness for her tipsy wobble and followed their whispering male hosts toward the pool table.

"You always got hiccups when you were boy-nervous."

"Are you kidding me?"

"No. I remember how you reacted when the football team coach, Mack first spoke to you."

"Huh?"

"You were nuts about him," Page explained to Eden's totally shocked face. "It took you until home time to get rid of the hiccups, that day. You seem to forget, I'm your sister remember."

"Oh, I don't think...hic... your memory's what it was, Page," she replied, trying to numb the comment as they reached their waiting hosts.

"So, you're James's huh...? Hi... hic.... I'm Eden and this is my...hic... big sister Page who lies through her teeth all the time," she said beginning to smile. "That's our...hic... dear girlfriend, Amelia. She's a girlfriend in the real way, ain't you Em?

"Yep. They do it for me," Amelia smiled.

"But don't you hold it her or anything else, or she'll chop it right off," she pointed to Claude's instantly saddened face. "We're gonna nail you guys to the floor, so you may as well say the... hic.... the drinks are on you, hic!" She said nervously offering her hand to shake her suitors.

"She chatters a lot when she's boy shy. Ain't that right, sis," Page admitted as James's softly, but strongly shook Eden's hand and politely pecked her cheek. She smiled back feeling a strong sense of emotion awake her senses. A long-lost feeling she'd forgotten began to flow back through her veins.

"You are boy-shy, and you know it!"

"Don't listen to her, she talks a lot of *BS* with big words," Eden explained, feeling a mountainous glow of attraction to him as well as wanting to quickly ring her sister's neck.

"You, and Em play with them. I'll sit this one out," Page sniffed feeling somewhat embarrassed by Eden's comment.

"Nail us to the floor you say," he said walking close beside her and calmly whispering in her ear with an unintentionally sexy voice. "We'll see about that, Red," he offered turning to face her and looking into her piercing blue eyes.

"Are you sure Page?" He politely asked as if something had offended her as everybody looked over at Page in unison. "There's no law saying we can't have three against two," he explained.

"Really, its fine, I'll just watch," she maintained grabbing a tall stool at the side. "I need to make a call home soon, anyway."

"Ok, well why don't we make this a bit more interesting... a little *passionnant,*" Claude added.

"How'd that be... hic...?" She frowned uncomprehending his words.

"Instead of boys against girls, how about mixed teams?"

"Ok, that sounds fair. At least we know they're ain't gonna hustle our asses," Amelia offered. "I ain't played this game for so long," she conceded pulling down on her tight skirt again. "The after-school club last time, I think? You'd better keep me right, Frenchman."

"You're darn tootin' they won't hustle us," Eden said arching her back and reaching into her skin-tight jeans back pocket and pulling out a dollar. "Right mister England... hic... I'll flip, you call. Heads, you're get Em. Tails you have me... I mean you get me... hic! I mean, it's you and me.... we're together, and a team... Erm... hic!"

"Stop digging yourself into a hole, Eden," Amelia said smiling at Eden's sexual connotated words as she blushed for the first time in a long time then flicked the dollar high into the air. "Oh, you know what I mean," she grumbled as the dollar came back down almost in slow-motion and she trapped it on the back of her hand.

"James... hic," she asked, waiting for him to speak, feeling somewhat more energized and soberer than she had minutes earlier.

"Tails," he announced, moving closer to her and placing his hand on top of hers, softly lifting her other hand from the coin.

"Tails it is! I guess you got me, partner," she said reluctantly moving away from him to show the coin to their opponents.

"Ok, it's me and mister UK won the toss, so it's us two to shoot off," she explained with another hiccup. "Hey partner, here's the dollar I promised you... catch!" She threw the coin in James's direction. "There you go. Set them up for the loser's, partner," she said walking toward him and leaning her shapely butt on the table as he knelt down to put the dollar in the slot.

"Are you good with a stick, James's? I mean at pool?"

"The best," he replied with a smile, as he looked up and quickly realised he was at eye-level, and talking to, her shapely butt, and flawless legs making him want to talk to her instead of putting the coin in the slot.

"So, you think we'll.... hic!" She gazed down at his lithe body, taking in his jet-black hair and broad shoulders. "Sorry, do you think we'll win, hic! Oh, hell and bananas! These damn hiccups."

"Eden," he said pausing yet again, "Do you trust me?"

"Erm, I guess. I only just met you.... but I guess I trust you... why?" She frowned lifting an eyebrow.

He stopped what he was doing, stood up and placed the dollar on the green baize. "Give us a moment," he said to Amelia as he pushed her feet apart with his, then slid his leg in-between hers. He softly moved his arm around her body and placed his left hand on the small of her back, causing her to breathe in unexpectedly after feeling a deep tingle run deep inside her very being. He placed his other hand in exactly the same place but at the front, on her slim, tummy. Making her audibly gasp and then look around the room to see if anyone was watching like she cared anymore.

"Take a deep breath and then hold your breath as hard as you can and force your tummy onto my hand. Just put your trust in me, and I promise this will work," he explained now getting quizzical looks from Amelia, Claude and Page who were standing, and still waiting for the pool balls to be set up despite being fully engrossed in what was happening.

"After three, are you ready?"

"Erm, hang on. I don't think I can remember all that," she weakly claimed doing exactly as he asked and enjoying every minute. "Something's working, but I don't think it's doing the things it's supposed to be doing," she whispered to his eyes, politely smiling, and flushing red as she felt his secure and firm hands caressing her body, knowing that this was the first time in her life she'd allowed herself to be openly touched by another man.

"Are you...hic... married?" she nervously asked out of nowhere, breathing heavily and changing the subject to the first thing that came into her head.

"Take the breath."

"Answer the question, then I'll take the breath."

"Does it matter?"

"Answer the question, James's."

"I was married. Now take the breath or this won't work. Talk later, just breathe in tight."

"Happily?"

"Eden, take the breath."

"Yes," he replied instantly thinking about Eden. "It was a very happy marriage, thank you. Now do please be quiet, hold your tongue and hold your breath."

Was married, she said to her silence. She did as he asked and pushed her body hard onto his strong hands. Then, for no reason at all, she closed her eyes. A minute later and bright red in the face, she slowly opened her eyes and let out a huge breath of air. "Phew, I think I went a little dizzy," she said as he relaxed his hands, then moved them away from her waist and onto her shoulders as she knelt her head and slowly recuperated her breath, secretly praying for another hiccup.

"I had a funny feeling you we're a bit dizzy anyway," he jokingly teased.

"Just a feeling, huh?" She smiled. "Woah, they've gone. Thank you so much," she sighed.

"Now you can talk. Why did you ask if I was married?"

"Erm, well I was gonna advise that if you we're... I mean are... or was married... I don't think you should have your hands on another woman unless you're a doctor. But erm, I'm glad you did mister hiccup. I mean... if I was your wife... not that I will... will be... would be... erm," she stuttered. "I'm sure I wouldn't be happy in the knowledge that you... you had your hands all over another woman. Well... on another woman. But, erm anyway, it doesn't matter now because my, erm: *My hiccups have all gone away, gone away for another day*," she sang loudly as Amelia tapped at her watch and Claude frowned across at them. "Yes, they're, *gone, gone, gone,* and that's more than nice," she profusely explained dragging their focus away from her singing. "It was butterfly, tummy, whoopee, nice," she said catching a closer glimpse of his smiling brown eyes. "So, thank you again, mister England," she said coyly picking up the dollar, opening his fingers and placing it into his healing hand.

"If I was still married, I wouldn't have dreamt of touching you," he pointed out with honesty.

"Well done James's!" Page interjected pretending to put her mobile away as she rushed toward them. "I've been her sister for thirty-two years, and she's never got rid of the hiccups so fast. You seem to have a magic touch with Eden. Which you'll probably need because it's you being her dream guy that set them off in the first place. Anyway, that was Mark on the phone, Eden. He needs me home A.S.A.P. Chloe isn't well. She wasn't feeling well when I left, but I forgot about that. Mark said she's been sick and she's been asking for me. Mark hasn't a clue when it comes to looking after them when they're ill," she suggested. "So, if you'll all excuse me, you take care and I'll call you," she babbled. "I really do hope I get to see you with my sister another time, James. It's really lovely to see her with a smile on her face at last." Page quickly hugged Eden, gave her a knowing and loving wink then waved her goodbyes and was gone, and almost forgotten just as soon as she walked out of the door.

"Are we going to have this game or what?" Amelia asked with impatience

Eden walked across to speak to her as James's knelt down to eject the pool balls again but stopping to wave goodbye to leaving Page as if he'd forgotten something as well.

"Did you hear that, Em? What a load of bull. Chloe's ill my ass. He said that because he's jealous. Just because she's out with us and she might be having a really good time. God! He treats her like dirt," she whispered angrily.

"Calm yourself and let it go. It ain't you're fight girl."

"Oh, he just annoys me. Has to have her there to wait on him, hand and foot" she scathed, deciding to clamp her mouth shut for fear of losing James's attention.

"To be honest Em, I'm a little glad she's gone," she whispered. "She was giving some of my secrets away."

"Yes Red, and we got a couple of stiffs to play with here. Sorry baby, I know you're hot on him, but I want lady-cake, not a crazy *Don Juan*," Amelia said with the volume of a fully blown Tuba in an attempt to heighten the awareness of her single status to the whole room.

"So, what are you two doing in good old Tennessee then you, big grouch?" She beamed as she chalked their stick as she waited for James's knelt who seemed to be fiddling at the side of the table.

"We're working on a number of assignments for the World Wildlife Federation.

"Oh?"

"Yes. Just updating statistics and checking on new developments. I work for *L.E.A.P.S* of London and Claude is with Extreme Ecology France."

"Huh?"

"London Environmental Animal and Plants Society. We're ecologists specializing in endangered animals and plants. We travel all over the globe. Not permanently you understand."

"Oh yeah?" She replied still unsure, but happy to watch and listen."

"This is the second time we've worked together. Anyway, this is a celebratory last night out cos we've just had a baby," he said bursting out laughing at his own joke that no-one else found funny. He looked up at her then over at Claude. "Sorry," he said looking back down to the coin slot and frowning, then back up and at her slim body till he saw her hand playing with her beautiful red hair. "This dollar won't fit in here?"

"Had a baby huh?" She replied completely straight-faced, feeling left out of his joke and waiting for him to elaborate as waiting Amelia was coached through another invisible shot by Claude.

"Yes, we've just finished a lecture in town and had some very positive news about a rare hippo species giving birth. I really can't get this dollar in," he said still struggling with the coin but continuing to talk to her with embarrassment. "I'll be on my way home tomorrow to take a look-in on mother and child in England."

Her ears pricked up and she turned around to face him. "Wow that sounds neat. I mean erm... not the bit about you leavin' and travelling home. I meant the hippo thing. Going home is just what you gotta do, ain't it," she sighed. "It's your job," she added trying not to look as concerned as she was feeling. "I mean... it sounds really good. It's just a dog-gone shame you're leaving so soon though professor fondle hands," she teased knowing he was still embarrassed at being on his knees with the dollar still no further on.

"Yes, I know, I really like it over here too. It's no problem though, I'll be back here in no time at all because there's so much work to do. Eden, can you get this coin in this slot for me, please," he protested as she happily bent down beside him. "What do you do?"

"I'm a music teacher. I teach history and general studies but music is my passion. I play guitar, and before you ask, I'm a single mother who's almost divorced and free again," she said secretly crossing her fingers.

"I wasn't going to ask. A gentleman would never ask such a question."

"Oh," she replied wishing he had.

"So, who's the lucky girl then?" She asked, moving on quickly and creating instant confusion in his face.

"I told you, I don't have a girlfriend, or a wife anymore."

"I meant the female hippo, James's."

"Oh, sorry. I thought you meant..."

"You have a one-track mind, mister nervous."

"Well, I am a little nervous. This is all new to me. And I still can't get this money in the slot."

"When you say; this is all new, what's so new about it?

"Because, I don't usually frequent bars or talk to beautiful women. In fact, I don't frequent bars, at all. It's about... hang on a second..." he said looking up and counting on his fingers. "Two years since I was in my last bar," he said to her open-mouthed surprise.

"Tell me about the Hippo," she asked warming to his voice even more.

"Ah. Now that's a subject I love. Her name is, Flora and she's beautiful. She's a pygmy hippo from Whipsnade zoo. Been there all of her days and her new baby's been called Harry after the new prince," he replied endeared with her interest in his work.

"That's pretty cool. I bet Flora looks just like my sister and vice-versa. Move out of my way mister amateur, let me at it," she said after watching him struggle with the dollar for long enough. She grabbed at his shoulder to pull him away from the pool table, then pushed him backwards off his feet to which he stealthily rolled back, then flicked himself up and on to his legs with almost physical effort at all.

"Oh, so you'll be coming back to these parts."

"Yes, the ecology tests have to be taken on a regular basis."

"It would be great to see you again, mister gymnast. Maybe we could go out alone... I mean together... alone... that is... not with these two," she motioned to Claude and Amelia. "Maybe a meal... or a gig... or even a *DATE* in Nashville?" She inquired leaving the *word* she meant him to hear first until last for fear of rejection. Secretly proud of the courage to ask in the first place and wondering where her boldness was coming from and deciding to blame it on the whiskey.

"I've never had an, erm... Englishman... as a date... or partner... erm, a pool playing partner," she said correcting her garbled words then deciding to change the conversation to stop herself from fluffing again. "Look, James's, you just have to be extra careful when you're pushing it in, the dollar I mean," she explained laughing at her own statement then standing back up and putting her hand over her mouth with embarrassment. "See, it's the small slot at the end, you know... for next time you can't get it in," she continued looking at him to see he was grinning at her somewhat sexual explanation. "Oh, forget it, you're not listening now, are you...? You, big jerk. Nope, you're not, you're just laughing at me," she said answering her own question, and softly slapping at him as he quickly twisted his body out of the way. "You think me real funny don't you.... you, big-pig." She crossed her arms and tutted, biting into her bottom lip until eventually, she started smiling. "I just hope you can shoot really well, mister clueless," she grinned at the naughtiness and decided to jump on the double-entendre, bandwagon of fun.

"See," she said bending down again and pushing in the release bar on the table. "The balls are out and on the way to the hole... we have lift off," she said as the table rumbled.

"Oh yes, you can almost feel the earth move, Red," he replied grinning as she carried on with the joke.

"Are you any good with your balls.... at this?" She asked, watching for Em or Claude to intervene and set them up.

"Oh yes, I've got a fast cueing action. You know, back and forward, in and out. But sometimes, it's better if you just feather and stroke your target ball right into the waiting hole," he said to her giggling delight. "Lead your opponent into a false sense of security before the all-important, final thrust shot," he joked walking across to her side and putting his arm across her shoulders as she held onto her stomach with the pain of laughter. "Always give your stick a good chalking up first though," he added deciding to quit while he was ahead but thinking innately about her almost identical enjoyment and sense of humor.

"Right! That's the balls set up," he shouted across the room to Claude and Amelia who had been waiting so long, they had almost lost the will to live.

"You'd better make sure we win, mister pool shark."

"Of course, we'll win. I was on the local pub pool team back home when I was a kid. I'd say I'm a reasonable player."

"Good, but tell me more about your work, James's. It's interesting."

"Really? Well, I travel all over the world for my job, but sometimes I'm at home a lot. I work around the UK and Ireland and quite a lot in Scotland. But because there's not a lot going on in my personal life, these days, the trips away are going to be a lot more frequent," he explained. "Which isn't going to please, Abby much," he added to Eden's secret and sudden, emotional gulp.

"Who's Abby?"

"Abby's my daughter," he continued. "This is the first real assignment out of Britain for a while which is great. It helps enormously when the place you visit and the people you meet are nice. Present company included," he declared as she gazed at him with a twinkle in her eye, still enjoying the sound of his voice. "I've been getting so bogged down in my work recently, or at least that's what, Abby keeps telling me."

"She's looking out for her Dad.""

"I suppose. She's eight, going on eighty but she keeps me out of trouble and on the straight and narrow."

"Where is she now?" Eden quizzically probed, feeling slightly happier she knew a little more about him as they watched their opposing team cue off.

"She's at Nathan's on the other side of town. My old friend from my school days. This is Abby's first trip out with me, and I think she's enjoying herself. Least I hope she is. It's pretty hard to tell. She'd normally be at home with her Nan and Grandad. They look after her when I'm away. Trips like this are great," he continued. "I've travelled all over the world for the cause. The job requires it because you don't get all the incredible stuff you have in Kentucky and the rest of the world in England," he reasoned, leaving Eden wondering as to where Abby's Mother was in the family equation. "I need to be in situ on site to observe all species in their natural habitat. It's just the same with everything else we're trying to protect and save throughout the world. I miss her so much when I have to go away. I'm so glad she's here with me this time." He stopped talking to watch Claude's first failed shot. "Maybe you'd like to meet her sometime," he asked gazing at his bewitching pool partner to her internal delight. "Then maybe we should exchange phone numbers first you, big hobo," she inferred feeling glad she'd secretly secured some future access to him.

"You're rubbish, French man. Get out of this a pool tigress's way… roaraow!" Amelia said, imitating her hands as scratching claws. "But just for the ladies you understand," she teasingly grinned as Claude's face turned despondent again. "Come on you two. Play the game, or before you know it, you'll have your tongues down each other's throats. Get with it, you're on yellow and it's your turn. This loser potted nothing."

"Ok, just hold your horses, we were erm, discussing tactics isn't that right mister dough-ball."

"Of course. Get ready for a victory beer, Eden," he said, touching her

41

shoulder and gently massaging his fingers into her clavicle. "With your hiccups gone, we can play the game properly. I think we'll play together perfectly," he added. He leaned forward on the green baize and concentrated his focus at the herd of red and yellow balls lying split across the bottom of the table. As he leaned his taut muscular frame, and powerful arms across the table, she gazed at him and watched his every move from behind. As he pulled back on the cue, she gloried in seeing his whole body tense up, and then relax as he took a practice for his first shot and briefly stopped to speak. "Yes, and a word of advice, Claude. I hope you have a jock-strap nearby. You might be needing it sooner than you think. Get this out of your precious crown jewels." He thunderously cracked the cue ball clean into the hive of color and a yellow ball wildly ricocheted off a cushion and into the corner pocket where Claude was standing.

"Oh, so it is like that, is it?" Claude grumped.

"Wow, you have an amazing touch," Eden whispered across the table in the sexiest voice she could muster as he continued.

She watched him intensely as he casually moved around the table and potted the balls so calmly yet succinctly into the pockets, one by one. Consciously following his concentrated and sexual gaze at every shot. She screeched an occasional yelp and whoop every time he sunk a ball and randomly and fervently whispered wildly in his ear at every possible chance. His quiet, controlled and skilled demeanor seemed to bowl her over with hypersensitivity and emotion. She was enraptured and overcome with a winning feeling that was also mirrored inside her being and her lustfully beating heart. A winning feeling of the game and of the man. As Claude and Amelia stood patiently waiting for him to make a mistake, they quietly began to talk about the overtly apparent chemistry between the love-struck pair.

As James potted the black, Eden jumped up and down madly, then threw her arms around his neck just at the moment when his mobile phone rang in his pocket.

"I think there's something strong there, can you see it, Claude?" Amelia offered.

"Oh yes, you could see the magnetism through a closed door. It's good for them," he paused. "I mean it's good very for him," he explained leaning on his cue looking across at her. "Is your friend Eden...?" He asked.

"What... available?" Amelia casually muttered through the corner of her mouth. "*Oui,*" Claude whispered back, waiting for an answer as he watched their intently playing adversaries being as carefree with each other like there wasn't another soul in the room.

"Yes, she is. Hold on a second," she frowned turning her face to meet his. "Is he...?"

The Frenchman rapturously whispered, raising both his thumbs up in the air, "*Oui mademoiselle, confirmer!*"

"Well she wasn't up until recently, but she sure is now," she replied with an easy winking and grinning at the Frenchman. "But we lost good and proper. Some player you are," Amelia cursed added frowning and sliding her redundant cue onto the table.

"We could ah, play again Amelia?"

"We could, but I think we'd better just sit on that, for now," she pointed out motioning to the winners who were all over each other.

"Oh, I see," he responded. "I don't think they need any of our help, they are besotted. You can see it in them."

"Now, I don't like the idea of spending the rest of my night suffering with you. But we need to stick together on this and help make things happen for them. Throw them together as best we can, Claude," she sighed.

"Agreed," he conceded.

"It's a hard job, but somebody's gotta do it," she declared looking up and loosening her top at the waist. "Those star-struck lovers stand to gain a lot for our penance, so are you with me?"

"But of course, Amelia."

"Good man. Hey Eden!" She shouted walking away from the table. "Come on honey, let's take these two dodos to the dance floor. I'm thinkin' we need to teach these good fellers a Tennessee move or two."

"Ok, in a second, Em. James's is just taking a call," Eden shouted as she stood in silence beside James's, feeling a little perturbed by his personal call:

"Yes Claire, that's right," he said frowning at his mobile as she grabbed his arm. "I can only just hear you," he said struggling to catch her words and pushing his finger hard into his ear as Eden playfully pulled him forward.

"No, I don't Claire, it's a bit hard to hear at the moment... yes, that's right. So just stay put and wait for Peter to give me a confirmation call? Okay Claire, I'll check the company emails first thing in the morning. Yes, thanks for letting me know, Claire. Bye now."

"Is everything okay, mister hot-shot?" She wondered literally pulling him toward the dance floor.

"Everything's just great. That was my secretary Claire. It looks like some things have changed. I'm staying in Kentucky until further notice. You'll have me right by your side," he said gently kissing her hand to her joyous surprise.

"Wonderful."

"Oh, and by the way, I can't dance."

FOUR: *Langdon*

"West, is that you...? Of course, it's you," he cursed, hastily reassuring himself he was being stupid. "In my office right now!" He shouted, swiftly slamming the phone down then picking it up again. "Valerie... are those damn papers here from my lawyer yet?" He inquired impatiently.

"The morning post hasn't arrived yet, sir. It's still too early for that," she replied playing with her huge auburn fringe then re-positioning her huge rimmed glasses and her yellow, flowered dress collar. "Milton can get the post today. I'm catching up on other stuff. You asked me to be in early because of the massive backlog, because of your holiday," she grumbled, accidentally dropping a magazine to the floor.

"Don't tell me something I already know, woman. I can see you through the office glass. I'm just making sure you're on your toes," he nagged. "Reading your latest trash magazine or beautifying yourself won't get the work done or make the mail arrive any quicker, either. Now, you ring my lawyer up now and find out what the delay is and get me a coffee in here sooner than yesterday," he proclaimed.

"What! But I…erm, alright… I mean yes sir… right away, sir," she fearfully replied, slipping her magazine into the drawer as Milton West hummed past her desk. He glanced at her then timidly knocked on Langdon's door. He was dressed in full cycling regalia and began unclipping his helmet and putting on his glasses from his chest pocket. She grimaced at Milton, then leaned across the desk to hide herself behind him and Langdon's view.

"Careful in there, mister. He's got a bigger burr in his saddle than usual. And he ain't got no clue as to which way is up," she advised to his nervous humming. She cocked her head to look at down his legs. Realising for the first time that he was so skinny, if he stuck out his tongue, he'd look exactly like a zipper. "Oh, coffee," she said, clomping to the office kitchen as she nervously twisted her gold cross necklace. "What did your last slave die of?" She muttered to herself, chewing on her pen. "It's you who's been away sunning your fat hide at the cost of the rest of us who made this humongous work pile in the first place. Humongous ape, humph! Lazy as a steering wheel on a mule. Won't let me do a single thing without his say, the control freak," she cursed as she filled the kettle then started to gaze out of the window to daydream and play with her earrings as it boiled.

"Come in man! Don't waste valuable time knocking on the damn door," Langdon shouted on hearing Milton as his roaring voice vibrated through the wooden office walls, and Milton's teeth.

"Yes sir… of course sir… erm, good morning, sir," came the wiry voice closing the door with a cache of folders tucked tight under his arm.

"What's good about it…? Oh, just take a seat man and be quick about it. Where the hell's your suit anyway…? You're only short of some polka dots. You got more bike jerseys than smart shirts," Langdon remarked, giving a solitary almost human smile and removing his tight and constricting black suit jacket to hang it on his coat stand. Revealing an even tighter fitting white shirt, with two dark patches of sweat underneath his arms. He lifted an arm then sniffed like a baboon and sat back down, completely regardless.

"I'll be changing into my suit shortly, sir," Milton encouraged making a bee-line for the chair at the front of Langdon's huge antique, oak desk. He quietly hummed to himself with his head purposely lowered in an attempt not to garner eye contact with his terrible boss, Langdon Stanley Dainty.

Mr. Acid. A nickname adorned from his initials that he secretly adored because of the negative connotations it conveyed to his friends, his cohort of workers and to his ever-increasing legions of enemies. A man with a veritable growth industry of hate. So much so, that Milton West and Secretary, Valerie Potts could secretly be the treasurer and vice-president of. Milton, or '*West*' had only recently gained his employment to L.S.D construction and industrials. The new kid on the block who had become Langdon's new right-hand man after its last occupier's demise from a heart attack. Milton had effectively become just another rubbing-rag employee for Langdon to taunt, belittle and completely abuse. A fix-it man who knew full well how to extrapolate ways around American laws and systems of rules succinctly for his employer's means. Such long forgotten laws that other people didn't even know existed. West was still feeling his way into Langdon's cut-throat empire and needed a little more time to grasp his ruthless business ways, and how he ran his underhand construction company. Milton's years of experience at the bar in both the supreme and federal courts of Dallas and Houston had furnished him with a second nature aptitude to understand what the other people's thought processes were, even before they did?

A humble and nervous soul, with a huge bag of brains. Mild mannered, and somewhat childlike in stature and character. A trait which sadly allowed him to be powerlessly bullied at school. But a sad attribute that in the end, became his most powerful tool, that more often than not, misled his challengers into thinking he would be a weak pushover, dependent on whosoever dared to try and bury him in a court of law. A nice man that exists as an encyclopedia of understanding, skills and knowledge needed to cope with every scenario any business could take. A health nut who also believes the planet is dying, along with everything on it which, in itself, purported him into a green thinking, clean machine that prefers to cycle everywhere for the countless health benefits it reaps his body and the planet. The other sadly demeaning qualities that set Milton West apart from others, was a particularly embarrassing motor-neuron based, neck-twitch. A myoclonic jerk, which varied in occurrence and severity, dependent on the situation he found himself in. Another failing that was currently of a severely pronounced state of affairs for him was an annoying ever-present weak, and annoying, oratory hum. An anxiety led noise, which over the years he'd fornicated unconsciously into almost every single sentence, except when he was confident and in full flow. The droning variations of which, altered on the complexity of the query or problem he faced.

After taking a doctor prescribed extended sabbatical from work after his last stressful job, and before joining Langdon. He and his wife Hilary began to think he'd belatedly got the twitch under control. But he'd sadly realised, after barely crossing the threshold of Langdon's construction company, it was back with more than a vengeance. The root of which, could only be put down to the pressure and stress and the ferocity of anger that Langdon spoke to, or shouted at him. ERGO: The fouler Langdon's mood or temper, the worse Milton's myoclonic tic and the hum.

Despite all his human failings, he remains just the kind of man, a ruthless take no prisoner's bad-egg like Langdon would be useless without. You could say they were as different as chalk and cheese. With Langdon residing at the other end of Milton's scale. Langdon being a particularly nasty piece of work, who'd clearly needed anger-management classes and a psychiatrist longer than he'd care to admit. An ex Vietnam veteran, who walked with a stick due to an old army shrapnel injury. A scumbag, who thrives on his low-down and mean son-of-a-bitch reputation, who cares not for understanding or owns an honest heart beating in his chest.

"Take a damn, seat man, we have work to do!"

Langdon's phone rang as West fearfully took his seat then meekly placed a bunch of files and papers he'd brought with him onto his lap. He placed his cycling helmet on the desk and began humming quietly to himself as he waited.

"What is it now Valerie? Can't you see I'm in a meeting?" He shouted. "And where's that damn coffee," he fierily added raising his arms aloft, leaning to one side and peering through the clear office glass partition, over West's shoulder so she could see him.

"I know you are sir, but I've got one of your foremen, Jed Gray on the line, and he says it's very important," she stuttered, glancing at his reaction through the glass. "Something about land drilling tests for the proposed 1-75 highway intersection you might be building... shall I put him through?" She asked politely.

"Put him through...? Oh Lord," he snarled. "I'll decide if it's important or not woman, and don't ever presume to know what I'm thinking or try to second guess me. And as for *proposed* or *might be*," he screeched, taking a deep breath and spitting his words in West's direction as he spoke. "You can get those thoughts right out of your stupid empty head. It's happening... and it will happen!" He stated red-faced and thumping his fist onto his desk whilst looking angrily at humming West. "Tell, Jed I'll call him back when I'm free and hold all my calls and get me that damn, coffee. Do you want a coffee man?" He sniffed, waiting for an answer and only getting a hum. "Oh, bring a coffee for cycle-boy, too," he added, about to slam the phone down and panting profusely before any of them had chance to say a word.

"SIR...! Someone else has called. An Eden Buckley from the Harlan Community Alliance. She wanted to speak to you, directly. She was quite abrupt, if I may say," she imparted giving him food for thought.

"Abrupt," he pondered recognizing the surname immediately. "That's Joe Buckley's meddlesome regurgitated offspring," he cursed. "Ring her back and tell her to limit her concerns to the road meeting that I'll be attending with West. Now, get me coffee woman!" He protested thumping down the receiver and looking across his oak desk at Milton with his meek finger held up in the air:

"Umm, I don't drink coffee sir, not for six years... um," West announced shaking his head and mildly twitching to Langdon's contained silence. "Too much... um... caffeine has too many negative impacts on the body."

"Where the hell did you get that clap-trap? I've never heard such cock-a-mammie nonsense, prove it!" He shrieked, issuing some kind of battle of wits challenge and pretending he was mildly interested as the door opened and Valerie walked in faster than a moth in a mitten, with two cups of coffee.

"All fact's sir... um... and all proven," West proudly stated, watching Valerie and looking pleased he'd had chance to open his mouth to put his flippant boss straight on one of his choices for a healthy life. Valerie placed the tray on Langdon's desk and scuttled from the office before he had any chance to brow beat her. He reached for his coffee and proceeded to fortify it with no less than six spoons of sugar as West looked on, completely dumbfounded and mildly twitched, then began to speak:

"Umm... white noise caused by too much caffeine can cause psychosis, and too much stress doesn't help things either sir. Umm... if you're on pain medication too... um, liver damage can be imminent, or at least...umm... a far-reaching possibility. That's just... um... for starters sir," he proudly announced, pushing on his horn-rimmed spectacles as Langdon stirred and sipped his sugar and caffeine fix. "And as for raising your blood pressure well, it... um... can go... off the scale. Excites the circulatory system you see. As well as the... um... well, having the side effect of the shallow breathing... um. Which doesn't allow you to... um... correctly replenish and regulate the air you... um... breathe. You leave stale air in your lungs, which can't be conducive for anybody at all...um... sir," he continued getting somewhat in his stride as Langdon frowned, scratched his bald head and looked into his sugar-gloop mixture.

"How well do you sleep sir? Um... if I may hazard a guess, not very well at all. Caffeine causes insomnia, irritability and irrationality... the three I's... um... It has a six-hour life and takes two hours to break down internally and pass through your digestive system. It... um... stymies the flow of oxygen to your brain also. Cripples it! That's a real truth, sir! So, that's the other two I's accounted for... um," he added very succinctly before Langdon had even processed the answer. He put his coffee on the table as his knowledge bound employee continued his factual bombardment.

"It also reduces your cognitive performance and has a negative impact on your mood. The only way to get back to normal is to drink it again. It's a legal drug.... sir... um... an addiction...!" He said clapping his hands together for effect and accidentally scaring silent Langdon, who was secretly beginning to worry about his heart.

"Go on man, continue," he asked as Milton austerely twitched and Langdon waited, wide-eyed and completely shocked.

"How do you pee sir? Um... sorry, don't answer that erm... no need. I already know how you pee," he confirmed making Langdon frown like a road map as West erratically smiled then continued. "I mean how's your bladder, sir...? Coffee weakens the urinary tract and peritoneum. Oh, yes indeedy, and that really is something for you to think about," he with a pointed finger, as he stood up. "Excuse me, I'm just going to get a small drink of water from your cooler, sir. My mouths a little... um... dry with talking," he explained as Langdon silently watched.

"Please do. In fact, get me some water, pl____," Langdon asked, instantly sighing at his own stupidity for almost uttering the word *please* as he placed his half-drunk coffee back on to the tray.

"Oh, sure sir... um... of course." He walked to the cooler and pulled two plastic cups from its stack. Filled them and walked back to his chair humming with victory to himself. He took a mouthful of his own, gargled and swallowed, then placed Langdon's down on his desk.

"But if I were you sir.... which...um... I'm not...um... I'd stick with the coffee for now," he said taking another nervous sip. "Withdrawal from it can add anxiety, drowsiness and fatigue...um. It can also make you depressed sir."

"Make me depressed!" Langdon shouted as Milton stopped talking to take another, much-needed breath. Langdon grabbed at the water and put his hand up like an Appalachian Indian.

"Just stop talking man...! Enough. That's more than enough! It's YOU that's making me depressed, not the God-damn, coffee...um." He put his elbows on his desk with his hands across his receding hair line, realising he'd just made a comparable humming noise then sighed deeply.

"Well sorry sir, but you did...um... ask," Milton announced with a particularly large twitch. Langdon looked across his desk, and then at Valerie through the glass in the background and said nothing.

"Um... it's a *good* job I didn't tell you all about all the detrimental and bad effects of sugar... umm... sir," he added to Langdon's angry stare which made Milton instantly retreat into his shell and bow his head down again.

"A *good* job?" Langdon shouted. "You'll have *no* job if you don't shut your mouth man. Now let's get down to the matters in hand. This new damn interstate access road I'm building through the derelict houses of those backward kinfolk and over Boyles swamp," he said, secretly happy he was already on a subject that would cause other people harm. West quickly picked up the folders he'd placed on the floor.

"Well, um... yes sir," he ticked. "I have looked into the current state of occupancy of the houses," he paused to open a yellow file on his lap. "The truth is, they're not all derelict... umm... some are, and some others are empty. But... um... the majority of them have been occupied for a very long time. I have all the correct figures right here, sir," he added with a twitch, pulling a paper from the file.

"Is that so Milton. Well, fancy that?" Langdon sarcastically answered, steepling his hands together so hard that West heard his boss's fat fingers crack.

"See the thing is," Langdon whispered leaning forward on his desk and beckoning Milton forward with his index finger. "I don't care... in fact... I don't give a flying hoot who's scratching around in those houses. That land is mine, do you understand me?" Langdon whispered with a clenched fist and tone of anger, feeling compelled to make some kind of statement by crushing Milton's cycling helmet that was sat on the desk beside him. "My road is being built on that damn land," he said pointing hard at his own chest. "Either with eminent domain law, or without. But straight over those lame delinquent's hovels and you're going to make sure it happens. Do you understand me?"

"Well… um."

Good. Because that's what I pay you for man. You're here to make things happen, West. This will be a very big money maker for me. The biggest in a long time. It took years, but now the money has been released for all Kentucky road improvements. Did you know this Harlan highway project was supposed to be undertaken over twenty years ago?"

"Um… yes."

"Oh." Langdon replied knowing Milton had his eye on every ball as he sat back on his huge chair and started rocking himself from side to side with his foot. "And then, the damn powers that be put a cap on the cash and decided to put it on the back-burner then used the money for something else," he sniffed pulling a silver snuff box from his top pocket. "So now they've seen the light and released the coffers for further development to try to bring Harlan County out of the dark ages. So, it's up to us… no," he corrected himself. "It's up to *ME* to make this happen," he exclaimed looking at Milton in a somewhat smug fashion as he sniffed a smidgen of pungent powder up his nose. "One way or another, the land is mine and the profits will be mine to," he said as his eyes watered and he sneezed a thousand germs straight across the desk. "Now of course, there'll be a few casualties along the way but hell, that's the way it's always been. In order to progress, some people's lives have to fall by the wayside." He pushed himself back again in his chair with a cruel smile as he waited for Milton to open his mouth. Milton said nothing, deciding to wait to speak after his thoughtless boss's egotistical speech. "So, all we have to do is get down there and start buying everything up. Slowly… slowly… catchy monkey!" He said grinning to himself as West twitched with distaste. "Every man has his price, you know that much man. Everyone can be bought. From low-down townsfolk, to high court judges, and that's the way of the world," he explained watching Milton's bowed head and wondering if he was listening to a single word. "Get me another cup of water man," Langdon said rising from his chair. He reached across to his coat stand and grabbed his gold, beast's claw walking stick from the umbrella rack. "I need to go drain the main-vein," he announced. "Don't you move a muscle man, I'll be right back." He walked across his office and yanked open his door. Blatantly, ignoring Valerie, and disappearing down the corridor with his walking stick making a loud, rhythmic, and scary thud against the hardwood floor as he went.

West had turned to watch him leave through the half-open door where he could see Valerie frantically opening the morning mail. He nervously smiled as she politely looked back with the knowledge he'd just had a pretty dismal experience and a second-nature, dressing down. The run of the mill kind that, Langdon relished dishing out on a daily basis. West flicked through his paperwork and gathered his thoughts.

Soon, the schizoid and rhythmic thud returned but then stopped. West once again looked down and entrenched himself into his paperwork of concerns and contingencies, but more overtly tweaking his ears for the return of the thud of his boss's cane. His excitable mind even envisioned the possibility of no cane thuds whatsoever and a close and heavy breathing fright episode happening right behind him. On hearing Langdon's raised tones, coupled with Valerie's timid voice behind him he breathed a palpable sigh of relief.

"Just tell Jed to stop bothering me... or he'll be off the payroll for good," he gurned. "Is this all the mail?" He asked leaning his stick to rest on her desk.

"Yes sir, that's all so far," she confirmed suddenly sniffing at the sweaty air and looking up at the overawing fat bull looming over her.

"What do you mean, so far?" He asked with a vacant frown.

"There may be a second post later, sir. So, if the Boyles swamp finalization documents appear in that, I'll bring them straight through," she replied. "That, is what you're waiting for, isn't it, sir?" She sheepishly asked, waiting for his fury. He didn't answer and instead, leaned on her desk and fixed her eyes with a steely gaze.

"You make sure you do woman. because I can't afford to waste any more precious time or any more damn money on this settlement. That cretinous farmer, what's his name again...?" He asked as he rested his weight on her desk and the cane inadvertently slid along and crashed to the floor. Making

West jump out of his skin and Langdon glance down and instantly see red.

"Henry Creech, sir," Valerie muttered.

"Creech! That's him," he affirmed lifting his arms off the desk as he tried to bend down for his cane. He lifted himself back up, cane-less and red in the face. "Anyone would think it was some kind of valuable salmon rich lake. Hell, it's just an old damn swamp, not a lake of gold," he assuaged as he watched with delight as Valerie jumped from her seat and scurried around the desk to retrieve his fallen stick. "Creech, more like leech," he angrily added. "He's living in a bubble if he thinks I'm going to pay his asking price."

"His son, Henry was on the phone asking to speak to you, yesterday, sir. But you were out," she said passing him his cane and returning quickly to her chair.

"There's two of them?" He asked with puzzlement. "Do they have no damn imagination," he furrowed. "Henry one, and Henry two? Heavens above."

"No sir... it's senior and junior erm, sir," she offered to his silent scowl.

"Brains of cows these townsfolk. I'll tell you this, if they think they can take on the might of me and win, they'd better be ready. I'll flatten them like a steamroller, I'm a human steamroller, do you hear me!" He shouted with anger. Valerie decided not to answer and keep her fat, bull, and pig thoughts to herself or she would wholeheartedly have to agree with him and lose her job on the spot.

"If they show up... bring the document's right away, if not, get on to whoever you have to and find out where the hell they are, and what the blazes they're playing at! Keep me bang up to date with all progress and bring me another coffee through, quick smart." He turned on his stick and headed back to his office. Pushed open the door with the stick and walked behind West's swivel chair, grinning to himself. He grabbed the top of the leather back for some added walking support. Then forcefully thrust it away from himself. As he did, West precariously spun around and almost slipped from the chair. Saving his glasses from falling off his face but lost his neatly organized papers across the wooden floor, as Langdon flopped his fat bulk back into his chair with his horrible, cackled laughter as Milton's chair finally came to a stop looking in the opposite direction toward Valerie.

Valerie peeked through the glass as he embarrassedly peered back, then stood up humiliated and anxiously humming to collect the strewn documents from the floor. "Oh, leave them there, West. Better yet, throw the crap in the trash or burn them. I imagine there's been no one else been in touch willing to sign over to me, has there?" He queried.

"No sir," West gulped.

"Well damn them all! They're of no consequence to me whatsoever and damn your stupid figures, to," he fumed. "I don't care who owns what, or whose land belongs to who, how many houses are derelict, or how many are occupied," he added with a heartless stare. "I want them all gone. Destroyed, flattened and history. The hovels, the people, the lot! Is that understood?"

"But sir," Milton timidly interjected as he scurried around to grab the papers. "I do understand what you require and I'll do my best to make it happen as lawfully as possible." He incongruently twitched. "But I have to know what kind of pay-off budget you're working on for this. My limitations sir... and the... um... minimums and maximums that you are willing to pay out." He sat back down on the chair, violently twitched then fished through the papers as Valerie entered the office and Langdon glared at them both for not even bothering to answer his question.

"Listen to me carefully, man. And you, while your stood there! If I had my way they'd get nothing. To be honest, I'd be happier them paying me for having the good grace and vision to build them a damn road in the first place. They'll get as little as possible... I'm not a bank, and I ain't made of money, either. Just get down there, A.S.A.P and every day hence. Grind them into submission fast. Any and every way you can and use every trick in the book. You must have ways to do that with your faultless reputation striding at the legal bar. After all, its sticky situations like this I employed you for. I want you to make them backward folk sick of the sight of you. Every time you hook one of the slippy fish, I want to know about it. Who they are, and how much you paid them off for," he badgered. "When they'll sign on the dotted line and any other mitigating circumstances in need know. When you snare them, I want you to find out every last detail about them. Their family history and any road into their financial situation that we can drag the price down. If they have debts, or a family illness they need ready cash for. You know the kind of thing, man," he said pausing to look up at Valerie as he carried on:

"A need. It could be a disease, drugs, alcohol, addiction, death, life, anything at all. Find all their weak spots. What the hell do you want, woman? Standing there tapping your foot as if you are important," he said with a scowl as Valerie looked at Milton who was frantically taking notes. She looked at Langdon as if she was searching for his conscience, despite knowing he was far from anything like that. Then, in a dangerously awkward and dangerous manner, she banged the coffee tray down on his desk. Then blatantly watched the coffee spill from the cups without moving an inch. Langdon looked up at her, then arrogantly grabbed for the spoon and the sugar.

"The Boyles swamp finalization documents sir," she said pushing them across the desk. "They're not finalized, and they're not signed, erm sir. In fact, they are torn in two." She said added with secret delight, imagining she was digging an invisible knife in Langdon whilst Milton clapped with his secret allegiance. Langdon ignored her and focused on stirring his gloopy coffee. "There's a letter though. Would you like me to read it out… sir?"

She asked narrowing her eyes at silent Milton, as she snatched the hand-written letter from the desk and proceeded to read it out without Langdon's consent:

Acid

Your new offer to me and my wife is an insult as I expected. Just the same God-damn crap you threw at us last time. I'm a proud man and putting a road through my land and over the Boyles is of no good consequence to me, or my family. My kin had the good sense to leave these parts a long time ago. Now granted, it would help the poorer folk of Harlan, my neighbors and the locals get better work and higher paid jobs to support their families. Better road links have been promised and forgotten by now, for far too long. That was the reason I would be selling

for. As well as making sure the wildlife and creatures get safely moved over to Craggy swamp or The Devils Dungeon, as I had asked. And heavens above, that ain't so much to ask. You know I'm close to retirement and more than ready to give up the lease. But hell, you'd kick a mule down if it only had three legs. All I can hope for is God to make you see sense to give me my original price. That's if there is a God in that low-down world of yours?

This is my last offer and it will be rescinded two weeks if you do not comply. And if that is the case, I swear by almighty God that before you get your fat grubby hands on my land I'll give it right back to the government.

But just before you choke on your whiskey or wine, let me give you something else to think on. I've had another offer, from another source in Tennessee. Maybe they'll end up with Boyles and the rest of my land right from under your fat, damn nose. Hopefully, they'll throw your sorry ass in the place before they fill it in.

Hoping to hear from you real soon.

Henry Creech Snr.

#

Langdon's blood began to boil. West and Valerie looked at each other, then at Langdon then back at each other feeling as if they should just hold hands and make a run for it and evacuate from the volcanic eruption about to resonate through the room and possibly the rest of Tennessee. Langdon arrogantly threw the teaspoon spoon on the desk as all three of them watched it drop to the floor. In a rage of fury, Langdon leaned down to his bottom desk drawer then tried pull it open:

"What the hell's wrong with this damn thing," he shouted with a red-face as he continued to yank on the jammed, drawer handle. After about thirty seconds, he managed to get it open just enough to slide his fingers through the top. Using his desk as leverage he jerked, wrenched and tugged at it, until he got it open half-way then took a panting breath as Milton and Valerie watched in amazement as he once again, furiously pulled on the handle so much that all muted West and Valerie could hear was the sound of glass, hitting glass until, as if saved by the bell, Valerie's phone rang from her office.

"I'll erm, I'll go get that," Valerie said thankfully making haste towards the door and realising a lucky 'get-out-of-jail' card from had gracefully been provided from above for this raging bull escape.

"Damn this useless piece of crap," Langdon shouted raucously to a somewhat possessed twitch from Milton. Once Langdon had gauged the drawer was open enough, a relieved smile appeared across his face. He reached inside and pulled out one, of two bottles of whiskey that had been clunking off each other while he'd been pulling on the drawer. West frowned negatively at his sad boss, and the bottle now clasped tightly in his hand he was badgering to screw open. Milton narrowed his eyes to read the words: *Glencrofter.* Scotland's finest single malt whiskey: *Share a dram with friends.* Milton could see the bottle already looked less than half empty as Langdon sat back up as West watched in trepidation for his boss's next painful move. He unscrewed the top, took two huge, grunting gulps from the neck of the bottle. Then, with the whiskey still tightly in his hand, he picked up his coffee, drank a mouthful and then topped up the mug with his whiskey. So much so, had to rest his chin on his desk empty some, to prevent himself from spilling it all over the top of the desk. After his chinned swig, he looked at Milton, to see that his twitch was almost reaching the high echelons of spasm. Langdon sat muted, said even less and gave himself a minute to ingest his much-needed alcoholic fervor and then calmed down. Then, to top everything he stood up, reached over to the coat stand and put his hand in the lapel of his suit coat to produce a small, brown, bottle of pills.

"Don't look at me like that, man," he shouted across the desk. "Nerves man, they're for my nerves, and my heart," he explained, tilting his head backwards and flushing two pills down his throat with his Mickey Finn cocktail of coffee, whiskey and sugar which astounded Milton almost to the point of intervention.

"These accursed people will be the death of me, yet," he alluded. "Right man, what we've just discussed," he said with a stagnant, gurgling burp. "Just put it on the back burner for a while. I want you to get over to Creech's place soon as. Sweet talk the lame idiot and pander to his every whim. Tell him I'm re-considering as you speak. But most important of all, get him on side. Make him believe in you and trust you, implicitly. Get him to like you, as hard as that may be. Try to drag the name of the other interested party out of him. I'm going to make some calls to Tennessee," he said sniffing like a bull with a blocked nose. "I might even go to Tennessee, if I have too," he hypothesized. "I ain't going to have no rug pulled from underneath me on this. I've put too much damn work into it for some other half-baked construction company to reap the profits. I've got a pretty good idea who it is. That is, unless the old, damn snake's lying? I just need to be sure of things before I go any further or make my next move. Hell, I might even have to call in the team," he alluded reaching over to take a slug of his whiskey. He opened his top drawer and fished out and threw an old black, char-edged Italian moleskin diary on his desk.

"Um… what team sir?"

"Oh, never you mind about that, man. It doesn't concern you for now. Well… what are you still doing still sat there? Time's a wasting! Get out of here, and get on it," Langdon exclaimed with his coffee mug in one hand and flicking through the moleskin diary with the other. Milton turned around to exit the alcohol and sweat smelling room. "Oh, and while we're on it, don't forget you have to attend that stupid community meeting for me, West."

"I thought you were attending… sir?" He quizzed.

"I wouldn't be found dead breathing the same air as those worms. Besides, I have to meet some other interfering English ecologist feller and put his nose straight with a few home truths," he dribbled with another mouthful of spirit.

"Which reminds me. That, Buckley girl," he seethed. "She's another inconvenience I can do without. I might have to sort out her incessant intrusions as well."

"Yes erm, well. I'll get on my way right away, sir," Milton twitched. "But, um... there's something you must know about the houses, before I go... sir. I think it's a fact that's important... for you personally... that...um... is," he said pulling another A4 paper from his folder.

"What the hell are you rattling on about man? What could be more important than this?" Langdon furiously asked, looking up from his flea-bitten diary.

"Well sir... all the preliminaries you have asked me to do have been completed. The groundwork into occupancies and tenancies, sir. I've already compiled a pretty extensive register and inventory. That was my first port of call when you assigned me to the job," West explained as Langdon looked at him like he was wasting his precious time. "Um... sorry... I have a full list here of all occupied, vacant, variant and tenanted houses," he twitched. "Full names... histories... backgrounds and occupations of the working tenants to." He held up the paper then apprehensively slid it onto Langdon's desk.

"Will you stop reeling around the fountain, for God's sake," Langdon exclaimed lifting both his open palmed hands into the air. "I haven't got time for you blowing your own trumpet about what a good job you've done. Just tell me what's on your mind. If you're going to dare sway me on this, at least give me something to chew on," he cursed.

"Well sir... ok... um... I'll just cut to the chase," Milton stated, twitching hard as Langdon sighed and took another drink of his coffee cocktail as his right-hand-man gathered his words:

"One of the houses on the land is occupied by your wife's great aunt."

FIVE: *Swim*

He drove his lithe body solidly through a punishing breast stroke. Kick after kick, turn after turn. Relentlessly and without falter, over and over. He turned his head to his left and took a much-needed breath of air. Replenishing his supply as his arms twisted back down to continue with the job in hand. From his snapshot breath and glance, he could gauge that he was over halfway, with less than halfway to go. *She* flashed into his thoughts from nowhere. He quickly extinguished her from his mind and then quickened his pace. He imagined a crowd was cheering him on. Chanting his countries name to the finish line and waving union jacks in his honor. Just as they had back in 2002, when he was representing his country in the commonwealth games.

 His arms raced after each other in a never-ending, wind milling spiral. In his focus, he felt no drag or no hindrance or hampering viscosity of the water. They were as one. He envisioned himself as a waterwheel, constantly twisting as if there was no break in between his arm revolutions as if a river wild was relentlessly throwing itself at him. He had become inanimate and an automaton. He was machine and a finely tuned river engine. Just like the *Waverley* paddle steamer he'd travelled on some weeks before that had him marveling at its aged, yet perfectly tuned steam engine, below decks.

 He tilted his head once again, then took a final glance up with another breath for luck for this final push to glory. In his mind's eye, he'd taken himself straight back to the commonwealth games with the imagined voices cheering in his head just like the real ones, he'd heard all the years before. He panted heavily, then kicked his feet in one final gesture of power. Threw his arms together with his finger-tips to bursting from the water and on to the tile. Thump......! As his hands hit the pool side, his body came to a fast and stifled halt. A delayed backwash of water crashed from behind, hitting his body then dispersing itself on to the poolside. He let out a loud and labored breath of relief then carelessly pushed his goggles off his eyes and head as they dropped aimlessly into the water.

 "Well, what can I tell you buddy," an American/Australian voice remarked before he'd even had chance to draw breath. In his single-minded struggle for perfection, James had completely forgotten about, Nathan. His long-time friend from his school-days who was crouched down above him, at the poolside. He ignored his friends call and continued to catch his breath as he bobbed up and down in the water like a tired buoy as, Nathan spoke again.

"Do you want the good news, or the bad news?" He asked as James reluctantly peered up from the water and pointed his index finger into the air.

"One moment, Nate," he said looking down to the bottom of the pool as he treaded water. He pinched his nose, took a deep breath and then disappeared from view. Swimming down to the bottom to retrieve his goggles that were now lying on the tiles thus leaving Nathan to his own devices. Or at least his stopwatch. Nathan continued to kneel at the pool side and checked his stopwatch again to be more than sure his facts were right as James reappeared faster than a bolt from the blue. But this time, he was at the pool steps just to Nathan's right with the reclaimed goggles wrapped firmly in his hand. He climbed up the steps as Nathan walked toward him;

"So... you ignoramus, I'll ask you again."

"Don't ask me again, just tell me, I'm shattered," James's croaked thinking timing wasn't Nathan's strongest point as he collapsed himself on the poolside bench. He placed the goggles beside him and rested his elbows forward onto his legs. Leant over and took his head in his hands to recuperate his breathing and his composure.

"Well, my old King Edward, you did pretty damn good, buddy," Nathan explained with his fast-talking allophone accent. "Only six seconds slower than you did in the final in 2002. And, another thing," he retorted as James sat back up and pushed his index finger over Nathan's lips.

"Six..." he mumbled behind the finger. "I think a lot harder training is needed, buddy," he concluded as his James's nodded as he looked down at the unforgiving water.

"What's the good news then?"

"Well, to be honest I don't think you're ever going to get your time down to.... what was it in the final again?" He asked looking at him for pointers.

"Forget the time fat mouth, what's the other news?"

"Ok, ok! Point taken. Sorry buddy. I know I have a juggernaut mouth. The good news... is... there's no bad news," he stupidly grinned beckoning James's to see the funny side. "Sorry again. It's your ex-father-in-law. I mean Jane's dad, Iain. He's... Iain has rung again," he corrected his slip lifting the stopwatch chain from over his head feeling uneasy with his below par choice of words.

"Finally," James brightened. "What did the old sod say?" James's asked picking up the goggles and twirling around on his finger.

"He said give him a call when you're free. Oh, and Claire from work called too."

"Oh. I must ring work, ASAP. Thanks, I owe you a pint, pal. Where's... that little girl of mine? I bet she's wrinkled as a prune down there," he said wondering and looking toward the shallow end of the pool and pulling the white goggle strap wide in his hands then playfully mounting them backwards on Nathan's blonde-haired head and strolling away with a smile.

"Did you hear me...? Work called," Nathan shouted, feeling somewhat perturbed. "She's up in the spectator's area and I have your phone right here, pal."

"Oh, Right." James immediately glanced up to the spectating area see Abby sitting at the cafe looking intently into her mobile as usual. He took this phone from Nathan and started walking toward the changing rooms as Nathan followed. "You owe me more than a beer, you... ouch! Scoundrel," he groaned pulling the surreptitiously placed goggles off his head and catching James up along the side of the pool. "Nathan," James asked turning around and stopping in his tracks.

"What now, James's?" He quizzed as James's put both his arms softly on his friend's shoulders and spun him around to face him with his back to the pool, looking eye to eye.

"What is it buddy? Would sir like a massage... a cocktail... or maybe a big Cuban cigar... to go with his big head," Nathan joked. "Or maybe sir's stopwatch... shoved right up sirs..."

"NATHAN, listen!" James's shouted, bringing Nathan's musing back to reality. "Sorry for shouting Nathan, but sometimes I haven't the first which cloud you're on, pal," he claimed. "I just want to thank you for today. I really do appreciate all your help with looking after Abby and the swimming training. Much more than you realise. This hauling myself back to some half-decent kind of fitness is hard going. But having Abby with me on this assignment is a dream come true. I couldn't have done it without you and Sato's help. I appreciate you standing in my corner, yet again. There is one thing though," he sternly asserted. "I met someone." He watched Nathan's face change from a silent frown to rapturous smile and decided to make his words quick before his friend began a full interrogation. "Her name's, Eden and she's wonderful. You, are the only person I've told about her," he conceded.

"James, that's brilliant news," he exclaimed patting him on the back. "Eden huh, cool name," he insisted. "How's Abby with it?" He questioned, expecting a positive answer. "She was the first one you should have… you haven't even told her, have you?"

"No, she doesn't know anything yet. Its early days, and nothing may come of it anyway. I only met her madness last night. That is, she's as crazy as they come," he explained with a smile. "All I do know is, that my instinct tells me she has a genuine heart. A small-town American girl, with an incredibly natural way about her. I think I might get to be with her more, so all her weird characteristics will reveal themselves in good time. If there is anything to be mentioned to Abby, only then, will I open my mouth? I don't want to hurt her," he said with a negative air. "Eden texted me this morning," he added.

"Wow, you got her number, too. Did you text back?" Nathan asked to James's silence. "I'm happy for you buddy. It's about time you finally moved on."

"Anyway, I'd better get changed and ring the office straight away. There's been some developments here, so I'm going to have to cancel this morning's flight home. At least for a little while. I only had to go back to England to take Abby home it doesn't seem to me like she wants to leave, at all," he declared. "Not a single word about missing anything or anyone from back there. I told Eden we might be staying on a while last night, but only briefly"

"Oh, you told your chick, but you ain't told the boss yet. I get it, you coward," he joked. "I'm really happy for you buddy. It's incredible what a good woman can do, eh pal," he mocked, suddenly turning somewhat serious. "Listen buddy, the truth is... Abby doesn't want to go back to England. She opened her heart to Sato and me, last night. She reckons this place might be a new start for the both of you after, erm, Jane. As for this Eden, it's none of my business as long as you're happy. So, while I have a chance to say anything at all, I'm going to say this:

Bloody text her back you idiot!"

"Right," James's said with a wry smile. "I never told her Jane had died. I simply told her I was married before."

"You really are something else, Ustinov. You need to get your act together quick smart."

They both walked toward the exit, in the deep and knowing sense that all of their years of friendship offered.

Nathan had been sat in his friend's corner on many occasions. He'd helped James through thick and thin more times than can be counted on both hands. After the tragic loss of his wife and childhood sweetheart Jane to cancer three years previously, James had found himself in some very dark places. He'd been at the mercy of the soul destroying, unforgiving bottle and at his lowest ebb, he'd even contemplated suicide. Heaven knows where things would have ended for him without the support of his Australian friend.

And likewise, James's had pushed Nathan the strong way through some pretty horrendous scrapes and bad life situations. There was Nathans brief crazy and hazy fall into the world of drugs after his short, and bitter marriage and divorce. The loss of his step father shortly after Jane had died was another tumultuous blow.

Their friendship went back to Cambridge, where they had found themselves irrefutably entwined together as inexperienced and naïve freshers with absolutely no idea of the scheme of things or slightest inclination of their path in life or what the big bad world had to offer. Their camaraderie and understanding of each other's foibles took hold of them immediately. Weirdly having a shared love of swimming, rugby and even the same taste in girls. They became a strong and tight coalition that has endured more knocks and set-backs than most could see in any lifetime. Yet throughout their ups and downs, both had become so much stronger individuals because of each other as a result.

They paused at the pool's exit corridor and Nathan stood strangely silent. Seeming to be further taken aback with James's news and his heart-felt declaration. "Anytime you need me, I'll be right here," he explained stuttering his words with his reply and quickly realising he hadn't stammered in such a long time. A shortcoming that was brought about by the incessant school bullying he'd endured many years before as a young scholar, but a negative foible he'd eventually shook off and thankfully grew out of with James help. Nathan calmed himself and regrouped his sentence, for a big *thank you James* speech as they stood shoulder to shoulder, opposite the tiled wall at the edge of the pool.

"I actually enjoyed watching you torturing yourself and putting those old muscles and bones of yours through that horrendous regime and thankless hurt," he quavered. "You're never going to get your pool length times down to anything near the commonwealth standard again. Let alone, your thirty-something destroyed physique back to the perfection it was when you walked away with the silver medal," he explained taking another breath. "I think deep-down, you know that." Nathan said taking a deep breath and continuing into an eloquently rehearsed long-winded spiel at James ears as his negative, foot-tapping body language which showed he was much less than zero interested in enduring.

James's listened tokenistically, as his mind wandered through thoughts of Eden and Abby, and Jane until he decided to turn his attention to working out a myriad of silencing techniques while Nathan continued his never-ending sermon.

James's looked hard at Nathan, then gave Nathan's shoulder the softest of nudges to see him blindly step backwards to try to feel solid ground where there was only water. His arms flailed wildly at his sides, and he fell backwards, right into the pool. A huge splash of water followed, then a passing female swimmer screamed as another furore of laughter erupted from all around the pool.

Nathan disappeared beneath the water, only to bob back up, both breathless and in shock.

"Thanks buddy!" He cursed, spitting out a mouthful of chlorinous water and thrashing his arms at his sides. "Thanks ever so much you, English lunatic. I'll get you back for that!" He shouted floundering as James smiled and threw his towel over his shoulder as Nathan immediately turned his attention to James stopwatch.

"Is this damn thing waterproof James... James?"

SIX: *Breakfast*

She opened her sleepless eyes and blinked toward the slowly spinning ceiling fan. Loose and laboring, it relentlessly spun above her head like the multitude of thoughts that had churned through her brain and kept her awake half the night. "*Mmm, it's his fault, but that's ok,*" she affirmed to herself as Jamie replaced *him* in her mind. "*Ouch...! It feels like my brain's bouncin' off the sides of my damn head,*" she groaned holding her head underneath the covers. "*That's all that liquor and amazing company for me,*" she subjugated, brushing her hand across her forehead and pushing her long red hair to one side. She sighed and tried to wake her piercing blue eyes to life.

Red hair and blue eyes, a blessed combination indeed. The rarest one percent of people in the whole world. Almost as exceptionally sublime as a four-leaf clover. But this one was as stubborn as a mule for free.

As she bravely pushed the cover from her eyes, the sun-kissed morning cascaded through the window blinds and across her face, creating a bright, aureate and laddered sun-hue across the white bed covers, and directly into her narrowed eyes.

She blinked and squinted, then turned her head away from its stifling glare. "Aargh!"

She grabbed for the spare pillow and pulled it over her head to make a temporary sun visor, then slid her arm back under the covers and over to the cold and empty, side of the bed. Deludingly expecting it to be warm. "*Maybe one day soon*," she dared, day-dreaming inside. The bed had been vacant and solo for a long-time now. That's except for when Jamie's hip was sore as it often was with his Perthes disease hips. On a painful day, he could always be found tucked up beside her, and hankering in for cuddles. Last night, Bailey had snuck into her room as usual, and settled for the floor right by her side. Happy and contented as long as he's near his matriarch. Just as she was when she camped out by his side, when he was born.

On hearing her wake up, he shuffled himself to life to secretly peep his canine snout up at the bed.

He was only the size of his head once upon a time. The only ball of fluff who found the strength to make it through the complicated canine birth with the single-handed help and care of a somewhat younger Eden, twelve years earlier. An ordeal that had forged an inseparable bond between them right through her teenage years and is still going strong.

At his birth, Eden had shown such commitment to her cause she'd been found sleeping numerous times beside the basket with Bailey's Mum, Judy and poor, fighting for life, Bailey. Once he'd got through the dangerous days, she'd noticed that he was at his happiest sleeping on his belly, and across her tummy. With his spindly legs wide apart and spread eagled across her chest. Making young Eden, refer to him as belly, until she changed it to the next best thing, and his true name, Bailey. Soon after she'd nursed him through the first touch and go days of his life, her mothering nature was called on once again when her own son, Jamie had barely reached the tender age of three. One morning, she was tearfully awakened to find him crawling into her room on all fours, crying and trying to make some sense of why his hips were in so much pain. There began eighteen, solid months of crutches, casts and traction on a daily basis to return his mobility to fuller and stronger capacity, albeit leaving him with a slight, pronounced limp. The regular regime of pain-killers and creams to alleviate the problem still remains today, until an operation can be acted upon and scheduled by the deathly slow doctors.

Bailey's Mum Judy lived a full and happy life, then shuffled off to dog heaven. Her owners, and Eden's grandparents, Sally and Joseph still remain. Not ready to shake off their mortal coil but only the ownership of the wooden porch-house where Baily was born to their two granddaughters and Jamie, who is their fifth grandchild. Sally and Joe's ways are still deeply ingrained and inexplicably rooted in the life of all their siblings, and grandkids, most particularly, partial invalid, Jamie. Who has grown to be completely unlike his wayward and abusive father, Kyle? A Name that has almost become a swear word in the Buckley households. Though despite being the biggest mistake of Eden's life, she was more than happy to thank him for giving her such a beautiful son as Jamie. The one good thing to come out of the whole sorry marriage, and the blessing, she thanks God for every single day. But then, loving a child is always full time... never part time.... never sometimes, and certainly not just on your time. It's all or nothing.

Joe and Sally gifted their ex-mining house to their grand-kids, then moved up to Eden and Page's parents, place Arlington Hall. Named after Joe's middle name and built on a beautiful spot overlooking the Cumberland River. Although ailing in health and in years, Sally and Pape Joe still have the major role in the ever-increasing Buckley legacy. They decided they could be better looked after in their twilight years at Arlington so they were on tap for the ever-increasing babysitting duties that came around.

Arlington stands a huge pile of a plot. The biggest of young Joe and Penny's homes. Of which, these days, there are more than one or two. This being thanks to Joe's entrepreneurial skill with business. He designed and built Arlington with his own hands. Overseeing every stage of its inception, its building and construction. From the first shovel of turned earth to the last blade of grass laid.

Joseph Arlington Buckley. A hard-working ex-railway man that had always worked hard and done his best for his family in every sense of the American dream. A self-made man, who has never been afraid to get his hands dirty. Self-taught, self-educated, and thoroughly self-disciplined. Just as his kin have turned out to be. A clever soul who had his eye firmly cast on the ground-breaking and inescapable introduction of computers and technology, as well as all the things that these days, now seem second nature that the whole world takes for granted.

 He was the brains that brought about, The Sentinel Software Corporation. Once a pin cushion dream that is now a giant in computers, software, industries and holdings. Now a vast international and globally recognized leader in all things, PC.

 A multinational of such success and size, it allows him to dip his toe into any other industry or field he sees fit to find a niche. A fortuitous business and family legacy that Eden is more than aptly skilled, but stubbornly reluctant to grab onto the reins of, or be a part of, at all. Despite this, she remains jealously and automatically linked to it by her peers, co-workers or so-called friends. Eden's stark refusal to be involved with her father's empire is a decision that him, himself has continuously and clandestinely tried change for years. And still, she draws the curtain to refuse. Remaining unassumingly happier to teach history, general studies and music to ne up and coming, Harlan county generations.

#

"I know you're down there, beast," she announced sighing and stretching her arms up into the air. She twisted her long slim body to the bedside cabinet to look at the time on her mobile. Secretly hoping to see a text or a missed call from *him*. James's. She groaned a yawn in duality with Bailey, as his head dutifully appeared. He'd instantly rose to his paws after hearing her laboured call. He rested his huge, Labrador head on the bed covers right by her side, as if he was awaiting further instructions. His tail incessantly wagged as he tried to land a lick toward her face. She watched his antics with a smile, then dropped her cell phone onto the bed-sheets and placed her hand softly on his head.

"Morning, shaggy head. Its 7-10, and time to get up, again," she explained as if she was waiting for him to answer.

"Yep, we were almost late again," she confirmed for him. "Oh, its ok monster face, we're always *lastminute.com*, ain't we boy? We should keep all these extra-curricular, late-night man-meetings to a minimum. Ain't that so, shaggy head? Don't you agree, Mister Bailey, sir?" She asked as she stroked her hand into his thick, brown main.

"We're doing far too much of everything, and not enough of something," decided, smiling and thinking about, James's again. "Meetings and marking and woofing and barking... and MEN!" She announced to a random tune as she slid herself back under the bed covers and put her hand under Bailey's jaw to nod his head in agreement for him. He shook his ears, and yelped a canine acknowledgement, as if he knew exactly what she was talking about, as he lifted his legs, and quickly tried his canine best to jump up on to the bed:

"Ah... aah! No beast, no men in the bed. Not even the dog kind. You know the rules by now, boy. We'll maybe just one man might be allowed," she said pointing her finger at his cold nose. "Uh huh, and today, we should get that construction company CEO to take a running jump straight into Boyle's swamp. It'd save all this crazy meeting stuff, heh boy?" She said with a smile thinking about the next few days and what lay in store for her.

"Now, are we agreed on this bed is out-of-bounds business, boy?" She asked quizzically, as she snuggled her white duvet up to her chin and feigned a deep voice and even sterner face. "Are we clear?" She asked with a frown pulling on the quilt and hiding from Bailey, then blowing him a kiss and playfully disappearing underneath the covers again. He let out another playful yelp as she reappeared and rolled on to her slender tummy and bent her legs up into the air. She rested her chin across her clasped hands on the edge of the bed to make her head at eye-level with his. They peered at each other, nose to nose, and dog to master in silence. Then, after a few more teases and tail wags, he jumped up and licked at her face for all he was worth as she laughed and turned her attention to her son in the other room: "Jamie...! It's time to get up, honey," she shouted still trying to fight off Bailey's incorrigible tongue. "So, we do see eye-to-eye then," she asked him again as he yelped even more loudly, somehow knowing that he could, now she'd shouted out of the room. "That's great Lord Bailey paws. Oh, yuck! I'm so glad we're erm, agreed and, erm licking from the same song sheet," she said with a smile, talking to him as if he was some official top-brass or interested party at the up and coming *stop the highway* meeting. Bailey wagged his tail and carried on trying to lap his tongue at her face as she lifted up and blew down his long Labrador ear to try to make him stop. She pushed her hands down onto the mattress and raised herself up onto her knees.

"Nope?" She shook her head from side to side. "You're oblivious to it all ain't you, boy? Good thing, I guess... you, lucky hound," she said with a nod as she stroked his coat and he launched his front paws up onto the bed, yet again. "Are you awake, honey?" She repeated toward her open bedroom door. "Come on now baby, time to get up. We're already running late."

She leant across and grabbed at her spring water, twisted it open and took a long, dry-mouthed swig. As she did, Bailey's ears lowered and his front paws crept further onto the bed. She screwed on the top and replaced it back to the cabinet then grabbed for Bailey's head and ears again. She gave in to his love and watched as he proudly lifted his hind-quarters up, on to the mattress. She grabbed him tight, then hugged him for all she was worth. "Go on boy, go get, Jamie." He barked and bounded off the bed and scampered through the door.

"I'm awake Mom," Jamie belatedly replied as Eden climbed from the bed and threw on her green nightgown. She grabbed her for her cell and then headed straight for the kitchen. Flicked on the kettle and then opened the bread-bin. Stares at the contents and pushing the two last and lonely slices of bread inside the toaster. She pulled open the cupboard and fridge at the same time, then poured out two glasses of orange then stopped dead in her tracks. Concentrating her gaze and her aim to get throw empty carton as masterfully as a dart player across the kitchen and slap-bang into the waste bin. "More recycle," she muttered as it thunked perfectly into the trash. She grabbed some school folders off the kitchen table and tucked them under her arm, then placed them on her brown, sofa-bed opposite and quickly returned to the kitchen for her mobile charger so she could recharge her cell. "Come on baby... breakfast. I got no eggs, I'm afraid. I must remember to remember get some groceries," she affirmed switching on the radio somewhat automatically as the toast popped up. She buttered the crisped bread then plonked two empty cereal bowls on the table. Opened another cupboard, and then grabbed the corn oats to lace the bowls. Finally taking a short step backwards to grab last of the milk from the fridge like some kind of kitchen ballerina or a psychotic, whirling dervish. "It's on the table!"

Jamie limped into the kitchen with his canine bodyguard watching his over-size blue pajamas pants being dragged nonchalantly, across the kitchen floor. His blonde bed-head hair was sticking up all over the place as rubbed at his ear, yawned and then took his seat at the kitchen table.

"Good morning soldier," she sang out, before placing a kiss on her little boy's brow.

"Morning Mom," he replied, yawning a frown and picking up his spoon.

"Are you ready for the play, honey?" Eden asked taking a sip of her orange and loosening her nightgown.

"Yes Mom, I reckon so," he confirmed, crunching a mouthful of oat flakes after his words.

"Oh good. If we have time, I'll get your guitar tuned. How's the hip today?" She shouted as she walked from the bathroom to her bedroom.

"Its fine, Mom," he shouted twirling a finger into his mess of hair. "Mom... dad said if he has time, he might come to watch the play today?" He recalled swishing the oat flakes around his bowl as she returned to the kitchen, fully clothed in flared brown slacks and a matching jumper in no time at all.

"I know baby. I hope he keeps his word and shows up for once. Let's just wait and see," she explained teasing her jumper down into place. "Please don't build your hopes up, honey." She bent down at his chair and softly rubbed her thumb across his cheek, secretly knowing the fate of his question. She could almost imagine his little spark of hope fade to gray. "I'll be there, and Pape and Grandma, too. I hope they're feeling up to it?" She kicked off her slippers, and then caught them at the same time. "Anyway, we're just faces in the crowd," she said exchanging the shoddy slippers for a pair of flat soled sneakers from beside the sofa. "There's going to be a big crowd today, baby. You just try to remember those chords honey. Ooh, with a big crowd comes traffic. So, driving in town will be a monster nightmare today," she thought as she poured more hot water into her coffee cup. "The Fourth of July celebrations are here next week as well, and everybody will be busying. On top of everything else, there's those damn road-works near Huff Park to contend with?" She grimaced. "I thought they'd have had them sewn up and done way before our Independence Day? Its backward progress, just like all that crazy road digging that's going on over at the dam. They seem to be taking forever with things, these days," she purported to herself. "Come on honey, finish that breakfast, or we'll be late. Oh, and H o n e y! Don't give the beast any more of your toast."

After less than five minutes, Jamie had almost finished his breakfast and Eden was pushing her school papers neatly into two large work bags with a piece of toast lodged between her teeth. Jamie crunched at his last piece as Bailey regimentally stood silently beside his chair, quietly hoping for any more tit-bits. Eden sat down on the sofa and flicked through her marked and un-marked essays, then stacked them into two quick piles. "Ok half done, half to go... shucks... not enough hours in a day," she explained to herself as she glanced over at his breakfast progress.

She moved from the sofa, back into the kitchen and began putting his dinner into his school bag. "*Apple, banana and pear, oh my,*" she said bursting out laughing almost immediately. "*Apple, banana and pear!* That reminds me of the *Wizard of Oz!*" She affirmed smiling across at Jamie. "*Lions and tigers and bears, oh my!*" She said, singing the songs refrain, and smiling and rocking herself from side to side.

She clicked his school bag shut in time with her song, and then danced across the room toward the wall mirror. She grabbed the hairbrush from the hall table and began her somewhat tumultuous task of choking it through her curly hair, whilst also singing into the brush and looking in the mirror at the same time. "*Lions and tigers and hair.... lions and tigers and hair, oh my.*" She walked back to the kitchen and continued her singing onslaught as Jamie listened. "*Lions and Tigers and... hair... OUCH!*" The brush knotted in her long locks and slipped from her hand and down to the kitchen floor. "Ouch, my hair!"

Jamie had finished his breakfast and quietly walked out of the kitchen quietly humming the same tune to himself.

"Don't forget to clean your teeth, baby. Oh, this hair... I love you honest I do. But you really are a handful," she said, still mimicking Dorothy's from *The Wizard of Oz's* voice. "I'm not talking to you honey, I'm talking to this bird's nest of mine... ouch! Where did I put that afro comb again?" She wondered still tugging the hairbrush through the stubborn knots. "Oh, darn it," she exclaimed looking at the clock. "No time... no time!"

Because of her rushing annoyance, she quickly decided a simple hair band would suffice. She dropped the hair brush on the kitchen table and walked to the hallway mirror. Picked up a butterfly clip, and hair-band from a plastic box below it and gripped them tightly in her teeth. She gathered her long hair with both hands, then took the hair-band from out of her mouth. Fed it over her fingers and across her curls, then looked back into the mirror to give it a quick, once-over. She turned her back to the mirror, then looked over her shoulder, and clicked the small, red, butterfly-clip into place. "Oh, this darn mess of curl. Thanks Grandma."

A pull, a twist and a tweak later, and her smart work ready look was complete. "Hey, will I do?" She quizzed bemused Jamie as he walked back into the room and nodded as he brushed at his teeth. '*I wonder if I'd look good enough for him,*' she whispered to herself, looking more than fit for purpose and amazingly beautiful at the same time. Eden didn't need make-up to look good, and she rarely used it at all. Just one less job she need worry about. She picked up her glass of fresh orange and gulped it back as Jamie grabbed the last piece of toast from his plate and pushed it into hovering Bailey's jaws. He returned to the bathroom to rinse out his mouth and within five minutes, he was dressed and ready to roll-and-roll, just like his Mom.

"Good to go honey?" She asked, kneeling and zipping up his coat, then filling a glass of water.

"Yes, Mom."

"Here, take your pills before we go, and don't forget to take the afternoon ones after your dinner."

"All gone. Come on Bailey," he said gulping down his pills and putting the glass in the sink as Bailey scampered out of the kitchen and Eden followed. She locked the door and they headed towards the garage. Jamie limped across the garden to throw a tennis ball for Bailey. "Oh, I forgot you have the car in the shop getting fixed. Am I getting the school bus today?" He wondered as she fumbled through her keys and pushed one into the rusted, garage door lock.

"No, you are not, Jamie. Today is a Mustang day," she eagerly explained smiling as she turned the key in the lock. "We'll just have to use Pape's car for a day or so, until the Jeep is repaired."

"Great! I don't like the school bus, anyway. They call me names. Peg-leg and Limpalot, and Long John Silver," he explained as she wiggled out the key and pushed the garage door away from herself. The creaking door opened halfway, then promptly stopped.

"Call you names? Who does?"

"The big boys at the back."

Is that so," she asked with a frown as she and yanked hard on the bottom of the door. "Oh, we'll be late at this rate. Come on... come on?" She put down her bags then grabbed the underside of the door. Deciding to give it a much heftier, helping hand.

"Well they did last time."

"They did huh...?" She cursed. "I'll have to be doing something about that kind of behaviour," she replied thinking about the cruel names that related to his limp. "Right, I need some big strong hands to help me open up this door, honey," she reasoned immediately thinking about James. "You pull at the bottom and I'll push up here."

"That old antique... does it even work?" He asked grabbing the underside of the garage door as Bailey waited on the grass for the ball.

"Of course, it works baby, it's a magic Mustang. They always work." As they began to push and pull, the garage door creaked, then and twanged and moved up a little, then suddenly stopped, as if it had jammed again. "Oh, come on you, rusty piece of junk," she panted. "Phew. Ok, just hold on now baby... let me just check something." She walked to each side of the door and looked up at its corroded springs and then pushed the door back down. "Ok. Let's try again, and this time, let's pretend we're opening a big can of beans," she smiled. He looked up at her with a quizzical face, smiled wistfully and nodded his head "Are you ready honey, this time after beans. Here we go... both together now," she said looking down at him as he gripped the bottom of the steel door with both hands. "*One, two... BEANS...!*"

They pushed and pulled at the door until it groaned and creaked then eventually released itself. As it did, it shot up to the top of the garage and banged itself to a stop. As they watched, they automatically hunched themselves over, cringed and then closed their eyes. Once the door had come to a stop they both opened their eyes and burst out laughing. It had been so long since it had been opened, it showered both of them with rust, paint and pieces of wood.

"We, did it Mom," he said shouting their victory then saluting hi Mom with a high-five.

"We, sure did honey," she agreed brushing bits off her coat and from his hair. "Wow baby, you're as strong as Hercules."

As they looked inside, they could see the old Mustang sitting undisturbed underneath some dusty bed sheets. Jamie had always known it was there but had never seen it. The garage was out-of-bounds to him specifically for that reason. He'd sneaked inside to play a time or two, but never paid it any interest at all. "Ok, now go around the other side of the car and grab hold of the sheet, like this," she explained lifting her corner of the raggedy cotton cover near the front wheel. "You take hold of that side and hold it tight in your hand and walk with me. But don't run, now," she pointed out. "When I shout, you have to lift it high above your head, honey. As high as you possibly can, ok?"

"Sure thing!"

"But be really careful though," she sternly echoed. "If it snags on anything just stop. Can you do that honey?" She asked as he looked over at her thinking that she seemed to be taking this lifting off the sheet thing very seriously.

"Of course, Mom, piece of cake," he nodded as he grabbed the sheet in his hand. "Can we do *beans*, again?" He asked with a smile.

"You bet we can, honey," she agreed. *One, two... beans*!" They walked in unison and silence and lifted the sheet off the car whilst moving to the rear of the car. As they did, the dusty sheets moved along with them without so much as snagging once. They slided and glided off the Mustang's paintwork like silk until they got to the rear of the car. Then, with their own weight, the sheets dropped off its roof down to the garage floor. As the mustang was revealed, the morning sunlight bounced off its gleaming ruby-red paintwork. Jamie seemed to be shocked into silence with its beauty as Eden simpered a big chuckle to herself.

"Wow, Mom. It's beautiful," he gasped still inadvertently holding on to the sheet.

"Yep, she sure is honey. This is *Betsy*. Let's just hope she's in a good mood today." Eden gathered the dusty sheets from the floor and placed them on Pape's old work bench, at the back of the garage. She took a single sheet from the bundle, shook it wildly then opened up the Mustang's passenger door. She lifted the seat lock and pulled it forward. Leaned over the top and lay the single sheet in her hand across the back. Neatly tucking it in at the corners. "Bailey, I hope your paws are at least half clean? There you go Jamie, get inside, but be careful with your shoes, honey. Pape like to keep *Betsy* spotless and so must we," she explained walking to the front of the garage and picking up her bags as he cautiously climbed into the back of the car and sat on the sheet as Bailey slowly followed, who also seemed to be in extra careful mode as he took his place beside Jamie less raucously than usual with the tennis ball gripped tightly, between his teeth. Eden walked around the side of the car, dropped her bag on to the passenger seat, and then walked back to Pape's bench, at the back of the garage. Leaving Jamie to settle himself into the glory of his new charger's, back seats. "Sit nice BEAST," Eden shouted to ball-biting Bailey from the wooden bench. His ears lowered and the tennis ball dropped to the floor of the car. She pulled on the handle of one of the wooden drawers on the bench, which was filled with oily and ancient looking spanners. "Yeuch!" She grabbed a heavy handful of the wrenches and put them on top of the bench. "Oh shoot! I'm filthy already?" She repeated the process until the drawer was completely empty.

"Mom what are you doing?" He shouted over his shoulder. "Can we get going? I want to ride in the Mustang. It is so COOOL."

"I won't be a minute honey. I'm just looking for the... where the hecks the...?" She wondered to herself.

"No, I don't want your ball, I want a ride in the Mustang," Jamie said to Bailey who'd retrieved his ball from the floor of the car and was currently chomping on it, right in Jamie's face. He grabbed the ball and threw it through the half-open car door, then turned back to look at Bailey. "Now park your butt, mutt," he shouted sounding somewhat reminiscent of his Mother as she continued to worry and rifle around at the bottom of the spanner drawer. She grabbed at the oily, cotton drawer liner at the bottom and lifted it between her thumb and index finger to reveal a key that was taped to the bottom of the drawer. "There you are! Ok, honey, I'll be right with you. I was just getting the car key." She put the key on the bench, then turned to her left and switched on the hot water tap beside the bench and quickly washed her oily hands in the sink. Quickly drying them as she picked up the key and walked over to the car.

"Right," she said quickly taking her seat and fastening the safety belt. She looked over her shoulder at Jamie, then Bailey and smiled: "Here goes nothing." She puckered her lips and kissed the key. "I do hope she's willing. *Betsy* hasn't been on the road for... ooh, let me see now?" She said scratching her head as she shook the gearstick from side to side as she pushed the key into the ignition. "It must be five years since she last moved. Give or take a year. "Ok, fingers crossed... In fact, cross everything, honey," she hollered. As she turned the key the engine kicked, coughed and spluttered, then cleanly revved and sprang to life. Then, she pushed down hard on the accelerator; *Vroom... vroom...*! Went the engine. Almost as soon as the noise reverberated around the garage, it faded and then stopped. Inside the Mustang, the happy smiles, turned to sadness.

"Has it got gas, Mom?" Jamie pointed out learnedly

"Has it got any gas? Tut, what do you think I am," she replied somewhat unsurely, realising he had a very, valid point. "Of course, it has," she frowned. "At least it did five years ago," she said quickly eyeing the needle on the dash. "Let's give her a minute. She's not used to all this excitement. Been sleeping for a long a while... hibernating. Ok, *Betsy*... one more time girl. Let's do this." She turned on the key again and then pressed hard once more on the accelerator. The engine reluctantly turned over and then let out a spurious bang. *'Vroom*!' She turned to Jamie to see he was already grinning from ear to ear. "Yippee," she shouted. "I knew she was in a good mood. Baby, we must remember some petrol on the way."

He visually agreed, as he silently nodded at her through the noise of the loud, revving engine. She crunched into first gear and trundled out of the garage. "Stay right there, honey," she said un-clipping her seat belt. "I'll just lock the garage door, then we're on our way." She momentarily walked behind the car, then jumped back in and looked over her shoulder at eager Jamie, and Bailey. "Drive Mom, drive!"

SEVEN: *School*

Eden arrived at Jamie's school at the same time as his class teacher and her old school friend, Laura who was fiddling with her glasses and trying to park her jeep with some trepidation. On seeing each other, Laura decided her half-hearted parking attempt was as good as it was going to get as she frantically jumped out of her car at exactly the same time as Eden.

"Hey Red, how are you? Come here sweetheart... let me give you a hug," Laura exclaimed running around her car toward her friend. Eden smiled and bent down to exchange hugs with her somewhat smaller friend as Jamie slid himself out of the Mustang and closed the door on Bailey to go and wait beside his Mom for his goodbye kiss.

"Where have you been hiding yourself girl? Let me take a look at you," Laura asked standing back to take a long look at her old friend. "What's with *Betsy* Mustang? I thought she was long gone?"

"Nope. Pape would die first."

"She's still as beautiful as she ever was. How about you girl. How's things with you after... well, you know what I mean," she intimated briefly nodding her eyes to Jamie who was quietly watching all the other kids walking into the school almost in procession.

"Oh, you know, I'm fine Laura, honestly. You always find a way to get through," she replied bowing her head at the unspoken subject matter that her friend was referring to, then changing the subject almost as fast. But you know the drill Laura, it's always the same. Music... marking.... tests... and marking... assignments and the endless student support. Oh, and did I mention the marking? It seems to be never ending these days," she sighed.

"I know what you mean. I'm always behind with that too. They don't make allowances for how much it takes over your home life. I seem to be putting ticks and crosses on papers all the time when I'm home. But I'm glad everything's okay.

"Well, everything except fighting to keep a roof over our head, and don't even ask Laura! It's a long story," she sighed not wanting to go in to any detail because Jamie was standing there. "As for the Mustang; it's only temporary until I get the jeep back. I'm thinking of coming in with him on the school bus tomorrow, though. Some of the bigger kids have been getting a tad nasty."

"Nasty, I don't follow, Eden?"

"Name calling," Eden said nodding her eyes to Jamie just as Laura had.

"Really. That's not good but I suppose it's just what we did. Not that I'm condoning it," Laura said shaking her head and knowing full well she wouldn't like to be on the receiving end of any nasty words from kids or a crossed word from Eden. "Anyway, listen, we should get out sometime and have a real catch up."

"I'd would love to if the constant exam marking would let us," Eden joked.

"Oh, and hey... and another thing," Laura stopped herself. "I heard some Chinese whispers," she teased turning her own voice to a whisper as she spoke. "I was told you had someone new on the horizon. Is the rumor true," she coaxed? "Maybe that's why I haven't heard a word from you in ages. Up to your neck with a new man," she joked as Jamie looked up to try to hear what all the whispering was about. "Good morning Jamie, your Mom's got you here bright and early today.

"Mom, there's Declan," Jamie said eager to walk in school with his best friend.

"Okay, honey, off you go and catch him up," she said planting a kiss on his head.

"Yes, just go with Declan and I'll be right with you," Laura said deciding her inquiring words might not be good for his ears.

"Oh, and it was the Mustang got me here early, miss. It's like a rocket on wheels. Bye Mom," he said as he limped away.

"Ok baby," she shouted. "Have a good day and I'll be back over before the *Play* to tune the guitar. What time is the Play this afternoon, Laura?" She asked, deflecting Laura's question and turning to watch him disappear through the entrance doors.

"I'm waiting," Laura smiled folding her arms.

"Nope. There's no one on the horizon, under the bonnet or within a thousand miles. And they're isn't going to be either. Not unless he's a Prince, or a King," she reasoned instantly thinking about James.

"Oh, really Red, is that so? Because that isn't what my little birdy told me, you, big fibber! You seem to forget that Amelia and I are still close. She's already told me all about your big new thing, or should I say you're British dashing King," she replied giggling intensely. "He's the king of England, isn't he?" She japed as Eden threw her hand over Laura's mouth and turned her head away laughing.

"I'll kill that girl. She has such a big trap and unstoppable mouth. You take no notice of that girl. She's making mountains from molehills," she chimed.

"Hey now hold on. Don't give her a hard time. Amelia want's what is best for your heart, and you know she does. She said he's tall dark and handsome. Is it true?" Laura asked waiting for Eden to speak.

"Well as I remember he wasn't bad at all," she sighed looking up at the sky and biting on her finger then growing inanimate as she reminisced. "I know Amelia want's the best for me, bless her heart," she paused. "He was a little bit of incredible," she continued. "At, playing pool, I mean."

"Nope. I'm not buying that, Eden. I think you've been smitten by a Britain," she giggled as Eden laughed.

"He potted every ball, one after one... he never missed a shot, Laura," she said as her eyes brightened.

"I think he potted all your balls to, didn't he, Red. Where is the dashing Prince now?"

"Hey! Nothing happened in that way you, big nosey parker," she insisted with a coy smile. "It was a kiss on the hand and a peck on the cheek," she said with a sigh. "He was a complete gentleman, and you know that's something that I'm really not accustomed to at all. And right now, I don't know where he is. So, let's just erm... forget him Laura, because I have to. I don't want to get in any more man-soup or be with him on the rebound. I need to put him out of my mind, because he's almost took it over as it is."

"Eden, allow yourself have a little happiness, for heaven's sake."

"We did swap numbers and I text him this morning, but I guess he's forgotten all about me now," she muttered feeling sorry for herself. "Last thing he said was he'd had a reprieve from flying home. So, I know he's in Kentucky somewhere. Oh, and he's got a daughter, and she's here with him. He's been married before as well," she explained feeling as if they were both from broken marriages and realising she had told Laura everything she needed to know in less than a minute.

"It'll take a little time. Give it time," Eden.

"Time is something we don't have. We both have such busy lives. From what he told me, he travels all over the world, all the time and that's far too busy for a small-town girl like me. Oh, I don't know. Maybe he'll ring me, and maybe he won't? But at least I didn't have to get hooked up by you this time you scoundrel. Do you remember when you fixed me up with that skinny guy... what was his name again?" She suddenly remembered, searching her mind.

"Oh yes. It was Lance, Lance Linton," Laura added putting her hand over her mouth in reminiscent shock.

"Lance! Pah, more like prance," Eden said, raising an eyebrow. "I could have killed you, Laura. Lance Linton...! Oh my, more like prance stinkin!" That skinny Nancy boy that smelled better than I did," she frowned. "In the end, I had to pretend I needed the toilet to ring my Mom and get her to call the bar, just to get away from him. Oh, no. Not my kind of man at all, Laura. About as rugged as a bunch of flowers," she explained to Laura's giggling horror. "I kid you not honey. A metro-sexual with eyeliner. I swear down. Golly, how much did he love his own ass? There was no room for anyone else in his life because he adored himself that much." Eden said as they both burst out in fits of laughter.

"I honestly thought his bow tie was a secret camera. I ask you honey, a bow tie? So, Sunday school," she cackled as Laura screamed with joy as they both looked around at the shocked looking school kids that were turning their heads at the unruly laughter as they were passing by as if it wasn't the right thing for teachers to have feelings as well as boyfriends, or a laudable sense of humor.

"Right, I'll call you, and we'll get the old agents together."

"OMG... Laura! The *Cotton candy agents,* I completely forgot about all that crazy stuff. What were our names again?"

"Oh, come on now Eden, you should remember them all off by heart," she whimpered:

"You were agent Curly Choc, I was agent Treacle, Page was agent Fudge and Kerry was agent, Jelly-Baby," she said pausing to think. "Amelia was agent Cherry Drop and big John was agent Sugar-Daddy. Ruth was agent Swizzle I think. Oh, last but not least, Kyle was agent Nougat. Just like the damn nougat and idiot he turned out to be!" Laura added as their laughter ceased and Eden remembered that Kyle was also in their youth, as well as the father of her child.

"Mmm, yes well Laura and on that sad note, its way past time both of us weren't here. I'll call you... and we'll have that get together. I promise honey."

"You make sure you do, Red. A little *us* time. All work and no play make's Eden a dull girl. I know Amelia will be up for it, and Ruth too. You make sure you ask Page, next time you're down in Tennessee. Hey, maybe we can even have a night out down there, and stay over at Pages, just like we did last time? Wouldn't that would be brilliant? Come on honey, let's make it sooner than later," she said grabbing Eden's hands and squeezing them together with her own.

"Well, there is a band coming to Nashville this month who I'd love to see. But me and Page aren't seeing eye to eye at the moment? I would love to catch them live if I can because they might not be over here again for a while. They are twin sisters, and I've heard so many good things about them, and..." she enthused, ardently carrying herself along with her musical vigor then pausing.

"Go on, Eden."

"Well, what's kind of weird is that they are British, just like *him*," she said referring to James's again. "Their first album is brilliant," she eagerly explained. "They sound like they've been doing it for years, and golly, they're so fresh and so young, and so *country,* and all that from over the pond too? I think they're going be playing at the *Bluebird cafe* or the *Grand Old Opry.* Or was it at the *Ryman*? Mmm, I must go check that out," she garbled as Laura realised she'd hit a nerve in her old school friend.

"Right, I really must go in. What's the band's name again?" Laura asked looking at her watch.

"Ward Thomas," she replied looking at her own watch and seeing she'd less than fifteen minutes get to Harlan County High School, and then realising that Bailey was still patiently waiting in the car. "Check them out on the internet, Laura. Ward Thomas...! Don't you forget now," she said, pecking her friend on the cheek. "I'll send you a link to one of their songs," she shouted climbing into the Mustang and fastening her seat belt.

"Ok, honey. Ward Thomas... I got it," Laura replied scribbling it on her hand and putting her pen in her teeth and waving. "One more thing, Red... I hope he comes back to you."

"Yeah, whatever. Speak soon Laura, love you," she said gulping as Laura's words echoed in her head. As she opened the car door, a strange girl's voice came from behind her

"Miss Buckley, could I have a quick word?"

EIGHT: *Music class*

"Ok so take the song; *every time we say goodbye* by Cole Porter. Does anyone know him, or anything about him?" She asked, questioning her morning music class to a sea of nodding heads.

"Yes Mam, he's a... I mean was a pianist and a songwriter from Indiana who went to Yale back in the day. I think he's on the Hollywood walk of fame. I know that song off by heart," came the enthusiastic reply from a young white kid who was sitting close to the upright piano and motioning toward it. Secretly dying to impart the whole room with his best Cole Porter impression.

"Good. I think most people know or have heard of him. The man's an American Legend," Eden acknowledged. "If you didn't know him, you wouldn't be sat here in the first place. And you are right on all of that, Shawn, but there's more," she continued:

"Cole Porter learned the violin at six and the piano at eight. That's some going, huh," she stated.

"Anyway, that song is a perfect example of what I'm trying to explain," she said picking up her guitar and throwing the strap over her shoulder. "He starts the song on *A flat* and finishes in *A minor*. Just listen to the difference," she explained stringing the opening chord, then quickly

switching to the other chord and humming along as she did. "He makes the change clearer and more visible with his lyrics too:
'There's no love song finer, but how strange the change, from major to minor. Every time we say goodbye.' It became a jazz standard and a benchmark just like so many others he wrote in his short life." She looked at her watch, then confirmed it with the class clock behind her. "Right people, we're fast running out of time. Thanks to Wendy and Josh for their lovely renditions of Sinatra's, *you make me feel so young.* I wish I did," she joked. "Very well done, you two. So, on that note, here's the bit you all hate. Homework!" She said drawling her voice. "Now I'm not asking for blood, but I want you all to learn a song that is in a key you've never played in before. A key you hate, or one you avoid like the plague because it's either too hard to play or isn't in your vocal range. You can pair up if you like? I'll leave it all up to you. And that's about it. So, put the instruments safely back where they belong, and if it's ok with you, we'll finish off a little early. I have to go tune my boy's guitar. And that isn't coded language for needing the toilet either," she grinned as the students quickly scuffled and screeched up from their chairs. A small black boy approached her desk at the front of the class as she knitted her guitar plectrum between its strings and carefully placed her acoustic into its case as she noticed he had a guitar still hanging across his chest.

"Miss Buckley, I've been erm... working on a song with some completely different chords. To be honest, I don't even think they're recognized chords at all. That's why I'm... a little unsure," he explained

"Really Abe? What's your song called? You can quickly show me the chords on your guitar," she asked clipping shut her guitar case, and thinking about the time.

"It's called: *Don't ever forget me.* It's about a boy and a girl, or erm... a man and a woman who are in love but get separated because of their families," Abraham shyly explained. "He's in America and she has to leave to go home to England," he continued tweaking and tuning his guitar strings as the last of the other pupils left the class.

"Mmm. England huh, go on, tell me more. No, in fact… play me more, Abraham. Because that's such inspiration at your tender age," she said excitedly whilst keeping a firm eye on the clock and secretly returning her thoughts to the England and James.

"Well ok, I'll just play it, shall I," he smiled, sliding his fingers onto his guitar fret board "It's a slow one, miss. The chorus chords are the same as the verse ones. That's why it shouldn't work. But it erm, it just does." Abraham smiled, stood back and looked down at his guitar. Quietly strumming and feeling the emotion of the song, as Eden relaxed herself into her chair with silent anticipation.

 He continued to play the guitar as he ran through the broken chord arpeggios at the introduction of the song with his voice humming along in tune. The poignancy of the song was somewhat more enhanced, due to the emptiness and ideal acoustic construction of the music room as well as the comparisons to Eden and what she was feeling. Realising Abraham's nervous sounding voice, she slowly put her hand up:

"Abraham, hold it one second. Relax a little honey, you're not on trial here. It's your voice, and it's your song. Are there any words with that?" She quizzed, standing up.

"Yes miss, I got words. I've changed them a few times until I think they're right. I'm happy with them now."

"Great. Sing the song with the words and let yourself go. Don't be so staid when you perform. Feel the song, and let it flow. You need the audience to really feel it. Be sure to hold your head up high, or people won't be able to hear you when you're looking down at your guitar strings."

"Okay. It's only usually me in my bedroom, but I know what you mean. Do you mind if I start again and I'll sing the words this time?" He asked.

"Of course. You do whatever makes you feel comfortable, Abe. But just make it real. Feel it from the heart. That's what performing is all about," she explained. "Now, in your own time." She watched as Abraham repositioned his guitar, quietly cleared his throat and then strummed into his intro:

"I'll nod in the break and the chorus, and then you can get a feel for it, miss," Abraham explained just before he hit the main chord, and then began to sing;

"It seems impossible to take…. a little piece of your heart.
But you know I, wanna make a claim.
A little finish to a start.
People say it's easy to say goodbye, with a broken heart.
But with nowhere to run, and nowhere to hide, my emotion is out of time.

I know that you're leaving and there's nothing I can do.
But baby there's just one thing, I want you to do… oh… ooh!

Don't, don't ever forget me, don't ever leave me alone, oh baby.
If I see you in my dreams, then maybe, maybe I can take you home."

#

She began to smile and calmly relaxed in to the pleasant sound that was emanating from Abrahams guitar playing and his young, yet husky, and soulful voice.

Abraham was a particularly quiet and unassuming member of the class and indeed, the school. He never got into any trouble, kept himself to himself, and didn't even hang around as part of a gang. He was a solitary soul who hung around with nobody, but himself and of course, his music and his guitar. He was particularly un-academic and struggled with arithmetic and English. But he was hands and heart above everybody else in more the artistic subjects. She had noticed his musical spark and his surprisingly mature and astonishing guitar playing abilities when he first applied for the scholarship. She harboured a gut instinct that this unapologetically astounding musical student would never become a 9 to 5 pen pusher or an ordinary, everyday member of society. And that he would eventually become a star in his own right. Reliant on nothing, but his voice and his musical adeptness.

She leant back in her chair, with her hands on her head and her eyes closed. Happy to be listening to Abraham singing and playing out his heart. As the song reached its climatic crescendo, and ended, she quickly opened her eyes, calmly looked ahead and suddenly noticed the clock. "Oh, hot sauce! You sent me a million miles away. That was beautiful, Abraham. It works with the chords for verse and chorus, completely. It's very accomplished," she explained. "You really must get it down and record it, Abe. I can imagine a string section running right through it, especially at the bridge, and before second verse," she explained throwing her bag on her shoulder.

"I've already recorded it, miss. I have a CD recording of it in my bag, just for you. I did it with my PC, and it has got strings on it with a quiet bass drum, like the beating of a heart," he explained to her amazement. Abraham fished into his bag and handed her the CD. "Here you are, miss."

"Oh wonderful. Thank you. That song has got *hit* written all over it. Okay, young man, will you walk with me," she said as he zipped up and pulled his guitar rucksack into place on his back, with the headstock pointing up in the air.

"Oh, I do hope my boy Jamie learns to play as well as you can. I'll play this to him, just to show him what can be achieved. Just you remember to keep your head up, Abe. You need to be able to see the whites of a crowd's eyes. Never sing to your feet. You will have them melting in their seats with that song," she added closing the class room door. "I'll have some time away from it, then listen again in the car on the way home later. I'm off for my son's guitar performance. You take care, Abe, and I'll see you at next class. Oh, and well done."

NINE: *Sheridan*

She walked into the staffroom after class and pulled out her silent mobile to briefly glance at the screen. It showed a missed call and a message. Both from James. "OMG, he rang. He actually rang!" She took a deep breath and opened up the message:

Hi Red.
Sorry I didn't text earlier
Work stuff came up.
Last night was just what I needed.
Thank you very much for your company
And for your kindness.
Let's do it all again soon.
In Evarts all day.
Try ringing you again later.
James X

"Wow, a kiss! Yep, I still got it!" She joked to herself, flicking at her long red hair and then shouting and kissing her phone screen. '*Oh yes, and as deaf as a stone, too. You were enjoying Abraham's song so much, you didn't even realize your leg was vibrating you, silly girl,*' she said cursing herself, despite being happy in the knowledge that a spark had been lit in him. "Mmm, I'll ring him back later," she decided tidying her hair but itching to press the call button. "*No, Eden. I said later. You don't want him thinking I'm as keen as a loose woman,*" she told her conscience. She flicked through her contacts in her mobile until she reached **K** then, called Jamie's father number. It rang for the first time in forever, then went straight on to his answering machine message:

"*It's your boy's play. I just sort of hoped you'd be coming along, for his sake. Guess I shouldn't have wasted my time,*" she snapped, slamming the phone down with anger. She looked at the screen again and kicked her foot against the table in front of her. Enraged, she took a minute to compose herself, and rang a different number to appease her temper:

"Hi Sheridan, how are you honey?" She asked folding some A4 paper, then slipping it in an envelope. "Nothing at all really. Just out with my sister and friends and a lovely Englishman called, James. Yes, he was, and no, I'm not. Yes, just good friends. Oh, that's good, and Toni and the kids...? Uh, huh. Clays birthday, cool. What's that? A bouncy castle, wow. He'll love that. But he'll have to be extra careful... thanks... yes.... Okay, I'll try to get over later. It's his big moment today and something else has come up... I just had one class today. So, I'm on free-time all afternoon, that's why I'm ringing. Yes... I've just done the last of the tenant letters for the next meeting. Yes, at school now using their stationary and printer. Nope... I ain't stealing, there's eight kids from the Coal Cut Lane houses attending here, so it's classed as school business. I know the head teacher, anyhow. Thing is... one of the kids came over to my car when I was leaving and said there's a big bulldozer and a gang of workmen down at the bottom of her road. Yes... my road. Uh huh. No, I'd already left for school, so I ain't seen a thing at home. The little girl had received a message from her Mom asking her to tell me if she saw me at the school. She said, they had hard-hats and we're moving fence panels and a blue container off the tail-end of a wagon. Should we be worried...? No, she said they were on the old waste ground, at the back of her house," she paused to listen. "So, you think Langdon's leased that land from the coal company to make his mark...? The little girl said two of the workmen woke her family up at the crack of dawn, hammering signs up on two derelict houses. Can he legally do that...? So, what should we do," she questioned sticking down another envelope and adding it to a pile sat beside her. "Ok, so let's say I drive over to your house with Jamie for Clay's birthday party. Uh, huh. That's right. Then, we can head over to Coal Cut Lane together and post the new meeting letters and see exactly what's going on. It shouldn't take but an hour or so... huh. Would Toni be ok with that...? She paused, intently listening and chewing on a paper clip. "Shall we say after five o'clock? It won't take us long. Yes, the play starts at one, so I should be free any time after two. I know you're busy with other Kentucky stuff, but this is very imp... yes. I know I'm a Rottweiler with a bone but... aw, would you...? Oh, that's great.

Yes, all the kids involved in the play are getting an early day for all the hard *work they've put in. So, he can come with us. No... I'm not eating, I never eat. I'm pickin' my teeth with a... uh huh... under my nails next,"* she giggled. *"Maybe we can give some of the Coal Cut Lane kids a lift home. If the head teacher is okay with it. Yes. We can take some pictures up there and speak to some of the folk who attended the last meeting when we drop off the letters,"* she explained. *"I was going to take Bailey over that way for a walk and do it after work, because it's not far. Yes, I know it'll be better with you there. Shows the folk our solidarity on this and... Yeah... I know... it keeps me out of mischief. Then, when we're all done we can head straight back for Clay's party. Ok, thanks I'm grateful, yes and you. I'll see you later. What...? No, I won't be bringing James's with me you, big idiot!"* Eden put the phone down then bunched the pile of letters together and bound them with a huge elastic and placed them in her large shoulder bag and peeked at her watch.

"Mmm, one more call," she affirmed as she picked up the receiver of the school landline. *"Hi Mom. Yes, are you all set at that end? Nearly, wow! Is Grandma and Pape with you? Oh, just Grandma? Is she ok?"* She paused. *"What... he's gone to work with Dad...? Oh, I'm sorry who's passed on...? William Cornett... wasn't he Dad's, caretaker. Yes, I think he came to my christening. Oh, yes, I do remember him,"* she replied with an air of sadness. *"When dad used to take me to the office when I was about seven, he was always there. I remember he taught me the daisy game when I told him I had a crush on David Cassidy. Oh, come on Mom... Cassidy.... yes, he loves me... he loves me not.... yes, the singer,"* she smiled thinking about her text from James. *"Yes, David Cassidy was the biggest poster on my wall. Oh, that's a shame. Mister Cornett was such a lovely man. He always had a white, bucket sun-hat on, with his smoking pipe glued in his mouth. He sprayed the water hose at me once, when he was washing Dad's car,"* she reminisced.
"Yes, I remember it like it was yesterday. My jeans were soaked. Another casualty of coal dust, I'm guessing?" She sadly concluded. *"Well, I hope Pape or Dad tell William's widow our thoughts are with her. Listen Mom, if you speak to Dad before you get over to the school, tell him I need his help. I'm not*

going into detail on the phone, because I don't have time. No, I'm not avoiding him. In fact, every time I call him at work I get fobbed off or put on hold by that secretary of his. I'll tell you everything when you get here. In fifteen minutes, okay. Yes, I'm just going to see the final rehearsals right now, so I'll seek you out in the main hall. Just make sure you save me a seat, bye Mom."

#

She placed the phone in its holster as Laura opened the door. "Come on honey, your assistance is required. It's almost time to get this show on the road. Jamie wants to make sure his guitars okay," Laura explained feigning an air guitar.

"I called Kyle," she sighed. "He never picked up," she said staring at her cell phone again.

"Then you ain't ringing his ass again, come on." Laura said pulling on her hand. "Is Jamie's Grandma coming?"

"Yeah. I just checked in with Mom. Do you remember my Grandma, Laura?" She asked as they walked out of the door and down the hallway.

"A little." They walked around the back of the assembly hall curtain to see fifteen nervous kids, with almost as many adults' milling around their siblings, making sure they were perfectly dressed in their period costumes. Some wore white wigs, and others had red, white, and blue American clothes. Above their heads, there was row upon row, of star-spangled banners and flags, from end to end, all across the stage.

"Jamie, let me hear those strings baby," Eden asked kneeling down beside him. "Ok Mom, but I'm scared rigid here," he affirmed.

"You'll be just fine, honey. Strum them again honey," she said concentrating her ear on the noise of the guitar above the noise of the other children. "Mmm, the 'b' and 'e' strings sound out of whack? Pass it here, and let me tweak it a little," she said standing up and lifting the strap off his head and over her own. She strummed her hand and tilted her head whilst humming at the same time. She brushed her hair away from her right ear, then strummed again, and twisted at the tuning pegs until she was happy with its sound.

"Hey now, everybody gets nervous, honey. Something would be pretty wrong if you weren't. So, you are doing *America the Beautiful* and *Star-Spangled Banner,* right at the end," she asked looking at his music notation. "Oh, honey, you'll nail it!" She said looking at the other kids. "Hey, who's Abraham Lincoln today...? They all look the same to me. All wigs and pens and nerves," she joked looking at the children all around the stage:

"Five minutes for curtain call. Can all parents say their goodbyes, and leave the stage area to the left or right and take their seats in the main hall," a voice shouted?

"Right Jamie, I'd better go find our kin out there," Eden explained kissing his cheek.

"Mom," he asked. "Did my Dad...?"

"No baby, I'm so sorry," she croaked. "I called him and left a message."

"Oh."

"I never heard anything back," she replied feeling saddened by his choked reply. "Listen, I'd wish you good luck honey, but you won't be needing any luck."

TEN: *Stuck*

"Please, just wait for us and stay in the car, kids," Eden said as Sheridan drew his kid bursting jeep along Coal Cut Lane. He looked stealthily through his side window, as they slowly drove past a small, blue cabin in a scrub field about half a football pitch away from the road. He looked across at Eden and pulled down on his somewhat unnecessary black shades.

Beside the blue, steel cabin stood a brand new black, ORV. "Oh, will you look at that fancy car," he said applying his brakes.

"Mmm, I see it. Kids, can we trust you to get these letters to where they need to go?" Eden asked nodding at Sheridan and looking at the dark and intimidating car.

"Yes, Mam. We can do that no problem. Thanks for the lift home. Can we get out now?" A tall, red-haired skinny boy replied, automatically ejecting himself from the car.

"Sure. Thanks kids, and don't forget to tell your parents we'll be around to see them as soon as we can," she added looking again at the black car and blue cabin as the kids dispersed. "Do you think that's his, Sheridan?" She whispered following the kids lead and climbing out of the jeep and walking onto the sidewalk with Sheridan as he gazed up and down Coal Cut Lane, looking like, Will Smith in Men in Black.

"Yep, that's his because the sorry ass is stood right there, inside the blue cabin. He's got some nerve being up here."

"Are you sure? You must have pretty good eyesight. All I can see is a light on. Hey, why are we whispering anyway?" She puzzled.

"I have no idea. I was whispering cos you were, you lunatic! Have you got Kentucky red-eye, you blind woman? I know it's his ass, cos that's what these babies are for," he smiled lifting up some mini binoculars that he was hiding under his suit lapel. "Didn't you see me taking a peep?" Sheridan frowned. "Are you up for a little confrontation?" Sheridan asked with a grin, fingering his moustache.

"Does a bear dump in the woods? He's either brave or just stupid? My neighbors would lynch him if they knew he was here. Bring on the confrontation, I was born ready, Sheridan," she replied, feigning some lightning quick karate moves, but beginning to pant immediately "The SOB is going to get my wrath for speaking to me the way he did."

"Ah aah," Sheridan said, nodding his finger from side-to-side, in her face. "I was joking Eden. We don't have to make this personal yet. Just you remember what I told you on the phone," he said looking at her clenched fists.

"Have you got a tire wrench in the boot of the car? Or maybe some of that nice hard cinder block right over there will do," she said pointing toward a large brick at the edge of the makeshift compound.

"Not the way girl."

"Sounds good enough to me."

"Get a grip of yourself, woman," he hushed, itching his black afro hair, then grabbing her arm and pulling her back from picking up a large crushed brick. "Come on, trouble. Yeah, TROUBLE! I'm going to start calling you that. Let's go and see what nonsense we can hear, over there," he said waving his arm and beckoning her toward the compound gates. "If we get confronted, stay calm, and don't let him or anyone see a hint of your crazy. If you show any weakness, he'll prey on it."

They walked to the gated entrance, and past an old yellow pickup truck. Sheridan lifted an open fence panel and walked into the compound. As the light faded, they blended in with the shadows and sneaked across to the blue, steel hut. As they got closer, they could hear footsteps from inside and Langdon Dainty's loud, booming voice emanating on the glass of the closed window and through the gaps in the door:

"I want this problem gone boys... disappeared. Then, I can go full steam ahead," he urged as outside the blue steel box, Sheridan put his hand over his ear and his arms in a *be quiet* motion to Eden so they could zero-in to the spoken words. He dipped his hand under his suit lapel pocket and pulled out a small device. Hastily, he fiddled about, then pressed a small, red button as Eden stood silently, almost welded to the side of the cabin as they unknowingly continued to listen to Langdon's voice:

"When it's all done and dusted, all Henry Creech's wallowing and beleaguered money demands on me will be over. There won't be a damn thing he can do but accept the inevitable. But, just make sure you're thorough, and get rid of everything. Any evidence, I want buried or burned. Don't leave a trace, do you hear? I don't want anything leading back to me in any way, shape or form," he grunted.

"When are we getting paid?"

"After things have died down, you'll be paid in full, and more than sufficiently rewarded with dollars and jobs as the real construction work gets underway. If you and your new team do a good job, there'll be plenty more interesting work I can use you for. I don't deal with the money for obvious reasons. Besides, I'm not that stupid. But this is also a test. A test to see how capable and conducive to my organization you can be. So, consider yourselves on trial," Langdon explained.

"A test? Hell, to that. I ain't submitting to no test. How do you figure that, big man?"

"SHUT YOUR MOUTH, BOY! Don't you EVER call me that, again?"

"Yeah, just shut it Josh, and hear him out." another voice mumbled.

"Thank you. I'm glad one of you have got some manners, and at least half a brain," Langdon sneered.

Outside, Eden's eyes widened as she moved closer to Sheridan. Trying to listen so hard that she almost pushed him up against the door. Accidentally letting out an audible gasp and throwing her hand across her mouth as she tapped Sheridan on the shoulder.

"Did you hear that?"

"Eden, shush," he whispered turning toward her and begging her to be silent and still. Pointing at the flashing red device he was holding up tight to the door handle as he did.

"The test is simple boys. Once you get the down payment, you'll have 24 hours to complete the job. If you do not act in sufficient time, the deal is off. The timing for this job is crucially important. If you don't burn every damn thing to ashes, you've failed the task. Then, you can wave goodbye to the rest of the money, and any other work that could have been lined up for you on my payroll. Have you got that, chumps?"

"Why don't you just ring us up, instead?"

"I said it's a test you dummy. To see if you're up to the task."

The cabin fell silent, making Eden frown at Sheridan for their next move.

"Right, I'm out of this God forsaken place. Make sure the shutters are secured on this place and it's all locked up. Especially, the main gate. I want everything up here like Fort Knox for as long as we're here. Or, at least until we've got these lame excuses for human beings evicted from their cesspits. I do hope I don't have to see either of your sorry asses again, either. Any future liaisons or meetings will be conducted by my attorney and right-hand man. He's an ocean sharper than me, so you'd better be good little boys." Langdon took a look at his cell, then walked toward the steel door and stopped. He put his fingers on the handle at the opposite side of the door to where Sheridan's hand was still holding the flashing, red device. Then, Langdon turned back to face his henchmen. "So, what are you all waiting for? Get on it!"

Langdon turned the handle and opened door and trudged his fat frame toward his ORV. Pressed its key unlock button and then navigated his huge bulk into his seat as his gang of three thugs walked outside the cabin and locked the door to see Langdon wind down his window "Excuse me gentleman. Could one of you idiots get the gate for me? I'm in a terrible hurry."

One of the men strode toward the compound gate as another other followed. They opened the gates to watch Langdon's jeep wheel-spin past them and disappear in dust.

"Damn, fat asshole. He's one mean Devil. I could get rid of his fat ass in a second."

"Oh, shut up Josh. Don't worry about him... stay loose! Come on, let's get the hell out of here. Time's a wasting and I'm shaking for a drink here. I'm gagging some liquor, and quick." Josh locked the main gate and followed his partner in crime to the yellow jeep outside the compound and they were gone.

"Eden! Eden...? Damn those... aargh.... look at the state of me... I bet this 500-dollar suits ruined," he said as she appeared by his side. "Where the hell did you disappear to?" He cursed, clambering from his stomach on his hands and knees, from underneath a yellow bulldozer that was parked at the side of the steel container.

"It's your own fault, Sheridan. I bet James's would be way smarter than that. You should have hidden around the back of the cabin, like me. Oh lord, but I should have just reigned in on him," she scowled throwing a large tree branch that she'd picked up back to the floor as she watched Sheridan stand up and frantically brush his hands hard into his somewhat ruined, city suit.

"Excuse me...? But in case you'd forgotten, we got my son's party to attend."

"I know you fool. My son's already there. And if it makes you feel any better, my clothes stink of diesel from the smelly tank around the back," she moaned sniffing at her tainted blouse.

"I should have had the good sense to change before I came anywhere with you. Look, my threads are ruined, and Toni's going to kill me. Damn Dainty and damn you," Sheridan said frowning and spitting on his hands as he rubbed at his dust covered elbows.

"And damn you, to," she replied as a smile arced across both of their faces.

"I don't think I got much on this old dictaphone, either? Which is a damn shame, cos it's admissible as evidence these days."

"I'd like to hear what you did get, though. I can't be sure, but I'm... I could swear that I've heard one of those men's voices before," Eden explained as they walked across to the gate to examine the lock.

"Oh great! How, the hell are we gonna get out of this place, now...? It's solid," Sheridan groaned looking around. "Quick, you go that way, Eden. Walk around the perimeter and check all the palisade fence clips. There must be one of them missing, or at least loose enough to spring open," he explained deep in thought, and playing with his moustache again as they separated. "If that don't work, we'll have to climb over the God-damn top," he said standing illuminated beneath a streetlight to look at his watch and ruined suit. "God, look at my damn knees."

"We'd sail out of this place if James was here," she muttered.

"James this... James that, will you shut up about him," he goaded.

ELEVEN: *Henry Creech*

"How many times do I have to tell you, I ain't selling to that crook? He's stabbing everybody in the back with his lies and deceits. Uh huh... I spoke to that attorney West, and he's a good skin. On the level and as true as myself." Henry senior affirmed, spitting his mouthful of tobacco out into the sink and putting the receiver back to his ear. *"Don't you dare try tell me I'm no good judge of character? West said he can't work out the fat man's, bad ass ways neither. He even told me he lured him into his job under false presences and I*

believe him. No son... I don't care if you can double the swamp money... the damn deals off......! I'll tell you another thing for free. If you go against my wishes here... you ain't no son of mine... do you hear me boy! I'll cut you loose, and out of my life. My land... and, my damn will," he growled. "You'll get zilch. Not a bow bean or a pot to piss in. I am deadly serious boy. I'm done listening to the same old crock of crap from you. Your brother is here for a visit for some house meeting. So, when he leaves, you're Momma and I are taking a break down at his house in the city. What with her illness and all, she ain't seen the grandkids for the longest time." He spat again. "I wouldn't be surprised the little darlings recognize us at all. It's all finished, you hear. Dead and gone. Oh, why don't you shut your fat mouth? You ain't got no idea. How you think it makes us feel, knowing we raised a one-eyed, lying crook like you. Every damn word you say is all bad. Henry junior is looking after stuff while we're down Tennessee, so you stay away. Henry and some good class English feller will be around. I'm giving Henry and James proper instruction to deal with your ass the best ways they'd see fit. Hell, they can lay a rifle on your sorry hide if the mood takes them. Now get the hell my phone and out of this town, Josh. I got your Mom to look after." He slammed the ancient bakelite phone on its holder and wrapped its long dusty cable back to the kitchen wall as a painful and wheezed cough came from the other room.

"Henry, stop shouting. Is everything okay?"

"It's nothing, honey. I ain't shouting. It's just the damn grain salesman bothering us again. They never take no for an answer! If I've told them once, I've told them a thousand times, no. Sorry honey, it just gets my beef right up," he said thinking about his son. "I'm bringing the pills through, right now."

TWELVE: *Community meeting*

"Where is the fat-lying, pond-life? He said he would be here. Oh, he gripes me. All these folks have to take time off work to attend. Argh! He's lower than a snake's belly in a wagon rut! He has no moral compass, at all. Eminent domain laws, my ass," she cursed, biting at her cheek and slamming her pen down. She stood up from her desk, and tightly clasped her clipboard against her chest. "Damn him, ouch my head."

"Stop getting your knickers in a knot. I spoke to his secretary yesterday and she assured me he'd be here. I'm just glad I got all that dust and crap off my suit. What the hell's up with your head?"

"Oh yeah? I bet she did Sheridan. I wager she was under orders to say that. Just like that scrawny, twitching parasite over there, with the in-growing chest," she grunted looking across the room at Milton West. "It seems to me like they all piss in the same pot! Dainty should be here to speak with these folks, to ease their worries and their fears. Nobody seems to have a damn clue what's going to happen, and it's clear to me he just doesn't give a flying…"

"Eden, please…! Keep your voice down:
Good evening sir… madam, if you could be patient and take a seat somewhere down the front. There's tea and coffee just over to the right," he pointed. *Please help yourselves,"* Sheridan motioned the couple down the large community hall, as Eden watched another middle-aged couple walk through the entrance doors who were talking in whispered tones. He put his hand on her shoulder. "Your head, Eden?"

"Oh, sorry. Nothing. I was out with James and my sister, remember. It's a delayed headache. I always get a headache, two days after consuming alcohol. Don't ask me why. Anyway, Langdon's a pig! I was going to forget about the abuse he gave me on the phone, and let it go as water under the bridge. You know, give him the benefit of the doubt. The ignorant loud-mouthed swine."

"Oh yeah, and I can see you didn't bring big, strong James, either," Sheridan teased.

"He's busy," she smiled not saying a thing. "If Dainty doesn't show up, this is war! He can't just take the land and our houses from under our noses, it's just not fair. Now, I ain't no Harvard graduate, but there must be laws against doing things like that?" She wondered as Sheridan half smiled at another couple walking through the door, and showed them down the hall: *"Yes, straight ahead, Mam. Free tea and coffee available right over there.* Busy my left foot. Oh, James... you are so amazing and so smart!" Sheridan said ridiculing Eden just for the fun of it, and quickly moving out of the way of her fierce slap as he winked at her and brushed his lips with his finger.

"You leave James's out of this, or there's plenty more where that came from.

"Plenty more. Now you listen to me. There's plenty laws, Eden," he paused again. *"Any seat at all mam, we'll be with you in a short while.* The sad thing is, most of the laws are there to serve the government, not the people. And if things change, or the coat don't fit. They just amend or put a new law in place that fits the next sorry ass, democratic process. Or, at least make it look democratic. They just change the goal posts, to suit themselves. Scrapped, changed or adjusted laws as they need," he added. "It's always so underhand and wrong. They say you can't fight city hall, but we can, girl. All you need is the right tools for the job. Find a good shovel, and that's some digging done good, if you know what I mean."

"Yeah, to bury the fat bas...!"

"Good evening sir......! Welcome along," Sheridan interjected cutting her brash statement off. *"That's right, go on down, straight ahead of you."* He said pointing another man down toward the stage, as he playfully slapped her hand and another thirty-something, mountain of a man walked toward them. He took off his hat to make a smiling, tip head acknowledgement at Eden's beauty.

"Good evening, Eden. Long time, no see," he smiled.

"Hi Jerry. It's great to see you here," she assuaged as the huge man walked away and Sheridan continued:

"A little fishing or knocking on people's doors to get the dirt. The whole damn worlds corrupt. We just need to find an in-road and find the skeletons hanging in his closet. The bodies concreted under the buildings. You know the sort of thing. I've already been doing some searching on Langdon's ass. And, let me tell you. It sure makes for some interesting reading."

"But we don't have time for any digging, Sheridan. Time is running out for these poor people."

"Hey! Calm down, you're just like a coiled spring ready to pop. Slow down and hold your temper," he said hushing her tone. "You're as stubborn as a God damn mule, woman. Sounds to me like you've let him get under your skin and hell girl, he hasn't got here yet. Now, you and I know he's got these townsfolk running scared and that's exactly what we're here for. So, you just put a foot in your mouth girl. I know you ain't versed in dancing around inside a court of law, but I am. And hell... I can do the quick-step and the Charleston upside down, inside out and back to front, and all at the same time." he joked as she began to smile. "There's even a slow waltz with bells on, if I need it. That's the one for reeling them in you see," he added with a light wink, nodding his head and feigning a fishing rod. "As a matter of fact, I got some red hot, Californian electric boogaloo, right here. You see that girl?" He asked as he slowly wiggled his arms that etched an overdue grin on her face. "So, we keep tight! We need to keep it together, for their sake," he said nodding toward the people congregated in the hall. "You know we can do this," he confirmed. "We can kick his ass down. *Good evening sir, madam, that way.* And hell, when he's down and out, you can just go kick him some more. We're better than him, and his corrupt skinny lawyer," Sheridan motioned toward the black suited skin and bones man, on the front row. "We don't need fancy education and all that crap. We don't even need no English dude's called James, either," he jived as she went to slap him again. "You just give me a few more days. Maybe a week, tops. Let me get another angle on him. Something really bad. Something Acid thinks is buried deep and long gone. Just a way in to make him think twice, so he'll do a complete U-turn. That's all we need. The deepest secrets are always hidden in the most unlikely places. Once we've got him running scared, you can spin around on your high heels and kick them right up his damn, fat ass.

Now are we gonna do this right... of course we are," he explained before she had chance to reply. "So, just for now, put up and shut up and get your hot skinny ass up on that stage, and talk to these good people." Eden lightly slapped his arm for his underhand compliment. "Play that funky music white girl! Oh, and remember, if the scrawny fella tries to get on your case, Poker face! You hear me... Poker face!" Sheridan shook his hands in front of his solemn looking face as she took a deep breath, then turned to walk towards the stage.

"Ok smart cookie, I'm on my way," she said as Sheridan winked at her and took a seat at the rear of the hall, amongst the whispering tenants and residents of Coal Cut Lane, who were gathered for the second, *Stop the Highway* meeting. She walked up the steps, and onto the stage of the Harlan community hall, then turned around to see what felt like two hundred eyes that were all trained on her every move. The noise of the gathered people petered off to a silence, as she gulped and acutely smiled:

"Good evening everybody, and thanks for coming along," she said watching their faces look around at each other as they nodded and confirmed that she was friend, and not foe. "Some of you know me... and some of you, I haven't had the pleasure of meeting. But, I live right here. My name is Eden Buckley, and I'm here to help you fight for what is right," she explained to the crowd's positive murmurs. "Now, because this is the first meeting, we need to get to know each other a little better. Cos we could be fighting this fight for a hell of a long time," she explained, coughing then turning to her chair to grab some papers. "There should be some printed papers on your seats, just like this, and there is another paper being passed around the room. Could you please put your names on them both, and pass the other one along?" Some people started talking amongst themselves, shuffling and raising slightly off their chairs and searching blankly underneath them, or on the floor. Others remained tight-lipped and focused on the red-haired woman that was giving them hope. "The gentleman at the door as you came in is, Mr. Sheridan Barley from the Kentucky state, judicial affairs office. He is my friend and he is here to support us in our cause." Sheridan stood up from his chair smiled, nodded, and then waved in a casual, but fixed, Afro-American fashion.

"Where's the fat man... why isn't he here?" An unsentimental sounding deep female voice asked, as Eden watched Sheridan calmly walk down the aisle and pass out some more papers.

"Mr. Dainty isn't here yet," Sheridan said smoothly intervening, and raising his voice above the chattering crowd. "His representative, Mr. Milton West is sitting right at the front, and will be happy to answer any of your questions in a little while."

"Representative? Don't you mean corrupt scumbag? And Dainty ain't no Mister!" A voice exclaimed as the jeering got louder, and Eden tried to speak, but nervously stumbled on her words. "Please could we... have some calm," she begged as Sheridan walked to the front and slammed the papers in his hand down on the stage like an auctioneer's gavel, just below Eden.

"Now, you people! Please listen to me. This woman up here is here to help you, as am I," he said pointing up at Eden. "And this place ain't no God-damn cattle market, either! We know you all want to say your piece. And we all want to listen to what your opinions are and want you to have your cases heard. Now, they will be heard. But not like this! In a civilized way, with one singer and one song. The ignorant among you need to learn to keep your damn mouths shut. If you can't do that, you should just leave this hall right now. In case you hadn't worked it out yet. We're all on the same side," he fumed glancing over at attorney Milton West. "And another thing..." he started.

"He's isn't," someone said pointing at Milton West.

"No, and who the hell do you think you are, mister... Richard Pryor?" Another angry voice interrupted as Sheridan quickly looked to where the voice had come from and quickly zoned in.

"Well, if you'd been listening instead of mouthing, sir, you'd know fine who I am," he sternly replied keeping his temper firmly in check and walking over to the hat wearing man, then throwing his hand out in front of him. "Mmm, Brother Richard is one of the finest comedians to grace this country, sir. In fact, I've been called much worse. So, I'll just take that as a compliment and I'll tell you again, just so you don't forget this time. I'm, Sheridan Barley from the state judiciary office, at your service! And your name is...?" He continued standing forthright, and directly in front of the vocal, but shrinking as he waited for him to answer. "I'm here to make sure things are done right, and to the letter of the law. And you are...? Sheridan repeated badgering the man.

"I'm erm, Frank Smith," the reluctantly crowd-shy man replied.

"Thank you, Mister Smith. Good to have you here." Sheridan solidly shook his hand as the man lamely took his hand back, feeling somewhat embarrassed. "Could you find some manners and take your hat off, Mr. Smith."

"I've heard your ill winds before, Frank Smith. So, keep your own damn counsel until it's asked for," a disgruntled woman shouted from the back of the hall.

"And thank you also, for your erm, input and time, Madam," Sheridan continued. "Now between you good folk and these four walls," he said motioning Eden to take her seat as he continued the speaking duties:

"I'm almost in the same boat as you people. Except, I've got a lot more axes to grind with Devil Dainty. I shouldn't really call him that because that guy over there might construed it a reckless character assassination and sue. But, I don't really care, because I've been grinding axes for years. Always waiting for the killer shot," he spontaneously clapped his hands together making a few members of the audience, and Milton jump.

"Yee haa! I heard that. But you won't get him axed tonight, mister Barley cos he ain't here. That lame rat couldn't find his own nose with a lantern," a voice shouted as Sheridan vociferously thumped his hand on the stage yet again and the room fell silent. "Now, what part of shut-up don't some of you people understand? You'll all get your turn to speak. But not all at once, like a bunch of selfish, ill-mannered school kids! It's like a damn kindergarten in here," he fumed. "We're on your side of the fence, just remember that!"

"He ain't!" A woman shouted pointing at Milton for the second time.

"No, mam, he isn't. And this ain't no damn pantomime either!" He growled walking back to his seat and nodding at Eden to continue.

"Thanks, erm Sheridan. So, as I was saying. Of course, we want the new link road, but not where it's been planned to be built. We want to keep our community together and our homes safe," she said giving them a minute to gather their thoughts. "So, as mister Barley said… one at a time. Mister West, could you join me up here on the stage, please. These people need some real answers," Eden asked looking down at Langdon Dainty's lawyer, meekly sitting on the front row as she grabbed another chair from the right of the stage and the crowd rowdily rumbled as Milton stood up.

"Why certainly, miss Buckley," he nonchalantly replied tucking a yellow folder under his arm, then repositioning his glasses before making his way onto the stage to the sound of vocal sneering, taunting and mocking murmurs from behind as Sheridan gave Eden a thumbs up, as she waited for Milton West to take his chair.

"So, if you want to ask a question, just put your hands up. I'll pick you out, one by one. Then, if that person could stand up and give everyone your name and some details and then call out your question. Is everybody happy with that?" Eden asked looking around the hall to see a hand already aloft.

"Yes?

"I have a question," the old woman shouted as some of the crowd turned around to look.

"Is everybody warm enough in here or is it just me?" the old woman asked to a small number of titters.

"I'm cold!"

"Could you turn up the heating a little, Mamie," Eden shouted lifting her hand in an upward motion to another elderly woman who was minding her own business and knitting quietly to herself, near the entrance doors. "Maybe we'll take two questions at a time, I know you all want a turn and you all want answers. So, let's just play things by ear, and see how it goes," she explained pausing for a breath. Milton West looked down at the baying for blood audience, and uncomfortably fidgeted in his chair. Looking somewhat like a twitching lamb to the slaughter.

"Right, okay everybody, first question please? You there, sir," Eden asked as the young man promptly stood up.

"Hi. My name's Henry Creech. Before I say anything, I want you to know that I don't live around these parts anymore. But my Parents do. Now, this construction company, I mean… this Dainty wants to build this road straight through my folk's land and over Boyles swamp. Now, he's offered my Pop peanuts for the pleasure of doing that. So, I'm here on their behalf to let you folks know, that whatever he wants, it ain't happening. That man understands nothing at all," he said sounding very sure of himself as Eden decided to sit back down on here chair.

"The Highway link-road plans involve the filling in of Boyle's swamp, which sits smack-bang, in the middle of my Pop's land. Dainty cannot fill that creature filled haven in at all. The fact is, there's other people in this world that will stop him. There's stuff in there that is precious to all of us for our survival. Species of plants, trees and animals and flora and fauna that a lot of cleverer folks reckon are very important and should be protected by law. Now, I know that all that might mean nothing at all to you, and the road is more valuable and should take precedence. I understand completely that it's being built will help service you people better and bring a better quality of life to you," he sniffed. "Jobs out of town and better links to Tennessee, and Nashville and all the other states outside of Kentucky would more readily available. But let me explain:

He needs to go and find somewhere else better to build the damn road.

I work in ecology, and Boyles is far too important to just bulldoze over. No amount of bribery or hush money can change that. I've already made some calls to the WWF and some others. Some of the animals and species in Boyles and places just like it, are bio-indicators. In both terrestrial and aquatic environments, which are the best and most accurate signals of environmental stresses and indicative of the biosphere of the world as a whole." As he continued, the audience remained silently listening and interested every word. "Those little green frogs in Boyle's swamp know precisely what's happening and what could come to pass for our fate. In their current form they've been here a hell of a lot longer than us." Sheridan silently whooped and smiled to himself, catching Eden's eye as he glossed his gaze over every silent head in the room. He rubbed his hands, smiled and rose from his seat giving the thumbs up to her, then pointed affirmatively at Henry Creech as he continued his speech:

"Two hundred and fifty million years longer than us to be exact. Ice ages, asteroid crashes and earthquakes longer. Or any other, God-damn environmental catastrophe. You name it, they've lived through it. And they're still here to tell the tale. We can and do study their behavioral patterns and learn a hell of a lot from it." In the silence of the hall, a chair violently screeched across the wooden floor, making Henry Creech stop in his tracks. As everyone turned around, the vocally uninterested female heckler from earlier, stood up from her seat, in the middle of the hall and headed brassily across the room to the tea and coffee stand as everyone watched as she recklessly and flagrantly bumped into the seated people's knees along her row as she passed.

"Yeah, yeah. Who cares?" She brazenly said looking around the room as she re-filled her plastic cup with tea, then walked back to her chair in the same stroppy manner.

"I'm just here for anything that's free," she ignorantly added as Henry Creech remained tight-lipped, waiting for her to sit down.

"Go on boy, say your peace and be quick about it. I got better stuff to be drinking in a bar, than this gnat's water," she loudly announced sipping her drink to a tirade of audience grumbling as Henry Creech looked at Sheridan to continue:

"They serve as an alarm call to us in case something drastic is wrong with the planet. They're our most accurate barometers of pollution, destruction and disease. They also help with physiology and medicine. Just like all the plants up there. They all have an irreplaceable employ in the use of pathogenic and antibiotic resistant bacterial strains. Again, please bear with me. I know that sounds just a load of old pants and plants, to most of you," he added clearing his throat and looking up at, Eden as, Sheridan walked past him, and toward the stage.

"Come on, man. That stuff means nothing to us. You're just on a one-man crusade to save the planet. I need to work out of town to provide for my family. I don't care about your damn plants, birds and fishes, or stupid frogs!" An angry man shouted, greeted with a succession of audience jeers.

"Please everybody, you'll all get your turn. Mister Creech could you finish your point. There's other folk who'd like to speak." Sheridan advised turning to face Henry Creech and the audience in a nightclub bouncer style. He folded his arms and leaned back on the stage to face their view.

 "Okay. I'll quickly explain. Some years ago, there was a species of frogs being observed and researched right here in Kentucky. These little fellas held great promise for further advances in medical research, to cure peptic ulcers. Which are common in more than 25 million Americans. That's right, 25 million of you! Sadly, the gastric-brooding frogs disappeared off the face of the earth from right under the noses of the scientists who were studying them. That was our doing. Through the chemicals and pollutions that we throw into our environment on a daily basis. We could have saved a lot of *us* if we'd had a little more consideration for *them*. Do you, or any of your family suffer from peptic ulcers, sir?" Creech shouted across the hall to his heckler, who quietly slid down in his chair. Remaining sullenly tight-lipped as his wife looked at him fierily and kicked at his leg.

 "We can't make monumental advances like that in medicine or human life if they're not here anymore. I'm gonna shut my mouth right now, apart from on last thing: There's ecologists in state, right now to help put a stop to this link road in its present form. So, go ahead and build the damn thing by all means. But not by destroying everything in Boyles swamp." He nodded for no reason, then sat back down as Sheridan watched the whole crowd's perplexed faces. Eden looked over at Sheridan, and sensed that everybody was growing restless, angry and visibly louder in the hall.

 "Okay, thank you very much for your enlightening words, Mr. Creech. After hearing those incredible facts, you certainly opened my eyes. I really do hope the link-road gets built, but not in the place it's intended." Eden said moving right along and pointing   at a particularly rake-thin, grey-haired, old woman. "Yes Mam. Could you tell everybody your name and your question?" She asked as the woman uneasily rose to her feet.

 "Erm howdy. That vagabond man offered me chicken feed for my place. I swear down as God is my witness. His nickel and dimes were nothing," she said as she coughed and caterwauled. "I apologize, but that man is uglier than homemade mud, both inside and out, and as treacherous as quicksand.

I wouldn't trust him as far as I could throw him." The community hall started to rumble and titter. "Oh, I'm sorry, I'm forgetting my place," she sighed as she composed herself. "You see my Mom is nearing ninety-two and I'm seventy-five," she added nervously wiping her nose on a crumpled handkerchief that she'd pulled from her homemade jumper sleeve as she quietly smiled at, Eden.

"Oh, I'm sorry Mam you wanted my name. I'm a little deaf and I sometimes forget the order of things, you see. I sometimes forget my own name," she said with a bowed head. "I'm Martha Hensley and my Momma is Mary Smith. We live on the Cutters Creek side of Coal Cut Lane, up where... well I think you well know where, cos you live right close you, kind girl," she said as if there was only Eden in the room. "Aah, ah choo...! Excuse me. Anyhows, we've spent all of our days here you see. At least the best of them. It's too late in what little time we got left, for us to be moving on anywhere at all," she sniffed. "Our men-folk are long dead and gone with the black lung. And Momma and I just want to live out the rest of our days here, where we've always been. Where we feel happy and loved and belonged. I just wanna know what's gonna to happen to us. You come on down here, wanting us to fight? Hell, we've fought all our lives and there's no fight left. What with the coal companies and the power people. It ain't never got us nowheres, but backwards. I just want to be able to go back home and tell my Momma that everything's gonna be alright cos she's frightened as hell. I think we all are." The woman looked around her at the hall of silent, empty faces and sat back down.
It was less than fifteen minutes into the meeting, but in the sad solemn silence, Eden felt her throat gulp deeply in the deathly hush of the room.

THIRTEEN: *Colville's*

"Fine sir, no problem. Just take the sidewalk straight down, until you see the Holiday shack on your left. Then, take a right and you'll see Colville's car hire, down on the left. The brown fronted place, with the antique car in the window," he explained looking down the road at Abby in the distance.

"Ok then. Thanks again, sir. I'll go find these wheels, then we can get moving, Abby... Abby?"

"Yeah, I heard him. So, hurry up slowcoach, or we'll be here all day," Abby shouted already reaching the end of the street and waving back at her Dad as she disappeared around the corner. He shook his head and followed at such a speed that his rucksack began to bounce on his shoulders, with his mobile phone tightly gripped in his hand and the vehicle papers flapping from his mouth. As he turned the corner, Abby was already sitting outside of the car hire shop that they had been looking for, and happily petting a small, terrier dog. As James got closer, it yelped at him, as if it was protecting her. Then, after a second or two, it happily wiggled its tail-less stump at him, then jumped madly up and down in an attempt to reach Abby's lap. Who was now perched on the shop window-ledge, visually overjoyed with her new-found friend. "Oh, look at him Dad, he's so cute. Why haven't we ever had a dog? Mum said I could have a puppy when I got older, and I'm still waiting," she inferred as she finally lifted it onto her lap. "Surely, I'm old enough now? I'd look after it," she suggested.

"I know you would. I've never had a dog, either. Let's just wait until we get back to England, and then we'll see," he agreed putting his open hand on her head as the little dog sniffed at his sleeve.

"Well, would you look at that," he glowed, looking over her shoulder. "It's beautiful. I bet it's in the same condition as when it first came off the production line all those years ago," James's said as Abby grabbed the stray dog in her arms, stood up, and turned in the direction of the shop window.

"Come on Abby, let's take a peek. We need to go inside anyway. Put the mutt back down, and let's go take a closer look at the beauty." She frowned at his schoolboy need to see the car, but did exactly as he said, and carefully placed the dog on the pavement, then followed him somewhat regimentally, into the shop.

"Hello!" He shouted through the seemingly empty shop. All that could be heard was a radio coming from behind a door that was behind the large wooden counter. "Someone must be here...? Maybe through the back," he surmised looking at the slightly open door. "Hello...! Abby, bob under that counter and take a peek through that door for me." She cautiously bent under the old flip-top counter, until she slowly appeared like a silent thief at the other side. She crept toward the other door, as James's impatiently turned away to marvel at the sleek beauty of the vintage 1954, Rolls Royce, wedding car that was sitting all ribboned and bowed on a trailer stand, in the shops reception.

 Just as Abby reached up to push on the door handle, the shop's front door was nudged open by the stray dog's nose, outside. He'd opened it just enough to allow him to dart inside the shop and through. As he did, he barked loudly, running both past James and then under the counter to where Abby was now stood, almost frozen with fright and obvious horror as if she'd been rumbled. At the same time, James had spun around to watch the mutt run frantically past him and he'd accidentally lost his balance. He'd reached out to grab at the car's shiny steel mudguard for balance and it had inadvertently come off the car in his hand, making a surprisingly loud bang as it clattered out of his hand and on to the floor.

 "Dad! What are you even doing?" She asked as he flumped to the floor beside the pristine, and mudguard shy car. The terrier continued to bark even louder at the noise, and had moved itself to some kind of safety, near the second door, behind the counter. Once there, it stopped, sat down and turned around to face Abby, with its mouth open and its tongue hanging out. Looking at her, as if it was waiting for her to follow. She looked at her Dad for further instruction where there was nothing but a silly adult, still lying on the floor. "Shush dog. Get up quick, Dad. I can hear footsteps." The stray dog barked again as the second door was finally pulled open and an old bearded man, with blue, oily overalls who'd obviously appeared to see what all the commotion was. He said nothing, and looked across to see James on the floor, who was not yet wholly aware of his presence, and still, slowly panting and grunting. Precariously picking himself up from the floor whilst using his rucksack and the car's wheel as leverage to help him. The kindly faced, tubby man, who looked somewhat like a mechanic Santa internally gasped, and then winked a smile knowingly at Abby. As, if he'd seen her before.

He quickly put his finger across his lips, motioning Abby to remain silent, then, slowly leant forward on the counter in front of him. Although totally perplexed at the scene, Abby and the man stood silent and motionless, and grinning at each other. On seeing the bearded man, James immediately tried to stand up from the fall as if nothing had happened. Totally embarrassed with himself and looking around the empty shop in case anybody else had seen his comical misdemeanor.

"Howdy sir, howdy Bethany... I mean, young lady," the bearded man exclaimed leaning deeper onto his elbows and rhythmically tapping his fingers on the counter, secretly winking at Abby again. "What can I do for you... sir? Maybe fix a Rolls Royce mudguard...? That much I can see anyhow," the man said answering his own question but remaining steely eyed as James quickly worked out what to say.

"Oh erm, howdy, I mean hello. I'm James, and that's my daughter, Abby. I'm sorry, I slipped back there, and this erm... came right off in my hand," he truthfully replied putting down his rucksack and giving his ashamed hand something to do whilst holding the shiny metal, mud-guard in the other and going beetroot in the face.

"Yes," Charles replied waiting for an explanation.

"I, erm... believe this is yours. It, erm... just fell off, when I touched it," he said looking at the mudguard in his hand, as if it was going to corroborate his story. James walked slowly toward the bearded man, then placed it on the counter just beside the man's elbow. "Fell off you say? It was connected to my car last time I seen," the man solemnly replied, now strangely beginning to sound just like Santa.

"Well, erm. Yes, so what happened was...very silly." James said turning around to the car to begin a further explanation of the calamitous sequence of events.

"Oh, never mind, it'll be fine," the man said turning his gaze back to Abby, who was now texting on her phone. "Your daughter reminds me of my dear granddaughter," he said, picking up the mudguard and walking past James with a quizzical grin on his face.

"Sorry. I was just having a little fun with you, nothing more. It's hard to find fun anymore, when you're as old as me. I can tell you honestly, that my own mudguards fell off me a long time ago. So, you like my little darling, do you?"

"Oh, yes I do," James concurred as the man clicked the shiny metal guard back into its housing within seconds.

"Yep me too. I'm guessing there's not many of them left in the world now. A dying breed, just like us all," he explained as Abby walked through the counter to join them, immediately followed by the scrawny dog.

"It's amazing. How the devil did you get a Rolls Royce in here anyway?" James asked looking around the tiny shop.

"Where there's a will there's a way," the man said. "And where there's a will, there's a damn argument too," he added smiling and looking down at Abby as she looked up at him from her mobile phone. "They ain't real bricks at the back of the counter, see. This whole desk comes right on out. Unclips here and here. It splits right apart," he explained pointing at some old locks at the side. "It even has wheels, but their hidden. You see the door I came through and caught you both up to no good. It's just a false, wooden wall. You unclip the bolts from the floor, and it peels right back on big shutters and hinges. Made it all myself you know…. back in the day. Many moons ago when I first bought the place." He explained as he violently coughed, then pulled a tissue out of his top pocket and covered his mouth as he continued to wheeze, sibilate and clear his throat. He turned away from them both, put his hand up and then spat into the hankie. Then, screwed it up and threw it into a bin. "Sorry. The old black lung. It's gonna get me in the end. There's probably not long to go before I see my dear Clara. But never mind, silly old me. So, what can I do for you good people? I'm Charles. Now, young lady, you just take a look in that cupboard right behind you. There's some candy in there. New promotional tittle-tattle from the parent company."

"Oh, we are here for some transport. It's a van. I have the paperwork, right here," James informed him.

Yes, go on honey. That's right, that's the one," The bearded man said as James fumbled with his papers and Abby pulled on the cupboard bolt and then looked back at his agreeable face. "Just release the latch and pull it toward you. Take as many of them their candies as you want. Because they'll only be stood there rotting for a long time, otherwise. Kids don't hire cars? Crazy promotion men! Especially kids who look the spitting image of my granddaughter. Oh, and you can take one of these things as well." He pointed to his blue, baseball hat peak, then bent down and pulled an identical, *Colville's car hire* hat from a stack underneath the open counter shelves and passed it to her. "There must be a dozen more in here."

"Thank you, sir," she said with a smile as she tried it on for size, whilst still ripping open the lollipop wrapper. She twisted her banded blonde hair through baseball cap the hole at the back, then pulled down on the peak.

"There you are. You only need to grow a beard now, and you'll look just like me," Charles smiled, turning his attention back to James who was now opening the correct piece of paper from out of his rucksack. "Now James, you can go ahead," he said as if Abby was more important than James.

"We're here for a van. The name's Ustinov, and here's the van confirmation papers, erm, Charles," he explained offering the letter across.

"All righty then. I'm Charles, as I said. And I'm sorry. Because, I'm darn forgetful sometimes. It's Charles Colville, and I'm very pleased to make your acquaintance. Welcome to my crumbling little empire," he said raising his arms into the air with a marked wheeze. "Oh, and you've already met my dog. Say hello, Archie." The small unkempt dog barked, then directed its attention to Abby's coarse biting of the plastic wrapping from off the lollipop.

"Aah, you're the LEAPS ecology guy. I'm sorry, your vehicle hasn't arrived yet. I know it says it has, but they rang and told me to give you a hire vehicle while the specialist interiors you require get fitted. They also said it'll be a few more days. Do you want me to call them, James?"

"Not at all. It'll get here when it gets here. We are in a bit of a rush, though. A temporary van will be fine. As long as we have some kind of transport until then," he replied looking at the Rolls Royce again.

"Ok, well you'd better follow me out back. Let's see what I can fix you up with. You can have the pick of the crop. Archie, watch the shop now, and don't you be going back outside and up to no good." He pointed at the scruffy mutt who growled a grumble, and then walked away from lollipop sucking Abby. Charles lifted up the wooden counter, as Archie unwillingly trudged past James, then masterfully leaped up onto a chair just near the Rolls Royce, and lied down and started staring without fault, at the front door as Charles beckoned James and Abby to follow him out the back of the shop.

"To be perfectly honest, there ain't much in at the moment. Where you both headed, anyway?" Charles asked, garishly coughing into his hand to Abby's worried frown.

"Erm, Harlan county hostel."

"What...! A hostel Dad," she asked scratching her head and biting on her lip. "That sounds scary. Do we have to stay in a hostel? It'll be full of strange people we don't know."

"That's exactly the same as what you do in a hotel, sweetheart. I haven't booked it yet. It's only written in the temporary instructions from work. Hostels aren't so bad," he advised to her shaking head. "I've stayed in worse places. It was practically a tree house in Venezuela," he said looking at his frowning daughter, but still not winning her over as they followed Charles. "There was no running water and the toilet was just the trees. There were snakes and..." he stopped. "Besides, I had to keep the travel costs down on this trip as much as I could. I paid for everything myself, and for your information, work doesn't even know you're with me."

"Don't start, Dad. It isn't my fault Mum isn't here anymore."

"Sweetheart, I didn't mean anything like that," he replied feeling suddenly sad. Look, if we can get our hands on the project house keys, and it's ready, we can do away with the hostel idea, completely."

"We have a house here... brilliant!"

"Ah, Harlan County, I know it well," Charles explained with a huge cough, feeling he needed to interject. "Just down here to the roundabout and take a sharp right. After that, it's a straight road. You'll soon be on the 61. Follow it to the 33, then north to Pineville. Then, the 119, through to Bell County. You should be in Harlan in a couple of hours, traffic permitting. There is some road works going on up there, though. A lot of road digging going on at Maynardville," he explained sniffing hard and wiping his nose on his sleeve, as they continued walking down the concrete car lot.

"I thought you said you were forgetful, Charles. You don't sound forgetful to me."

"Comes with the territory, James. You can stop awhile on the way if you got time. It's a beautiful drive. You got the Chuck Swan state forest over to your left. Then the Cumberland historical park on your right. There's 14km of underground caves to see in that place. Beautiful, black bear country.

"Bears!" Abby exclaimed almost swallowing her lollipop.

"Let's get you some nice wheels. There're some ordinary town cars over there. Oh, and that. And that," he pointed at the random vehicles. "Bigger estate cars, or even one of those vans, if you got a lot of lugging? I got a couple of strong and solid jeeps over at the end there. They'd see you right whatever roads you get them on. You're in Kentucky, and we're a little more laid back than those city folks. But expect the worst of the highways and roads," he said with a sniff as they walked down the other side of the forecourt. "Take whatever you like. In fact, take two. I'm only going through the motions now. These old overalls never get dirty, these days. My times of making a buck or two are over. It's just become a little something to keep me and Archie busy. A hobby, until the big man calls." Charles explained grabbing his handkerchief to wipe the congregating dribble from the end of his nose, and then visibly hocking on the concrete, as Abby watched him looking worried.

As they walked along the sun baking concrete, she turned back to look at his blood-filled spit behind them. They continued past the small saloon cars, until they stopped in front of a new, red jeep. "That's very kind of you, but one vehicle is more than enough," James joked. "We'll take whatever you recommend, Charles. I've driven a jeep like that one before though. In Malaysia. It was very rugged terrain and in monsoon season," he inferred looking through its windows for any familiarity.

"No problem James, the keys will be underneath the sun visor. It was serviced last week, so I'll just take the wheel clamp off for you." Charles felt his pocket for his keys, then bent down and released the lock and pulled the cumbersome, yellow chunk of metal from the wheel. "Drive it through the back gates, and park around the front of the shop. I'll have the paperwork ready for you to sign when you get inside. Here, catch." Charles shouted flipping a dollar in Abby's direction. She crowded her fingers together and caught it.

"Thank you erm Charles," she smiled wondering what it was for.

"Go with your Pops and get yourself a soda from the shop next door. I'll see you both when you get around," he confirmed picking up the heavy wheel clamp and walking out of earshot, then violently stopping to wheeze, clear his throat but more importantly, to regain his breath. He rabidly spat the contents of his mouth onto the floor, yet again, and then paused to lean on the side of a large, wooden storage box. After a couple of minutes, he placed the wheel clamp inside it. As he did, he grabbed hold of the box again to steady himself, as he continued to violently cough Abby ran toward him to comfort him as best she could. "I'm ok honey, go get that soda," he said as she reluctantly walked away to climb into the jeep with her Dad.

"This is too high off the ground," she said grabbing a handle inside the door as she tried to climb into the jeep. "We'll be okay sweetheart. These things have the pull of a hundred horses. They are much better than those little dinky toys over there," he added as he pointed through the jeeps front window.

"It has four seats, as well," she said looking into the back, but still watching Charles out of the corner of her eye.

"Yes, they have so much power. Probably far too much for me. I'll have to be very careful driving this thing," he explained, about to put the key in the ignition and then peering across the forecourt. "Hold on, look at that old girl right in front of us," he said pointing through the window again. "There, in the little garage with the open doors. How about that instead, Abby?"

He asked as he eagerly jumped out of the jeep and onto the lot, leaving Abby watching him and un-clipping her seat belt. He walked excitedly across to an old pea-green camper van on the opposite side of the lot.

"Hey dad, wait for me."

He turned around, looked at her, and then turned back to view the dilapidated, vintage camper van sitting inside the tiny garage that was almost enveloped around it. On seeing it up close, he shouted across to Charles "Excuse me, Charles! Sorry to be a pain, but what about this?" Charles looked back at him puzzled because he wasn't able to hear a word and just put his thumb up. Then, he began to walk back, as Abby walked to her Dad's side. "Well, what do you think? I know it's not the best-looking van, but I like it. I wonder if it's roadworthy." He kicked the flat, front tire as Charles appeared and then leaned forward with his hands on his knees, both puffing and spluttering.

"What do I think? Are you being serious? It's the color of sick, Dad. It's horrible," she griped as he walked tightly between the camper and the wooden walls of the makeshift garage to take a closer look while Charles fought get his breath back. "Oh, come on Abby, what do you reckon?" He jokingly pulled on her ponytail as she followed him beside the camper.

"It's just a bit... well, I've never been camping before Dad, and there's just two of us. What about charging my phone though? If I can do that, then I guess it'll be okay."

"Come on, you're the one turning your nose up at staying in a hostel. I think this will be a perfect solution. And of course, you can charge you're mobile, he explained looking though the dusty windows. "It looks all self-contained as well. All we need is food, water and petrol, we'll be sorted. Oh, and some gas," he added.

"I asked about my mobile, Dad."

"All you need for that is a car charger. You just plug it in the cigarette lighter, and that'll do the trick."

"Phew, I ain't as young as I used to be," Charles said appearing at the side of the van. "Like your pop said, it'll be a whole lot of fun. The wife and I loved every minute of it. Meet, Clara two," Charles smiled. "This is my old girl. My wife Clara and I spent many a year out and about in this. It's a bit ramshackle now, but oh, the fun and great memories I have are still in here." He said tapping his chest. "I was going to get rid of it when my Clara passed. But I didn't have the heart. Oh, and don't let the soft tire fool you. I've taken real good care of it. It's got close to 300,000 miles on the clock, but it'll rattle off 300,000 more," Charles coughed. "I've taken the engine apart and re-built it twice. From new pistons, right through to skimming the cylinder head," he sniffed.

"I got the keys right here in my pocket, and she's all kitted out at the back to. Everything works dandy, just as it did when we had her on the road. There's no need to even try her out, because I kick up the engine every single week. I'd state my life on her reliability. In fact, she's never let me down. I used to keep her in the main garage back of the shop, but when I sold out to the multi-national, they wanted her out of sight. Some bad image rubbish, they said. I built this little place for her instead. Here, let me throw some air in that tire. Abby, grab me that air hose from down on the floor inside would you honey." Charles pointed across the garage floor. "You can take her with my blessing. Just make sure she gets back here, safe and sound." He said as his face tightened and he violently coughed again.

"Are you sure, Charles? You don't even know me... I mean, us. How can you place so much faith in a couple of complete strangers?" James asked scratching his head as Charles looked down at Abby. "Because I know that your daughter here will keep you right. What's the worst that could happen?" Charles replied, connecting the air the hose to the tire as James took the keys from his hand. He opened the door until it touched the side of the garage and he furrowed himself inside. "Turn her over James, while I pump this up a little. James, there's a secondary spare wheel underneath as well as this one on the front, and tires will always stay up longer when you're using them regular. All the changing tools are inside. As well as pots, pans, fresh blankets and bedding, and all the cooking stuff you'll need. There you go, 32 psi will do just fine," he shouted above the compressor noise. "That's you, good to go. Try her out first though and be sure."

"No need, Charles, I'm sure she's the one."

"Okay. Go out the gates and drive around to the front of the shop as I said before. I'll get you a new gas bottle from the garage store. I'm sure there's some in there, somewhere," he said walking away.

James kicked up the camper engine with Abby alongside him and trundled through the gates to the front of the shop. "Dad, he spat blood out again. He's not well, is he?" She lamented.

"No, sweetheart, he isn't. He doesn't sound good, at all. It's a shame. I did some research when I was here last. Well, when I was down the road, two months ago in, Tennessee," he replied in a saddening tone. "This whole area has a huge coal mining history. Especially in Harlan. It stems from way back when, to right through to the present day. Charles mentioned black lung. I'm afraid that just about says it all. Years ago, coal mining was carried out by men with picks and shovels on long shifts and hard hours. Nothing like the machines of today. There was no health and safety laws back then, either. As a result, many men lost their lives," he explained turning the corner to the familiar front of the shop "With all the terrible conditions they had to endure, many have contracted black lung and breathing problems since, and they are still losing their lives, many years later. At some stage in his life, and somewhere along the way, Charles must have been a coal miner, or at least, been involved. That's why he's like he is… the poor fellow. What's even sadder is… there's nothing anyone can do about it now," he solemnly explained. "He just has to get on with it and live out the rest of his life as well as he can." James looked across at Abby and watched the sadness grow in her eyes.

"Nothing?"

"I'm afraid not. There's nothing we can do to help him, except maybe just understand," he said reaching over to Abby's hand to reassure her. He drove along the road and parked at the front of the shop where Charles was waiting on the sidewalk with Archie, and a gas bottle at his feet.

123

"Here you are, James," he said opening the side door and putting the gas bottle in the back. "No! You just sit there, and stick to staying sitting, little one," he smiled. There's no need to get out. Oh, and there's no paperwork to sign with Clara. Now, James's. Don't you forget about the road works now, you hear? Have a lovely time, and I'll see you both when you bring Clara back." Abby suddenly narrowed her eyes, then intensely focused them on Charles face. She unclipped her seatbelt and burst out of the camper van door. She ran around the front, and threw her arms tightly around, Charles legs. "Hey, little one, come on now. I'll be here when you get back. We're always here ain't we, boy?" He said looking down at Archie who also seemed somewhat sad to see her go. Abby let go her grip on him and bent down to pet Archie on last time. "You keep your Pops outta trouble."

"I intend to," She said running back around the front of the van to re-join her Dad who was smiling at Charles as Abby buckled up. "Thanks for everything, Charles. We'll see you in a few days." James shook Charles hand through the window. "Right Abby, let's get this big green, swamp machine on the road. We can pretend we're Bonnie and Clyde" he smiled.

"Who's Bonnie and Clyde, Dad?" She inquisitively frowned.

FOURTEEN: *The bump*

"So, did you have a good time?" She asked as Jamie stuffed his face with Clay's birthday cake.

"It was great, Mom. I don't want anything else to eat, now. I did have a proper meal as well," he explained tucking into the cream sponge. "What happened to you and Clay's Dad?"

"A proper meal my butt. You'll tell me anything to keep me quiet. As long as you had fun, that's all that matters. Sheridan and me. Mmm, we erm, had a flat tire up at Coal Cut Lane, delivering the letters for the next community meeting. Oh, look at the time, we'd better go get Bailey, pronto. And that isn't going to be a barrel of easy," she intimated as a lump of Jamie's cake dropped from the corner of his mouth to the floor of the Mustang "Mercy me, will you look at the queue of traffic here, Jamie. This town's grid-locked. Aunt May will be wondering where we are." she cursed reluctantly joining the bumper to bumper car-jam and slowing up the car behind a pea-green, camper van. "Shoot! And they're all heading in the direction of our house. That means after we leave Aunt Mays, that queue of metal mayhem is what we've got to look forward to. And well, would at those lazy, high-vis men over there. Just drinking coffee and smoking and not much of nothing else. It's darn typical. So much for getting the road reopened. They're just shooting the breeze, and watching the world go slowly by. God, did you see that! This idiot in front keeps slamming on his anchors. Aargh...! This one-horse town! I wish we could get out of here, and permanently. Sail away to another life and make a new start somewhere. Oh, now wouldn't that be a wonderful adventure, Jamie?" She looked in her rear-view mirror to see his reaction. In doing so, she took her eye off the road for a split second, and the Mustang softly coasted forward and touched the rear of the camper van, that was sitting stationary in the traffic queue in front.

"Oh crap! OMG Jamie, did I just hit that thing?" She asked twitching, then rubbing her eyes. "Did I....? Shi... ne a light! I wonder if they felt it. It was nothing really. It didn't do a thing," she explained to Jamie, who wasn't even listening. "It's his fault with all his stupid, juddering. No. It wasn't a hard tap, at all. Must have felt nothing. I never even felt a thing, did you? She asked feeling nervous but making out it was an everyday occurrence. "Their fault with all the fitful stopping and starting. Probably using his damn cell phone and driving at the same time. Camper vans, argh! Damn tourists! They could make a career out of causing accidents," she added trying to push the blame as far away from herself as she could. "Oh, I hope he doesn't get out. Is there anybody looking out of the mirrors, Jamie?

"I don't know. I'm full up with cake," he mumbled.

"If he's damaged Pape's Mustang, I'll..." she seethed turning the tables on the blameless driver.

Jamie, simply couldn't speak, due to the sheer amount of cake that was still in his mouth. Plus, the fact he was secretly grinning from ear to ear, at his

Mom's stupid error. As she looked over her shoulder to see his reaction, he darted out of her field of vision for fear she would see him laughing as the camper moved forward, then stopped again.

"Look, there he goes, again!" She angrily lifted her hands off the steering wheel into the air and frowned back at Jamie for some kind of support.

"Look Jamie, he's driving like a jumping jack? He must be running out of gas or full of road rage or crazyitis. He doesn't even know it, either. The dangerous fool. I think I'd better hold back a little. Just in case he does something else stupid." She pacified herself, apportioning the blame elsewhere again. Sensing his Mom's anger, Jamie pulled down on his seat belt. Leant over the passenger seat through the half-open window to have a better view of the traffic, and the notorious, green camper van that was enraging his Mom. She held the Mustang back a short distance from the camper until she reached the junction, then quickly drove down Jones Street for her Auntie's house, in Oak lane. She indicated left, then drove the Mustang through a swift gap before the car coming in the other direction passed. As she turned the corner, she caught a brief glimpse of the green camper driver in her rear-view mirror, as the oncoming car parped his horn at her. "Phew. That was chaos. I hope the traffic frees up a little when we get back there, heading for home. I hope I don't come across that useless camper clown again, or there'll be some seriously harsh words. There isn't a vaccination for stupid. I'd sure give him a piece of my mind," she convinced herself. "I need to check the front of the Mustang. Oh, and not a word to aunt May, honey. Right, here we are. Oh look, she's sat out front with the water sprinkler on. Look Jamie, can you see the rainbow crescent in the water?" She asked pointing at the arced and glistening band of color.

"I won't say a thing Mom, I promise. The rainbow's cool. Look Mom, Baileys sleeping beside Aunt May." As May waved, Eden she honked the horn, and Jamie waved through the window as she pulled the car on the driveway and they climbed out of the doors like female batman, and a limping robin. "Sorry we're a little late. We had a few stupid people to deal with. The traffic's crazy in town tonight." She explained walking casually around the car to secretly inspect the front. She looked down at the bumper for any damage, or any sign of green paint. Then, turned to face limping Jamie and gave him a sly wink.

May stopped knitting to watch, almost saluting at them by shading the sun from her eyes as she squinted through the fly fused, and warm night air as they walked toward her. "Oh, there's no such a thing as late in my world. I have all the time in the world, these days. I could hardly see you for the setting sun. How was the guitar playing today, Jamie? Did you steal the show? Oh, Eden, I haven't seen my brother's car in such a long time. I see it's still looking great, after all these years," She said as Eden smiled and looked back at the Mustang, feeling a slight twinge of guilt even though the bumper showed no visible sign of damage. Before long, Bailey was rambitiously running around the garden, barking at their arrival and the shock of his furry coat being systematically soaked by the sprinkler.

"Oh Lord. Would you look at the daft, mutt? He makes more noise than a guinea hen. He's as fractious as a moony horse. So, I take it the play went well?" May asked leaning back in her rocking chair.

"It was great. I'm going to learn some more songs and start a school band," Jamie said walking toward the house to hug his aunt, and then settled himself on the porch step, just beside her. "I'm sure you are honey, but go on inside and wash that sticky, cakey chin. Then, get us all some lemonade." "Ok."

"So how are things, Eden? We hardly get a chance to sit down and talk these days. You're here and you're there and you're gone. Always busying yourself," May said as she picked back up her knitting needles and replaced her glasses on the end of her nose. "How's Jamie's hip holding up? Any sign of an operation yet?"

"Oh, we're ok, May. You have to be, don't you," she sighed. "We heard nothing about the operation. Not a damn thing. I'm beginning to think they've forgotten all about him. How can it take so long?" She asked wrapping her arms tightly around her legs and turning away from her Aunts gaze to watch the sprinkled water falling on the grass as May continued:

"It'll come honey. Just have faith in the Lord. You're far too busy for finding a man or settling down again to, I suppose?" May asked to Eden's silence. "That boy needs a father figure."

"Oh, come on. Don't you start giving me a hard time, as well," Eden replied thinking about James. "That's all I seem to get thrown at me these days," she said feigning a mock voice. "Get yourself a man... find a dude... hook a hunk. Yeuch! That's all I hear. Thanks, but no thanks. It gets plain boring after a while. Besides, I'm in no position to do anything like that. I'm far too preoccupied with Jamie and my work at the school. But more than that, I couldn't trust another man. I will not compromise who I am for anyone. Not after what Kyle put me through. What he put us both through. He's still doing it to. He even wants the house we live in. Can you believe that? How could I be such a fool?" She rested her chin onto her hands and stared at the dancing water, then fell silent again, getting lost in the water as it slowly mesmerized her into some happier thoughts. She concentrated on the sound of water, then unconsciously opened up her heart, and her feelings:

"I wouldn't have the patience to see it through. James, is from the other side of the world anyway. Another world. How did I get it all so wrong? I wanted a happy ending just like Cinderella. I wanted a knight in shining amour, or a Prince among men. Not a pretender, dressed in tin foil that turned into liar and a cheat. And, I don't want my heart shattered in pieces again, either. So that's it. The brick walls are built tall around my tender heart, and they're staying put."

"Who's, James, my darling?" May asked, almost waking Eden from her lucid state.

"Oh... did I say, James?" She asked uncomfortably, shifting her posture and wondering what to say. "I meant they're staying put... the darn bricks." She said quickly tailing off to go back into her enjoyable trance.

"Be really careful, honey. A *darn* is more righteous than a tear."

"Look Auntie. It's just like a little Cumberland River Moonbow, isn't it?"

"Yes, it is," May agreed as they watched the flickering colored kaleidoscope of water forming randomly in front of their eyes.

"The Moonbow is elusive, and it doesn't happen often. Making it so much like love." May explained as Eden's heart gently melted as she listened to her

Aunts voice and closed her eyes. "Love comes quickly. Just like the Bow. Only when the full moon is low in the sky, and the night is as dark as coal. When the night is clear as crystal, and the breeze blows silent, with the feeling just right. Only then, will the Moonbow appear. When all those tiny intimate and important connections are made, the magic happens. Exactly like love. And it will come to you again. I know it will. And when it does, there's not a damn thing you can do to stop it. So, you grab it with both hands and never let it go. Life and love are precious and must be enjoyed in togetherness. But let me tell you something else, honey. There is no glory in the Moonbow's birth and blossom, until it is looked on by both a loved and loving eye," She explained smiling and putting her hand on Eden's shoulder as she sighed.

"What are you saying?" She acceded.

"In order for you to love again, you have to find the courage to stand up to everything that's gone wrong and say: *'I forgive you, and I'm finished with you.'* Being honest with yourself and your feelings will allow you to move on." Eden took it all in, said not another word, and then quietly rested her hand on May's leg. "You'll never lose by loving, but you'll lose holding back. Open your heart, again. Please, don't let it ache so. Because when one door closes, another door, and another chapter will open. Just you remember that, dear."

Eden squinted at May, stood up from the steps and intimately put her hand on her Aunts shoulder. Then almost as immediately, formed a pessimistic impression on her face.

"Oh, I don't know? Do you honestly believe in all that magical nonsense?"

"I believe in love, honey. And love has been happening that way for centuries," she explained, calmly picking up her knitting needles once more. "Hope is everything."

"You're crazy, May. I do wish that were true. But, I guess I'll just have to wait until forever until something wonderful like that happens to me. Until then, I'll consider myself well and truly educated." She said with a smile as Jamie came clattering through the porch swing doors, with two glasses in his hands, followed by sniffing Bailey.

"Have you been stewing the lemonade yourself?" Eden asked.

"No. I was just having a sit-down. My hips sore today," he explained as she took a glass from his hand, and he sat down beside May. "Did you remember to take your pills this afternoon?"

"Yes, Mom."

"After your drink, get him straight home then Eden. I insist on it. A hot bath and your night time pills, will help." May said standing up as they drank their glasses of lemonade.

"I'll rub some cream into your hip as well. But we really must call and get some groceries from town first. There was nothing for us to eat for breakfast this morning. Oh, and there's that darn traffic to contend with, as well," she remembered. "Jamie, Bailey, go and get yourselves in the car. Aunt May, thanks for everything. I honestly don't know what I'd do without you," she said kissing her auntie's head as they watched Jamie carefully navigate the wooden porch steps and waddle toward the car with his sore hip.

"Thank you for the kind words. I wasn't mocking what you said. It was lovely listening, but it's just so hard for me to believe in. Could be a dream come true if it were to happen," she paused. "But I'm just a pessimistic unbeliever. I never used to be either? Oh, I guess Kyle put paid to that lovely kind of thinking," she said before walking along the driveway. "Or, maybe I will take your advice and plump for some healthy optimism for a change. Better get going. We'll try the other way home this time, see you tomorrow with Bailey," she shouted, slamming the car door and thinking about the heavy traffic that lay in wait for them, around the corner.

"Oh, it doesn't look that bad, Jamie," she said turning off Oak street onto Highland avenue to where the traffic situation had somewhat eased. "We'll head to Donny and Mack's grocers, just on Island Street. Get a few bits and pieces, and then do a big shop another day," she said flicking her hair from her eyes. "We should have the jeep back by then. There's nowhere near enough room in this Mustang for shopping. That's my excuse anyhow." She drove along in the main streets tail of traffic that was moving at a reasonable pace. Then, she turned sharply into Island Street, and straight onto Donny and Mack's car park, in to what looked like the last vacant car space. "Bailey, watch the car," she stated edging herself out of her seat and onto the tarmac. "Do you want to wait in the car while your hips sore? I promise I won't be long," she asked grabbing her purse and dumping her school bag behind her seat, and out of sight. "No. its ok Mom, I'll come along," he replied, already climbing through the door. "I can put you in a basket if you like," she teased.

"Mom, I'm fine. But erm... Mom... look," he said climbing from the car.
"Yes... honey, what is it?"
"What is it...? Don't you mean, who is it? Look over in the far corner of the car park."
"OMG!
"Exactly!
"The green camper van that was at front of us in the traffic queue," she said wondering what to do next.
"Mom. Keep your temper. Remember, it was partly your fault."
"Partly my fault my butt. He was the big bag of nerves in the jumping jack van."
"Mom!"
Okay... okay! I suppose I'd best go and give the darn fool some kind of apology. Or at least a piece of my mind." She looked at the camper again, as her conscience ate at her thoughts.
"Mom!"
"Its lights are on? Mmm, I'll just go and say a quick sorry," she said as if she was under duress. As they walked over to the rear of the camper it seemed to look that everything was okay. Unmarked and free from damage, just like the Mustang. At least it was, until Eden walked closer, and for no other reason than to clear her conscience, she lightly kicked at the bumper with her foot. It rattled somewhat loosely, and then dropped to the tarmac beside her feet. "Oh no!" She shrieked, as Jamie burst out laughing. She put her hand across her mouth, expecting the driver door to open as she looked

around to see that Jamie had already turned around, and darted back toward the Mustang, leaving the culprit standing on her own, beside the camper.

"OMG! That could only happen to me. Jamie! Come back here this instant! Help me get this damn thing back on before somebody sees it. Oh God! I'm a complete idiot, I'm for it now." But despite her worry, the camper didn't move. She crept around to the front to see that both front seats were empty. She looked back at Jamie. Then, for no apparent reason, pulled on the driver door to watch it open in her hand. Her mouth fell open, and she emitted a shocked yelp as she looked back at Jamie, once again, who was now in hiding mode, and peeping over the bonnet of the Mustang, with a huge grin.

"Oh, thanks you traitor. Where's your loyalty?" She frowned trying not to smile at her self-made predicament.

"I'll get you back for this." She bent down just like Jamie, as if that would help make her invisible, and closed the camper door. Then, she returned to the clearly injured bumper at the back of the camper. She knelt down and cupped her hand around the white metal, then lifted it up. Attempting to return it to its former glory. As she struggled to put the bumper back, the metal clunked and chinked loudly in her ears. Obviously sounding so much louder because of her secret, guilty conscience.

As she pushed on the bumper, all at once, it seemed that something had firmly clicked back into place. As she carefully took her hand away, it stayed exactly where it was. In silence, she quickly retreated backwards in commando style, to where Jamie as he shook his head with amusement.

"Mom, I just can't take you anywhere, can I? You can't leave it like that. What if it falls off when he's driving? I know I'm just a stupid kid, but he's parked tight to the wall and he has to reverse that green hunk of junk to get out of there. What if he reverses over the bumper?"

"Well, he'll know he has a slight problem, won't he."

"Mom, that isn't right. And when he does, don't you think he might ask the shop to look at their CCTV cameras to find out what happened?"

Eden frowned at her sense-making son, as they both leaned on the Mustang bonnet looking across at each other for an answer. "How did you get to be so annoyingly adult, Jamie? Oh, darn it...! Ok then," she said admittedly and blatantly folding her arms together. "So, I'll just own up then, shall I... huh...? My stupid Mom broke your van, sir. Why don't you just go in there and tell the whole shop, son," she arguably whispered into his ear. "It was fine until I kicked it?"

"No Mom. It was fine until you hit it with the Mustang. You always taught me to tell the truth. No matter what the consequences. You always said; honesty's the best policy"

"Oh, shush. All right... all right! Don't rub it in.... you trainee police man. You don't have to make me feel any worse than I already do," she said as they both folded their arms at exactly the same time.

"Ok, we'll go in the shop and I'll explain everything. Are you happy now Judge Jamie?"

"Mom, I just...? I didn't mean," he innocently crowded his hands in the air. Secretly smiling inside as he watched his Mum wince.

"Shush. Come on then honey. Let's go watch as Mom makes a total chump out of herself."

As she stomped across the car park, Jamie followed her, looking down and giggling to himself as she muttered a plethora of impossible explanations to herself under her breath. She pushed on the front door of the grocers and they walked inside and then headed straight for the customer service desk. Behind the counter, there was a small dumpy lady wearing glasses around her neck and writing furiously on a small pad. Eden looked at her, then stared around the shop in a feeble attempt to avoid opening her mouth at all.

"Evening Madam. Can I help you?" The woman said as Eden quietly zoned in on the woman's name badge clipped on her white uniform, and then looked up to face her:

"Excuse me, erm.... Miss Dipsey I'm erm, looking for the owner of the green camper van that's, parked outside."

"It's Dempsey. Gloria Dempsey... and I have absolutely no idea who you are talking about. Everybody, including God uses our car park. Are you sure they're even in here?" She nonchalantly replied looking back down at her counter notes and lifting her glasses appropriately on to her nose.

"Well how the hell would I know?" Eden flippantly countered. "I'm sorry, it's just sat out on the car park, so I just assumed?"

"Isn't that something you should never do, Mam?"

"What?"

"Assume. Now, as I explained. The world and his wife park on here as you can see." She motioned her head toward the busy shopping aisles. The shops always full to bursting at this time, but what with Independence Day next week, its complete chaos." She said as Eden turned away from her to see the body bustling aisles of the shop.

"Thank you, Gloria. Thank you very much," Eden replied sarcastically as she looked down at Jamie and gave out a deep, mortified, and ungracious groan.

FIFTEEN: *Groceries*

"Abby, can you calm down with the sweets, we're fast running out of basket room here. I really think we should have used a trolley instead. Oh, I think I should buy a tin-opener while where here? I wonder if the camper van has one on-board. Charles did say it was all kitted out?" He pondered as she joyfully threw another packet of sweets into the almost overflowing basket. "I think I'm going to treat myself to a couple of beers, seeing as you're immoderately treating yourself to every single sweet in the whole shop," he cursed watching his automaton daughter concentrate as she scanned the whole content of the sweet and chocolate aisle vortex that he now seemed to be permanently trapped in.

"Dad, this is obviously just research. There's some strange and wonderful yummy stuff in this place. All pretty cool. I do have to check some of it out for quality purposes. We don't even have edible money, back home."

"Oh really, how thrilling? Just stay here with the basket, I'll be right back," he mumbled putting the sweet-heavy basket on the floor tight beside a full shelf of peanut and lime dippers, as Abby frowned at him for his sweet impudence. "This is getting totally ridiculous. I'll be right back with a trolley," he said walking between two elderly ladies. Posthumously deep in conversation and vindicating the high cost of bananas and their vehemently brilliant qualities as Abby continued to smile at her abundant cornucopia of sugary delights nestled in the basket below her. She plonked her backside scurrilously down right down on top of them. Both salivating wildly and innately smiling to herself as he walked away.

"Ok Dad," she shouted as he disappeared. "I'll just get one or two more vital, lifesaving essentials from here," she consummately explained. As if she was a professional sweet shopper. As he walked down the sweet aisle, Eden and Jamie were walking in the opposite direction. But in the coffee, tea and drinks aisle instead.

"Oh Jamie, I'm such a klutz. Excuse me sir, madam, do you have a green camper van parked outside?" she muttered. "The back bumper is..." she said as their silent and shaking heads confirmed they didn't. "This is going to take all night, and more people will be coming in as I'm asking. Oh shucks." Jamie looked up at his Mom, and flailed his arms wide open, lost how to give her an answer. "Excuse me sir, sorry to bother you. Do you have a green...?" Jamie shook his head to himself and walked to the end of the drinks aisle, deciding to leave her to it. He walked up and down the width of the shop. Then settled himself down on a two-box stack of cooking oil, that was involuntarily left sitting on a wheeled truck between the meat and fish counter, that exactly mirrored the other end of the shop, to where Gloria was currently stood.

"Erm, excuse me, miss."

"It's Gloria, mister. Read the damn, badge."

"Oh, erm, of course, sorry. I just want to break a dollar... Gloria. That's what they say isn't it?" He smiled at her stern and unimpressed face.

"They say. Who is they?" She replied as he passed her a five-dollar bill.

"Just for the erm.... getting a trolley.... oh, you know. I have far too many things for a basket, you see," he smiled purporting an invisible basket in his hand to a bemused Gloria, who looked him up and down, then *beeped* open the till to furnish him with some change. "Thank you so much... bloody camping eh...! Who'd be so stupid? Especially with six children," he implied lying through his teeth completely straight-faced to even more stun her already confused expression. He turned around to walk into the drinks aisle as Eden walked around its far corner.

"Mmm, where's Abby gone now...? And where's all the sweets gone?" He mumbled to himself, glancing over at each side of the aisle's contents. "She must be on that side. James, you dope! I may as well keep going to the end now," he assured himself.

Eden strolled down the almost empty sweet aisle before her, then glanced down at Abby who was diligently immersed in reading the contents of a packet of *'Crazy Squirrel Fizzers.'*

On hearing Eden's footsteps, Abby looked up and politely smiled: "Hello."

"Hello," Eden replied as Abby returned to her candy education whilst Eden looked up ahead and decided to write off the aisle off as null and void in her camper driver search. She walked to the end of the sweet row and turned into the condiments and sauces aisle.

James turned the corner of the chocolate and sweets aisle and almost mowed the trolley into his own daughter. Who was still happily basket-perched, and patiently trying to understand the premise of *'Buttered Unicorn Horns.'*

"Hi Dad. These things are supposed to make you dream of Unicorns and Dragons. That's weird!"

"No, you're weird!"

After yet another tumultuous aisle that she hoped would be the last. Eden decided she'd had more than enough and headed back to see Gloria. Whereas, James was feeling extra happy, now he'd extricated the basket contents into the roomier trolley and had finally made it to his place of choice. The beer and liquor corner, at the far side of Gloria's desk.

"Mmm, I'm spoilt for choice. I could try some of that black draught beer. What do you think Abby?" He asked as she stood unconcerned on the front rail of the sweet-packed shopping trolley.

"Excuse me again, Gloria. I've really had enough of this now. This feels like

Ground-hog day. Could you get your manager, or someone to turn off that stupid, damn music and put an announcement over the tannoy for me," she asked feeling somewhat sick of asking the shoppers the same question and hearing the constant elevator music in the background as Jamie appeared at her side.

"Ok lady, keep your hair on. Lord above, there's some awfully weird people in here tonight," she grumbled. "I can do that for you from right here. What's the registration?"

"Erm, I have no idea."

Gloria looked at Eden like she was stupid. "What's the message then?" She appeased, patiently waiting as Eden scrambled her words together.

"Slug green camper van owner to the Gloria desk, please. No, to the main customer service counter," she replied in an instructing tone as she looked up at the sign above their heads. "Could you give them your name as well, please? This is unusually important, and I have to get it right."

"Sure thing, honey." Gloria bent down below the counter and turned the piped music down. Turning the shop strangely silent and making the shoppers suddenly realise they were talking rather loudly.

"Good evening you lovely shoppers. May I have your attention please? Could the owner of the green camper van on the car park report to Gloria at the customer help desk, please. That's the green camper van owner to little old me at the main help desk, thank you."

#

"Mmm, Germando export bier wins, I think. Well, after all, when in America, go for German," he affirmed with a smile. "What was that? An announcement? Where's the music gone, Abby?"

"I think you're wanted at the helpdesk, Dad. Come on, grab your beers and let's go see what you've done now," she calmly explained, systematically grabbing the beer four-pack from his hand and dropping it into the trolley. Then, she pulled the trolley handle away from his hands and headed for the front desk, leaving him puzzled and scratching his head, but slowly following right behind.

Eden leaned impatiently and silently, as Jamie sat beside her on a temporary, washing powder stack as a thin, and black suited store manager came into her field of vision, who seemed to be aiming straight for Gloria. "What seems to be the problem?" He asked looking gaudily at Eden then Gloria. "There's a problem outside, sir. Just waiting for some clarification about a vehicle," Gloria imitated. Looking straight back down at her tick sheets.

"I don't understand," he frowned glancing at tight-lipped and dour-faced Eden who really didn't want to have to explain herself again.

"You're supposed to run everything past me before you decide to cut the music and announce anything, Gloria. It's company policy and scribed in blood, in the employee handbook. Have you ever taken the time to educate yourself in that area?" He asked as she raised her head up, almost in slow motion to meet his eyes.

"So, sue me... you... yes man!"

"I beg your pardon?"

Look, this young lady here has a life or death emergency, right here and right now! And what do you do? Nothing! You are more interested in laying down company policy to make yourself feel good? Jeez, I've got a damned mind to report you to the union, or the companies' higher powers, or both. I think on my feet, and if that's not good enough for you, sir well, you can take this job, and shove it where the sun doesn't shine." Gloria looked at Eden as she instantly turned to face the store manager. Clearly opting for Gloria, as she watched the battle of wits unfold between them.

She winked back at Gloria and folded her arms to annoy and impede the store manager's obvious female problems. Which automatically increased his jumpiness, lack of eye contact, and his insufficient ease to resolve the issue.

"Don't start, Mom," Jamie implored. "Mom... just leave him alone." Eden looked down at Jamie, smiled and turned back around as the store manager decided to ask Eden nothing, and simply rotated himself to face Gloria. "Well, you carry right on, Miss Dempsey. You're handling the situation very well, and everything is just as it should be."

Eden turned to face the desk where the manager had joined Gloria at the back of the counter. "Excuse me. But maybe you should throw that out the speakers one more time. You know... just to be sure everybody heard. The owner must be in here? The thing's out there on the...."

"Hi there. I remember you from the sweet aisle."
"What?"
Oh, never mind. I'm Abby.... and it's my camper van," she explained after appearing beside Jamie. "Actually, it's our friend's, Charles. We met him today and he's not very well. But he said we can use it for as long as we like. But you don't need to know all that stuff, either. Anyway, my Dad is on his way." Jamie looked intently across at Abby and gave her a smile. Realising she was almost the same height as himself.

"Hi Abby. Pleased to meet you, I'm Jamie," he said as she spontaneously smiled back and put her hand out to greet him as James came sauntering around the corner as Eden turned away from the desk to suddenly be faced with him and yelped louder than she ever had before. Her mouth open, and she went bright red. She smiled at him whilst secretly glowing inside.

Rather than jump into a joyous hello speech. James decided to put on a huge, false front. "Evening. My names James Ustinov, and I'm the owner and the driver of the vehicle outside. Sorry... I was a little beer-beverage-busy-back there," he answered choosing his words like gloop because he was both nervous and happy to see her as he thumbed over his shoulder to the beer corner to show them all where he'd been.

He looked back at the desk huddled group and thought about the nonsense he'd just uttered. Then, smiled at his stupid mastery of tongue twisters and words beginning with the letter **b**. As he stood there, he had become particularly aware that he was fighting a losing battle with his eye sockets and their innate need to turn to the *left,* to where Eden was standing. So instead of fighting his eyes, he decided to single out the manager with his words and his gaze. "My daughter informed me that there was some kind of problem?" he said as Eden stood silently in the full knowledge that she'd just heard herself yelp like a wounded cat with a euphoric mixture of utter disbelief and joy. On top of that, she could also feel that she was slowly crushing her own abdomen with her arms because she was so over the moon to see that it was, *him* standing right in front of her, all over again. She slowly lifted a hand up to hide her gaping mouth, or at least to close it, before something possibly more detrimental escaped, as all the while, Abby and Jamie looked at each other, thinking that they had hopefully just found a brand-new friend.

#

Eden, moved her hand from her mouth to caress her throat. Feeling far too excitable and giddy to even attempt to speak for fear of such a high-pitched, or abnormal sound coming out, that the close congregation of the shop would begin to believe they were clearly in the company of a talking Hyena that was masquerading as an ordinary, everyday Harlan girl.

James glanced at Eden, then cleared his own throat. Subconsciously mirroring her actions as she secreted a slight knowing wave at him from one of her stomach clasped arms.

"Hi, mister Ustinov erm, may I call you, James," she asked looking deep into his dark brown eyes.

"Of course, you may, Eden," he replied, relaxing his tense shoulders and looking around at the bemused and gathered faces. Eden looked across at the store manager, and then at stony-faced Gloria. Who instinctively felt that something wasn't on the level with the two *strangers*? Imagining at worst, an unmitigated armed assault on all tills and cashed-up areas from the unknown adults, and children before her.

"Excuse me, mister store-man. Sorry, I didn't get your name. I think I can take things from here, if that's okay with you, sir?" Eden quickly inferred to the manager before Gloria had a chance to break any of her concerns. The manager looked over at Gloria for some kind of invisible permission as she simply shrugged her shoulders at him. "You're the boss-man. Do whatever you want. But, I'll tell you, sir. There's something about those two, and that just don't add up," she shouted pointing at her head.

"What do you mean, Gloria," the manager asked feeling somewhat in the dark.

"Oh, never mind it. I got figures to tally and shelves to stack," she conceded picking up her papers, and walking away.

"Of course, you can take things from here, Madam. I'm sure that will be fine. I'll put the store music back on now that we're all sorted out," the smiling manager said to Eden as he rubbed his hands together.

"Dad," Abby said tugging on his denim jacket. "How come you already know her name?"

"What?"

"I said, how do you already know her name!"

Before James had time to answer, Abby's statement echoed rudely inside everyone who was there's heads. The store manager glanced at departing Gloria as he felt his demeanor shrink again. "Yes, how do you know her name, sir?"

Well, I erm... I'm sure somebody said it, didn't they," James suggested as Abby looked at him with crossed arms and the manager tapped at his chin with his finger.

"Mmm well, they didn't. So, I think it would be better if you all take your, erm.... camping business or whatever your sordid enterprise may be out of my law-abiding shop. Then we can get on with running our own business, and you can get on with yours," he announced realising he shouldn't have assumed anything about the situation.

"Look, we've met before, Abby. The last time I was here on assignment, a couple of months ago. It's a long story, but it was only in passing. So, brief an introduction, it was hardly worth mentioning to anyone," he explained as Abby looked at Jamie and her petulant frown remained.

"We, we... were working on the same project, you see," he continued trying to redress the balance, but failing miserably, as Abby stayed silent, leaving Eden to intervene and grab the crux of the sentence to try to recover the increasingly, possible train wreck. "Your dad's skills in his work are invaluable to the cause... Abby."

"They are?" Abby replied unsurely.

"Of course," Eden gulped.

"What cause?"

"My cause!"

"What skills?"

"His ecology skill, I mean," Eden said with a cough, remembering his pool skill and some of the conversations from Brannigans Skoolhouse. "Yes, his skills in ecology are a credit to him. I really learned a lot. I even love ecology more than he does," she lied as she tried to remember more of the things that he'd told her.

"Really?"

"Yes, he told me about the ecology company and erm, everything."

"He told you everything, did he? Mmm, so, what's his company called?"

"Are you trying to catch me out, or something?

"The name," Abby asked getting a little irate as James began to contemplate jumping up and down, to give Eden a clue in case she'd forgotten."

"It's called… LEAPS."

"Which stands for what?"

"It stands for… London Endangered Animals and Plants Society," Eden replied to James marked relief. "Nice camper van you, and your Dad have, Abby. He… your Dad, did tell me that he would be bringing a different type of strategy to the table on his next trip. Maybe that strategy, is you?" She announced blatantly lying through her teeth for a second time and excessively smiling. Swallowing deeply and tilting her head away. "Sorry to be harping on about our work kids," she fibbed. "That's where the problem lies, you see." She pointed to the shop door as the store manager watched on, still believing in his own damning conclusions as he gave up, winced and walked away. "I think your camper's broken."

"I bet you didn't expect to see me, then?" Abby confidently added, deciding to give the somewhat squirming, but beautiful red-head the benefit of the doubt by taking her questionable explanation at face value.

"No, Abby. I certainly didn't."

"This is my surprise holiday trip," Abby explained to Eden with a smile.

"That's brilliant! When these two are working together, we can hang out."

Jamie shouted, finally opening his mouth with a more positive note.

"So yes, we... were coming in here to stock up on groceries for the camper van."

"Same as us. I've run our cupboards dry at home, erm James," she explained flicking her red hair and wondering why she was mentioning home to somebody who didn't even live there. "Anyway, as we drove into the car park Jamie and I noticed your rear bumper was hanging off.... didn't we... Jamie?" She clenched her hands under her chin and looked across at her son. As if she was praying for him to back her up.

"Yes sir, that's correct," he piped, grabbing the baton. "Hanging on the floor, it was. My Mom took the amiable step of trying to re-secure it for you, sir. That's why we came in here to raise the alarm. Before someone experienced a possible fatality from the irascible bumper erm... sir." Jamie succinctly explained to his Mom's astonished look. Wondering how he'd so easily attuned himself with his auntie Page's diction, and managed to lie through his teeth, as honestly as herself.

"Oh, I see. Thank you, that's very kind of you both. Please call me James. I did mean to give you a call yesterday... Eden, you know. To inform you...I... we, were on our way here to the project, but," he added. Still randomly making it up as he went along. "You know how it is. There's been so many other things going on, and we've been so busy with everything," he explained feeling a little more relieved he could see an end to the bare-faced skullduggery, that he was alighting to both their children. "We'll go and take a look outside in a minute. You have shopping, and I want to get some more of those German beers. Why don't we all head back into the aisles and get our things together. Then, we can load up and inspect the damage on the camper. Maybe I can do a temporary repair, then we can all be on our way."

"I'm glad we're going back to the aisles, Jamie, there's sweets called; 'Snakes Tails,' have you heard of them? I think that's a name derived from lies," Abby sarcastically sniffed as she turned the trolley around and beckoned Jamie on-board as they walked back into the shopping aisles ahead of their parents.

"We're you born crazy, Ustinov!" She bluntly asked turning to face him and almost clashing her nose with his, then leaning close to swap whispered words, as they followed the children.

"Not as crazy as you, Red."

"It's Buckley, Eden Buckley, and slow down, daddy long legs. Or you'll have us catching them up before we've even had chance to get our lying asses straight."

"Not as long as your legs, and not as pretty, either. And stay off the preaching horse and take it as the compliment it was meant to be," he replied. "Anyway, I like this whispering thing, don't you?"

"Lies? Don't you call me a liar, you cheeky, SOB?"

"Ok then, your distortion of the truth."

"Now you sound just like my damn sister. You lied through your teeth as well?"

"Hush about the lies and concentrate. We need to get our story straight quick."

"Ok, what's your thing?"

"Huh? My thing?" She replied, feeling herself going red and smiling at the same time. "You, sexist pig!"

"Sexist pig... me.... charming. That's not me, that's your mind in the gutter girl," he playfully linked her arm and almost danced her along the aisle. She didn't resist his touch one bit. Then, she looked at the kids and realised she was experiencing a long-forgotten thrill or a new family feeling. It seemed to her senses, that this was the first time in a long time that she'd felt at least a little happy. She bit her lip, and playfully yanked him backwards. Watching ahead in case any of the kids turned around to see their playfulness.

"Hey, the story. Come on now, please. Can you be serious for one minute, James?"

"I was. That's what I meant when I asked you about your *thing*," he explained. He softly released his playful grip until they were still linked together, but with no force or strength incurred from either party. To them both, it felt right, and she didn't want it to end. Just then, he released every tension in his arm, and allowed it to drop back by his side, naturally. As it did, his hand brushed across hers and he wrapped his little finger softly around hers and squeezed into it. Then, he let go and let his hand fall into its normal walking sway.

"Okay, you win. I'm guessing there'll probably be a lot of that," he inferred. "Right, the story, Eden. I'll tell you my *thing* and you can make up whatever you like. Look, they've just turned the corner. I'll just run with whatever falls out of your mouth. As I told you at Brannigans. I'm an ecologist, but things changed as I said in the text. I've had to stay on here to check out a swamp A.S.A.P. It's called Boyles. We are camping over there tonight. Tomorrow, I have to do some testing of water, plants and check on the wildlife. I need to verify all the animals in and around the vicinity and that's about it. Oh, and I have to set up a future development project house."

"OMG! You're working at Boyles swamp... how long for, James?"

"A while at Boyles, and eventually, six others. So, I might be around for quite some time, I'd guess. We're going to try to get some of the waters registered with ecology status."

"I said, how long?"

"Oh sorry. On and off, for about two years."

"Do you know Henry Creech?"

"I don't know him, but I know the name. He's one of my contacts here." Eden took a second or two, before she answered. "I know Henry and he knows me," she looked at the kid's progress, then looked up, at *him.* "You must be here for the new highway extension?"

"I'm here for verification and to register the swamp as an untouchable wildlife haven, as I just told you. My company has told me there's been some heightened concerns about these special places. I have to find out what those concerns are yet."

"One of those concerns is a big fat one."

"Excuse me?"

"Listen James. We aren't lying to the kids and listen when I tell you, that we really are working on the same thing. I'm trying to stop a highway link road being built through our houses and across Boyle's swamp.

"That's really weird."

"Yep, an amazing coincidence," she smiled, stubbornly kicking him. "And that's for your cheek. Right, if the kids mention anything else, I'll do all the talking. It's virtually the truth anyway," she beamed, knowing they we're destined to have their paths crossing so much more than she'd anticipated. "Everything Henry said at the meeting, makes complete sense, now."

"Eden, don't look ahead, but they've turned back around. They're on their way back to us."

"That's okay. You've just filled in most of the blanks, James. I'll tell you the rest of my side of the story later. They're almost here. Oh, and hey, mister camp-stove. I don't like the fact that you and Abby going squatting on someone's land at this time of night, without permission."

"Oh, it'll be fine."

"Hey kids, are you getting to know each other?"

SIXTEEN: *Decision*

"Well whatever you did, it seems to have done the trick. It does feel quite solid now," he said wiggling the bumper, then kicking it hard to be certain before he stood up. "Let's dump the shopping in the back and head to wherever we're going."

"So where are we going... Dad?" Abby pertinently asked grabbing another bag from Jamie who was stood inside the shopping trolley.

"Erm... to be honest. I thought we might just head to the swamp and set ourselves up somewhere, nearby. Wherever it is? We've got everything we need right here. I do have to meet Henry Creech at some point, tomorrow. But we can cross that bridge when we get to it," he replied taking the last bag of shopping from grunting Jamie's hands and then lifted him from the trolley.

"I think you've done enough work for one day, James. Do you even know where Boyles is?"

"No. I didn't run any of the surveys here last time. But I was close by."

"Welcome to my world, Eden," Abby interjected.

"But I can soon find it. Let me have a quick look on the map," he explained opening his ruck-sack. "I do have a map in here, somewhere. And a sat-nav."

"You're not organized at all," Eden stated.

"Not organized... nonsense! All I have to do is change the country settings, plug it in, and that'll do it."

"James, you're not going anywhere tonight and, that's final," Eden said sternly as the kids looked at each other and smiled.

"Abby, would you take the trolley back with Jamie, honey? You get to keep the dollar. Your first American money.

"That was my dollar, and I had to face Gloria to get it!"

"Oh, be quiet, James! Jamie, I know your hips sore, but go with her, and make sure she's okay," Eden asked in an attempt to speak to James on his own, realising he wasn't taking a blind bit of notice.

"Sure Mom. Hold on tight, Abby," Jamie announced pushing the trolley as the casters rattled over the speed bump and away. Eden waited until they were completely out of earshot, then turned to see James, randomly flicking through his rucksack papers. "JAMES! I said, I don't think it's such a good idea to be driving over to the swamp and camping out for the night. Anything could happen. You have no authority or permissions to do that?"

"Oh, where is it now? It was right here, on the plane? Well, you are right in a way. I was supposed to get in contact with Henry before I ventured up there. He did say he'd meet me to clarify everything and arrange things. But we never got the chance to meet because I've been travelling and sorting out the project house all day. My company changed everything around so fast, because of the possible threats to the swamps. Oh, here it is, hiding right at the bottom. It's always the last thing you find when you're looking for it," he smiled.

"Are you listening to a darn word I'm saying?" She asked tugging on his arm. "I don't think you should be rushing things. Especially seeing as you haven't a clue where you're going. In strange place and in a strange town, with even stranger folk," she explained feeling a little unsure of their predicament and not wanting anything bad to happen to anyone.

"What do you mean, strange folk?"

"Look, remember when you asked me to trust you in the Skoolhouse? When you got rid of my hippy-cups."

"Of course, I do."

"Good. Because now it's your turn to trust me. Until things are ironed out proper, you two are coming with me and Jamie."

"But, just hang on a minute. I think you need to fill in some more blanks for me about our story. While the kids are gone."

"I know I do, but all in good time. Now shush your button mouth. They're almost behind.... hey kids! Are you all done?" she shouted mid-sentence.

"We are."

"Great! Right, Abby. Your Dad's agreed that tonight is not a good night for swamp sleeps. Isn't that right mister, last-minute?" She announced looking steely-eyed and waiting for him to answer, as she hastily continued. "So, you and your Dad are coming with us to our house," she furrowed as he tersely looked at her, then down at the cheering kids, before he had chance to answer.

"Well, I suppose exploring to the swamp in daylight will be much better."

"Yep, that's right. So, the swamp will be the thing, tomorrow. And as long as I've got anything to do with it, that's settled," she said pointing in to his chest as he shrugged his shoulders. "Now granted, you won't be staying in the house. But you'll be outside on my driveway, but safe. Strange arrangement, I know. But you'll be sheltered and safe, and under my wing," she said in a motherly and caring manner as she glanced at Abby, then back at *him*. Still lightly tapping her finger into his chest. "And until things are sorted, your permissions and your meeting with Henry and whatever else it takes, that's just how it's gonna be mister, rush-a-lot. After that, you can go and camp and sleep at the swamp to your heart's content Ustinov. Now is everybody clear," Eden asked looking at him and the children. "Can I get a high five on that kids?" She asked opening her hands at her sides, as Jamie looked at Abby, then they slapped both her palms on either side of her at exactly the same time. "That'll do it for me, kids. I hope your Dad's a good driver, Abbey?" She questioned as if James wasn't even there.

"Yes Eden... he's a good. What do I... erm call you, anyway? I know he calls you... Eden, but? Auntie Eden?" She asked throwing another of her searching, but extremely valid questions into the mix.

"You can call me, Red, if you like."

"Oh wow, I like that."

"So, do I," James confirmed. "Very much," he whispered beside her ear as he looked at her smiling eyes.

"Right, it's getting dark. So, it's time to move. You make sure he follows me, Abby. No deviations. We don't want to have to come searching for you now, do we? Our house isn't that far. Twenty minutes from here, tops. Ok kids, jump right in, you're chariots await," she encouraged as the kids smacked each other's hands and separated.

"You have a wonderful way about you," he announced.

"Oh hush, mister, crazy-horse," she said blushing but feeling wanted. "We can have a talk about everything when we get home. I mean to my house," she corrected herself, realising the words had fallen from her tongue far too easily. She jumped in the Mustang with Jamie. Then showered patiently waiting Bailey with kisses, until James and Abby were right behind them in camper. "Are you with me?"

"Lead on Red. I'll be right with you, all the way!"

SEVENTEEN: *Home*

"It isn't much, but its home," Eden said slamming her door as James climbed out of off the camper, onto her driveway.

"It looks very homely. What the...! Where did this fellow spring from?" James asked looking at Abby's beaming face as she watched Bailey dart toward her from out of the Mustang.

"Oh, I forgot to tell you we had a dog," Jamie said.

"That isn't a dog. It's a dog and a half! I bet he can smell Archie, Dad," she said fervently watching his wagging body as he sniffed at them both. Bailey seemed to take an instant liking to James and jumped on his hind legs to get closer to his face. As he petted the somewhat, mad dog, something else grabbed Abbey's attention. "Dad... listen... can you hear that?" She said as Bailey ran toward the house and his mistress and savior.

"That's the crickets, lovely isn't it? You'll be hearing at lot of different things like that, sweetheart," he explained as Eden turned the key in the front door.

"Come right in. Are you two hungry? I'll rustle something up nice and quick. Hey, just you calm down. I've never seen you so crazy...? In your basket Bailey."

"We'll erm thank you, I'm absolutely starving. Dad thinks of his work rather than our stomachs."

"Bailey eh? I didn't even know he was in your car. I like him. I like this little place too," he retorted looking around the bungalow as the dog reluctantly spun around in his basket and obediently sat down.

"How about some salt beef, with a little lettuce, on rye? That'll fill you up good," Eden explained emptying her shopping out onto the kitchen top. "Are you cold? I can kick up the fire," she pointed at the lounge. "Oh, Dad look, a real fire... how cozy. I'm warm enough thanks. Salt beef? Mmm, that sounds good. Have we had that before, Dad? It's so much warmer here, than at home. Oh... but it'll be cold outside. We're sleeping in the swamp machine," Abby fretted. "I don't like the cold. I hope there's enough sheets dad?"

"I'll make sure you have plenty warm covers, honey. Jamie, your pills are on the way baby," Eden chirped, liking that fact that she had someone else to look after.

"Jamie where's your room? Oh, I love this place. So much nicer than home, Dad." After the barrage of positive comments, Abby followed limping Jamie into his bedroom.

"I'll holler when food's done. Please... erm take a seat, James. I want you to treat this place as your own," she requested, secretly wishing to herself. "Are you a coffee, or a tea man? You look like a stiff upper-lip tea man to me," she giggled faking an English accent. "Or maybe something stronger after your long haul? The strong stuff keeps the snakes away. Least, that's what we were told as kids."

"Don't dare say that to Abby. I'll have one of the beers. I'll just go and get one from the camper."

"Ah aah... no need. One ice cold beer, coming right up, mister Dumbo." she said as he promptly sat back down and silently watched her.

She stood on one leg, tucked the other under the worktop and leaned across to the fridge handle. Pulled two bottles from the top shelf and leaned back upright, without moving one step from her position. Then, she grabbed two orange drinks from the shopping, swiveled to face him, and sat the beers on the kitchen table. Returning to her lettuce cutting, without even flinching.

"And I suppose you can do swan lake in the bath?" He said secretly marveling at her supple moves.

"Only on a full moon," she joked. "Ok, the beef's cooking up good. So, our story. Best get this stuff straight while we're alone," she said adopting a firmer tone, but thinking of the other things she'd much rather do with him when they're alone. She continued to prepare the food, but intermittently turned to face him. Working on the kitchen top food, as they drank their beers.

"I think I got a good idea why you're here. I know Henry junior, quite well. He was at my school. Anyhow..." she said tailing off and turning the beef over on the grill. "He was at our community meeting, the other night. We're trying to stop the building of a link road. An intersection link, that if it happens, will run right through where you have your English butt sat, right now," She said as his enthused facial expression dropped. She sliced through a rye loaf, and ballet twisted herself to the fridge. "There's a fat, mean SOB called Langdon Dainty. He's about as dainty as a rhino in a tutu. So anyhow, he's going around to my neighbors, to try to get his hands on their homes and this land. He also wants Boyle's swamp and some other fields. I think he's building a bridge as well? Anyhow. Some of my neighbors have been here a lifetime. Most all of their days, in fact. When the coal was found in Harlan and around, they'd come to work the mines and the strip the fields to make a living. They've suffered every damn hardship you can imagine at the hands of the coal bosses. It's always been a land of struggle round these parts. But now, Langdon is making this fight, the biggest one of their lives. The folks are old and tired of fighting. But I, for one, will not go down without a fight."

She buttered the rye bread, then covered it with lettuce, and the cooked beef from the grill. Replacing more beef from the worktop, onto the grill as he intently listened and she turned back to face him.

"Could you put those two orange bottles in my pockets, James? But no tomfoolery now. I'm gonna have my hands busy right here." She smiled, picking up a food plate in each hand then turning to face him. "I'll take it on through for the kids, then we can have more time to talk."

He gulped a mouthful of his beer then stood up. Picked up the plastic bottles, silently in each hand. As he moved closet he looked at her defenseless face waiting for him to load each of her pockets with the bottles. He smiled a wicked grin as her heart began to race as her waiting seconds felt like minutes. He edged closer until, using the bottles as levers he opened her pockets and slid them inside, below her taut waist, as she waited and held her breath. He pushed them down until they wouldn't go in any further. "Golly!" She gasped, biting her lip then taking another deep breath as the chill of the bottles hit her skin through her slacks. She felt as if her own inner temperature had begun to react automatically. She secretly shuddered, and then breathed out deeply.

"Ooh! They're just a little cold. Come on quick... stop your fooling. You know my hands are full. You, big lummox," she said beginning to grin.

"That's you all loaded up. Mmm, food smells great... almost as good as you," he said looking at the kids prepared food with his head close to hers.

"I... I'll kick you where it hurts for that. You, big tease," she stuttered, trying to self-consciously blow a flock of hair from her eyes, then turning away and walking toward Jamie's room with a bigger than huge smile on her face.

"Hey you two, salt beef's up. Everything okay in here?" She asked putting the plates onto Jamie's chest of drawers. "Yes, Mom. Abby's teaching me about her phone. It does everything look... we're playing *'Perilous power'* he smiled.

"Uh-huh. Well get this down you, then you can take your pills and you can both play some more. James and I are going out front to get your camper sleeping arrangements ready real soon. I'm thinking he might just need a hand setting up, because he's a little new to it, and you haven't camped before."

"I'll take my pills when we've eaten, Mom." Jamie said as she walked out of the room to the kitchen, where James was brandishing a knife and attempting to cut the rye bread.

"Oh, sit yourself down, and drink your beer. I can do that," she said pulling him back with his belt.

"So, we're going out to get things ready in the camper after this? I heard you," he explained swallowing a small corner of the bread crust he'd attempted to cut.

"So, tell me more about your story?"

"Well, my work in Kentucky will eventually take me to every swamp mass in the state. There's really no set time limit. All ad-hoc, dependent on getting access to the places. That's dealt with back in London and passed to me over here. Wow, this beer's sure hitting the spot," he gulped. "What has come through the grapevine is; the parent body has secured the project house for all the ecologists on a global scale from every country involved in the project," he explained as she listened, and nodded every time she faced him. "It's equipped with living and sleeping quarters, and the necessary. In-situ tools for the job, along with the worldwide communication protocols needed to pass on the information to the relevant people. Word is, it's completed and truth be told, I'll be inspecting the place and giving it the final word. I'm a senior partner of the organization in England."

She licked at her fingers from the grill, then, sarcastically *whooped* at his comment. "Get you mister, big-gun, CEO."

"The green camper van is just a last-minute fallback measure because the new site vehicle isn't ready. Plus, Abby didn't like the idea of a hostel. She's not even supposed to be with me. The site vehicle... erm, thank you..." He stopped as she put a plate down at his nose. "...will be in much the same vein as the swamp machine. But that's maybe, a week away."

"Tuck in honey," she said biting into her sandwich, as he secretly thought of tucking into something else. "The text you sent today, said Evarts."

"That's right. My initial thought was somewhere within easy reach of all the swamp waters we have to evaluate. I've only been on the outskirts of Harlan until now and my original guess was a base near, Tennessee. The company make things so secretive for no reason at all. Eden, this is excellent. I was so hungry for something," he said, as she blushed.

"Glad you like it. I guess our stories truer to life than we realised. You want to save the world, and I want to save mine, and the other folk's houses," she joked. Washing her snack down with her beer, as his smile instantly faded.

"Hey come on now, James. I wasn't mocking you, I was telling the truth. We can help each other out here. Don't you agree?" She implied.

"I know, I'm sorry. I just get so wound up sometimes, with people's flippant nature. They have such a throwaway attitude to life. The world's a precious place, and it's the only one we have. I wish it was all treated with a little more respect, that's all. It honestly won't last forever, if we don't look after it," he explained, swigging at his bottle.

"Hey honey, I do understand what you mean when you say that." She quietened thinking of her loveless circumstance. "Some people have no regard for nothing but themselves. We're all casualties of something. I agree with you a thousand percent, mister, big ears," she said pulling on his earlobes. "Anyway, not so serious mister, sad-face. I liked you more when you were smiling. Now, I told the kids we'd get things ready. So, come on, mister, stuffy pants," she said playfully grabbing his hand. "We got bags to unpack and beds to make," she said grabbing her plate and walking to the sink and turning her back toward him, as she filled the bowl with hot water. He grabbed his plate and followed behind. He stood inches from her, and then put his left hand on the drainer and swung his plated arm closely around her body. Trapping her right in front. So close, that he could whisper in her ear. He slowly dropped the plate into the water and rested his chin on her shoulder. As she closed her eyes, he grabbed a handful of the soap-suds in his hand and pretended to rub it in her face.

"I like it when you are happy," he said tickling her hips. She smiled, screeched and dropped the plate she had in her hands in water, and in the sink. Still trapped, she turned around to face him, and he flicked the suds in her face, for real. She shrieked again, and then pushed him away. Then, she chased him with a handful of the suds toward the front door. Flicking them from her hands and across the room at his head. He impatiently grabbed at the door handle for escape. But she ran at him and pushed his muscular frame onto the front door as her body landed on his. She put both her arms either side of his head to trap him against the door, then moved slightly away.

"How do you like it, mister, now you're trapped?" He turned around to face her smiling eyes.

"I like being trapped by you. You got me."

"I wish I was locked up with you," she replied looking into his eyes. He wrapped his arms around her body. Tilted his head down and passionately kissed her neck.

She returned every motion and emotion, with the same vigor. As if it had been a lifetime since her last loving embrace. For them both, the moment felt as if it was in slow motion.

They separated millimeters, and her body sighed, as her eyes slowly opened. Now fully dilated with passion. She rested her hands on his shoulders to savor the moment. Then broke away, and joyously smiled. "Come on then, mister, freaky-deaky, let's get to the bed…! I…I… meant making the camper bed. Oh shoot…! You know what, I mean." They both smiled as she blushed and flushed with emotion as they turned the door handle together, with his hand on hers.

EIGHTEEN: *Camper*

"Oh, here, mister-slow. Let me help you… you see… it flips across like this," she said realising he was struggling as she pulled the camper bed down into place. "Now you put the sleeping bag, and covers on," she crowed standing up from her knees and closing a small, built-in, bedding box. "There's no pillows, though. I could go get you a couple of cushions from the house. Hey, would you look at that! It's as big as a double bed. Abby, has the bunk across the back window there," she pointed to the back of the camper. "And you have your butt right here, see? Cover on top... and that's you both sorted for sweet dreams. It's no wonder we stereotype all you men as dumb-asses. Abby's doing that about you, even at her age," she said laughing and touching his chest. Oh, I'm just foxing with you honey," she admitted. "You'll be cozy as two bugs in a rug. You might get word about your project house in the morning too. So, you might not have to do this camping again. What do you think, mister-confused?" She asked with her hands on her hips as he unraveled a sleeping bag onto the bed.

"I'm not sure," he said shaking his head, and deciding to goad her into some fun. "You're as tall as me. Just lie down on the bed, please," he asked feigning a quizzical look. "I just want to see if your feet hang over the edge."

"Oh Lord, there you go at that dumb-ass stuff, again. You ain't that big? There's plenty room, watch." She said innocently climbing onto the bed on her hands and knees as she moved herself into a full-length sleeping position, on one side of the camper bed, in an attempt to show *him* how much room he had. "See, tons of space. You could get three adults' side by side, quite comfortably on here. Four at a push," she explained looking up from the bed as he paused and smiled. He knelt on the bed and dropped his muscular frame down on his hands. Then, he turned himself onto his back so he was right by her side. "I don't want enough room for four. Room enough for two, will do," he joked, leaning on his arm to face her.

"Uh-huh. Well, I got a perfectly good bed indoors mister, sleepy-head. So, it's you here, and Abby over there in her little side-stack," she grinned regimentally sitting bolt upright and shimmying herself down the covers to escape his clutches before he decided to pounce despite secretly enjoying the physical attention in his eyes. She stood up at the edge of the bed and pulled on the light-switch cord hanging from the roof.

"Come on, go and get Abby. It's time for your beddy byes. We all got an early start tomorrow. What time are you out of the sack...?" She asked as he joined her on the driveway.

"Oh, I was thinking about seven."

"Okay then. When your ready tomorrow morning, get yourselves into the house and I'll make us all some breakfast. I'll be up. We leave for school about, 7-45. Ham, eggs and honey drizzled pancakes and coffee. How'd that be?"

"Brilliant. I don't normally bother with breakfast."

"Long as you're here with me, you'll be bothering," she replied walking through the front door to see Jamie and Abby, sitting at the kitchen table. Still talking but looking as if they were fading fast.

"Time to say goodnight, you two. You're all set for sleeps out there, Abby. Come on Jamie, let's get ready to hit the hay!" Eden waved them off as they headed through the front door and into the night air, toward the camper. As they slammed the door behind them, Eden locked her front door. Everyone was wrapped in their beds, minutes later. Eden lay silent and she replayed the wonderful evening's events through her mind. While outside, James and Abby had settled into their sleeping positions and were whispering, as they listened to the Cricket's and all the other strange noises, echoing through the dark, Kentucky night air.

Along with the noises of the night, soon came a quieter, but contented snore from Abby at the window of the camper. James smiled to himself and turned over on to his usual side. As he did, he smelt the slightest whiff of Eden's perfume on the pillow, where she'd been lying minutes earlier. He thought of her lying alone, in the house. Just as he was alone, right now.

In her room, she picked up her cell phone from the cabinet to look at the time. Although it was minutes, it seemed to be hours since she'd been lying by his side in the camper. She flicked through the cell phone and read his text again. Then, she ran her hand under and across the cold and empty side of her bed. She smiled, closed her eyes, and wished a wish.

NINETEEN: *He's gone?*

"Ooh, time to shake a leg, Eden," she said turning off her ringing mobile phone alarm as she jumped out of bed, quicker than ever before. She was so fast, she stood on sleeping Bailey's tail, which made him yelp into the bargain. "Oops, sorry boy... shush now.... they'll all still be sleeping out there," she whispered as if she might wake James up in the camper on the driveway. Bailey sat motionless, wondering what all this fuss was about. "Come on boy, we're going on silent manoeuvres," she grinned throwing on her nightgown. "Think you can manage that, boy," she asked stopping dead and deciding to slow down. "Ah aah, nice and calm girl... and not so keen," she encouraged. Pointing her finger at herself, for her own benefit.

She looked blankly at her bedroom window, quickly remembering that because her room was at the back of the house, she couldn't peep through the curtains, to look at the driveway. She walked toward the bedroom door, as Bailey stood up, wildly shook his body awake, and then followed her through the door. As she turned the handle and teased it open, a slow drawn-out squeak emitted from the mechanism, making her look down at Bailey. "Shush!" She frowned, putting her finger across her lips, as if it was him that had made the noise. She was feeling like some kind of morning intruder, or burglar as she tip-toed across the lounge and, Bailey obediently followed.

She listened hard to her miniscule footsteps that seemed so much louder against the creaking, wooden floor. Making her even more self-conscious as she glanced across at the wall clock's tick, deciding that seemed to be unbelievably loud as well. When she reached the front door, she pushed the quarter-light window curtain aside, and then wiped the condensation from the window. It was a misty morning outside, leading her to wipe over the window again for a better view as her heart sank.

There was no camper van. Nothing, only three black chirping cardinals picking at scraps of bread where the camper had stood. With no sign whatsoever, of what she wanted so much, to see. She quickly opened the front door to be sure.

She, angrily kicked the front door shut, and walked back into her bedroom in completely the opposite manner that she walked out of it. Leaving Bailey standing puzzled at the front door, waiting for any possible chance she'd come back and open it so he could disappear into the garden to alleviate himself. She grabbed at her phone and stared at its blank screen. Nothing was different. It showed the date, and the time, and nothing else. She walked back into the lounge, feeling saddened and downhearted, and looked back at Bailey who was still sat at over the door with a somewhat; let *me out... or I'm going to wee* look on his face. He stood up, looked at her and wagged his tail and she listlessly walked across, unlocked the door and watched him disappear out of sight.

'*Not a word... not a damn thing. Men! Humph...! Men, all the same,*' she cursed giving James a hard time in his absence. She walked back to the kitchen and put the kettle on with a vacant look, then sat down at the table and stared into space, twirling her red hair.

'*Maybe I scared him off? Or maybe something came up, and he just didn't want to wake me,*' she wondered as Bailey reappeared looking somewhat more refreshed as he sat close beside her chair. '*You wouldn't desert me without so much as a woof would you boy,*' she said stroking his coat then rubbing his ears. '*Mmm, not in a heartbeat. I wouldn't let you anyway. Oh, I guess he must have his reasons though. Who am I to ask why or stop him?*' She asked resigning herself to her plight and feeling a chill breeze through the room from the wide-open, front door. '*Brrgh, you could have shut it on your way back, beast."* The kettle clicked off, just as she closed the door. As pushed it, she noticed a slight bulge in the curtain at the bottom.

There was the usual, grated steel mail box bulge, but it seemed more pronounced than usual. She slid the curtain over to find a note pushed haphazardly into the metal box. Jammed through so much, it was sticking through the holes in the grate on her side, and into the curtain. '*Mmm?*' She looked around at Bailey, smiled then turned back to try to pull the scrunched paper cleanly from the grate. She got it half way out, and then it stuck tight.

She knelt down closer to the door, and fidgeted with the paper, between the steel. Then, pulled much harder in her anger and it released itself as the grate twanged back hard onto the door. Leaving half the note in her hand, and the other half sticking out of the box.

'*Shoot! You, impatient, brainless mare. Why didn't you just put your hand in from the top, like any other normal person,*' she conceded doing exactly that. She pulled the other half from the box, then replaced the door curtain before walking back into the kitchen. She put both pieces on the table and leaned herself on the sink and folded her arms across her chest, looking over at the rag-tag papers. She turned around to the wall, deciding to leave it, and make herself a coffee first, as her minds growing anticipation rose and she silently stirred her drink, and then sat down at the table.

She glimpsed at Bailey as he waited in silence for her next move. Hoping it was somewhere in-between breakfast scraps, or a full canine banquet. She placed her coffee on the table as her curiosity continued to grow. She unraveled the papers and fitted them together like a two-piece, jigsaw:

Hi Eden.
Very sorry we had to leave.
Work called about
The project house.
There's been some positive developments.
I'll call you later.
I'll text, if that's not possible.
Love and regards, James X

"See boy," she said ecstatically. "He wrote me a letter, see...? Well, a note. There it is boy, right there," she exclaimed pushing the torn papers into his cold nose and gladdening herself. "So, don't you be doubting him, again?" She smiled, apportioning all her earlier blame on Bailey, as he innocently wagged his tail.

"Do you think I should text him back? Tell him I got his note, and I miss him and want him to kiss me all over my body and have my babies?" She brightly asked, picking up her coffee and waiting for the dog to answer. "Mmm, maybe not, huh boy. Besides, he might be driving, so that'd be stupid. Especially on these roads. Mmm, I don't want him deader than road kill do I boy?" She decided as she thought for a minute. "Nope... that's just what you did when you woke up," she corrected herself. "You're far too keen, girl," she agreed to Bailey's wagging tail. "Nope. You're exactly right, Bailey. I am not going to appear as some kind of desperate woman, on a man-hungry mission."

TWENTY: *Phone calls*

"Morning to you, Miss Reid." She walked past the school administration secretary toward the staff room for her free period. Happily spinning Abraham's CD on her finger. As she reached the door, she felt her cell vibrate in her pocket. She elbowed the door whilst lifting out her mobile to see it flashing *his* name on the digital green. She glanced around the office to see it was empty. Apart from old history teacher, Bob Hensley who was sitting in the corner, with his headphones tightly clasped over his ears. He hadn't even noticed her come in and was happily listening to his music without a care in the world. She bent her head to hear him humming along to what obviously looked like a classical piece. Every so often, his hands would rise and fall, as if he was proudly conducting an invisible orchestra. "Oh, bless his heart," she said taking a seat near the window where she could see the kids outside, playing a particularly explosive game of soft ball. After her morning thoughts about not chasing *him*, she calmly clicked answer on her phone screen and put her feet up. Across the long seat:

"Hello mister, disappearing-act. Thanks for running out on me like that. How

are you, you, big-pig?" She teased waiting for a posh, or sexy, English reply.

"Hello, Red. So, sorry about that. Didn't you get the note?" He asked feeling happy to hear her voice.

"What note? Sorry, I was so busy this morning, I plum forgot about you camping outside."

"Oh, I'm sorry about that too, but I can explain. How are you?"

"James, I'm just fooling. Of course, I got your note, Bailey helped me find it. Thank you for leaving a note. It was very considerate of you. Most men wouldn't bother their hide. Not that there's been a procession of men," she said smacking her head with her palm for her stupid mouth.

"I can be thoughtful, sometimes," he replied. *"Anyway, because of the time difference, Claire from work called as soon as we got in the camper last night. So, I had to be at the project house this morning, to give access for the internet provider. That's where we are, right now,"* he said sounding as the phone crackled. *"I think there's been some kind of mix up, though. They've apparently arrived with the wrong equipment, or so the man tells me."*

"Uh, huh," she replied enjoying the sound of his voice so much.

"Eden, are you there?"

"Yes sorry, I was just trying to hear what you said. You sound pretty distant. I missed half of that. Could you say it again," she asked wanting to hear his silky-smooth voice once more?

"Oh, everything's okay here. But I really wanted to get up to the swamp today to do some initial setting out. But it looks as though I'm going to be stuck here until these engineers from Sentinel get this thing sorted out. It's not a big problem, but I might not be able to get over to see you later, though."

"Oh, I see," she replied. *"Sentinel, huh?"*

"That's right. They should be back shortly."

"Is the project house okay then?"

"It's fine. A bit desolate and off the beaten track. The road is very winding and littered with carcasses of dead animals. But it's great inside and has everything we need. I've started some work without an internet connection just to keep me occupied. But I don't want to leave until the internet is

connected. Then, I know it's working for certain."

"*Leave?*" She replied sitting up straight.

"*Yes, for the swamp.*"

"*Oh, I see. I know that company quite well. They're actually the main web provider in, Kentucky,*" she mused, almost skipping a heartbeat. "*I know some of their workers. Did they give you any idea of how long the screw up might take to put right?*"

"*You know them?*" He pondered.

"*Yep. Good folk.*"

"*Oh, they erm, said a couple of days.*"

"*Couple of days, huh? Listen, leave this with me mister, web-page. Let me see if I can ruffle a few feathers. How's Abby.... is she enjoying herself?*"

James shouted across the project house office to see Abby, playing with her mobile phone. "It's, Eden sweetheart, she wants to say hi," he elucidated.

"*Oh, hi Eden, glad someone's phone's working. This thing's had it!*"

"*What did she say there?*"

"*Oh, she's ok,*" he lowered his voice. "*To be honest, I think she was really excited to be seeing the swamp until this internet problem came up. She'll see it soon enough though. Oh, and her phone's given up the ghost, too. It'll be like she's lost an arm, until I get her another one,*" he added. "*That'll be like me losing an arm, and a wallet full of money.*"

"*You can tell her from me, she'll be seeing that swamp, today. I'll get the Sentinel things fixed up. Will you be able to come over tonight? I could cook us all a big family... I mean a nice meal,*" she asked omitting family from her question.

"*We'd love that. But we'll have to play things by ear until we hear something.*"

"*Oh, you'll hearing things alright, mister-mobile. Anyway, I have to get off the phone and make another call. I'm picking Jamie up from school later, so text me if you need me. Anytime, at all. Oh, and by the way, where is the house and what's the name of those people you're working for, again?*"

"*It's on the main Evarts road, about twenty minutes from you. I'm working for the World Wildlife Federation.*"

"Okay, got it. And, I know exactly where you are. Right, speak soon... you take care now." She said blowing him a kiss.

"No problem. Oh, here's one of the internet men now, I'll have to go to speak to him," he explained to the disconnected tone.

#

"Hello, this is Eden Buckley, put me through to Joe Buckley, right away." She said standing up and looking out the staff room window again:

"Oh, hello miss Buckley. This is Lynne, could you give me a minute, please. I'll just check and see if he's available."

"Hi Lynne. I hope you and your kin's well," she said with an air of familiarity. *"Now I don't want to be sounding harsh, but you're only getting a minute, because I need to speak to my Dad, and this is very important. So, while you're speaking to him on the extension to find out if he's going to tell you whether he's in or not, you can just tell him from me, that if he doesn't come to the phone, I'm personally, going to come over there and kick his butt if he doesn't. I hope you got all that?"* She bemoaned, without breaking breath. *"You can also tell him, I'm sick of ringing here, and being put on hold by you, and everybody else. He seems to forget that I'm his God damn daughter,"* she said to the silent receiver. *"Lynne, Lynne are you still there?"*

"I know well enough that you're my little girl honey, and you're always darn quick to remind me of it. How are you, honey?"

"Oops, sorry Dad," she stated wondering how much of the dressing down he'd heard. *"I'm good, thanks."*

"How's the little fellow? I bet he's getting as tall as you, by now?"

"Oh, he's doing okay, Daddy. He's still waiting on the operation, though," she said realising she should've kept her mouth shut, knowing what he was going to say next.

"You've been told about that, so I'm not going through another crazy shouting match," he said remembering the unholy spat they had last time he'd tried to convince her he'd pay for Jamie's operation, and how she blown her stack at him. *"So anyway, Lynne said this was important. Why don't you*

tell me what's on your mind, sweetheart," he asked in father-daughter fashion?

"You just might be able to help a friend of mine out, big time, Pops."

"Go ahead Spark... I'm listening," he said realising how long it'd been since he'd seen his Grandson and his little girl.

"Don't call me that, Pops! I told you already to stop that when I was ten years old, and you're still doing it."

"Sorry, honey. You remind me so much of my own stubborn, and pig-headed nature, when I was your age. That's why I called you Spark in the first place. So, don't call me Pops, and I won't call you, Spark," he joked.

"You're just pig-headed, cantankerous, and as stubborn as a mule about wearing a tie," she laughed.

"Exactly... now tell me your woes."

"This friend of mine is waiting for your engineers to install some internet stuff, over at Evarts."

"Oh yes, that Evarts job," Joe replied, pretending he was fully aware, despite not having the slightest inclination as to what she was talking about.

"Uh-huh. So, you know the contract, do you?" She asked waiting for him to answer, as she waved at mister Hensley, who was quietly leaving the staff room.

"Well as a matter-of-fact, honey...."

"You don't," she interrupted finishing his words for him. "And you tell me you crack a mean whip? Poppycock. You, big soap," she taunted.

"I can't keep my eye on everything that goes on in this place," he offered trying to pacify her.

"That's BS Pop, and you know it," she snapped. "I'll tell you who the messed-up contracts are for then, shall I," she offered.

"Go on," he replied being extra careful not to trip himself up again.

"The W.W.F," she answered trying to intimidate him even more.

"A bunch of wrestlers?" He muttered trying to make light of the situation and his employees' goof.

"No Pop, the other WWF," she paused. "The World Wildlife Federation."

"What!"

"Yes, that one. My friend is working for them. Now, from what I've been told, they'll be working in Kentucky for quite a long while," she said smiling to herself and plucking a ball park figure out of thin air. "Three years' worth of work. So, I reckon they might just be able to throw a whole lot of dollars your way, or maybe not, after this sorry-assed performance. What you think Dad? She replied knowing she was going to get her own way.

"Thank you for the information, honey. Now, you can tell your friend, that the CEO of Sentinel has informed you this situation will be alleviated forthwith, and by him, personally. Tell then they'll also get an extra six months internet usage, absolutely free."

"Well I would, Dad. But I've been trying to contact him again, and I've just found out his mobile phone is shot," she white-lied. "I don't suppose you could do something about that as well, could you? She crossed her fingers and waited for his reply, then pushed on the exit call button.

"Yes, you can tell your friend I'll have the newest, top model phone sent out with the correct internet parts for the job, post-haste. Along with all the missing kit. I'm going downstairs now to kick someone's ass. So, you can be sure everything will be there this time, cos I'm gonna be loadin' it all up myself.

Hello...? Eden... are you there?"

TWENTY-ONE: *Project house*

"Hello sweetie pie, nice place you got here," she said throwing a kiss and a big hug on Abby.

"You like our new, American house, then?"

"Oh, it's neat. Bit dark in there, though? How are you both getting on with things? Is the internet sorted?" She whispered.

"Ask him. He's in the back room with the engineer. He was unpacking delivery boxes and trying to get it up and running, the last time I looked. I'm still trying to fix this rubbish," she said lifting up her defunct mobile phone.

"There's tons of boxed stuff been brought over. Shame the engineer couldn't fix my phone at the same time. I'm bored, Eden. Hey, I could make you a coffee. We have cups now," she said throwing her mobile to one side.

"Load of stuff, you say. That's good, and yes, a coffee would be lovely, honey." Eden sat down on a cardboard box and lowered her voice. "How would you like to get out of here? Go exploring at the swamp? It's a lovely day outside," she enthused, as Abby's face lit up.

"I wish we could. But Dad said he needs to get his work done, before we go anywhere."

"Listen, you just sit right here, and leave him to me. We'll be out of her in no time at all. I have a little surprise for you as well," she said winking as Abby smiled back, wondering what she was talking about.

"Great. I'll go and put the kettle on."

"Okay! Back room, you say...? I'm on my way," she shouted. Amplifying her voice so *he* would hear.

"I'm through here," he shouted, instantly recognising her voice.

As she walked toward his voice, she looked around the room, smelling at the damp and leering at the cobwebbed and dowdy, living-room decor. Realising the place had been empty for quite a while.

"Oh, there you are," she said lighting up inside.

"Hi Red, come in. Lovely to see you," he said loving the fact that she'd turned up unexpectedly.

"Thanks mister, pc. Kind of easy to get around when you're a local girl. Abby's making coffee, want one?" She asked brushing a cobweb from her hair.

"I thought you said this place was all finished, mister, bad-decor. It needs more than a good lick of paint, that's for sure. I know it's been empty a while, because it was boarded up, last time I was in Evarts. That was... well, over a year ago."

"You're right. The rooms upstairs aren't bad, though. But the downstairs is dirty and damp. But I'll get around to that secondary stuff, in time," he said pointing toward the back door, where one of Eden's Dad's installation team was busying himself in a cupboard surrounded with wires, plugs and pliers.

"Dad, we need water for the kettle, and I can't pick that big drum, thing up," Abbey said appearing at the door.

"Okay, leave it. I'll come sort it out."

"Right, I'll be outside, Dad," she said walking away.

"You sure could do with some light bulbs around here. I hope they get the internet things sorted out for you today," Eden said following James into the kitchen.

"Hello Eden. I thought I heard your voice. Has Joe got you checking up on me?" The smiling, and spectacled man with a veritable comb-over hairstyle said as he looked up from his electrical haberdashery of wires. She narrowed her eyes to look closely at his face, through the dark of the room.

"Oh, hello Devon. How are you, honey? Dad, I mean... I thought you'd left *Sentinel* and branched out on your own?" She asked pulling an invisible zip across her mouth behind James back and using her best sign language moves to ask Devon to put a sock in it.

"Oh, I'm much better now I'm out the mire. My *Teletech* business went to the wall. I had no option but to come crawling back to... here, with my begging bowl."

"Oh, I'm sorry to hear that," she replied frowning and watching James wrestle with a full, five-gallon container of water, and spilling a lion's share on the floor, as he tried vainly, to fill the kettle.

"You're sorry," he frowned. "I ain't. Damn good thing it happened, as far as I'm concerned. Nearly lost my house with that crazy venture. I got a lot to thank... Sentinel for."

"Sorry about this Eden. I'm waiting for the mains water to be turned on today," James clarified finally clicking on the kettle switch as he tore bubble wrap off some new *Sentinel* branded cups. "At least the electric's on. I don't know who your company contact is," he motioned spitting out a mouthful of plastic wrapping. "But all the missing parts appeared soon after we spoke on the phone. There's all sorts of freebies," he said lifting more cups out of the cardboard box.

"Company contact?" Devon chiseled in finally deciding to open his mouth.

"She is the damn company. At least her Dad is." Eden sharply turned her head and looked enmity at him, like there was about to be a human sacrifice making him bend his head urgently back down to his screwdriver and wires as James looked at them both, totally confused.

"Oh sorry, I should have kept my mouth shut before I opened it. I really must get on with this," he apologetically explained.

"It's ok Devon, no harm done," she smiled. "Just tell me which box the new cell is in, and we'll say no more about your wrecking-ball mouth. And as for you, I'll explain everything to you, later," she said to head scratching, James.

"Oh, the cell phone. It's in the dash box in the van outside. Joe put it there himself. I'll go, get it," he explained scurrying out of the room as she turned her attention to James, who was still struggling with making the coffee.

"How do you take your coffee? I got milk and sugar this morning in town."

"Milk, no sugar, I'm sweet enough, honey," she smiled as James shouted for Abby who was still in the other room.

"What is it, Dad?"

"Do you want coffee, or are you sticking with juice!"

"I'll have one later," she replied appearing at the door. "Are we going to be here all day? You said we could go into Tennessee, to get this mobile looked at?" She asked pulling her somewhat deceased mobile from her pocket.

"No need, Abby. We can stay right here until your Dad has finished what he needs to do. You mustn't be long from finishing now?" She asked standing beside him helping make the drinks.

"But my phone?"

"Well, I've got to stay here, until things are up and running," he said as Devon reappeared.

"Devon, are all the parts here to complete the internet fix?" Eden sternly asked.

"It's in the schedule for a two-day fix and test. But I, erm was delayed starting so…. I can keep working and get it all finished. You'd normally need about 24 hours for the tests and completion certificate, mister Ustinov. But that's only for the red tape signatures. I'll make sure it will be ready to go by end of the day."

"My phone?" Abby reminded them as Eden winked at Abby and then at James.

"If we leave you the keys to lock up Devon, can we meet you back here at, erm…"

"Whatever time you like. It's a priority one job, so I'm on call to attend this anytime, day or night."

"Great. What a dedicated service. That'll give us time enough to check everything," James said as Devon handed him the boxed, brand new mobile phone.

"Yes sir, and that's your new mobile phone to replace the broken one."

"It isn't for him, it's for you my girl," Eden cut-in.

"OMG, omg, OMG!" She screamed, stamping her feet with excitement.

"A Lexicon tip-tap," James said looking closely at the red box. "This is the one you kept telling me all about, wasn't it? Here!"

"OMG! A Lexicon, wow, oh wow, oh wow!" Abby said stunned into silence.

"Right then, I think that's us, isn't it?" Eden announced.

"Just the house keys."

"Oh yes. Here you are, Devon," she said passing them over.

"Have a good day, then."

"Wow, you're some woman," James muttered running his hands through Eden's hair admiring her beauty, her wily nature and verve.

"You like it, Abby?" Eden asked as she walked out of the room. "Back in two seconds, I just want to catch Devon before he leaves and ask him about his wife."

"Thank you so much, Eden. You said surprise, but I never expected anything like this. A Lexicon…brilliant! I'm in with the in-crowd now," Abby shouted toward the front door, clasping tight onto the box and walking into the lounge. "Oh, it'll need charging though?"

"Oh, here we go again," James sighed.

"Hey…! Devon, listen. I need some paint."

"What!"

"Bring some paint back," she whispered outside the front door. "Just tell my

Dad the client requires it. Very important Devon," she explained tapping on her nose with her finger. "I'll speak to him all about it on the phone. White and Magnolia and plenty of it. If he asks you anything, just tell him it's just some more extra's, courtesy of *Sentinel*, get my drift?"

"Ok Eden, no problem."

"Thanks, Devon," she winked. He was gone before she'd returned to the living room. "James, you can go take Abby a look at the swamp now. I could come along, but I have to be back in town to get Jamie from school, at five so it's a little late for me now," she said looking around the dreary living room. "I'll come up there another day. Are you planning on working the whole weekend?" She asked hoping for a big fat, no.

"I haven't given it a thought. I had some diametric testing planned for tomorrow. But thanks to you, I can get away from this place now. So, the diametric's can be done later today," he said realising she'd already got him way ahead of his schedule. "It would be nice to spend some quality time with you. We haven't stopped since we arrived, Eden. So, I'm going to write the weekend off from any work at all. I don't suppose you'd be free to show us some of the sights and... Erm, be our personal tour guide?"

"I'd love too," she radiated. "But on one condition."

"Which is?"

"Wherever you want to go, I can bring Jamie, and Bailey."

"Eden, we wouldn't have it any other way."

"Great. Listen, Boyles is a bit of a distance from here, so, you be careful on the road's, mister-collision," she encouraged straightening his T-shirt. "If you don't make it to my house tonight, don't worry. Just keep yourselves safe in here and get back over to my place, whenever you can. Will you promise to text or phone me later, so I know you're both okay?" She asked looking at him caringly, but cautiously.

"Yes, I will. I promise," he replied grabbing her hand.

"Won't forget?"

"No."

"Double promise?"

"Yes!"

"Great, thanks. I know we aren't together today. But whatever happens, I promise we'll get to be doing something lovely, real soon," she affirmed openly wrapping her arms around his neck and pecking at his cheek, as she stooped to do the same to Abby, who was almost in another world with playing with her new phone and being silently in tune with every word and emotion being shown close by.

TWENTY-TWO: *Argument*

The next day, James pulled up on her driveway as Abby jumped out and darted toward the house.

"Good morning, Red. I feel funny calling you that, Eden. Is Jamie inside?"

"Yes honey! He's out back with, Bailey," she shouted as she killed the loud whirring of the lawnmower in front of her. "Just go on through and make yourself at home," she explained as Abby smiled, and walked toward the house.

"Thanks."

"What happened, mister, late-again?" She asked standing on the trimmed lawn, in an arm-crossed manner.

"We got caught up there with the diametrics and the ubillations testing. They needed carrying out on the same day, and then they have to be logged and sent over by email to them, all within 48 hours. I forgot about that stipulation. It's a timescale thing, you see. With the residual air flow current and the different conditions that vary so much over a day. Just boring stuff really."

"Oh," she replied unsympathetically. "Who's, *them*?" She asked purposely turning on the mower to drown out his answer.

"Head office! Erm, back home, in England! London Endangered Animals and Plants Society! We make giant leaps forward in ecology and science!" He shouted over the noise to her untalkative, and unmoved expression. Realising his joke had fallen on deaf ears.

"Uh-huh," she said switching off the mower again. "We... I... kind of expected a phone call or a text if you couldn't make a giant LEAP back here. Or even something on a Lexicon mobile or your own mobile or the landline which Devon made work at your project house," she sarcastically over hinted, picking up the grass rake and secretly wanting to hit him over the head with it.

"We had a problem with the charging the phones. Plus, it's erm, a micro-sim. We didn't know that and we, I almost lost all of Abby's numbers. Anyway, you said it wouldn't be a problem if we couldn't make it back to your place," he replied, as if he didn't like his actions being questioned, and realising he'd been single and on his own so long, he'd stupidly forgotten that there were now someone else's feelings to consider, instead of his all-encompassing work.

"Uh-huh. Well, I don't have much of a clue about that kind of technical stuff mister me, myself, and I. Just a quick thirty second call would have been more than enough. You did promise not to forget to text. Maybe you conveniently forgot on purpose. I was... we... were worried. There's been a lot of road traffic accidents in Kentucky recently. It's not the getting back here I'm talking about. It's the missing phone call," she sneered pursing her lips and thinking that he hadn't listened to her reasoning. "I just needed to know you were both safe," she echoed, angry at his thoughtlessness and selfishness, as she tried to guilt-trip him. "I did cook us up something nice," she added wondering if there where such a thing as *us* as she picked up the brush to clean the underside of mower with her bad mood.

"Accidents, you say," he said crossing his own arms.

"You heard me." She said giving him another apathetic look, yet fighting her feelings to be angry with him, and then pointed toward the house. "I'll be inside shortly. There's the door, the kettle is in the kitchen and the cups are where they should be," she implied being purely indolent and obvious. He hesitantly smiled and started to walk away. Still thinking he'd done nothing wrong and how he didn't like being made to feel that he'd crossed any line.

"I'm a confident driver, Eden," he answered stopping in his tracks but continuing to hold his nerve and his point of view. "I'm sure we'd have been okay, if we hit a snag?"

"You didn't listen... I said a lot of RTA's... drunk drivers, head-on collisions. Even off-road accidents because of the damn varmints. The roads around these parts are not your usual thing. Especially out by swamps!" She knelt back down brushing harder at the mower.

"I did listen. I'm aware of the driving conditions. I hold an advanced driving license in England."

"You just don't get it do you? That don't mean squat around here. You can get your ass advance licensed right into a tree easy enough anywhere here, and killing yourself in an automobile here, is as easy as blinking!" She cursed raising her tone and upsetting herself.

"I've driven all over the world, and in much worse places than this," he retorted, raising his voice to match hers.

"Please don't shout at me."

"I'm not!"

"Yes, you are. Welcome to my world. Where being me, is never good enough. And don't you tell me everything's gonna be alright. It never works that way for me. I know... I lived through crap like that, before."

"Hey now, where did all that come from, Eden?"

"Oh, just you never mind."

A raised voice frightened Eden. She was full of hurt and hate, and sadness and scars from Kyle. Shouting made her feel negative, and frightened. No competency to trust another, for fear of rejection and humiliation. The worry and fear of being hit, punched or any other kind of physical violence, like she had, many times before. As well as having her heart burned. She quietened and looked away from him. Scared to make eye contact with someone who might be capable of the same things that Kyle had made her feel. She'd questioned her own incapacity to feel, or commit after that abusive, and loveless marriage. Almost believing it was her fault and it had also tainted her in a way that would never allow her to feel some kind of wholeness in love and in and life.

"Look, I'm sorry. I'm sure you are a fine driver, James. But you can't blame a girl for worrying or caring," she explained, dropping her head to the floor and bursting into tears on the spot.

James ran straight to her side, suddenly feeling a heartless fool

"You certainly can't. Eden, I'm so very sorry," he said realising she wasn't in the argument just for a fight. The genuine tone and teary look on her face, truthfully conveyed everything she'd meant.

"I was worried. I'm sorry, I was just worried, James."

He knelt on the grass beside her and grabbed both her hands tightly in his. "I'm sorry for being so utterly thoughtless. I'm sorry, for not knowing you cared this much. Oh, I'm so rubbish with all the hearts and flowers stuff. I wasn't brought up that way. My parents were both war-babies and made of that English, stiff-upper-lip stuff. They didn't convey any emotion at all. Not even behind closed doors. All my life, all that not showing your feelings rubbish was in abundance from every corner. I can't blame them though. I'm still stuck in the past with so many other things," he said thinking about Jane, and the invisible wall of bricks that he'd built up around himself for her memory. "There's something else about me you should know, that I never told you," he said taking a deep pause. "My wife Jane, she died. She died of cancer. I've been locked away, deep inside myself ever since. And since then, I've never allowed anyone as close to me, as you are now."

"Oh God, I'm so sorry. Come here honey," she said wrapping her arms around his shoulders. "Why didn't you say something? Why didn't, Abby say something?" Eden asked in shock, as she looked deep into his sad eyes.

"It's not the type of thing you speak out about. Especially, to someone as special and wonderful as you are. I didn't know things between us were going to end up being like this. I was going to say something. But I think after a while, I felt afraid you might walk away just as fast as you'd appeared." He sat down on the grass and pulled her body to the side of his. "I've made a big mess of this, haven't I?"

"Oh, rubbish, James. After what you've been through. Of course, you haven't. I'd never run away from you. But when you raised your voice, you reminded me of him. Kyle. No one's ever been in my heart since him, either.

Not until now anyhow. I've probably been as scared as you. Maybe I even scared you senseless as well?" She faintly smiled. "I was resigned to never letting anyone into my heart again after all of his violence. He beat me black and blue. Then you came, mister, ecology. You've succeeded to change every thought and feeling I was resigned to believe." James crossed his arms over hers and they rested their heads together. Staying silent with their revelations and in the moment.

"Do you think you're too far gone to try to change," she whispered. "Maybe I can pull down those bricks a little?"

"I'm trying," he smiled. "I'm really, trying."

"Then, let's both try, honey. I for one, reckon some things are worth fighting for," she explained.

"I agree one hundred percent. I'll try to get out of this stupid mind-set, even harder now. Because I do believe you're pretty great."

"Only great... huh?" she teased, despite still doubting herself.

"Hey!" He said rubbing her knee. "You're amazing, just the way you are and don't ever let anybody tell you any different. I'm the one who has a whole world of changing to do."

"James... I was fooling."

"There's so many other things that haven't been said as well," he said zoning into her lips and kissing her cheek.

"What things?"

"Just things that I have to go through. Acceptance and fear and forgiveness. Abby's grieved for Jane. But, I don't think I have."

"We can work through anything, as long as we're together. Because I've got tight hold of you now, and I am not letting go."

"Are you sure?" He asked.

"I swear. Now come on honey, we need to get inside to the kids." With their agreement, they both looked away from each other and turned to face the house, to see both Abby and Jamie, sitting silently on the porch steps. Playing, but watching and listening to there every word, as Bailey dozed just beside them. They looked back to each other, then walked across to the kids.

"Dad, I didn't want to interrupt but, Claire's been on the phone. She gave me a message for you. The project house internet is ready. Eden, my phone's working great now it's fully charged. Are you both coming in the back garden now? We were playing swing-ball until the phone rang. She asked me to get you immediately. Sorry for interrupting. Are you both, okay?"

"Of course, we are. Let's get that mower away, Eden. If it rings again, tell her I'm unavailable, Abby. There's other things more important," he explained walking away, arm in arm with Eden, as they grabbed the mower.

"I'll put this other stuff away. Then get some drinks for the back garden.

After five or so minutes, they we're all sitting in the back garden:

"Shall we all do something together, tomorrow?"

"Eden, I screwed up big time yesterday, so we can do anything you want."

"We could visit the Moonbow. Heard of it?"

"Moonbow. Mmm? I know of it. Have you seen it, Eden?"

"Never! My aunt believes it can't be seen by mortal unless they're blessed with love," she added. "Jamie is kayaking the Cumberland river tomorrow. Would you like to go watch him and see it after that?" She said as she sat the juice on the garden bench and they sat opposite each other.

"I would," Abby chimed in as her and Jamie got up to go play swing-ball again.

"It's lovely. It's the only bow in the western hemisphere. It's on the Cumberland River waterfalls and a once in a lifetime chance, if you get to see it."

"When does it appear?"

"After midnight. The reports said it started to be seen, yesterday. It rarely comes along, but when it does, you must try your hardest to see it because you might never see it again, in your whole life." She looked across at him in earnest, making obvious reference to what they'd been talking about and what she was feeling about him deep inside. He secretly wrapped his leg around hers, under the table. They sat for a minute as he ran her words though his head, again and again. Comprehending their total affinity to the situation. She poured the lemonade into four plastic cups, as he tucked her hair over her ears. Making her red earrings come into view. He drank his drink and looked at his watch.

"I erm, think we'd better go and see it then."

"What! Right now?"

"Yes, miss, bossy-boots, right now," he smiled. "How far away is the Cumberland?"

"OMG, the Moonbow... today...? You're certainly making up for things." She said kicking at his leg. "Did you hear that kids?" She asked as they stopped playing swing-ball.

"Honest dad?" Abby exclaimed.

"Yep, Eden said after midnight, so we've plenty of time. Be a shame to waste the rest of the day, don't you think?"

"He'd better not be fooling, Abby," Eden wondered.

"We'll go in the camper. Extra room for Bailey. One day, I'd like to take you, Jamie and Bailey to England with me," he said as her eyes and mouth opened wide.

"Now that would be a triple-fun adventure!" she replied, instantly musing at his statement as she jumped up from the bench to get ready.

TWENTY-THREE: *Drive!*

"Can you slow down a little mister, hi-ho silver? It's only a little after eight and there's plenty of time," she asked cautiously tapping his leg.

"Certainly, I'm not going too fast for you, am I?"

"Not at all, it's the car in front that's bothering me. I just want you to ease off a little, and don't get too close. They're weaving about. Some folk take their life into their own hands on these back roads. They aren't taking lives into their hands, as well. I just don't like the way he's driving, let alone the colour of the thing," she pondered to his frown.

"The colour. Are you ok?"

"Sorry, it just looks familiar," she said scanning her memory. "Yellow pick-up... yellow... oh, my God. I think I know where I've seen it before. Remember the fenced compound near my house that I pointed out when you first arrived...? Where Sheridan and I went? Come on, the state department guy. We snuck in the place and heard some bad whispers. Anyhow, I'm sure that was the truck I saw there. Whoever it is, I swear they'll be up to no good. Abby, the sun's awful bright in the front. Could you throw me your hat? I get sun stroke really easy. Oh, and your shades, too," Eden asked tapping James's leg then pointing at the truck and watching every move it made.

"Yes, she does," he agreed, seeing the look of fear in her eyes. "She's going a bit red in the face with it. Oh, and fasten yourselves in, at the back," he asked totally on her side. Abby, popped through the camper's middle window from the back and passed through her hat and sunglasses. Then disappeared to do as James asked as he watched through the interior mirror. "You all strapped in?" He asked to the kids raised thumbs.

"So, you think they're up to something, Eden?"

"By the looks of things, they're either drinking or getting high." She quickly donned the hat and shades. "Can you get up a little closer, so I can see the passenger, James? Not too close, though. I don't want them to see me and start anything stupid. The children are with us."

"I'll try. I don't want to sound like a coward. But if their drink driving, it's not really our fight," he said speeding up.

"Maybe, but...." she slid down in her seat and pulled down on the hat to hide herself. "Langdon Dainty had them meet him in his cabin. He was asking them to do something for him. We recorded the conversation but couldn't make out what it was. Did you go to the swamp this way yesterday, mister, sat-nav?"

"Not sure, nothing looks familiar."

"I know this leads in the swamps direction, but I don't recall for certain. There're some cut-offs on the way. Not even proper roads, but you can definitely get to it this way."

"And your theory is...?"

"Oh, I have no idea. He said something about worthless. Make it less than worthless."

"Look! He's turning off," James announced as a small farm track came into view and the yellow truck slowed, skidded, and took a sharp right, onto the tiny, dust road. As he did, the back end of the yellow truck slid across to the edge of the dirt track. Making the driver over-compensate, skid and create a plume of ash, stone and dirt behind it. As it billowed up into the air, the trucks horn sounded as it disappeared. Leaving the dusty cloud of smoke in its wake. James wound his window up to save them from choking on the dust coming through. James reached across the camper to hold her hand and instill some kind of safety and care to her fears. She grabbed his hand so tightly; his fingers began to hurt.

"What do you think that meant?" He asked watching her lift herself up from her hidden position as she slowly released her grip on his hand.

"I don't know, maybe it was a sign. A sign to let us know they're on to us," she replied, looking through the back of the camper to check on the kids. "I'm sorry James. That was stupid and reckless of me," she admitted putting her hand across her forehead. "What the hell was I thinking? I know it was the same pick-up. I'd wager it's the same men. Thank you for being here."

"Hey, I like being at your side," he replied feeling his role was to protect her in a way he couldn't protect Jane, from dying. "Promise me you won't do anything stupid if you see that truck again. Especially, if I'm not around. I don't want anything bad to happen to you, Eden. I need you to promise me."

"Oh, like you promised, me?"

"This is more serious. We need to stick together. We're stronger together than apart. You taught me that much woman," he said squeezing her hand then letting go to hold onto the steering wheel.

"I know we are. Okay, I promise. Is everything okay in the back, kids?" She asked.

"Yeah Mom. Except she just beat me at blocks on the mobile, again. I need a wee though. Can we stop please," he shouted?

"Sure thing, Jamie," James replied.

"This road widens out soon. Take the signs to Corbin and the Cumberland River."

TWENTY-FOUR: *Kyle & Josh*

"So, this is the so-called, money maker," he said slamming his rusty pick-up door, causing a colony of nesting birds to flee from the surrounding bushes and trees from the green, and pleasant place.

"Uh huh. Don't seem like much does it, Kyle? The swamps at the back of the trees over by. I think he's going to be making this dirt track the main route of the intersection. It doesn't need no permission to be built, cos it's already here. Then, straight through them, there trees, and up and over where the swamp sits. Then, into Cutters Creek and beyond. Here dude, get another of these down your neck. I'll soon be needing more supplies the speed that you're drinking." He pulled on a small tarpaulin at the back of the truck to reveal a plastic crate, with six, dust covered, beer bottles. He threw one across the back of the pick-up, to Kyle.

"I need to take a leak, Josh." Kyle put his new beer on the top of the cab and walked off the dirt road and disappeared into the nearby trees. He gulped the last of his bottle, then willfully threw it into the bushes, at his side. Josh took another beer from the crate, unscrewed the top and leant on the truck, waiting for his partner, in crime.

"When we doing the deed Josh?" He questioned clearing his throat, and hocking as he returned from the trees, still zipping up his flies.

"Has the fat man called?"

"He ain't. I've heard nothing, from him, or his dumb ass, lawyer. I think we're being left in the dark with this one. But hey, if that's the way he wants to play it. It ain't no skin off my nose. All we need is a whole load of plastic drums full of a whole mess of gas and diesel. Mix them up really good, and... Kaboom...! That'll do the trick. Bang goes the swamp, and any evidence. We burn the drums, along with every other damn piece of crap in this critter ridden place. Right up there's where we are heading, dude," he said pointing Kyle toward a path with his beer bottle, as they walked into the long grass.

"Why don't we haul the fuel up in the next couple days Josh? We can stash it right here, out of sight," Kyle suggested kicking aside the overgrown panicum grass from the path beneath his feet, as Josh followed. As he continued through the shoulder-tall grass, an array of somewhat sleeping or disturbed stilt-legged flies navigated in all directions, from the grassy terrain. "Nobody will see any petrol drums, in this thick mess of reed and weed," he said walking into a slight clearing, and spotting the main sedge-grass covered water of the swamp, in the distance.

As Kyle walked through the clearing, he stopped and looked down at his wet feet. The moist, and boggy undergrowth had smeared and muddied his boots.

"Hey Josh! You could have warned me about the ooze. My dancing boots are ruined. I ain't going any further into this God-damn, cat-tail swamp, I've seen quite enough. Agh...! The damn flies are getting right up my nose, as well," he grunted waving his hand across his face. "I'll be bringing some rain boots next time. We can burn them in the fire. Or maybe I'll just get you to be doing all the Donkey work," he quipped laughing to himself.

"Look! There's the green-eyed, swamp water. There're plenty nice flowers around this place as well. I might even take some home for my Mama. Keep in her good books like the good little boy I am," Josh said as he walked into a piece of tight string that was running through the long grass.

"You are a flower, Josh."

"What the...!" Josh shouted as it nipped into his neck with its tightness. "Ouch! Who the hell put this thing here? Damn thing almost slit my throat." He grabbed it and pushed it down, then trapped it underneath his boot. "What the hell is this Kyle?" Josh asked grabbing at the twine. He reached to the side of his boot and pulled out a small, flick knife, and cut through the string to watch it ping through the grass at either side of them. Which in turn, disturbed and released even more flies and insects from the bushes as a result. "There has to be damn trappers up in this place. They won't be trapping much longer... Wow...!" Josh shouted. "Did you see that muskrat dart from the water into the bulrushes?" He asked replacing his knife to his boot.

"All I can see, is more damn, flies, you idiot!"

"It was like a giant rat! "Now hold on here. Be quiet a minute, Kyle. Some trappers might still be here?" Josh whispered stopping to tune his senses into the strange sounds around them. "That muskrat must have been three-foot, nose-to-tail. Yuk...! The dirty marsh rabbits."

"Never saw a thing."

"I saw it, Kyle, and there'll be plenty more where he came from. They breed as fast as vermin. They can birth a whole generation or more, in less than sixty days. I should have brought my rifle then I could have taken some home to eat.

"Hey, Josh. Talking of swamp water, I think it's high time we started making out ways back? I could kill for a good slug of whiskey."

"I like you're thinking, Kyle. We's seen all we need to see here. Don't have to make it any harder than we have to.

"Hey Josh, maybe we should bring another pair of hands along when we do it. I ain't awful keen on all this muck. I have a mud affliction. It hates me, and I hate it."

TWENTY-FIVE: *Moonbow*

"Oh, what time is it? Wow, we're here already? Much sooner than I thought. There's a space for the camper, over near the gift shop, mister-fast. It's a busy old place when the Moonbow is due to appear," she pointed out, rubbing her eyes from her nap. James put the camper into a parking spot, and touched a little hard on the brake, on purpose. Jerking, Eden forward in her sleepy daze.

"You thought we got her quicker, because you fell asleep, lazy bones," he smugly added. Eden looked across at him, said nothing but gave a sharp, slap on his thigh.

"I'm hungry Mom, come on Bailey," Jamie shouted.

"Me, too honey. We'll go get something, now," Eden agreed.

"You have an appetite like a horse. How come you're so slim and toned?" James asked shaking his head at her.

"I know, I'm so bad. I've always been as slim as a fence post. Always been able to eat a bellyful of everything, twice over. I'm terrible. My metabolism's fast and burns all the calories away. Hey hold on, are you calling me skinny?" She asked, yanking up her T-shirt and checking her smooth tummy for flab to James's secret delight.

"Can't you ever take a compliment, miss, paranoid?"

"I don't see no point in them, mister-cheeky. This is a great place on Independence Day," she added moving on. "We celebrated here in style when Jamie was still in nappies," she pointed out, thinking back to a happier time. "They did a great job, back then. We had a great big, food fest. Some drinking and lots of singing. Oh, there was a country band, too. Then a big firework display at midnight. Jamie, you remember that, don't you?" She asked to his expressionless face.

"You had ice cream, from here to here," she explained pointing at her lips. In fact, I'm gonna get some for home. It really is the best around. Can you get the cooler box from the back, mister-freeze?"

They all climbed out of the van and made their way to the refreshment stand in the corner. "Hi, Mam. Four cheese burgers with fries. No, make it five, the beast will need something. A tea, a coffee, and you two tell the lady what you'd like to drink. What's the conditions like for the Moonbow? I mean, what are our chances for tonight...? My friend's come a long way to see this. Isn't that right, mister-binoculars," she shouted watching James walk toward her with the cool box in his hand.

"Erm, yes I have. I'm from England."

"Aaah, England, huh. You're a bit of *wow* if you don't mind me saying, mister," The lady replied winking and lifting her eyebrow up at Eden. "You could well be in luck tonight. Maybe in more ways than one," she teased dipping the freshly made ice-cream into nuts, chocolate and some fizzy sherbet, and then passing it over the counter. "The best bow I ever did see was on day, just like this one, three years past. I lost my dear Angus, you see. That's how I remember it, so well," she added turning somewhat animated.

"That's a good, strong name," James commented.

"He was Scottish and proud of it. But oh, time and life move on, huh," she smiled. "He's up there. High above the Moonbow.

"When the Moon's on ice, and the rain is falling, your heart might hear the Moonbow calling," She added, singing in a way she'd been programmed to sing, but also sounding honest and genuine with her words, in a way that made you feel that the day, was such a better place. "You do know that true love is tied up with the Moonbow? All you need is a low harvest moon, and a sky that is darker than raven's wing. Just add a little sparkle of rain, and your all set. Tonight, you got a full, rose-moon, honey," she explained to Eden's smile.

"Is it easy to get up, there?"

"Sure. Take the smooth path up, where you see the lights on the rails. Head for the upper lover's leap, overlook. Its uneven, natural rock up there, so be careful. Your better up top. The lower overlook is a little more slippy and dangerous," she explained watching Jamie limping away with his burger in his mouth. "It's not that far to the waterfalls. Ten minutes, or so. Just head for the lodge up there," she pointed. "Its minutes from that. You're a lucky girl..." she quietened.

"Eden. My name is, Eden"

"Lucky girl, Eden. A lovely name to, honey. Grab your happiness while you can. Hold on to each other real tight, and never let go. Because, before you know it, it'll all be gone."

"Thank you so much, Mam. Hey Abby, you can try out the new camera on your phone," she shouted as Abby and Jamie got more distant as their talking continued.

"Wait kids! Before you disappear. Just remember, we need to be back at the project house early in the morning, to meet the engineer," James chirped up, making everyone aware of his important work, yet again.

"Oh, let them be. They're having fun. And anyway, we don't? You're only picking up the keys, mister-grumps. I could ring and get Devon to hide them instead. He might even still be there, now. What's wrong... don't you want us to spend some time together, up here?"

"Of course, I do. Why didn't I think of that? You think of everything."

"It's just being clever and flexible, James's."

"Yes. So, I've been flexible with you. It's time for you to be flexible with me," he joked as some people walked past and looked at them both, strangely.

"You want me to be more flexible...? Oh, honestly James. You wanted me to be more flexible last time we did the swan-lake position. Surely you don't want that up here, of all places. You sex maniac. Can't you think of the children's fun, for once?" She grinned pushing his ice-cream into his nose.

"At least wait until we get up in the trees, and away from prying eyes darling," she added in a louder, more imitated English manner, with a face of pure pretense. "That would be lovely, honey," James replied looking over at the frowning Moonbow visitors, enjoying the wicked sense of humor as a bespectacled man walked past, and overly winked at him as Abby and Jamie walked back towards their deathly slow parents.

"What's wrong honey?" He asked in a poorly imitated American accent, and sounding rather like, Nathan "I thought you enjoyed flaunting your naked body in front of an eager audience. I'll wait until we reach cover of the trees before I ravage you then, because I have a new position. We can take some of this ice cream with us and have some real fun," he inferred shaking the cool-box ice-cream as the people walking by, listened in shock.

"Dad... Eden, come on. What is taking you so long? Stop, messing around and acting like a pair of love-struck teenagers, it's embarrassing?" Abby said, raising her hands in the air with a long sigh, and looking at Jamie as Eden walked away with laughter.

"Have you heard those two, behind us? What's going on with them, Abby?" Jamie asked, licking his ice cream as Bailey fervently watched.

"Oh, nothing. They're just in love."

"What?"

"Yes, love. They've been like this for ages now. You saw them kissing at the house before. I thought you knew, Jamie?"

"Not really noticed. I didn't see any kissing either? I just thought they liked each other."

"Oh, they do," she casually replied. "Love's the next step up from that. I must admit though, it's really nice to see my Dad happy again. I could just do without all the daft swooning and silliness. It's so hum-drummingly boring."

"Oh well, if they're busy doing all that, at least they're leaving us alone."

"My thoughts exactly. Wow, look how bright the moon is tonight, Jamie. Listen, we'll have to keep an eye on those two as well. This love thing's only going to get worse. At some point, they might just need a little help to make things happen for real. If you catch my drift." She said turning around to wink at him.

"So, what's the deal mister, bad-accent?" She asked as they looked up the path to the kids.

"We stay here and try catch this Moonbow. Then head straight to the project house and stay the night. Then, you can get an early start back home tomorrow. It'd be far too much to try make it back to your house tonight. There's more than enough room upstairs in the frog house," he said sounding as if a once in a lifetime experience wasn't as important as his work.

"Frog house?" She puzzled. "OK, deal. I'll send a text to Devon and see if things are on track down there. I hope you don't snore?" She grinned, happy that she had a good man at her side, as he secretly delighted in her showing an interest in his work at last.

"The reason I said Frog house, is because I'm here to study everything in the swamps. Particularly the Frogs. The biological data we get from them has been ground-breaking. Diabetes, stroke and cancer patients benefit from the mini-proteins in their skin. In a word, Angiogenesis. It's interesting stuff that in the long run, could save a lot of lives. Frogs are a recognized natural healer in north and South American native customs. As well as the Celtic traditions of transformation and magic. Our unsung heroes. There's so many things we have to thank them for. That's why we have to keep our eye on the progress of their species over here. The last survey done, was five years ago."

"Uh-huh. I know a cure for peptic ulcers was almost found in their skin," she said to his shock. Secretly used remnants of Henry Creech's speech as matter-of-factly as Abbey had earlier, about love.

TWENTY-SIX: *Morning after*

James woke up on the couch with Eden beside him, and Bailey snuggled near their feet. As he tried to move, to look at his watch without waking her, she fell to one side, then opened her eyes. "Sorry, Eden," he said as he slid himself from under her and she got herself comfy, without him. He walked into the kitchen and put on the kettle as she pulled the cover over her shoulder and lay half asleep, and half-awake, but listening to him moving around. Happy that his body heat had kept her warm and safe, the whole night.

He walked back in the room to see her stirring:

"Thanks for taking me to see the Moonbow, Eden. It was incredible. I didn't think the kids would stay awake so long. I'm so glad they did. Abby loved it, and so did I. A totally magical place. I'm so silly, sometimes. I'd never give myself chance to explore or see things like that, ordinarily."

"Because you never make the time. Always so wrapped up and obsessed with your work. Life is for living, James. It's time for you to start living it properly," she yawned.

"I adore my job like you do, James. But sometimes, I always try to make the time for other things."

"I agree. But it's totally different when you're with another person. I really wouldn't bother to look at things, if I was on my own," he explained. "But, I like exploring with you. In fact, one day, I'd actually like to explore you," he teased to her smile as he sat back down beside her.

"Falling asleep on the couch. Jeepers! We must have been out for the count," she added, snuggling in to him.

"I'm sure you'll find things as interesting at the swamp today. You can help me with the test results when I've got them sorted out, this morning. You know how to use a computer, don't you?" He asked, standing back up to make the coffee.

"Sure, I do," she said holding tight to his arm and refusing to let him walk away, then, playfully letting him go once he'd got the message. He was back at her side within minutes, with a coffee in each hand.

"There you go, milk, no sugar. I'll have to get going soon. I need to get up there," he explained sitting down again.

"James, I need to go home for Jamie's pills. He's all out. I'll come straight back to help you if that's ok. I'd like to learn some more about your work," she said sitting up, still entrenched in the blanket as she took her coffee from his hand. "It's a bit cold in here," she intimated putting the blanket across his knees in an attempt to feel as close to him as she had all night.

"Hey, last time I was at Boyle's swamp. There's a little amphibian called the Gray tree frog. He's an astounding breed. He freezes himself to death in the winter. He produces glycerol that changes to glucose and freezes his body. The water and blood freezes the heartbeat, and his breathing stops. Then, the little guy thaws out when the temperature warms up," he explained taking a drink of coffee. "Hard feller to find though. He blends himself in with the trees. You hear him before you see him. His mating call is so tranquil and hypnotic."

"And all almost in my back yard too," she said blowing on her drink. "How would you like to spend the fourth of July together James? We could go to Tennessee."

"You said Jamie was going to a kayak event?"

"Yep, I just was thinking we could do everything together and go to a firework display afterwards. Maybe go into Tennessee the next day, and you could meet my sister again. We could stay over at her place and go out together to a gig. I think that would be swell, don't you?"

"A gig…? It sounds great to me. I just hope I can fit all the work in and get it out of the way. Once I get started properly, I don't let up until all the preliminary stuff's measured. If we do decide we're going to do all this other stuff together, we need to decide right now. Then I can keep too some kind of schedule or be able to increase my work rate and priorities. I don't want to let you down again."

"Is that a yes, mister-obligation…?" He stayed silent, but quietly smiled thinking into his coffee.

"Oh great… it'll be terrific," she said sitting up, secretly overjoyed and planting a kiss on his cheek. Feeling as if she was part of some kind of family team for the first time in years. "I'll go and wake the kids then… they need to be getting up. After all, it is…." she glanced at her watch.

"Seven thirty," he duly replied, smiling at her sudden rushed insistence.

"Erm… I make it seven thirty-seven. Golly, half the day will be gone. Hey, mister- boogie, can you line dance…?"

"Nope," he cupped his mug. "Two left feet."

"Then I'll be teachin' you good and proper. Kids…!" She shouted. "Come on now, time to rise and shine," she yelled, turning on the lights. "Oh, the paint…? Is that the paint?"

"Erm, Devon brought those boxes on his second visit. He said it was an extra part of the order. I haven't had time to look what's in there yet?" James purported. She fervently ripped open the box, to find exactly what she'd asked him to bring back. "Brilliant, and brushes too. Yippee! I'll just give this a quick try before I leave. Come on kids, wakey, wakey!" She pulled a large plastic container of white paint from the box and manically ripped off the plastic lid. Then pulled one of the larger paintbrushes out of the DIY home decor pack. Shamelessly daubing *EDEN* onto the one of the lounge walls in three-foot letters, as James watched, astounded at her lunacy. "Tell Abby I want her name painted on that wall," she pointed. "With *JAMIE* on the other, when I get back."

"You are nuts, Eden! When did you become such a hard-ass dance teacher and an even crazier interior designer you, mad woman? And you can tell them yourself, they're here. What about my name?" He puzzled.

"So, what about it?" She laughed.

The kids arrived at the bottom of the stairs. All sleepy and forlorn looking puzzled at her behavior. "Oh, I'm getting a bit carried away, aren't I. Better wash my hands and be gone."

"Yes, you are," he shouted. "I'll make sure I keep in touch this time," he said reassuring her as she began to get ready to leave. "That's your job Abby, can you handle that?"

"Of course."

"Sure, she can. Jamie come on with me to the kitchen and take the last of your pills, before we go," she said walking out of the room to the kitchen, with him in tow.

"Right, do you need any credit for that phone, Abby?"

"Nope, it's on a contract in Eden's name, Dad."

"Wow, that woman's something else."

"Yes, she is, isn't she? You really like her, don't you dad?" Abby said from nowhere.

"Erm, yes, I do," he replied frowning at her no-nonsense forwardness.

"It's okay Dad... I do too. Jamie's brilliant, too. He's like the little brother I never had."

James remained silent. Stunned by her resolute approach, that put him in mind of her mum, Jane, and Eden, too.

"She's a little wacky, don't you think?"

"Oh yeah, she's crazy, Dad. Good crazy, though. She keeps you in your place, just like Mum did. I think she's good for you."

"What...! Good for me... that's very nice of you to say. Where's all this coming from?"

"Just an observation, Dad."

"You're as bad as she is," he said, happy she approved.

"Shush, Dad. She's coming back."

"So, what have you and Abby been talking about, Jamie? I feel like I haven't spoken to you in ages, and you've been with me all the time," she said as she drove along the road toward home, and ultimately, Jamie's pills.

"Oh, this and that. Nothing, really, Mom."

"Did you like the Moonbow?"

"Oh, it was the best, Mom. I'm sore with the walking, though," he said pushing his hand into his thigh. "I'm never sore here, it's always up the top?"

"Ooh. We'll have to take it a little easy, today. We don't want you off school again. It won't be long before we get home, and then you can take another pill to help. Are you getting to know Abby a little better? She's a clever girl with that phone, isn't she?"

"She was telling me about where she lives, and her friends. She's got loads of friends. She's learning to play tennis. Oh, and how she's going to get her Dad to buy her a dog. She told me that she doesn't have a Mom anymore, either. She died."

Eden's eyes opened as wide as her mouth, as she struggled for what to say or to keep herself from slamming on the brakes or something worse. She gulped hard, calmed her nerve, and turned down the radio.

"Yes, I know she died, honey. She died from a terrible disease. But Abby's glad she came here with her Dad, though. She said it's all a great big adventure," Eden replied, changing the subject and thinking Abby was such a strong and brave girl to have not even mentioned her Mother's passing, at all. "We're going to spend the Fourth of July with them. So, we'd better make sure Abby has the best time of her life. And her Dad, too."

"I know, Mom. I think it's great that when we visit England, we can stay with them just like they stayed with us, here. And for as long as we like. I think that's so cool, Mom."

"Yes, honey, when they leave," she sighed. "Hold on…? What did you just say…did Abby really say that?"

"Of course, Mom. I think your accent is going a bit English. That's with hanging around all the time, with Abby's Dad," he giggled.

Eden stopped talking and stared at the road ahead, thinking about what Jamie had just told her. The blinding truth that Abby and James wouldn't be around forever, was beginning to dawn on her, so she quickly moved her thought to something else. "Jamie. Remind me to ring Sheridan when we get home, honey. We've been having so much fun, I plain forgot about the road meeting, tomorrow."

"Mom. I should have gone to the toilet before we left, can we stop?"

Eden looked along the road to see a parking area, just in the distance. "Yes honey, right there. I'll pull over," she weakly smiled, still contemplating her predicament with James as she stopped, and Jamie quickly jumped out of the Mustang, with Bailey.

"Come straight back when you... and don't go too far away from the road," she shouted climbing out of the car to stretch her legs. She started to walk around in circles, kicking winsomely at the dirt, below her feet. "James games, James games?" She looked over at a dusty camper van that was parked further up in the rest area and then walked toward it "Hi there," she said, waving and being polite. "My son. He's just taking a leak. I might be doing the same when he gets back. Busy road, huh?" She said, making conversation waving to the nosy family, sat inside the camper who were questionably glaring across at her unscheduled stop into what they seemed to think, was *their* own personal, road-side retreat. With no attempt at communication from the staring family, Eden reached for her mobile:

"Hey, how are you, sis...? Good, and the kids?" She asked kicking at the dirt and leaning her ear in her mobile. *"Oh, well that's nice. Listen honey, you remember the guy from the night we went out in the Skoolhouse...? We played pool together. No, not the French one, uh-huh, yes, him. I know, he was. Yes... let's just say he's staying around, a little while longer. No, we're not together. Oh, shush! Well erm, we is, and we ain't. Will you hush your damn mouth a minute, and let me get a word in edgeways? Yes... good. Thank you. Look, the*

Fourth of July celebrations. Yes, we're coming to visit you, so we're going to be together. Will you shut up already, and simmer down?" She said laughing at her sister's continuous digging into her affairs as she self-consciously flicked her hair from her shoulder, and her unwanted audience continued to glare over.

"Yes... a little... yes I do like... I think he does. He doesn't say much, apart from work. Yes, I do think he's lovely, and..... NO...! We have not miss, dirty-mind," she replied listening to her sister's comments and laughing. *"Though, I kind of wish we had. Just a kiss or three. Yes, he is.... oh, he is so.... huh...? How the hell would I know?"* She replied looking up to the sky and closing her eyes as the trees and bushes rustled behind nearby. *"Yes, now listen; I want to take him to see a country group in the city, so can we stay over after the fireworks? NO! Not those type of fireworks. See you and your dirty mind girl? It has nothing to do with sex! The federal holiday fireworks, gutter brain. Yes, and you got a one-track mind, you know that! No honey, he has everything. A sophisticated soul, with an intellectual mind. A beautiful hearted, mature-minded daughter as well,"* Eden replied thinking about Abby, then Abby's Mum.

"Yes, Jamie and Bailey. Listen, he has a camper van, so if you don't have the room. Uh huh, it'll be his van we come in. Well, if they're going on a sleep-over we can have their beds, can't we? No! Are you deaf...? I said we haven't slept together...No Page, I'm not lying, and you should know me better than that! I said we don't need a double bed you, big fixer! Stop putting ideas in my head." She burst out laughing and decided to wave at the nosey camper people who were now beginning to annoy her with their looks. The holidaying father got out of his camper and went to the back doors to put the terrier in his arms, and on to a leash.

"Oh, thank you... thank you so much, sis. Yes, the group, they're called, Ward Thomas. An English country music band. No, he didn't.... I don't know if he does. I'm not even sure what kind of music he likes. But I'm still going to teach him to line dance, whether he likes it, or not. Yes, it'll be great. Ok then, I'll have to go, Jamie's back now. I love you too, honey. See you real soon. Love to the kids."

"I'm all done Mom," Jamie said standing by her side.

The self-appointed, patrolling family man looked at Eden as she put her phone between her teeth as she knelt down and brushed some greenery from Jamie's hair. "Where's Bailey, Jamie? Beast...! Get out here, come on now honey, and get in the car." The weird man walked across to Eden, as Bailey bounded out of the bushes and instantly saw the tiny terrier on the lead, who was sniffing interestingly his master's leg. "Morning, sir. A fine day we got ourselves?" The man said nothing and stared at Eden like she was trespassing. "He got a name, sir?" She asked looking down at his puny, and noisy dog.

"Mojo," he muttered with duress, as his terrier snapped a feeble bark at her, and Bailey sniffed toward the scrawny dog and calmly growled. He lifted his jowls to stand his ground and showed the terrier his sharp white teeth.

"Mojo, huh?" She said nodding and loading her brain with sarcasm. The man looked at her, then bent down to pick up his frightened excuse for a canine up from the floor. "You should have your dog on a lead, miss," he inferred.

"Uh-huh. And maybe you should have a muzzle on your mouth, mister. Bailey... go!" Bailey, obediently looked up at her, then darted into the Mustang beside Jamie. Then, as if by design, the terrier started to wildly bark at Eden in Bailey's absence. "You know sir... that mobile home of yours sure could do with a good old wash. I reckon Mojo would be particularly helpful with that," she said eyeing the yapping and shivering terrier.

"Oh really?" He spat.

"Oh, sure. I figure he'd fit inside a water bucket, just dandy," she said to his shock as she turned on her heel and walked towards her car. "You go on have a good day, sir," she said to the man's anger and Jamie's delight. She climbed into the car and quickly pulled out onto the main road with a sarcastic grin, all over her face.

TWENTY-EIGHT: *Statistics & music*

She closed the car door and walked from the hot, afternoon sunshine through the open front door, of the project house.

"Hi honey, I'm home," she joked, "Hello baby," she said running her fingers through Abbey's hair, who was busy demolishing a packet of crisps from the shopping that was still sat on the floor, beside her. She went through to the back room, to see James, sat at the computer and quietly mumbling, to himself. "Hey!" She shouted putting her hands on his shoulders from behind. "Everything okay?"

He looked up at her and said nothing. Continuing to add something up in his head, and instead, silently nodded. Then, he carried on transferring his figures from a notepad, onto a computer spread sheet.

"Can I help?" She asked, leaning over and resting her head close to his. Massaging her hands into his muscular collar bone as she waited for him to reply. "Oh, doing my job for me, huh? You, said I could do that bit. Let me help you, mister-abacus."

"Sorry, I was stuck on something, there. Of course, you can help. Just keep doing what you're doing on my shoulders, because it feels amazing," he said feeling the tension in his shoulders ease away. Feeling glad to hear her voice and feel her soft touch. "You can help here, then up at the swamp later. Just let me finish this page, then you can take over. I'm just putting the data into the red boxes there, see." He said pointing his chewed pencil at the screen. "They turn green, once you've put them in the box." Eden moved around to his left side, to get a better view:

"I know what they do. I've done spread sheets before, honey. I'm not completely dumb," she replied, sitting herself impedingly across his knees. "I've had a bit of a problem up there."

"Oh? I hope there's no big snags mister, boss-man, we're on a pretty tight schedule here," she joked.

"It won't slow us down. I'm just a little bit of data, short, if that's what you mean. One of the sensor cables was snapped. It happens from time to time. A weak spot in the string line or possibly the wildlife getting to it and breaking the line. I haven't had time to take a proper look at the damage, yet.

But I over compensate with the wire links, so the end results should come out, just as they should." He put his notepad down and pulled her closer toward him. "Which reminds me, there's wellingtons, weather coats and walkie-talkies over there. Find the best fit you can. I'm afraid we're slumming it with the sizes."

"Great. So, we do get to go up there with you, today. I can't wait to see what all the fuss is about," she wisecracked.

"We'll head right up once these results are emailed, and we've had a bite to eat. I got a bunch of ready-made sandwiches from the Evarts shop, this morning. I need to take some more photographs up there, as well," he stated with a sense of urgency. "There's some new species of flowers. Least I think they are. I don't recall them being there five years ago? Pink ladies' slippers, shooting stars and some hummers, and white leafed leathers. The hummingbirds love those," he added eagerly. "The place has its own ecosystem. Everything has a purpose for everything else. There's just so much bio-diversity."

"Right then, I'll go sort the food out," she explained standing up from his lap and leaving him to his figures. She retreated to the lounge to grab the shopping bags and put things away.

"The Kentucky States Nature Reserves Commission, has provided so much care and so many habitats for the endangered species, the animals and the plants," he shouted. "It's a credit to them. I think this place can be another natural community to consider as a reserve for their list. Especially knowing that just Kentucky alone, is losing over one-hundred acres of forest a day through deforestation and clearing."

"What! Is that true?"

"It's actually an underestimation, Eden. The correct figure when I was last here was, oh, let me think now?" He looked up to the ceiling to remember his figures and noticed a huge cobweb hanging down in the corner.

"In 2008, Kentucky was losing 135 acres of forest and 100 acres of farmland a day. Put more simply, 46,000 acres of wildlife and its habitat, per year. That's as big as Lake George, which is the second largest freshwater lake in

Florida," he stated as she walked past him to the kitchen. He looked up from the PC at her stunned and shocked expression.

"That isn't right. It can't be."

"As I remember, it is."

"No, I mean it's wrong. There'll be no greenery left in the state at all if that's the size it's disappearing. Golly!"

"That's why we're fighting so hard to change acceptance of the need for natural environments, and habitats, like Boyles."

"Then we'd better keep fighting really hard, then. That's really bad news to hear, James. But it's good for me, because I like keeping busy. But what I don't like mister, facts-and-figures, is not being able to go to the firework's because of too much work. What do you say, kids," she shouted to her allies from the kitchen?

"We're going to fireworks?" Abby shouted back.

"Yes Abby, on Independence Day, at night," Jamie pointed out.

"We'll be staying over at Pages. She's got plenty of room, and you two can go with Chloe for the planned sleep over, if you like? That's where you'll see the fireworks."

"What?" Jamie said limping into the kitchen.

"Chloe's going to her friends, and you two can go along with her, if you like. Or, you can just stay with Page, and baby Bradley, in the house."

"What about you, Mom?" Jamie frowned.

"James and I are going to a music concert, in Nashville. But we'll see you in the morning, honey."

"Jamie, their doing the love thing, again," Abby whispered.

"Okay. That's cool, Mom. What's on the sandwiches, Mom?"

"You'll find out soon enough. Here, these are for you. If you want more, just holler." She pulled a chair up beside James at the desk, then took a sandwich off the overflowing plate.

"Get some food James, then we can go and you can get me a lovely bunch of swamp flowers," she derided.

"I'll never eat all these on my own," he said offering the plate back to her.

"Nope, I'm on a strict diet. So, you just shift your butt, and let me get my head around these here figures. You get them eaten, because you need to keep your strength up," she said dryly, as he turned to face her with a piece of ham, hanging from his mouth. "If you can't eat them all, there's a canine waste disposal unit asleep outside. Now can you give me peace for my grindstone?" She grinned, poking more fun at him.

"Figures," he bit. "I'll be able to put my arms twice around your figure at this rate." He moved out of her way as she nestled down on his seat. She shook and banded her hair with an elastic band from the shopping, then stuck his pencil behind her ear. James headed out of the room, passing Abby who was coming in the other direction. She passed her Dad, then stopped and leant on the desk, just beside Eden.

"Who are you going to see?" Abby asked with anticipation as Eden stopped looking at the computer screen and lifted Abby up, and on to her knee. "It's a country music band, honey. They play the best hoe-down music in the whole wide world. They're even from England, as well."

"What's a hoe-down?" She asked as Eden straightened her hair band.

"A whole lot of dancing fun, honey. They're twin sisters called, Ward Thomas and they're soooo... good."

"Oh, right. Catherine and Lizzie, I know them," she said glancing at Eden's hand in her hair, and feeling somewhat strange, because the last time she'd had her hair pampered in such a similar way, was by her Mum.

"Oh, wow. You know their names," she said with surprise. Yeah honey, they're getting well known in America now. Particularly in Nashville. This is their second or third visit, I think. I, just have to go see them. It's my kind of music."

"I don't think you understand, when I say I know them... I mean, I KNOW them," she frowned. "I've got their number in here... see?" She scrolled through her mobile contacts. "Here they are; C & L... Catherine and Lizzie. They were on the plane coming over. We made friends. My phone died you see. They went to Europe first, then came here. They were even on the music system on the plane. *A town called, Ugly,* I think. I tried to tell Dad, but he was sleeping. He's a stick in the mud, with music."

"OMG! That's just so cool. So, you like your music as much as me. I wish I'd have known that. Hey, how about we all go together, instead?"

"No. Its okay, Eden. I can see them when I get back home. They said I can go backstage. They live pretty close to us in, Hampshire. All I have to do is give them a ring, and they'll arrange it," Abby explained as Eden's mind wandered.

"Hampshire. Mmm, sounds quaint. Do you live in a nice place, then?"

"Yeah, it's a great place. A bit lonely at home without, Mum, but I have lots of friends when Dad's away. I think you and Jamie would love Hampshire, just as much as you love Dad."

Eden swallowed hard, feeling lost as to what to say. "Oh erm, you must come with us Abby, to the gig."

"No, really, it's okay. Besides, I think you and Dad need to spend some more time together. Because he really likes you," she replied being totally forthright and honest, yet again.

"Yes... I... like your, Dad. I really like you, too," she answered feeling impassioned with Abby's real honesty. "I hope you're going to look after me at the swamp. I don't like snakes," she smiled.

"Me neither. I didn't see any, though? All hiding, I expect. Dad will be looking after you, and I'll be looking after, Jamie. Has he taken his pills today?"

"Yes baby," she said as she eased her down from her lap. "You run along now and let me finish this tabulation work for your father." Eden watched Abby leave, thinking what an extraordinarily level-headed girl she would grow up to be in light of such a terrible loss to her personal life. Her maturity of years for such a young girl was abounding. So much more mature than, even herself.

"Okay. Oh, and Eden?" she turned back.

"Yes sweetheart, what is it?"

"Nothing. Just a little funny because you sounded a bit like Dad, then."

"Hello... yes. It is him, speaking," he puzzled shrugging his shoulders, then waving his arm in the air.

"Oh, I see... yes that's right, Colville's car hire, if possible. Oh, you're there now...? Erm...great. If you could leave everything with, Charles, I'll come and collect it today. No, this afternoon, in fact," he said imitating an invisible steering wheel to Eden as he held his mobile on his shoulder, as he drove. *"I can sign and scan, then email the inventory straight back to you. Yes, James Ustinov... USTINOV,"* he repeated, spelling out his name. *"LEAPS. That's right, okay, thank you for calling. Oh, and you can tell Charles, I'll see him with Clara 2, later. What! He isn't...?"* He said stopping talking to catch every word the girl was saying. *Mmm, okay then, Miss Rosen... right, thanks again... bye."* He pressed on the mobile, then turned to face Eden. "That's good news. The project van is finally ready. That was the company dropping it off. Things seem to be coming together quite well. We can pick it up after collecting the diametric cables and showing you around this little cornucopia of life," he confirmed pulling up the van, and turning off the engine.

"So here we are. Time for you to get your boots on. What do you think, Eden?" He eagerly emoted, secretly raring to go and playfully pushing her out of the camper door, as she opened it.

"These rain boots are huge, Mom," Jamie shouted through the van looking down at his over-size wellingtons, as Eden opened the side door. She smiled as she looked at the state of Abbey and Jamie's adult-size footwear.

"I'm afraid it's either wear those or get wet and muddy feet. Up to you honey. Wow, it's beautiful here. Come on kids. Pretty eerie too, in a sweet kind of way. Listen to the noises, what the heck's that beeping sound?" She wondered following James closely, through the thick and lush bushes. As they continued, James pushed a tree branch out of his way and it rebounded backwards, thwacking her in the face. "Ouch...! Thanks mister, me-myself and- I," she protested, spitting and rubbing her face, and then looking back to see the kids openly enjoying her misfortune.

"The noise you asked about, is the gray tree frog's mating call. It'll get louder as it gets darker, and the rest of them join in. Eden, take a look at these spring time treasures," James encouraged, stopping below a tree as the kids caught up. "This little beauty is called the, American Mayapple, or the umbrella plant. Specifically, it's nothing only a common weed. It hides under the tree leaves just like this one. Any idea what it's used for?"

"Mmm," she pondered. "Is it for rubbing on nettle stings?"

"Not quite," he grinned to their bemused and interested faces. "It's for Cancer. It has a compound that stops the cell division and helps with treatment of lung cancer, testicular cancer, brain tumors and some forms of Leukemia," he continued to her shocked face as their surprise deepened. "It's got many other derivatives of its compound. Mostly for treating psoriasis, malaria and rheumatoid arthritis."

"I'd have never known, James."

Oh, I nearly forgot. There's a little story about it, as well. It's believed that the girl who picks the Mayapple flower, will fall pregnant.

"Is that, so?" Eden replied frowning at his comment. "Oh my God, James! All those deforestation figures you told me in the house," she gulped. "All this greenery will be gone," she announced, somewhat mesmerized as the brevity of the future finally dawned on her as she watched him cup the small, white, and unassuming flower, studiously between his forefingers.

"Yes, and that was only the clear-cutting and logging figures that I told you. Climate change and other factors will have a direct impact throughout the whole of the planet. The disappearance of animals and plants sends ripples through the other species who feed on them, or are hunted by them, or interact with their disappearing environment. All the waters of the world run on the same processes as this. It truly isn't sensationalization. With over half the world's amphibian indicator species population in decline, we are all potentially in big trouble. If we don't find the answers to our problems, we ourselves are going to be another victim of these, Holocene extinction events. These conditions are what we're part of and are also partially or maybe wholly responsible for. Some scientists believe, that we are already in the sixth-wave of extinction to affect life on earth," he continued with a stony expression. "Our sheer preponderance is driving the slide to oblivion at speed."

"And there's me, worrying about filling up with gas to get Jamie to school," she said with her mind now fully open to his words. She continued to follow him, then suddenly went to swat a large bee that went buzzing past her head.

"Careful with that little fellow, as well. According to other statistics, those pollinating creatures might not be here in three generations time. Many species like him keep us alive. Pollinating crops, purifying water, fixing nitrogen, recycling nutrients and waste. Plants and bacteria carry out photosynthesis, which produces the oxygen we breathe. The trees absorb the carbon dioxide and other greenhouse gasses given off by our activities. Little souls like bees, bacteria and microbes, run this world. One estimate tells us that within fifteen years, a fifth of Africa's forests will have gone."

"Oh, hell. Really? That's unbelievable, James," she said with a palpable gulp looking back at the silent and listening kids.

"Yes really... and really, means forever," James added moving through the taller grass.

"God. We... I, should care so much more than I know."

"There's a song about the Mayapple flower, kids," he said on a lighter note. "That's if I can remember it."

\#

"Down in the shady woodland where, fern-fronds uncurl
A host of umbrellas are swiftly unfurled
Do they shelter fairy people from the pelting showers?
Or are the leaves only sunshades for all the waxen flowers."

\#

"That was lovely, James."

"Come on you lot. Let's move on. There's a lot to see and lots to be done,"

James continued leaving them all smiling at the poem yet dumbfounded with the facts. "This place is just like a mini, Murphy's pond without the bald cypress trees," he noted. "The diametric cables are just up here," he explained brushing through the bushes toward the sedge water in the middle of the small, and untouched oasis. He stopped again, to look to his left and then right for visual pointers. "Aah, there it is, I know where I am, now. See the ticker tape marker in the tree, just there?" He pointed. "The snapped line should be close to it."

"Murphy's pond? Where's that, Dad?"

"The other side of Tennessee. It's Kentucky's largest, bald cypress swamp. A K.S.N.P.C living classroom for kids like you."

"It's getting boggy... yeuch," Abby bemoaned realising it was high time to put her phone away as her boots squelched into the waterlogged grass she'd already walked through, earlier that morning.

"Here we are. Could you take this for me," he asked bending down to pick up the snapped line, and then tying the end of the wire to a small plastic roll. "Could you start wrapping it up? Just follow it along its path, through the trees. I'll go and find the other end of ticker tape and do the same. Once we've both wrapped it up, we'll meet back here. I'll leave this thing stuck in the ground as a marker," he explained pulling on a red telescopic flag that was hanging out of his backpack, then pushing it into the grass as he looked up at Eden's confused face. "As you walk, wrap the line, and release the tree clips where the line is secured, and then put them in this bag, as well. The cable runs within four meters around the diameter of the main body of water," he said glancing at his watch. "It should take us about fifteen to twenty minutes to get it all in. I'll see you over the other side," he said pointing across the swamp. "Think you can manage that, kids? Oh, and listen Jamie, you're the man of your team, so look after your, Mum. If any of you get into any trouble at all, just use this walkie-talkie. It will be secured on this belt, I'll just make sure it's..." he explained, openly tucking his hand inside her jeans to check the radio was secured as she watched him manhandle her waist and did nothing but flush red with embarrassment as she felt his strong grip, clearly enjoying every, last second. He yanked up and down on her jeans as she stood silently happy, rocking side to side. "Yep, there we are. It's on channel three, but the volumes down," he said kneeling down to fidget with the controls.

"The volumes down...huh? Wow... careful there. You got the touch of an angry monkey. Anymore yanking like that, mister-rough, and you'll have my pants around my ankles," she announced with another bug swipe.

"There you go, all done," he winked, gently patting her bottom. "Get wrapping, and I'll see you somewhere on the other side." He looked into her blue eyes, and then kissed her on her cheek as they separated. After about ten minutes of wrapping up the cable, Jamie looked up at his Mum:

"Wow! I'm glad I'm not on my own. This place is just like a maze. Everything looks exactly the same. Look, at those cool birds in the tree. You could play a great game of paintball in here. I hope we don't get lost, Mom. My hips still a little sore. It doesn't help think it's pulling these giant's boots out the sludge all the time."

"Maybe you should have just worn your trainers instead, honey. I should've remembered to bring your wellingtons from home. Sorry. Come on partner, we'll soon be done," she said rubbing on his head. Another ten minutes found them still wrapping. "Ouch."

"Come on my little soldier, we're nearly done. We can't have long to go. This ball of string's getting quite big. Isn't it wonderful here? All these kooky noises and it's so calming? There's more of those Frog's beeping now, too. Ooh. I hope we don't get set on by a herd of angry frogs. Is it a herd?" She wondered. "Maybe a gang. Hell, who knows. Are you enjoying getting to know Abby, honey? You two seem to be getting on real great," she asked trying to take his mind off his hip pain and throwing another tree clip into her bag as she swished away the flies.

"Yes Mom, she's great. I told her all about my school and how I play guitar like you... I wish she could stay." Eden listened to his sad sounding words and felt exactly the same way.

"It would be wonderful, if they could. But they have their own life in England. Ouch! These damn, biting bugs."

"She said we could go visit and see the tower of London and even Big Ben. That would be cool. How long before they have to leave, Mom?"

"Oh, I don't know honey. We should just hide their passports, and then they can't go," she replied winking at him as she heard another noise and her mind wandered. "Hey... James never mentioned anything about poisonous snakes?"

"Why don't you ask James to stay a bit longer, Mom? He might stay if you ask nicely. I like him, he's clever."

"Yep, he's certainly, mister-brains," she agreed as a loud and close whistle came loud through the air above the bird trills, warbles and skirls.

"I think that's him... he can't be far away. Oh, there we go; *another clip bites the dust. And another one down, and another one down, another one bites the dust*! She sang, beginning to sing the song in tune to her quickening footsteps.

"Hey! Don't destroy a perfectly good, rock song. That sound's nothing like, the original Queen classic. If you were anymore out of tune, I'd say you were drunk," James said appearing right in front of her.

"Oh, hello stranger," she smiled enraptured to see him. "Hey mister, plant-life, I got a question," she said as he kissed her cheek. "What are frogs in a gang?"

"An army," he said pulling the last clip off the tree and taking the reel out of her hand and then carefully lifting a spider from out of her red hair. "With toads, it's called a knot."

"A knot, huh...? Weird," she frowned. "Knot's, armies... shucks we learned a lot today," she said smiling at Jamie.

"We can walk back around now," James decided. "I've some more things to show you. Oh, look at that... a Turks-Cap lily, just beautiful. I found some wild, red strawberry's just like you, on the way over here," he inferred to her grinning gaze. "And, there was something else I found when we separated back at the red flag." He explained lowering his voice. "A beer bottle in the grass below the end of cable. So, maybe it wasn't the animals that snapped the lines?"

"What broke it then?" Jamie asked.

"Maybe poachers, hunters or trappers. Who knows Jamie? But if it was, they mustn't have been too happy when they saw the tree cables up. We could be in their territory. I'll have to speak to Henry and see if he knows anything about who comes in here and uses this place. I must speak to my people and start the detailed report for the Kentucky preserves commission, as soon as I possibly can."

"Oh," she mused plucking up some courage. "Jamie asked how much longer you might be staying in Kentucky." She said motioning to her son, but secretly asking for herself. "He was hoping it might be a little longer?"

"How long's a piece of string...? I could be... everything starts off fine, and then the external human complications come from all over the place. I've no idea how long things will take. You really can't put time limits on work like this," he purported, moving beside her and lovingly pushing his hand gently into her jeans back pocket.

"Human complications. You never give a straight answer do you, mister avoid-the-question. I swear, you're as difficult as nailing jelly to a tree. I'd prefer it if you just said you'd be here a long time.

"Come on. Let's start heading back," he smiled pulling on her jeans with his hand in her pocket. "There's some red clover on the way back. I'm going to take some with me for when we get home. It makes a lovely cup of tea."

"Oh, shut up, mister, Earl-grey," she moaned as he wiggled his hidden hand in her pocket, making her smile both inside and out.

"Mom, can we come up here, again?" Jamie asked. "I'd like to stay a bit longer, but my hips just about had it, with these boots."

"Oh, no. I never thought about your hip. I'm so sorry, Jamie, I didn't think."

"No, you shouldn't have to think, James. His hip is sore, and it's my fault entirely. I'm sorry honey, I should have been more prepared."

"Right! We're leaving this minute. Jamie, stop right there, son," James commanded. Eden watched James march across to Jamie and pick him up from the grass, like he wasn't even there. He lifted the young boy over his head and then perched him safely, behind his neck. With his legs dangling either side of his ears. Jamie smiled and held on tight on to his charger's chin, as Eden moved forward, then pulled the offending boots carefully off her son's feet. "You okay up there, son?" James asked as Eden cupped the boots under her arm. "I'm great, thank you, James," Jamie replied looking at his Mom with sheer delight in his eyes.

"Look Eden, the beer bottle's over there in that bush, can you see," he pointed as she walked toward the offending article and picked it out of the grass to take a look. Not having the faintest idea that it had been thrown there by her ex-husband.

Once they had walked the last fifty yards through the trees to the camper, he put Jamie down on the dirt track, and then wiped a small bead of sweat off his brow as the kids took off all their weather gear. "I'm so out of condition, I really must do some more swimming to get fit."

"You could have jumped in the swamp with the frogs, for a swim."

THIRTY: *The swamp*

"Hello. I had a call about the new ORV, for L.E.A.P.S," he asked the strange and uninterested woman behind the desk at Colville's car hire. She looked at him as if he was interrupting her from her important nail filing, and slowly, sucked her chewing gum into her mouth, then blew it back out in his face to listen to it pop. Instantly reminding Jamie of the Gray tree frog, up at the swamp. He smiled and whispered in Abby's ear, then stood behind James and did a mocking impression of her. The woman bit the gum in-between her teeth turned away, then half-heartedly spat it into the waste bin.

"Yeah?" She said moving back from the desk to face them and picked a half-eaten donut off the counter and took a particularly substantial bite.

"Dad, see if they have any lollipops left. The ones Charles gave me last time we were here. Is he around?" Abby asked, grabbing his leg and plucking up the courage to peep around him, to take a peek at the chubby, forty something woman with dyed hair, and huge, rimmed glasses that were perched on her nose. Suddenly, and after hearing her voice, Archie barked behind her, and appeared from behind the workshop door. He ran swiftly under the desk and straight up at Abby's legs.

"Right…sir," she replied, with her mouth still full of donut. "Hey, you get back outside right now you, flea-bitten waste of space," she snapped looking at the lovable mutt, as Abby frowned at her, happily stroking him. The repugnant woman reached under the large desk just as Charles had. "Yeah, you just got to check things off this here list, and give them a confirmation call. Then sign it, and I'll send it right on out."

"I think I can manage that, thanks. Is Charles around?" James asked again, completely unimpressed with her candour.

"The old goat, ain't here. He's in the hospital getting himself fixed up again. That's if they can fix him, this time," she added as the donut finally disappeared. "He's gone and had the last-rights. He ain't got much time left on this here earth. Which is not a poor old shame, because I stand to get all of this when he croaks. Well, at least half of it. I wish he'd just hurry up and get on with it," she nastily proclaimed, as the smile on Abby's face turned to anger and rage.

Eden walked through Colville's front entrance, loaded up with soft drinks from the shop next door. She took one look at Abby's face, and then looked straight at the woman. She strode across to Abby's side, and linked her arm. "Are you ok, baby?"

"Charles isn't… here. SHE… said he's dying," she said as she bowed her head and looked at Archie.

"Dad, I want to see him… we need to go see him!" She exclaimed rubbing her face onto her sleeve as a small tear rolled down her cheek.

"I hope it's a good hospit… which hospital is he at, lady?" Eden asked standing up beside saddened and silent James.

"There's no good hospital for the black lung. Once you get it, you're gone."

"Look. Don't give me any smart mouthed crap, just answer my question," Eden raged.

"He's at the medical center in Powell. I can tell you exactly where it is," the woman angrily replied.

"We don't need no directions from the likes of you. I know where Powell is you, excuse for a human being."

"Hey, watch it, ginger top! I don't like you're tone, either. I don't have to stand here taking your B.S," she replied gulping with fear of donut as she moved away from Charles desk.

"Just follow the signs for the 275, and the 75," she agitatedly pointed out as Eden's face tripped.

"Oh, save the directions, lady."

"We need to get there, right now," James offered.

"You can't leave that old camper out there blocking our trade," the stuffy woman blurted out, chewing again on a new piece of gum.

"Right...! The camper's going back in its garage where it belongs, and that's NOT, negotiable. I'll be straight back for the new van after we've made sure he's alright," James explained to the air-headed woman, as Eden waited for her to answer him back. "Eden follow me," James implored frowning angrily at the shop slob.

"I'm right with you honey," she said tapping his shoulder. They ran from the shop and jumped into their vehicles, and shot around the corner. He pulled up around the back, followed by her and Jamie in the Mustang. He put his thumb up to her through the windshield, as she flashed her lights to concur. "Abbey, you get out and open the garage doors, I'll get this thing parked inside."

She dove out of the camper and pulled on the doors. But they were so stiff, that and she was really struggling. As she continued, she suddenly felt an invisible force helping her from behind. Eden had already jumped out of her car and was yanking at the door along with Abby. Somehow feeling that broken garage doors were her forte. As the doors moved, they scraped across the concrete. Eden kicked a brick, and rolled a tire at each of the doors at either side, to make sure they stayed open.

They both spun around to see James, already reversing back into the tight-space, and right toward them. Abby quickly moved out of the way, as Eden breathed in, to hear the camper brakes squeak, and the engine die. James opened the door, until it touched the side of the garage, and then edged along the gap, until her was stood right in front of Eden. In the frantic rush, they could feel each other's beating hearts pounding as they stood close together. He knowingly touched her hair as they closed the doors quickly across. James pushed over the hasp, and clicked the lock shut. Then, they all turned and ran toward the Mustang, as the chubby woman watched from the doorway, at the rear of the forecourt.

"Come on Dad, hurry up!" Abby beckoned through the car beside Jamie.

"It's locked and going nowhere. Do you want me to drive?"

"Nope. We'll be quicker if I drive. I know the way."

"Whatever you say," he said realising it was not a good time to start a debate.

THIRTY-ONE: *Hospital*

James ran through the automatic double doors of the hospital.

"Hi, we're here to see Charles Colville," he said impatiently to one of the two uniformed women, who were sitting in the hospital reception desk.

"Afternoon sir, erm of course. Do you know which room he's in?" The nurse asked, lifting up some paperwork from the desk in front of her.

"I'm sorry, I have no idea. I think he was admitted a few days ago? Tall man, long, grey beard. It's black lung," James replied looking over her shoulder into the adjacent café that was milling with people.

"I see, pneumoconiosis, one second." She looked down at her computer to scroll through the in-patient's names. "Aah, Colville, he's right here, and he's up on the second-floor, sir. Take the lift at the end, and when you get out at the second floor, you'll see a small nurse station," she explained pointing toward a sign saying *elevators.* "He's in room twelve. His personal nurse will be outside the door. Erm, sorry, but I do need to ask, are you all family...?"

They looked at each other, wondering what to say for fear of rejection.

"Not immediate family, but we've brought this little one with us you see. Sorry, we feared the worst," Eden purported as James, Abby and Jamie looked at other and appreciated Eden's bare-faced cheek. Knowing that she hadn't even met, Charles. The two receptionists watched as two small hands appeared on the front of their desk, followed by a small, blonde head.

"Hi, I'm Abby. His granddaughter."

"Oh, hello there," the woman smiled as Abby lodged her chin on the top of the wooden desk, to stay partially visible.

"He's not expecting us... expecting me... There's no need to inform him I'm here. I really want it to be a surprise, you see," she explained adapting the biggest winning and pretentious smile, she'd ever faked. Enchanting the nurse, immediately.

"Oh, it certainly will be then... that's lovely. You'll be pleased to know, he's in good hands. It's very patient oriented here, and he has his own room. Only met him the once. Lovely man, though. I think he's slowly getting on his feet again. But go easy, he's still very weak. The nurse will take care of everything, and don't rush yourselves. We don't have any specified visitation limits here," she said as the phone rang in front of her. "Second floor patients are in recovery. He'll be taken home towards the end of the week and transferred to our home care team, if he's strong enough." She picked up the phone and silently motioned them toward the elevator sign. "Good afternoon, Powell Hospital."

"Phew, well done. You little fraud," Eden whispered to Abby as they made down the corridor to the lift. "I'm a fraud?" Abby said smiling. "You have a mind to talk."

After about two minutes, the lift doors opened up on the second floor:

"Hello there. You're the one's here to see Charles. I thought so. Go right on in. He's just had something to eat and he even had a little walk around on his Zimmer. But he's all settled down now. There's tea and coffee inside, just help yourselves."

"Thank you, nurse." James said lightly tapping on the door before they walked in to the antiseptic smelling room. Charles was lied in bed looking like he was fast asleep. As soon as she got to the side of the bed, Abby began to smile, due to the fact that he still had his Colville's car hire peaked cap perched on his head. Eden and James quietly sat on different sides of the bed, with Abby and Jamie on their knees in a somewhat whispered silence. Abby frowned at the beeping heart monitor and a steel frame that was holding a clear bag of liquid connected into Charles's vein. Then, as if he knew, he breathed a deep, wheezy breath and his eyes opened. He looked up to the ceiling and then side to side. Seeing Abby's face immediately.

"Hello little one, lovely to see you again. Did you look after your Dad while you were away?"

"Mmm. What are they pumping into your arm, Charles?" She asked, sliding off her James's knee, and leaning onto the bed to get a closer look at his arm.

"Oh, I don't know, honey. Something to make me better. Water-food, I think," He said with a smile, lifting his weak hand onto her head. "A bit late for that kind of stuff," he said placing his hand back on the bed, as if he didn't have the strength to hold his arm up any longer. "How's things, and who's that? I see you have a lovely lady with you, James. Aren't you going introduce me?" He asked running his tired eyes up and down Eden.

"Yes, I have Charles. This is my lovely, crazy lady, Eden and her son, Jamie," he replied deciding to go with the flow as she nodded and smiled. Swooning inside, at his description. "Afternoon, Charles. I heard a lot about you, sir."

"We got the news when I went to drop off the camper. How are you feeling?" James inquired.

"Oh, I've been better. I got a little of my strength back, now. You didn't need to bring Clara back at all," he said with a cough as he moved both his hands to his sides to try to sit himself up on the bed. James looked across at Eden and they both automatically acted upon his wishes. Lifting him carefully, then sliding him backward as Eden carefully moved his head forward. She raised his pillows, then they gently rested it down again making his face strain, as he fought to clear his throat. Instinctively, she picked up the cardboard pot from beside the bed, and put it under his chin. He knowingly smiled, and then spat in to it.

"Oh gee, thanks Eden. This thing's certainly got the better of me, this time. I got troubles holding food down?" He said settling again, as she sat back down. "James, listen to me carefully," he wheezed. "My last will and testament is locked in the safe, at the garage. I had it changed quickly. It clearly states; Clara's yours along with some other things."

"What?"

"Oh, hush up, and heed my words. I don't have time for you to start questioning my judgement. Its lawyer legal, and I got it witnessed by Jake, from the shop next door. So there ain't a damn thing that, unrespectful toad of a niece of mine can do," he coughed. "But anyway, that's a done deed. So, tell me, where did you get this pretty young thing?" He shamelessly asked to Eden's blushing embarrassment.

"Oh, we got together last time I was here, Charles," he explained, deciding to keep him happy and looking at Abby to stay quiet. "She keeps me on my toes more than Abby," he said looking across the bed.

"She's almost as beautiful as you, Abby," he said laughing, then coughing up another mouthful of phlegm. "Well, you keep tight hold of her. I imagine she has a temper full of fire, with a heart of gold.

"I'm a Harlan girl, Charles. I keep him in real good check," she added nodding her head.

"That's good," he added breathlessly. "Harlan girls, can breathe fire. I should know. My dear wife was one and the same. I sincerely hope you're going to make an honest woman of her?"

Eden looked at James, as Abby looked at Jamie as the room door opened in the silence.

"Mr. Colville. It's time for your injection and the doctor is on his way. We have the test results this afternoon."

"Oh yes… tests," he frowned somewhat serious-faced, as Abby caressed his needled hand.

"Tests… Abby, more damn tests. I feel like a pin cushion. There's that many holes in my skin, I'm probably leaking out. The tests are only going to tell you what I already know. The devil dust is the death of me."

"We'll get out of your way and come back again, tomorrow," Eden said to the nurse who was watching at how upset Abby was becoming. She climbed onto the chair between her James's legs and planted a kiss on Charles's cheek. Then, she carefully climbed back down to the floor.

"Yes, we'll be back tomorrow. You'll probably be feeling a little better by then. You'll be back tinkering under the car bonnets before you know it," James assured Charles, as everybody stood out of the way to let the nurse do her thing.

"I won't be going anywhere, anymore," he smiled acceptingly. "So, give my love to Archie when you see him. Because now, he belongs to you. Look after the little scamp for me and look after my Bethany, I mean Abby. She's the double of my granddaughter, Eden," he added coughing profusely as the nurse stared at Abby.

THIRTY-TWO: *Face-off*

"Abbey will be just fine at Aunt May's," she informed James's thinking she was glad Abby wouldn't be able to see her at her worst, should Langdon wind her up. "There was a hell of a lot of folk at the last meeting. Brrgh, it's a bit cold in here, again. I hope this works out," she sighed. "I hope Dainty hasn't got his claws into anybody else, and we get as much interest for NO again. Oh look, there's Sheridan," she said smiling as he came rushing through the community hall doors, toward them.

"Sorry I'm late. Big family emergency," he explained panting and gathering himself together, and then looking inquisitively, at James.

"It's okay. I... erm... we were late. I had to ask Mamie pass the papers around while I went to the little girl's room. Anyway, this is James, but I call him mister-ecology."

"You call me anything, but my real name."

"Oh hush, mister-moan."

"Aah. So, this is the man you've never shut up about. Real pleased to meet you, James. She's talked about you so much, she's worn out your name." Sheridan said shaking his hand, and he nodded his head in acknowledgement.

"Oh, you shut up you, big liar," she blushed. "It looks like there's a lot more faces here tonight. Word must have got around at last," she said scanning the back of the audience. "What was your problem at home Sheridan? Oh, and is the fat parasite showing his face tonight?"

"We think Clay's broke his wrist or thumb playing cricket. His hand's like a bowling ball."

"Cricket? How did he get into that game? That's strictly for the English upper-class, isn't it," she teased looking at James, and then over Sheridan's shoulder as the halls outer doors opened.

"OMG. He's here.

"I know. I was just getting to that. He was getting out that black O.R.V, as I arrived," Sheridan explained motioning his eyes at her dumbstruck face as she turned around, to see Milton West opening the outer doors as, Langdon aggressively walked through the first door, then glanced through the internal door at straight at them. He abruptly stopped, to tokenistically look at a notice board on the wall. Scanning the advertisements as if he was either wasting time, or gathering a storm. As Milton waited beside *him*, like a frightened lap dog. Holding onto the inner door, as *he* casually cast another unforgiving eye at the countless flyers pinned on the cork. He snatched another glance at Eden, and then, at all the other silent onlookers.

"Oh, look West; *After-school programs. Educate, empower and encourage,* how very sweet," he shouted, sarcastically sneering to himself. "Ah, and another one here: *Have a happy, safe holiday time,'* pah...! Boloni! Pointless junk for pointless people and waste of good paper if you ask me. Open that damn door man, let's get this crap over and done with," he said prodding at Milton with his cane.

Milton opened the glass door, and stood with his back to it, as Langdon limped himself into the hall and gave another, steely eyed glance at the whole of room. Then, as he was nearing the front, he stopped at Eden's leaflet table. "Good evening Mr. Dainty, sir. I'm Sheridan Barley and this is Eden Buckley, and this is..."

"Yes, I know. James Ustinov from L.E.A.PS of London," Langdon replied fixing James with a blink-less stare as he turned his head and focused his attention at Eden. "Mmm, so you're the famous Buckley girl," he said to her silence as she wondered how the hell he knew James. "The one who refuses to take over Daddy's empire. I admire your spirit, and your tenacity, but nothing more," He said banging the tip of his cane on the floor, making her jump.

"Admire me... that so, huh? I can't say I admire anything about you. In fact, we were just wondering where your swollen fat ass was, before you so rudely walked in." She folded her arms and kicked her wooden chair onto the pew behind her, imitating his cane trick to good effect. "I'd say you're pretty much swollen in head and stomach, but weak in legs, and though sharp of tongue... you are obviously empty of brains you, ignorant piece of...!"

"Now... now, come on, people. Let's not turn this into a slanging match before we've even started," Sheridan said trying to calm the warring factions.

"And I believe a Harlan county girl, too. Now I heard a whisper that this whole place was overrun with witches back in the 1850s," Langdon continued, seemingly unaffected with her comments as he bent forward and moved into her personal space. "You may well be of that stock, lady," he stated grinning to himself. "Maybe, a second or third generation throw-back or even a direct descendent of the Clay's and the Turner's. Did you arrive here on your broom tonight, missy," he shouted to her offended disdain. "I'd advise you to get back on it, and be gone!" He cursed, pointing his cane in the air as the room silenced behind Eden.

"Hey, come on now. There's no need for that kind of talk. We're here to listen to the worries of the people. Not your personal agenda's or any other stupid-foul mouthed, crap."

"You're absolutely correct, Sheridan. There's no need for any of it, at all," James said, instantly putting himself in the firing line between, Eden and the fat man. "Let's all be civil. That goes for you, too, Mr. Dainty. You know how to be civil don't you?" James sternly questioned Langdon, who was now standing proud and turning to look at Eden before she had chance to say a thing. He shrugged it off, and limped away with Milton, rabidly twitching beside him. Then, he stopped once again, and turned around:

"A Garden of Eden family of witches? Mmm, quite plausible, don't you think."

Eden began to bite into her lip so hard, she almost split the skin. In the unexpected silence, a small queue of people was trying to get to some seats behind Langdon's walking bulk.

"Look, just head down there, and settle yourself into a seat," Sheridan asked in an angry tone.

"Yeah, move your fat ugly hide, before I do," Eden said gritting her teeth, and still trying to hold back from exploding.

"I wish you luck tonight, *Miss* Buckley," Langdon said curling his lip. "You'll need it," he added. "Oh, and it is, *miss,* isn't it...?" He asked in a false tone, looking over at James. "I just wondered, you see," he continued as he walked away. "I heard from a new employee of mine, that you are a *miss*, these days. Or was it, mess?" He added making her blood boil.

"You heard from who?" Eden asked, still biting.

"Oh, just a good man of mine. Very good, in fact. He sorts out certain kinds of problems for me... if you know what I mean," he paused. "He doubles as my chauffeur you know? As a matter of fact, he's waiting outside for me, as we speak. Kyle Tucker. He certainly knows you," he said turning the knife into her as deeply as he possibly could as he derided an evil wink her way, then turned and walked away.

"Damn him," she swallowed. Feeling shocked to the bone. "Damn the pair of them," she added looking at Langdon and Milton, but secretly thinking about Kyle.

"So, that's the nasty fellow you were telling me about," James falsified, somewhat under prescribing her fuel-filled hatred toward Langdon. But feeling even more relieved that Langdon had opted not to reveal that they had already met. "Maybe I'll have to have a little chat with, Mr. Dainty," he said cautiously. Annoyed with the way he'd spoken to her as he openly threw his arm around her for all to see. He hugged her hard and then whispered in her ear. "Sweetheart, I'll be right down at the front. And just you remember..." he said pushing her hair away from her face. "I'm by your side and, I believe in you." He said moving away, just far enough to drop his hands into her pockets, like he'd done before.

"James, stay here, with me. I need you to stay, forever."

"We'll talk... there'll be time for us to talk. Now go… and knock him dead," he said pulling her toward him and passionately kissing her neck, and sending shivers of hope down her spine. She looked up at the stage, and then sighed hard.

"Better to keep your distance, man. He's bad news," Sheridan said picking his papers up from the table as James watched his woman clench her fists, then walk away "I've got a little secret on the dirt-bag, that I'm saving for later. Oh, and by the way... I hope you do stay in her life, and do the man thing. She needs someone like you, James. Permanently."

"Ok people, can you hush down please," she shouted through the hall as she walked down the main aisle, striding calmly, confidently. Completely rejuvenated by James's positive words and almost ready for the fight of her life.

"I can hear a certain someone's presence is creating a noticeable stir in here tonight. Can we have a hail Mary for that?" She asked clapping her hands as the audience cheered. "It should make for some healthy debate, once our friend Sheridan from the state office opens a can of worms or two," she explained walking from the side aisle, across to the stage, and feeling all fired up and ready to get into her stride as Langdon looked at her, and fiddled with his cane.

"Just fill your papers in like you did last time, and pass them to the end of the aisle. Mamie will do the rest. There'll be a question and answer session again. But this time, you can fire all of those at your good friend and mine, Langdon Stanley Dainty," she explained to create a rowdy atmosphere. "Let's give them a nice round of applause," she said sarcastically, as the whole room began to jeer.

"He's a double-crossing double-dealing, scumbag," came a shouting voice.

"I'm gonna get a contract out on you, fatty," came another above the loud voices.

She proudly climbed the steps of the stage, turned around and threw a destructive glance at Langdon. Then, she looked at James, who gave her a smile, whilst looking at a somewhat nervous Langdon, with twitching Milton beside him. She lifted up her papers and was just about to speak. Then, she looked into the audience to be staggered numb by a somewhat slight wave from the back of the hall. It was her Mom and her Dad who had been sat listening to her, just two aisles down from her leaflet table.

As she acknowledged them, the hall doors creaked opened once more. This time, in strode Henry Creech with his Father, right by his side. As Henry senior took a seat, Henry junior stayed behind to hold the door open for someone else. As the whole hall waited with anticipation, Langdon's wife appeared in the silence, and pushing a wheelchair, which was somewhat heavily laden, with none other than, Langdon's great aunt.

THIRTY-THREE: *Colville's*

"Yes honey, we're on our way down. No, don't even talk to me about, James. I don't even want his name mentioned. Uh-huh... yeah. He introduced himself to Mom and Dad and stayed with them for a little while, which was fine. Then, he went talking with Henry which was great for the cause. But after all that, he went and spent the most of his time with the fat man. I couldn't hear a thing. I was talking with the Coal Cut kin. Oh, I nearly forgot, then he went and spoke to the fat man again, and you know what... I ain't seen the English pig, since. No... I know that, Page. I ain't stupid."

"Excuse me Mam. You're not supposed to use your mobile phone in the garage. That'll be thirty-bucks please," the man said waiting for Eden to pay her for the gas and food.

"Here's your thirty dollars. Oh, look. I'm awful sorry sir, I know that, but this call is very important... *No Page... I'm talking to this fella, right here... I've tried his phone more than a dozen times. He could be plain dead for all I know. Yes, it's working fine. He just won't pick it up, the English toad. I've just been to the project house in Evarts, and he isn't there, either? Oh, sorry. That's his work place. Oh, and another thing,"* she said taking a deep breath. *"You'll never guess who the fat man has got working for him. Huh? Hello?*

Sorry, you broke up there. Yes, of all people, Kyle. He was outside in the car to pick him up after the meeting. No, to pick up the fat man not, James. God, Page, are you even listening to me? I got no idea what the hell's going on, but he'd better have an explanation. No! I'm not jumping to conclusions... I'm just worried about everything. Wouldn't you be, if Mark disappeared? I know he's not my husband.... but he's my friend, and it's just well, strange. Yes.... it is! I told you we we're coming to you."

"Excuse me Mam... the phone... it's against the law..."

"I know... I know... I'm sorry. I'll take these to, please. *Yes Page... we're going to the kayak race on our own. Stuff, James. After that, we'll be on our way to you. We're meeting* Stephen *Foster at Clover fork, just above Evarts. When they set out on the river, I'm driving down to the finish line at the other side of the tunnels. Yes, Stephen Foster, from school. I didn't want to leave Jamie up there on his own. It's his first-time. Once he sets off, it's all downhill. Hah! Just like my damn love-life. Yes, I know. I'm stressed out of my head with Jamie's big day as it is. Abby should have been with us as well. Oh, I'm fuming inside. Some Fourth of July this turned out to be. I know... I'm being plain stupid. It's just that, whenever I think I've found something really good, it seems to disappear through my hands like water. Listen... I'd better switch off this phone or this gas-man will stare my ass to stone. Would you try get in touch with Dad or Mom, and see if they've heard anything since yesterday. Oh, I don't know, there's nobody else I know. It's worth a try. Ok honey, see you later, bye."*

"I hope everything's okay, Mam? That'll be another three dollars erm, for the drinks."

"Look, I'm very sorry, sir. I'm all over the place at the moment. My apologies for ignoring you, about the phone. My head's up my butt today. Oh, and sorry again. I shouldn't be burdening you with my personal crap anyhow."

"That's ok miss, we all get days like that. Try not to think about it too much. I'm sure things will sort themselves out. Sometimes it's better talking to a complete stranger."

"That's easy for you to say, sir," she said fidgeting in her purse. "I don't know where I am with this, and that... with him... and with my damn heart."

"Does he, love you?"

"Oh, I don't know... I think... I... hope so?"

"Do you, love him?"

"As much as I could at the moment, the pig! Sorry."

"Everything happens for a reason, honey. One more thing. Do you trust him?"

"With my life."

"Then just trust in him. It'll all work out fine. You'll see. Here's your change. You might be deceived if you trust too much. But, you'll live in torment, if you don't trust at all. You have a nice day, Mam."

THIRTY-FOUR: *Kayak race*

"Come on, Mom. Oh, look there's Jayden from school. He's doing it as well. He's talking to my sponsor. I'm going to see him," he excitedly explained, forgetting all about his hip, and running toward his waving friend who was stood amongst the others on the warm summer day. Eden followed him as yet another dozen kids that were roughly the same age as her son happily climbed into their own kayaks, bobbing on the busy river.

"Well, I never... Stephen Foster. Golly, small world," she joked as she neared her school friend and Jamie's sponsor. "How are you, man of watery talents," she exclaimed throwing her arms around his shoulders from behind.

"Look who, it isn't, Eden *the crazy*.... OMG, come here, honey. How the hell are you? In fact, when was the last time I saw you?" He announced turning around to hug her, and resting his rotomolded, dual-kayak from a trailer on to the grass and giving her a kiss and a hard, high-five.

"Oh, come on," she perked. Leaning back with her arms wide open, as James completely slipped from her mind. "The fresher's ball at Lexington remember. We were a double-blind date. That was when you could be bothered to get off the damn guitar long enough. I hated that guitar so much back then. Are you still playing?"

"Of course, I am. I got my little recording studio and practice room built onto the kayak center in Putney. My guitar, and Harlan county campground are my two life constants. Along with the boss-lady and kids, of course," he joked. "My son was going be competing today. He's the same age as Jamie too. But he's off to the black mountain, with his Grandpa. Anyway, little fella how is you today? I see you're all ready to run. Does everything fit ok?" He asked looking at Jamie's wet gear. "I was sorry to hear about you and... you know," he whispered spelling K.Y.L.E out, and motioning drinking a glass of beer.

"The helmet's a bit loose, Stephen," Jamie replied, pulling down on his loose lid.

"Oh, that's ok. Life goes on, and we move on," she explained playing things down. Thinking about Kyle, and then James and his absence from her day. "I'm happy, Stephen. I got this little blessing now. Everything will be ok today, won't it?" she asked looking down at Jamie.

"Don't listen to her getting all sorry for herself, Stephen. Ask her about James," he tweaked, with a grown-up style similar to Abby's.

"Oh, James, huh? Take the lid off and let me alter the strap. Who's he then?" He asked laughing, as Jamie passed him the black helmet. "Your Mom always played her cards close to her chest. As long as she's happy, that's all that matters," he confirmed. Moving on to a different subject that he could see she seemed more anxious about. "Listen, Eden. He'll be totally safe. There's not a single thing to worry about. There's been a little heavy rain the past few nights, that's all. It just means the clover gauge runs a little higher and faster. But it's a nice, short class 3/2 race with just ten Kayaks, per race. So, it'll be over and done, in no time at all," he explained pulling the safety strap tighter and replacing it on Jamie's head. "Try that, little man."

"He's English, and we're moving to England," Jamie added, grinning and fastening the cap brace.

"Oh, take no notice of him. He's teasing me again, that's all. He was around, but he's, up and, he's gone now, I guess I scared him off. Just like I did you," she added feeling sorry for herself. "He was supposed to be here with us today. But I'm sure we'll manage just fine without him. Isn't that right, baby?"

"That's us kid," Stephen said checking the helmet a last time. "I think we're about ready to jam. See this Kayak Eden, number 7? It's the only blue one in the line-up, so you can't miss us. It's called a perception tribe. It puts our feet level with the body instead of the normal, skew angle. So, it helps with posture, control and comfort which will be good for his hip. It ain't no slower either Jamie, so you'll still have hold on to your ass.

Get a good spot at the end of the tunnels, and it'll either be the first or second tunnel from the right we go through. We'll hit a bit of white-water when we come out. But we'll soon slow down, into the calmer wash at the end. You need to keep your wits about you, little man. When we come to the tunnel *in* mouth, keep your blade out of the water, and leave all the paddling to me. Lay it across the boat until we get back side, and I'll get us over the finish line, safe. Oh, there's two other bits of the water run you need to know." Jamie listened hard trying his best to grasp all the information.

"*Whitefield* shoals is our first, 100 yard rapid. Then we hit *Bounce the baby*, where we stay river-right, down the wave train, until we see the tunnels."

"*Bounce the baby...* hah, sounds really cool, hey Mom?"

"Now... the tunnels sound pretty scary. But there as smooth as a baby's back-side, and also rapid free. The ride *in* tunnel is fast and choppy, but don't worry too much about losing the light. There's enough light to see our way through. Once we're at the *out* section, we're on a big tip-slide to glory," he confidently explained. "There might be a strong *Edie currents*, because of the high waters, but nothing to worry on. I'll be taking all the slack, and real good care of everything. Are you both okay with that?"

"Just you keep my baby safe, Stephen. How long will it take, from top to bottom?"

"End to end, about a mile, all told. Which is fifteen to twenty minutes, all in? Once we're down in the play-boat holes, you can mess around a while before my van-man comes and gets me for the next pass, okay." He looked at Jamie's face of fear and excitement. "Ok, little buddy, let's go. We'll see you when we get on through to the other side."

"I know you could have picked him up at the bottom, Stephen. But I just wanted to come and check, to be sure of everything"

"It'll be great. I'm sure of it. Just you make sure you take some pictures of us for him. Then I can pinch copies, and mount some on the walls of the kayak center."

"I will. What's the start time? I hope I have enough breathing space to get down to the finish?"

"Oh, chill Eden. You have a world of time. Ok, let's synchronize watches. I make it 13-15, check?" He said in a teasing manner, seeing she was already worrying and looking at her watch.

"I have 13-18."

"We're off at 14-00. That gives you 45 minutes to get down there. Hell, I can walk it in that time, with my kayak on my back... twice!" He smiled. "Now get your ass out of here girl!" She waved at her excited son, and rushed away. Trying to be brave as possible. In her head, it felt like she'd allowed her pride and joy to risk his life, just for an adrenalin kick. Which made no sense to her whatsoever? She walked out of the wooded area, and the 20 yards to the car, constantly looking at her watch, and feeling like forever had begun. She got back to the Mustang to see Bailey's head, still hanging out of the half-open window. With his long tongue hanging to one side of his white teeth, as he panted in the warm, afternoon sun. She looked behind the car and could see someone else had pulled up, and partially blocked her in. They were all smiles, and oblivious to her time constraints, and kitted out to enjoy an afternoon of much the same as Jamie. The muscle-bound Dad was pulling a kayak from the top of his car, as if it were a twig, while his two sons watched and waited, talking rapids, and water and waves.

"Excuse me sir, I gotta get my car out of here, like... yesterday."

"Yes Mam, I get that. But I'm just dropping this hulking piece of junk for these two, kayak fish." He said as he placed the striking, bright-red kayak on the grass beside her feet.

"No. You don't understand. You, need to move, right now. I'll have to get down to the tunnel *out* side, pronto. My own son is in a race at 14-00, and it's his first time."

He looked at his watch as he opened his car door. "There's a pretty reasonable gap right their lady, but I'll just reverse a little for you. Time's only sitting at a quarter past," he smiled, looking at her confused face in the same manner as she watched his actions. Wondering who the hell she was to give him any of her time constraints.

As she waited, she quietened her thoughts. Realising, that because of her worries, she was totally over compensating for absolutely everything. She decided to stop her fears at once. Deciding that things will go just as her trusted friend, Stephen had planned. She reassured herself again, as she watched the stocky man reverse his car to leave a gap so big, you could drive a truck through it.

"Sorry, sir. It's my first time as well. I'm, just a little...."

"That's okay. I don't blame you. I was exactly the same when my youngest took a hold in this crazy sport. Turns out, I was just being darn stupid. Worst is, I couldn't even swim you see. I looked a complete fool, because he's the best in his class now. As a forfeit, he made me take swim lessons after that," he affirmed, pleasantly smiling and lifting the tip of the kayak already being held up in the air at the other end by his two patiently waiting sons.

She arrived at clover fork tunnels in less than ten minutes. Ten minutes to long to be thinking about James. As she looked down to the waterside, the on-site ambulance entered her vision, and bad thoughts appeared, in seconds. She blocked them out, and put on Bailey's lead as her mind wondered back to thoughts of James. 'Are you alive...? Why are you as unreliable as Kyle...? Why haven't you called, and what made me trust you in the first place...?' She muttered, shaking her head, and feeling she was pushing herself into overload. "Oh, shut up Eden. Just forget him for today girl. He must have a perfectly good reason. I need to learn to trust him. Come on Bailey, I've been neglecting you, haven't I? You'll always be my number one, man," she said clipping on his lead and grabbed a small bottle of water, and tucking it into her pocket. She locked the car, then glanced at her silent mobile sat in her top pocket. Wishing it would ring. She walked down the hill, some thirty yards to the congregation of onlookers who were waiting around at the edge of the fast-flowing water.

As she walked down the path, she glanced over the river to see five kayaks in the calm water. Just play boating, as the watching congregated people chatted and patiently waited for the next cavalcade of eager, kayak kids to arrive. She made her way toward the finish line that was visually and physically suspended from each river bank, on two tall steel poles with a somewhat older man, similar to Charles, standing beside the pole on her side. He was smoking a rolled-up cigarette, and constantly looking at his watch. He looked up, and spotted her through his sun shades, as she walked slowly toward him.

"Afternoon, miss. Lovely day for it."

"Oh yes sir. It's a beautiful day," she replied nonchalantly, not giving a fig if it was hail, rain or snow. "I heard the water's a little higher today?" She said motioning to the swirling wash, coming through the ends of the four tunnels.

"Oh yes. The river's much busier today. Are you okay, Mam? You look kinda... hold on," he said clicking his fingers. "First time... huh," he smiled.

"You got that right! I'm a kayak virgin," she sighed as he nodded back, realising she was looking pretty damn clueless to everything, as he puffed on his smoke. She sat down on the bank beside the man and started chatting about all things water, until a hand tapped weakly on her shoulder. She turned away from the man and the busy river, to see Milton West stood behind, and looking at her with a huge camera, that was dangling precariously around his neck. Almost, as if it was pulling his weak body to the floor. Beside him, was a somewhat, *mini-me* version of himself. Dressed in a lifejacket and removing a large pair of goggles. "Erm, hello, Eden. Nice to see you relaxing and not taxing yourself with work," he said pleasantly smiling.

"Oh. Hello, Milton," she replied deciding to be as polite as possible and staring at his doppelgänger son. "Are you both having a nice time?"

"Nice time... it's my first time, and its brilliant, Mam. My Dad took some pictures of me on the water. By the way, I'm Gregory. Pleased to meet you. Do you work with dad?"

"Erm, I suppose, I do," she garnished. "We have our little work fights from time to time, but your Dad's a good soul," she smiled. "Did you have a good ride? It's my son's first today. It isn't too choppy and dangerous is it?" She asked turning her attentions straight back to her vacant son.

"No. Nothing like that, Mam. It's a blast. I'm going to get changed, Dad. Nice meeting you, Mam."

"Ditto Gregory," she said as he walked away, leaving her looking at Milton.

"I... I erm. Look, I know you don't like me much, miss, Buckley. But as I was waiting for my son, I saw you coming down the path."

"Uh huh," she agreed waiting for him to elaborate.

"I just wanted to say, that I admire everything you're doing, in regard to the people and their homes, and the swamp," he said taking a deep breath. "I think you're a very brave woman, indeed. I truly hope everything works out the way it should under God's eyes, and to your advantage."

"My advantage?"

"Yes, everything you're fighting for, is the right thing to do. To be perfectly honest, I hate my job. I hate working for that insufferable man, as well. We shouldn't even be talking about him, anyway. This is your son's big day, so you just have a great time with him."

"Thanks Milton. It's very kind of you to say that." She said as he walked away leaving her lost for words, as she instantly turned her attentions back to the old man in front of her.

"Have there been any problems today, sir?"

"Nope. Just a few disturbed tree limbs floating around. But the river and kids can deal with those, as they appear. Maybe you should be having one of these things to calm your nerves," he joked pulling his cigarette from between his lips.

"Drover one, drover two, that's a go... I repeat, that's a go." The man's pocket hitched radio shouted.

"Oh, hey now. That's the two o'clock shot on their way down." He pulled the radio from his pocket, and took off his sun shades for a clearer view upstream:

"*Drover two, copy that, loud and clear, over.*" They don't take long to get down here, Mam. There're ten kayaks in the soup for this one. Conditions must be the same, or they'd have let me know any different," he said pulling down on his peak to shade his eyes from the sun.

"My son has a hip disease, he's plenty mobile but you know how we worry."

"Is he in a dual?" The man asked continuing to focus his gaze at the tunnels.

"Oh, sorry yes," she replied gulping on her water, then replacing it in her hand with her mobile from her pocket. She dropped Baileys lead to the grass and threaded its leather hand strap loosely over her training shoe at the bottom of her skin-tight jeans. Realising, somewhat stupidly, that if Bailey saw Jamie and made a sudden bolt toward the water, she'd be going for swift and unscheduled dip as well.

#

"Hey, great start little man! Can you hear me okay, Jamie? How you feeling fella?"

"Wow, this is sooo great. I can hear you just fine, Stephen. It's so fast, huh."

"Sure is. Whitefield shoals is faster than usual, today. We're all pretty much spread even across the water, see." He nodded to the line of kayaks either side, as he glanced again to see more vessels to his right than to the left.

"The water's going to change when we take that right corner ahead," he said as they navigated the kayak toward the bend and looked at the twigs, tree stumps and roots along both the sides of the river. They turned the river bend, and a rushing spray of water hit the main body of the boat. Splashing hard onto their goggles.

"Okay now. Just be aware. It'll get a little choppy for a while."

"It's okay, I'm good... wow the white waves, cool," Jamie shouted above the loud surge of water as a kayak came bouncing across the white-water from their right side, overtaking them in the middle, and pushing them over to the left.

#

James parked the project van right behind Eden's Mustang. He looked
inside, as Abby joined him, holding Archie on the lead beside her. Archie
sniffed madly at the grass as they noticed the Mustang window, partially
open.
"They must be down the bottom, sweetheart," he said motioning toward the
river as they took the same path toward the people in the middle distance.

#

"Right, that's us in the *bouncing baby*. Brace yourself Jamie, this looks awful
choppy today! We didn't need the stupid line he's just made us take, either?
There's another kayak coming through behind us as well," he shouted seeing
the burgeoning water riding kayak appearing from nowhere, right by their
side. Realising he'd better shut his mouth as not to alarm his rapids partner
to the trickier and more technical, rocky tree line that they were now,
unwittingly taking. Their kayak slid and slewed closer to the bank, giving
Stephen the distinct feeling that they were now committed to river-right,
with nowhere else to go.

#

"How long before they come through the tunnel end, Mister?" She fretfully
asked the old man who'd moved lower to the rushing river edge, to improve
his view?
"Couple of minutes, I guess!" He shouted leaning perilously over and above
the vast surge. "I need to blow this whistle once when the first come

through. Twice, when they cross the line."

"Hold on, real tight, Jamie. The tunnel entrance is right there," he shouted, guiding the kayak slightly to the left with his paddle. The cross-water hit both their goggles with another water smack, as Stephen remained silent and concentrated on his paddle strokes. He compensated fast, plunging his paddle into the water, hard right. Somewhat slowing them down, and guiding the kayak's front tip, so it would shift across to the same path the other three kayaks had just taken when passing. As he did, Jamie shook his head to rid his goggles of the spray. Once he'd wiped them, he saw a large tree stump bobbing in the center of their path toward the second tunnel. "Stephen, look! There's a..."
"I see it!"
The riders at the front quickly glanced back, to survey the blue kayak's progress, in light of the obstacle in front. Then, they disappeared into the far-right tunnel, as Stephen ran through a busier water shoals, just before the entrance. Just then, another kayak appeared and overtook them. Heading for the normal, right tunnel path. He glanced across at them, then back at the stump, simply that hadn't moved.
"Hold tight, little-man. I need to pull us right, before we hit that damn..." He thrashed his paddle into the water, to pull the body of the boat right. But it was too late. The side of the kayak made a dull and deadened thud into the much larger looking stump at Jamie's left, making him scream at the top of his voice.
"NOOOO!"
The strength of the hit had shuddered the kayak almost to a stop, and caused enough force to rip Jamie from his seat, and through the plastic liner, right out of the vessel and its polyethylene body. Aimlessly ejecting both

him and his paddle into the cold, fast water. Stephen quickly corrected the boats path, but it was now, one passenger less. Jamie had disappeared beneath the water, just as the kayak slipped into the tunnel.

#

"Oh, look. Here we are… here's the first one," the man said blowing on his whistle to the crowd's cheers, as Eden sat with a worried face, beside him.

#

"Look, Dad. At the edge of the water. There she is. Her red hair's given her away," Abby said picking Eden out from the crowd. Huddled near the finish line with everyone poised at the tunnels edge with their cameras and mobile phones as the first kayak journeyed itself expertly through the faster water and into the slow rapids. Then, through the slower backwash, and finally, into the white swirls, as it closed in on the finish line. It was quickly joined with another three boats, who were nestled together, just behind.
 The man strenuously blew on his whistle, as Eden stood up with her hand across her mouth.

#

"Are you alright, back there?" He shouted watching Jamie courageously holding on tight to the rear of the kayak.
 "Yes… it's freezing, though," he replied, still smiling as he received a mouthful of water for his troubles.
 "Now just you hold on real tight, we're almost through," Stephen shouted as his words echoed through the tunnel as he sensed the daylight become brighter. "When we reach the end, I'll jump out and grab you," he said,

looking back and seeing another kayak, close behind. "You can let go of the boat when you feel my hands. Our life-jackets will keep us safe. Now keep a tight hold.... just a few seconds more."

#

"How many is that now, mister? I've lost count," she asked kneeling back down so he could hear her above the noise.

"That's eight, Mam. Just two left. I'm guessing your boy isn't out yet?" He said without looking at her and continuing to concentrate on the tunnels.

"No, he isn't. Oh, I don't like this, at all," she ventured as the blue kayak suddenly appeared upside down from the tunnel mouth making her scream, and helplessly fall forward onto her knees. The two bobbing bodies rapidly followed the kayak into the white-water backwash, then disappeared beneath the waves.

#

"Abby, there must be something wrong. Go straight to Eden's side," he said recognising her screams in seconds. "I'll be right with you," he said furiously running across the grass to the furthest point to his right, and as close to the tunnels edge, as he dared. Within seconds, his mind was in a zone. Just like it was, at the commonwealth games. At full tilt, he galloped to the edge of the river, took a last look at his targets, and dived into the swirling, abyss of water. He crashed into the waves, almost twenty feet from his launching spot. Then, disappeared under the fierce, white swell.

"Hi Eden. It's me. Look, don't worry. My Dad's on the case," Abby explained, putting her hand on her shoulder as Bailey and Archie got to know each other.

"What...! Abby, where's James. And, where the hell, is Jamie...?" She shouted, shocked and scared out of her wits. She turned back around to the watery scene to see the two heads were still bobbing, but much closer together. And another, swimming perilously but adeptly through the water, and toward them from the opposite side.

"In the water. They are both okay. Dad's a great swimmer. They'll be out in no time. He'll make sure Jamie's fine," she inferred as if this was the type of thing he did on a daily basis. Eden stood up, feeling more than overwhelmed, and in disbelief. After less than a minute, the three floating heads had traversed themselves through the heavy waters to reaching the calmer swells to be greeted by a multitude of resounding claps, and cheers from the assembled crowd. They continued floating downstream together, until they could safely walk freely, through the shallow flows of water. Everybody watched delighted, as James disappeared under the water, soon to quickly reappear with Jamie sitting on his shoulders, for the second time. As they got to the river bank they were greeted by a mass of camera and mobile phone flashes. As James lifted Jamie onto the side, he ran straight into his mother's waiting arms.

"OMG! Thank you, mister-dolphin! I don't know what else to say," she shouted lovingly hugging her son.

"No problem, Eden, I enjoyed that. A very brisk swim, indeed," he explained climbing up the bank with Stephen as she looked on, still astounded and puzzled.

"I enjoyed it to, Mom. I didn't expect to fall out though," he said with a smile.

"Neither did I. Because that wasn't supposed to happen. I'm sorry Eden, the high water loosened up the dead tree roots far more than we expected. It was a mighty big stump we hit back there, huh, little feller. Almost as big as a house eh?" he suggested smiling at Jamie.

"Yeah, it was."

"Yep. But you held on like a clamp to the kayak. A full 590 yards, and all the way through that tunnel. So, well done, little man."

"He seems fine. Please accept my gratitude, the pair of you. I'm eternally grateful. Now, come on trouble. We need to get you out of those wet clothes. I put some in the Mustang, just in case. Good job, huh?" She swished his wet blond hair with her hand. "I'm afraid I've nothing that'll fit you, honey," she said frowning and looking at James soaked attire, and grinning.

"I'll be ok," he smiled.

"My drivers here in the van. You can go get changed inside, Jamie, away from the crowd. I'll see you over there," Stephen said walking away and deciding to leave the ready-made family alone.

"Give me the keys, and I'll go and get Jamie's clothes," Abby perked.

"Here you go, honey," Eden said throwing over the keys. "As for you mister breast-stroke. YOU, must be out of your damn mind!" She replied thankfully, but still dismayed as they walked together towards Stephen's van.

"I'll give you a breast-stroke if you don't shut up, come here." He said grabbing her arms and throwing them over his shoulders as he kissed her so hard, he almost took the wind out of her lungs. "I missed you," he said as she sighed and burst out laughing with a tear in her eye.

"Not half as much as I missed you. I'm so happy to see you. I thought you'd run out on me, again?"

"That would never happen." he replied putting his wet arm across her shoulder.

"Hey, mister-soak! That was some incredible swimming back there. Are you some kind of human robot?"

"I told you he was a good swimmer," Abby added, walking away with the keys and both the dogs.

"I represented England for the commonwealth games in, 2002. Maybe I forgot to mention that?"

"Really...? Now I know where all those muscles come from," she said totally over the moon.

"I only got second, though."

"Oh, and so modest. You, big chump."

Stephen opened the kayak van door, and Jamie jumped in. Waiting for Abby to return with his dry clothes and leaving his mum and James sitting alone on the grass.

"What's going on, James? I was so worried. I haven't heard from you in three days. Have I done something wrong? Have I pushed too far, too soon? I don't want you to keep running away, I want you to stay. You did say we could talk. I need to know you feel the same?" She said furrowing her brow and touching his wet hair as she watched Abby walking back with the clothes.

"It isn't like that, at all," he said to her confused expression. "There's just some difficult things happened, since I arrived. There's more happened since I was last with you, as well. It's all bad news," he said seriously, then zoning in on her eyes and putting his hand softly on her face.

"Did you get them, honey?" Eden interrupted, as Abby appeared beside her, laden with clothes. "Go on, inside the van and help him out. When you're all done, go and get yourselves something from the refreshment tent," she explained, palming her five dollars and pointing across the field as Abby slid open the van door.

"Will do," Abby replied as Eden closed the door tight, to stop them hearing anything.

"Charles has died. And I have to find a way to break the news to her."

"Oh no. I'm truly sorry. She really took a shine to him, didn't she?"

"Yes, and he took a shine to all of us... especially her. That's why it's going to be so bloody hard telling her."

"What else has happened?" she asked, listening hard in case the van door opened.

"It's complicated, Eden. But it's nothing for you to worry about."

"Oh great. That sound's incredibly familiar," she tutted thinking the worst.

"It's nothing to do with US.... sweetheart. It's just work."

"Of course, it is. And now we're just going to go around in more damn

circles," she said crossing her arms and nervously spinning her foot.
"Now you just hold on a minute."

"No, James... you hold on... I want to know that you're going to at least be around. I need you.... Oh, sh... ucks! There you go, see. You nearly made me say it," she grimaced realising her heart was now firmly on her sleeve.

"I didn't make you do anything... I never would. There're some important decisions for me to make and to do that, I might have to. NO, I will have to go back to England, and as soon as possible," he said as she put her hands across her ears in a negative way.

"Ah, just go on ahead and run away again. Typical man. I probably won't even see you again."

"Will you please stop being so bloody melodramatic? I can't go until the other things are sorted out here."

You know what Ustinov, you're sound like the riddler. A riddler of a web of lies and deceit. And while we're on the subject, are you in cahoots with Langdon?"

"Cahoots! Oh really, Eden? Well, if that's how you think of me, then maybe we're doomed before we've even started?" He retorted as a van door opened. In the heat of their words, they'd both forgotten about the kids who were still happily talking in the back as Stephen slammed the front door back over again. Eden and James sighed, gave each other a black look, and continued their argument.

"I couldn't get in touch in case my phone has been bugged. Abby's phone to, for that matter," he explained as she stormed away, heading for the refreshment tent. He quickly followed, squelching in his wet shoes as he gave chase.

#

"What's going on out there, Abby?"

"Not a lot. I think it's their first argument. Oh well, it happens. We can't all live in complete harmony, all the time," she said as calmly, that if she were any more laid back and wise, she'd be lying horizontal, and creating world peace. "I'm going to have a go at that kayaking one day. It looks great."

"Argument?"

"Yes. It's what adults do best. The love things are getting quite serious between them now. I think they're going to be needing our help sooner than I thought. So, you need to be with me on this. It's for their own good, and ours."

"Oh, ok then. Cool by me. Tower of London, here I come."

"Now. Here's what I think we might have to do."

#

"Go away, James!"

"I won't."

"You're workin' for the fat man, ain't you," she said in the most Kentucky drawl he'd heard her speak so far."

"Don't be so bloody stupid, Eden. Listen to yourself, all Harlan tongue again. Seems like you do that, the angrier you get?"

"Uh huh. And you ain't seen nothin' yet! Listen to me, stupid ass. Cos you ain't even seen me angry, yet."

"Then maybe I should. Just to see what you're really like, and what I *might be's lettin' myself' infers,"* he drawled, goading her accent.

"Don't you dare imitate me? Oh, never mind. Just shut your stupid English mouth. Why do you do this to me, all the time...? I love you Goddammit!" she shouted to his silence. "Argh! You see what you made me do now! Aargh! You are insufferable, James Ustinov."

"Maybe I am. And maybe that's why you love me?"

"Huh?" She stopped in her stride and turned to face him.

"Well, as were saying things as they should be. I love you too!" He affirmed looking back toward the van, and the kids. "So, while you're ripping truths out of me, I'll tell you something else," he explained as she stood silent, with one leg crossed over the other, and her arms tightly folded, biting on her lip.

"Abby's not biologically mine," he said to her open mouthed, shocked and contorted face. "She knows it, and now, so do you. Talk about laying my life on the line for love? He frowned angrily, as he regained his composure and pulled her arms apart to hold both her hands. "If *we*, are to be here with *you* and Jamie, I need to get permissions from her other guardians. And that isn't going to be easy."

Eden, are you ok? Are you even listening to me?" He asked to her mummified shock. "There's other things," he continued to her staid silence. "But they're achievable and nothing to do with us being together. I can and am, working them out. So, you just listen carefully to me. With my hand on my heart, I all need to know is that you'll understand. Even though at the moment, I can't tell you everything. Remember the trust thing we said. The pledge we made to each other. It still stands, and it needs to be stronger than ever," he said softly rubbing a tear off her cheek with his thumb as she bowed her head.

"The other things are almost as important as our future together. It wouldn't be so bad, but they're not even my doing. I'm just lumbered with them. I need to sort them for the good of you, me, the kids and the people at Coal Cut. So please, will you try to understand," he pleaded wrapping his arms around her. I'm acting the way I am, for the greater good of everyone. I shouldn't even be here. If what's happened at this event and the kayak race gets reported by some local newspaper. A certain someone's going to put two and two together, and be hunting me down. That's another reason I can't see you. If anyone touches a hair on your or Jamie's head, I couldn't live with myself. You're as deep in this as you need to be. I won't have you involved any deeper than you already are. If anyone works out me and you are an item, I'll have ruined everything for everyone."

James stopped talking, and they looked at each other as if they were somehow feeling the same force of understanding. She kept quiet for a minute longer, then, she took his hand.

"How long will you be gone? I... we... could come to England with you?" She said throwing her head into his chest as he wrapped his arms tighter around her body. He gently lifted her head to face his. As he did, he saw two more identical tears rolling down her cheeks. He wiped them away, and pushed her head back into his chest as the door to the van opened, once again.

"Back in a minute, Mom. We're going for sweet treats. Have you been crying?"

"Erm, no it's this idiot making me laugh so much. Ok baby, take your time. We'll see you both at the Mustang." Abby gave them a silent knowing look, and turned on her heel. As they both walked toward the refreshment tent, Eden and James walked to the car park, hand in hand.

"I'll be here for a few more days, and then I'll have to leave. I need you to bring the next road meeting forward, and then I can attend, before I go. That's honestly, all I can say." He stopped and pulled her toward him again. "I know it's what I want, and I know Abby will want it."

"Bring it forward?" She stopped and looked up at him as her heart beat out a rage of emotion.

"Yes, forward. Please, now no more questions, I think we've said more than enough. I can't see you again, until the meeting. I don't want to blow this thing, because there's a lot of people's lives involved. I'll make everything up to you after the meeting, I swear."

"How do you know it's what Abby wants, James?"

"Because I'm her father."

"Okay. I trust you and I'll do as you say," she whispered. "In fact, I'll do anything you ask of me. It might take a bit of work to move the meeting forward. But I'm prepared to do anything for what I have in my hand and my heart right now. If we have to be apart to be together, then so be it," she said as they reached the crest of the hill.

"So, I guess, this is it then," she said gripping tight into his hand.

"Yes Eden, for now.... just be patient, and be strong."

THIRTY-FIVE: *Arson call to arms*

"Who's that?"

"Me. I decided to ring you, myself."

"That right?"

"Don't give me any lip boy, it's time to do your thing, right now."

"Huh? You said we'd be doing this under the cover of night. I don't like the idea of..."

"Just shut you're God-damn mouth, boy. By the time you get up there, the light will be fading. I don't want some half-assed job, either. I want ashes and cinders. Desecration and ruin. All burned to the ground. I got torched at the housing meeting by every single idiot there. So that's what I'm going to do back to them, and to this damn swamp. Burn every last piece of ground at the place, you hear?"

"I hear you..."

"How much fuel are you taking up?"

"Six, 5-gallon tubs of gas and four, 5-gallon drums of diesel. More than plenty."

"Did I ask you for your opinion?"

"Erm, no sir."

"Take ten gallons of each."

"But sir. That'll hardly fit in the pick-up, if it even does at all."

"You know something, you don't even talk proper? Get a bigger vehicle. I don't care what you have to do, just do it. I'm making a point here. Teaching people a hard lesson that they don't wanna ever mess with me. Particularly our swamp owner and that red-haired witch. I've got an English biologist on my side now. So, this'll be the final flame to the coffin. I've been building this fire a long damn time. Now I'm ready to strike the match on all their sorry asses."

"As you wish."

"I do. You sound much better, when I hear nothing at all.

"Mmm," Josh said to the dead phone line.

THIRTY-SIX: *The trap*

"I hope this works, Joe?"

"Oh, it'll work just fine. I'm just hoping on these idiots coming when the fat man told you. Otherwise, all it will be all for nothing. I don't envy your quandary either," Joe replied.

"Listen up. You two can go soon. Me and Abby can finish everything up here, and then go check on the recording gear in the van. I'd just like to speak to the Chief of Police you tipped off, before you leave. He has to be familiar with my voice."

"I don't envy any of either, and I'm embroiled in the middle of the whole damn thing. Ouch my hand! This is the worst Fourth of July celebration I've ever had?" Sheridan grumbled.

"Personally Dad, I think it's pretty cool. A stake out in the old green swamp machine. Never done a stake out before, and we don't celebrate the Fourth of July in England," Abby shouted, passing a screwdriver to her Dad as Joe walked toward him and she walked away.

"It must be just like our bonfire night at home. I don't like bonfires. Abby, go get me another ball of cable from the van," he asked fastening another tree clamp as she nodded, and ran through the bushes. "Sheridan, get yourself out of here now, you've done more than enough. Get home to your family and the celebrations. That's an order."

"I think you're right, James," Joe said watching Abby disappear, and then taking out his mobile. "Keeping her busy, will take her mind off, Charles."

"I know, I don't think it's sunk in yet. But she'll be okay. She's better with grief than me. I was a wreck when we lost her Mum. It was Abby I got my strength from."

"James. I need to ask you something one more time. Just to help me understand," he bluntly inquired. "You say you're going to look after my daughter. Are you gonna marry her after all this crazy mess is over?" He quizzed. "The thing is, I just need to know that you mean what you say." James was about to speak, as Joe continued. "She's had a lot of heartaches and lonesome time since that SOB, Kyle. I don't want you breaking her heart and her spirit, like he did. I honestly don't think she'd could handle that hurt again."

"Here you go, Dad, I'll go and help Sheridan with the last bit. I think he's struggling over there," she affirmed reappearing with the cable and overhearing them talking. Instinctively knowing to get out of the way.

"I promise you this day, in this beautiful place, and on my child's life. I'll try to be true to her, for the rest of her days. I also need you to know that I haven't gone into this lightly either. Every day, I've spent with her has been a day of pure joy, and that is something that started the faint flicker of light at the end of a very dark tunnel inside me. It's only been a fleeting romance, I'll give you that. But I know how I feel in here. It's grown and it's still growing She doesn't know how I feel deep down, because I'm too bloody stupid to show it. Plus, I blame my Mum and Dad for hiding my feelings. God bless them. Bringing me up to wash over every single emotion or word. I never imagined I'd feel this way about any woman, ever again. Your daughter is a woman of special beauty. Inside and out. She's also naturally gifted with grit and determination. She has a natural loving way, with heart of pure gold. She has an aura around her that I can't explain, and cannot ignore. From the first night I first cast eyes on her in the Tennessee bar, and every day since. She has continued to glow brighter and stronger in my eyes. She beguiles me without even trying. Look Joe, with me, you get what you see and she's exactly the same," he said putting the screwdriver in his teeth.

"Good. Well James, I think you've told me everything I wanted to hear. You won't hear another word on it, from my direction. Sorry for the close interrogation," he explained patting him on the back. "Now I can't speak for her Mother, though. Hell, she can speak her mind just fine by herself. I guess she will, given time," he said looking at his watch. "Talking of time, I have to move or she'll have my Fourth of July roast cooked tougher than where there ain't any at all."

"I didn't expect to be so candid, Joe," he smiled. "Anyway, we can manage fine without you both, now. I'll go and ask Sheridan to leave as well. We have a full 24 hours before they're supposed to be here. Thanks for all your help over. I'll be seeing you again when I get back from England."

"Sure James. You get yourselves over to Arlington on a weekend, when your back. Sunday's usually best. We can have a good, sit down meal proper ways. Now I'm just going to check in with Harvey, and let you speak to him before I go." He tapped a number into his phone.

"Dad, look at his blisters," Abby said opening up Sheridan's palm.

"Damn screwdriver. That's what I get for having a career in an office all my life. It's turned me into soft, brown putty. Eden's got tougher hands than me," he complained, touching the swollen welt on his palm. "Are we about done, Jimbo?"

"Oh sorry, yes of course. There's about a dozen clips left to fix. But we can finish that ourselves. Get out of here, and I'll see you at the meeting. You have my other phone number, haven't you?"

"Yeah man. It's right here in my cell. Hey, I'm going to be getting one of those new Lexicon things, just like you, Einstein," he said lifting his good hand in the air for Abby to slap. As she hit his hand, they heard a horn sound in the distance. Making them freeze solid.

"That wasn't no critter... what the hell was that?" Sheridan asked looking at James and Joe.

"Abby, you're the youth. Go take a look, but be very careful. Get straight back here."

"What the hell do we do now?" Sheridan asked looking at them blankly, as Abby sprinted through the tall grass.

"We wait until she's back. Then we do whatever needs to be done," Joe stated in an air of finality, cancelling his phone call on the spot.

"The cameras are already up and running, and recording. I hope they're camouflaged enough. The sensor's and sound recorders aren't online yet. I might not even use them."

"So, what you're telling me is, I got these sore hands for nothing?"

"Sorry Sheridan, I was just being thorough. I like to do that," he whispered. "I knew we didn't need all the sensor cables because there's only the dirt track entrance. Why would they come in any other way, and make it hard for themselves? Besides, we don't need the sensors now. If this is them?"

"If this is them... oh, brilliant. Bye, bye Fourth of July feast."

"Who else could it be?" Joe asked.

"That crazy daughter of yours has made me miss my dinner," Sheridan said looking at Joe. "Ouch, my poor hand," he moaned feeling sorry for himself as Abby darted back through the trees. Excessively nodding and giving them the thumbs up, and looking like she was enjoying every minute of the stake-out.

"Yellow pick-up truck," Abby whispered.

"Oh, shut up Sheridan you big pudding. I think we'd better make ourselves scarce and head over to the van. Then, I'll alert Harvey to get his squad up here, right now."

"Wait Joe!" James put his hand up until Abby got back to his side.

"Yellow pick up with two men, unloading drums," she panted.

THIRTY-SEVEN: *Douse*

"I hate that fat man, if payment don't arrive as he said, I'm going to be burning his own damn house down. Never mind this place," Josh said as his partner in crime lit a cigarette. "Hey man come on... put that damn thing out. I don't wanna be going up in flames."

"Oh, shut it you, big girl," Kyle moaned, dragging a five-gallon drum off the pick-up as It bashed on his leg with its own weight. Depositing petrol on to his jeans.

"Hey man, why didn't you carry two? I ain't doing all the lugging around here. We're supposed to be equal partners. Who made you leader?"

"I did, you idiot. Now just shut your big mouth and do as I say. You should have told Langdon to take a running jump. Fancy taking orders from that fat piece of crap like him? How the hell would he know how much petrol we use to torch the place anyway? You, crazy fool!" Kyle moaned swigging on his beer.

"I'm just want paid right. So, I'm doing the job right."

"We got six gallons, and five gallons as agreed. That's more than enough."

"Oh, fire expert now, then?"

"I said, shut it. We'll bring all the drums to the clearing first. Then we can do the spreading," he said skull-dragging the plastic container against his leg again. "I'm going to get bruised easy as a peach at this rate? These drums are damn heavy," he exclaimed smoking whilst panting for breath, as they reached the edge of the wooded clearing. "Josh, there's something wrong."

"How so? Did you grow a conscious overnight?" He sarcastically replied dropping his two, five-gallon drums on the grass.

"I threw an empty beer bottle into that bush last time we were here."

"Golly Sherlock, ain't you the big detective. Whoosh, I'm so out of breath," Josh replied planting himself down on one of his drums.

"It ain't there, now?" Kyle said squinting and giving Josh a black look.

"Well done, you solved the case," he said clapping his hands. "Who cares...?"

"Listen a minute. When we were last here, all those God-damn flies and bugs sprang from the trees straight out. This time, there ain't been nothing. As if they'd already flown their nests or already been disturbed. I say something ain't right?"

"You're paranoid man. You know what I think... I think you ain't done a big job since the Team days. You've gone all soft, man."

"Your nose will go soft in a minute. Soft, and spread halfway across your face. Someone's been here, I can tell... I just know it," he cursed walking away from the bush. He took another slug of his bottle, and then threw the empty beer bottle in the other's place.

"You're completely in... sane!" Josh squealed. "Come on man, we'd better go get the other drums before you have a mental breakdown."

"I ain't likin' this at all," Kyle moaned, spitting into the grass as he followed Josh back to the pick-up.

THIRTY-EIGHT: *In the van*

"The cameras pictures are great. How did you get them so high up in the trees?"

"Oh, simple. Just an eight-year-old daughter who doubles as a monkey. A telescopic ladder and some ankle spikes. I do hope this old van battery holds out? I've never run a system without the engine running before. Thank heavens for Charles having this camper van rigged up the way he did." He said looking across at Abby's sad face as she glanced up from the CCTV screens, at his mention. "I can't say as much for the microphones, though. I'm scared to touch any of these connections in case we lose the pictures. Maybe I've done something wrong," he said wondering why the sound wasn't coming out.

"That's the fire-starters through the high grass. How long are we gonna let them carry on?" Sheridan asked as his stomach rumbled and he thought about his backyard patriotic barbecue with the luscious potluck salads and food he was missing.

"Long enough to incriminate themselves," Joe replied. "Or, as long as it takes for Harvey to arrest them. I spoke to him while you were outside and told him no sirens and no damn squad cars on the dirt track. He's got a little walking to do. I hope he's still got some of that army training in him? After this is done, I might be landing one or two on Kyle's jaw, like he did to Eden. You didn't hear that by the way," Joe said as Sheridan shook his head with comic style.

"Look, while they're gone back to the pick-up, I'm going to try something," James said aloud. "The microphones are low, to keep the bird noise at a minimum. Maybe, they might just need a little jolt of electricity to wake them up. They got submerged in water last time I used them in, Venezuela."

"No James. Leave them be, or we might be in trouble. We can live without sound," Joe thought pulling on his arm.

"Dad, they're coming back!" Abby said as James fiddled with the connections and the pictures flickered on the screen."

"James, don't be messing," Sheridan said, watching him blatantly pull off a battery connector as the screen went black. He recklessly played about with the micro-sound clip connectors at the back of the wobbling console that was perched on a small camping stool. Sheridan closed his eyes and put his hands over them. There was nothing. Nothing, but a blank empty screen, and four even blanker faces. They all looked at each other lost for an answer. Looking perplexed, Abby angrily, and randomly kicked the whole set-up.

"Charles, do this for me," she whispered to herself as she looked up, closed her eyes and crossed her fingers. She kicked it one more time, and the screen flickered back to life. Once again, semi-functional with no sound coming out of the speakers.

"Hell, and high water, you did it! You mad, crazy girl!" He said as his face filled with glee.

"I didn't. Charles did," she said, kneeling back down as they looked at each other, somewhat amazed by the event.

"Is it still recording?" Joe asked as James looked down at the flashing red button. He gave Joe a nod as his phone vibrated in his pocket. He pulled it out and pressed it on loudspeaker:

"Hello Joe, I'm at the bottom of the track with a four-man squad. What's your status?"

"There's two of em as we suspected. Abby's been out sniper. They're offloading the fuel now. We're holed up, in a green camouflaged camper, to the right of the main path. I don't know how this man got this old van here. Could be divine intervention. Anything's possible with this fellow."

"What about your tire tracks, Joe?"

"None to speak of. It's been hidden here a couple days, so the grass has risen back up. There's no sign of us at all. They have no idea. What's your plan of attack, Harvey?" Joe asked watching the CCTV screen;

"I got everything you just said from my scouts. I see the yellow truck and I see you too buddy boy. Special binoculars courtesy of Kentucky State. I got two of *my men shimmying through the long grass, either side of the track right now. But we're gonna keep an eye on the suspects and wait a little longer. Looks like they have a lot of propellant to be dealing with, judging by your communiqué. We'll sortie up to your position in slow stages. Let them wear their asses out, before we go in for the ambush. Just hold tight buddy, when we spring them, it won't take long. I've been after Josh Creech a long while now. He's a slippy customer. I owe you one for being able to pin this on him. They're low-down small fry who can't say no to a buck or two. Talk to you real soon Joe, Harvey out."*

THIRTY-NINE: *Burn*

"Hey, slow down on the booze, pretend boss. You need to be saving some that beer for our high flame celebration. We have a lot of drinking to do as we watch this place burn to ashes."

"Yes, and a lot of running. You've planned all but nothing, have you Josh?"

"Huh? How d'you figure?"

"Because my arms feel as long as an Orangu.... as long as an apes. Once we're done, we need to high tail it out of here. Get ourselves down to my pad for some clean clothes. Then straight to the railroad bar afterward. Did you think of any alibi yet, you brain dead cretin?"

"Nope. I was just gonna head out night fishing? Make myself scarce that way. I thought that would do as good cover."

"Yes, and who's gonna corroborate your being there... the damn fish?"

"I guess you're right, Kyle. We got three more barrels each to bring on through. Daylight's almost away. You think we can make it back to the railroad in time for a good night's drinking? We've gotta douse all this damn stuff out yet," Josh said realising Kyle seemed to have thought things out more thoroughly.

"What waist are you? You might be needing a belt for yer britches amongst other things," Kyle asked laughing to himself.

"Stop calling me a waste and threatening me you bully. Oh... waist, I get you now," Josh puzzled.

"You'll have to throw on whatever clothes I have spare. Washing clothes ain't my strong point. Oh, right now, listen! I've had right enough of this crap. We're leaving the last of his God-damn fuel in the truck. There's plenty enough here."

"There's plenty when I go get the last of it, Kyle," Josh said pointing his finger. "I told you, I'm doing this right, and I stand by my word. I don't want no comebacks from him or from you, either, do you hear me? If we don't get paid because we scrimped on something, I'll know it ain't down to my ass. Now, you can just sit right here on your damn fat lazy butt, and have the good grace to wait for me to get back. I'll be about ten minutes," he groaned disappearing into the scrub.

Kyle remained sat on a gasoline drum and dangerously lit another cigarette while everyone in the camper van watched.

Joe, dialled Harvey's number;

"Hey H, they're separating. The one you want is heading back to the truck and the other low-life is sat in a clearing, about eight minutes from the end of the track. What you want us to do...? We have a little girl with us. The English ecologist's daughter. I don't want..."

"You do exactly nothing, Joe. You just leave this to us. My men are almost in position and we're almost on top of the truck. The fact they're apart will make our job easier. It'll be my pleasure to keep this clown quiet and stick a muzzle on his mouth. My other boys will be getting ready to apprehend the fellow in there. You just sit tight, and wait for my next call."

"Oh, this is too much. I feel like eating my own tongue. Please tell me you have something to eat in this thing?" Sheridan crowed as his stomach rumbled again.

"There's biscuits and crisps up in the top cupboard," Abby pointed out. "Sorry, I thought you knew?" She explained wondering why he hadn't ventured for them before.

"What?" He replied, frowning and standing up to wrench open the cupboard door. "Oh Lord, in heaven. I thank you," he said taking three, packets of biscuits out. With his mind on his empty stomach, he sat back down forgetting about the covert situation and thumped his butt onto the seat. The camper van suspension wobbled severely, and the CCTV picture disappeared. Only to reappear seconds later, vilifying him with three pertinently angry stares in the process.

"Sorry, people."

Then, Joe's phone rang again. He looked at everyone then scrambled to his pocket to retrieve it. "That was quick, if he's ringing to tell me he's got him, he's done well. The old buzzard's almost on retirement, but he's still fast!" He said looking at his mobile phone screen and expecting to see *HARVEY*, flashing green, but instead seeing; *EDEN* beaming brightly in his face as it continued to vibrate in his hand. "James," he said turning the screen to face his eyes.

"Just take it, Joe. It might be important. Our hands are tied here, and we can do nothing for the moment."

"No, here James, you take it. If she still wants to speak to me, I'll take it, then"

"Dad... hello.... phew, finally! I need to talk to you right now. It's really important."

"Hi Eden, its erm... it's me."

"What...? Where's my Dad. What the hell is going on?"

"He's here, right beside me. Remember, I asked you to trust me."

"I did... I do... is he ok? Are you ok? What the... he's.... you've both got some serious explaining!"

"He's fine. Would you like to speak to him?"

"Erm, well okay, but what the hell are you doing with him?"

"I'll pass you over, then he can explain." James gave Joe his phone and he turned it to loud-speaker.

"Hi Baby, just be quiet and listen, and please don't interrupt. I'm expecting a very important phone call from Harvey Swanson, and I need you to hang up, right now. We're all okay, here. It's just hard to explain, right now. Suffice to

say, that Abby sends her love."

"Love you Eden, MWAH," she shouted puckering a kiss as Eden's heart was in her mouth.

"So, does Sheridan."

"Oh, I'll save a biscuit for you girl," he said with a mouthful of crumbs.

Her face lit up with confusion as she burst into a smile at the same time as her eyes began to well up.

"Jimbob says hi, as well," Sheridan added crunching into another biscuit like he'd never seen food.

"Love you sweetheart!" James shouted across to the phone as her heart skipped a beat and she burst out laughing with tears of joy.

Joe turned the phone back to earpiece and listened intently to her words.

"Ok Daddy. Tell him I'll see him at the community meeting. It's been brought forward, just as he asked. I'll get off the phone. I have no idea what you're all doing. But I'm guessing whatever it is, it'll be for the best."

"What we are you up to. Erm...Mmm, you could say that we are, saving Eden," he confirmed looking over at the others in the camper.

FORTY: *Victory*

"Evening everybody. I'm Eden, as you know. Thank you all for coming along at such short notice, again, to this extra, and unscheduled meeting. Now, before we get into the thick of it, may I quickly introduce tonight's guest speakers?" She said clearing her throat.

"We have Langdon Stanley Dainty, and you all know who he is. There's lawyer, Mr. Milton West, who most of you have seen before. We also have Mrs. Helena Chase from Defend and Defer, Human Rights Management for the first time tonight. And last but certainly, not least, we have, Mr. James Ustinov, whom, I'm told, is a world-renowned ecologist over from England," she said with a wry grin on her face. Now because we have as little time as ever, please feel to ask them any questions at all. They are all here to provide us with answers.

So, as I say, we don't want to keep you from your homes any longer than we need to, so if everybody's ready, we'll let you have a quick minute to gather your thoughts, and then we can jump right in with the first questions of the night. She walked away from the microphone, and took a small sip of her water, as the audience glared at the people on the stage just as the show was about to begin.

Oh, and just before we start," she said taking another sip, and then placing the cup on the floor. "I also have to inform you that I have a strong suspicion that the majority of you... of us... will be going home rather quicker than the usual three hours, and with more than just a spring in our steps, tonight," she announced feeling the most naturally confident, and positive that she'd felt with herself, in a long, long time.

"So, from what I've heard, there have been some major developments over the past week. Quite big, *fat* developments, in fact. Yes, I can see in your faces that you're all hearing me say that in a positive manner. That's because I'm feeling absolutely delighted, tonight. Let me be the first to tell you that the road in its present form is history. It's dead and it's done!" She said as Langdon shuffled uncomfortably in his seat, frowned and looked at Milton in contorted disgust. "Not only is the road finished, so is this fat excuse for a human being, right here." She swung her pointing arm around to face Langdon. Directing the audiences glare straight at him as she kicked at the cane in his hand. He was already going red around the gills and she'd just made things a hell of lot worse. "Yes, I said excuse for a human being. Now tell me, is that libel or deformation of character, Mr. West?"

"Erm, I'm not really sure which, but it's very good news miss, Buckley," he explained slightly smiling and lightly clapping his hands together, finally swopping sides as Langdon frowned at him not knowing what to say. Milton looked ahead at the cheering crowd in front of him, then reminded himself he was actually on stage representing the man beside him. But feeling inside like he was almost on show, due to the people applauding him so much. Thus, began a furious show of twitches from his neck as she leaned over to speak into his ear.

'I found out the truth, and they know that none of this is your fault, and you did tell me you admired what I was doing,' she whispered as he gave her a secreted wink and then twitched as she smiled in a manner not dissimilar to Langdon and moved away from his ear lobe. She turned a full 720' degree spin on her heels, then stopped her body right in front of the confused fat-man?

"WHO'S BEEN A NAUGHTY BOY THEN?" She shouted for all to hear, feeling sober yet giddy, and full of excitement. Imagining she was at the circus or in a court of law, all at the same time to the crowds amazed, and chattering delight. "I can just imagine you with a nappy on, with a dummy in your mouth. You, big dummy!" She teased, snatching his cane as his mouth dropped wide open at her antics.

"Okay, okay, enough of the silliness I hear you cry," she shouted stopping every last hint of the fun in its stride. She placed his cane back beside him and turned back to face the audience:

"As you all know, the road was planned to go through *OUR* houses and Mr. Creeches swamp. Last night, two thugs employed by this man. Mr. Langdon Stanley Dainty were caught by Kentucky police at Boyles swamp with thirty-five gallons of highly flammable liquids and propellants to burn the whole place to cinders. To burn alive the critter filled oasis that contains of some of our most endangered species of animals and plants. Plants that are used as cancer treatments. Animals, amphibian's birds and insects that are natural indicators that we look upon and are able to study and learn from to make this world a better place." Langdon coughed loudly, and took a hankie from his top pocket, to mop the nervous sweat from his brow and hide his embarrassed face.

"I have absolutely no idea what this crazy Witch is talking about."

"I have," came the shy and twitchy voice from right beside him, silencing both him and the rest of the hall.

"I know everything, and I'm willing to testify against you in a court of law." Milton announced as the silence turned to quiet whispers.

"Shut up man. Get me a drink of water... oh never mind. I'll get it myself. Oh, and you're fired." Langdon stated as Milton remained seated and steadfast. "Do you have any water in this place Witch? I need a drink my throat's..." he said falsely coughing and continuing to speak. "The swamp is full of nothing but bugs, bugs and more bugs. It needs bulldozing into the ground, then I can build the road for the betterment and the greater good of Harlan County," he coughed.

"Oh, I see. So, he's fired, and you want some of that water stuff, you put fires out with for your damn, nasty throat!" She pointed, now angrily kicking his cane back to the floor. "Sheridan, would you pass me cup of water here, please. No, make it two," she asked worried he might have a heart attack on the spot as the false cough had now turned into a real gasps for air and breath.

Sheridan walked to the foot of the stage, as James stood up beside her.

"That makes two of us that will testify against you. See, you think you've had me in your money pocket, and on your corrupt side from the beginning. But all the time, I've been on the side of the swamp, and the side of these good people, here tonight. What's so charmingly ironic about it, is that in all this mess, I think I might have found the beginnings of a new species of frog up there," James said looking at the audience, and then facing off Langdon at the same time.

"Did you honestly think I'd be so thoughtlessly narrow-minded, as to let you destroy God's creatures for your own selfish gain?" He growled looking at Langdon and picking up a file from under his chair as Eden bent down and grabbed the water from Sheridan, then quickly moved out of the way to let James continue to speak. She reluctantly gave Langdon a cup of water and stood with the other cup in her hand. Proudly listening to James:

"Here in my hand, I have signed and stamped declarations from a few people who care. Please bear with me as it's rather a long list," he explained, taking a deep breath:

"The World Wildlife Federation. The Kentucky States Nature Preserves Commission. The Tennessee Wildlife Agency of Resources. The United States

Fish and Wildlife Ecological Services. The Endangered Species act, as well as, Healing Earth, Endangered Earth, and on it goes. In fact, I have over *EIGHTY* other email correspondence and communications from various other interested parties in America, and throughout the rest of the world's ecological community. I think if I read them all out, we'd be here all night," he explained nodding at Sheridan, who stood up and clapped his hands, deciding it was time for him to say his piece until, all at once, the main door opened, and in walked Harvey Swanson, in full uniform.

 "People, over here!" Sheridan said grabbing everyone's attention:

 "Before the Lieutenant joins in with the party, I also have some more letters right over here!" He shouted, waving his papers in the air and pausing to let the crowd turn around. "Oh, and I hope you're listening to hard Dainty, cos this one's by far the best, ball cruncher. "The Kentucky state office now prohibits the sale of any properties, on any designated ex-mining land or otherwise." The crowd went wild and a dozen cowboy hats were thrown into the air. "But just hold those hats, for one more second," he paused. "The big bopper, is right here," he said shaking a paper in the air. "Eminent Domain does not apply to any lands under... what's that say?" He said making a meal of his words, knowing he'd already scoured the document from top to bottom. "*KRS416.450*, blah blah, blah, and so on and so forth... and listen to this Dainty... you might learn a thing or two. "Any lands that are deemed a safe-haven, nature preserve or recognized natural habitat, can NEVER be touched!" He casually orated to all the intently listening eyes.

 "Hell, what that means is, your houses and homes and Boyles swamp are fine. That beautiful place... and you people are safe, from him. And until a full public inquiries findings results are found, nothing will change at all. Well hell, I might have a big, long and lonely beard by then. So, I suggest you all go home in the knowledge that you'll be able to sleep soundly in your beds for a heel of a long time," he said to the rapturous, and cheering applause. "I'd say this meeting has just about had it, people. Apart from a little personal business of mine. So, you can all leave and get home to your families and tell them all the good news," Sheridan said looking at James for approval as the whole room remained seated.

"Ok then, well if you're staying a while, then simmer down a little. Because I ain't quite finished up yet," he said turning to face the stage. "So, ever expectantly now, and at long last. I get back to you mister Dainty," he said pointing his papers sharply at Langdon, then briskly walking to the stage stairs.

"Now I told you I'd get your sorry ass, and I have. I could've starved or choked on biscuits in the process, but hey, the things we have to do to achieve our goals," he said rubbing his stomach as Eden and James wryly smiled across the hall to each other. "You ain't no man of the people... In fact, you ain't no man's man, at all. I'm glad I wasn't in any damn war trenches with your sorry ass," he said as Langdon's wife suddenly stood up at the back of the hall.

"He isn't a man of mine, anymore either," she said as she brashly moved through the seats, sliding her handbag onto her arm as the others on her row, automatically and politely twisted their legs to the side, so she could walk through. She walked along the middle aisle and down to the stage, like a hell clicking storm. Then, she delved into her bag and threw some of her own papers willfully onto the stage. "I was going to leave this until you got home. You don't have a home now. Your Aunt Phyllis is in the spare room where you where, and that's where she'll stay." She said as the papers slid across the wooden stage, and Eden quietly bent down to pick them up.

"No! Miss Buckley! Let him get down and pick them up himself. He deserves to be on all fours like a pig, the fat heartless swine!" She said storming out of the hall within seconds. Prompting others to do exactly the same, as they stood up from their seats and followed her lead. All looking and sounding as mutually disgusted with the man that was now wincing defenselessly on the stage in front of them.

"Yo, ACID! See the uniformed man right over at the back there?" Sheridan shouted. "He's waiting for you. I'd say it's time for you to leave."

FORTY-ONE: *U-turn*

"It's a shame we couldn't get the fireworks trip on the Fourth of July with all that Langdon hassle. But at least we can we make the Nashville gig hand in hand. I'll make this a last dance to remember you with, until you're back."

"Hardly be a dance with me. I've never been able put one foot in front of the other. I could pogo when punk music was around," he explained as they drove down the Tennessee 1-40 highway through the warm night air, and the crickets sang their usual refrain.

"This is the first time I've actually felt no pressure from any of it all. It's all done," she said looking into the back of the camper, to see the internal light on with the kids still talking as she slid the separating glass to one side with a thunk. "Hey, come on now you two monkeys. Time to get a little shut eye," she appeased watching them talking to each other wrapped tight in their sleeping bags.

"Dad, I thought we were calling at the swamp before we leave?" Abby shouted as Eden looked over at him for confirmation. Even though she already knew.

"Yes, sweetheart, that's where we're headed. Then, a quick stop at the project house, to check something out. Then off we go, to Tennessee."

"We can go to sleep after we've seen the swamp, then. It'd be nice to see it at night," She said looking at Jamie and winking.

Eden closed the window and looked back at James, as the kids turned back to themselves.

"Oh, I brought this with me, James." She said pulling a CD from out of her coat. "It's Abraham, one of the kids at school. I could have sworn I'd told you? Oh, I don't know. So much has happened. Anyway, he put this together for me last week. He's only 14. I think he's really got some talent. Do you mind if I play it for you? I'd like to see what you think."

"Go ahead. What's it called?" He asked looking in the mirror to see a large truck coming up behind them.

"*Don't ever forget me.*" She said as she pushed the disc into the player and waited for it to start.

"Oh, no. Abby... we need to turn back," Jamie said seriously climbing from his bunk and grabbing her dangling arm.

"Why, what's wrong?" She asked sitting up on bed and taking a drink of water.

"I've forgotten the passports."

"No way!" She gasped looking through the glass where their parents we're sitting.

"This is my mess, Abby. Leave it to me," he replied. Groaning at himself and feeling pretty stupid. He launched into action by grabbing his bag and secreting his supply of pills under his covers. Then, he banged on side of the van, making Eden and James jump as Eden pulled open the middle window with shock.

"Mom, I need some more tablets for my hip. I think the bumping on the road is making it sore."

"Huh... bumping...? There's ain't any? Anyway, they're in your bag, aren't they? We'll pull over and let you have a good stretch and a walk around."

"I picked up an empty box by mistake. I don't need a walk, just the pills," he said looking up at the window to see if she was watching, then stashing the contents deeper into his pillow case as Abby pulled the quilt over her head, to hide her grinning face.

"James, sorry we need to," she thumbed through the window.

"No problem, we've only just set off, anyway. I'll pull over and spin us around. It's a shame you couldn't come back to England with us. It has some of the best healthcare in the world. It must be terrible for Jamie, walking around in pain all the time. I have a private, well-being plan that we've never used," he explained pulling in to let the truck past, and then turning around the camper.

"Wouldn't we have to be married for something like that?"

"I think so," he replied without as much as a glance. "Isn't that what we both want?" He asked looking up and down the road before turning safely.

#

"See Jamie, there you go. I knew he'd say it in the end," Abby said looking across at Jamie.

#

"Yes, of course, it is, James," she replied caressing his leg. "It just sounds funny hearing you say it like that. Let alone, at all? I never thought something like you would happen to me, again."

"Now she's committed," Jamie whispered, coughing resonantly to remind his Mom to close the internal window.

#

Once they'd got back to her house, Eden pulled open the door for Jamie, then went running down her path followed by Bailey and Archie and opened the front door. "Back in a tic. I'll get some extra pills for you and a bottle of water for the dogs. I forgot about the mutts as well, honey."

"Cool. I'm just getting a comic from my room, for Abby," he declared.

"Ok baby," she said walking into the kitchen and turning on the tap as he tracked her movements, then disappeared.

Reappearing in minutes, beside her in the kitchen.

"Wow that was quick! What did you say Abby wanted?" She asked passing him a glass of water and a new box of pills."

"Oh, just this comic," he said throwing it disinterested, onto the kitchen table. He swallowed his pill, then drank the water.

"Now, where's that...?" She asked herself, rifling through the clip box in the hall.

"What are you looking for?"

"This," she replied holding it up. "My lucky red hair clip for the gig."

"You don't need any luck, Mom. Everything will work out just fine without luck. We'll make sure of that."

"What are you talking about? It's just my hair clip. Crazy superstition and nonsense on my part, granted?" she furrowed. "Come on, let's get out of here. Jamie...the comic? You said it was important," she said motioning toward the kitchen table.

"Oh, it doesn't matter mom, let's just disappear.... to England and beyond," he said as they walked out the door toward the van and his mom shook her head.

"Strangest boy," she puzzled locking the door and jumping into her seat beside James. As Jamie got to the side door Abby looked at him with clear anticipation. He gave her the thumbs up, jumped in and slammed the door shut. Almost trapping Bailey's tail in the process.

FORTY-TWO: *Frogs & face-masks*

"James. Abby said she'd like to see it again before you leave, but look... they're both fast asleep? Maybe we'd better leave them as they are," she thought as they pulled up to the top of the dirt path at the swamp.

"I think you're right. We'll leave the dogs with them for safety, and have a quick walk in there on our own. Just for old times' sake? We are here, after all?"

"Oh, listen you... mister, big-romantic," she said pushing him back.

"We've all had a busy few days, it's probably caught up with them," he confirmed.

As they disappeared toward the trees, Abby and Jamie lifted up their covers and opened their eyes, then laughed at each other.

"Wow, it sure is peaceful here tonight. The light of the moon makes it feel magical. Listen to all those contented creatures. It's just so silent and calm, there's not even a breeze," she said nearing the water's edge. "Abby said she wanted to look in on these little fellows," he explained shining his torch at the water, and gently pulling on her hand, as he beckoned her to follow. "She knows I'll make sure they're fine," he affirmed squelching into the reed grass and crouching down. "Look, can you see the spawn in the water?" he asked carefully pulling the reeds bed apart and shining his flashlight onto the star bright glistening lily's that were floating in the water. "This is the new breed of frog. Not actually new, but new in Kentucky. Something quite amazing must have happened with the ecosystem for them to even be here at all. I can only put it down to global warming or climate change? That, or maybe by complete accident?" he explained as she knelt carefully beside him.

"A bit like you and me," she smiled.

"What?" He asked as the small frog moved across the loose sedge, and on to a taut lily-pad. As they looked at him, he seemed to be looking back, and watching their every move.

"He's a frog prince," she joked looking at James's confused face. "I mean you. A new breed that has happened along, who ain't supposed to be from these parts. Something quite amazing for him to be around here at all," she declared squeezing his hand, as she lay her head intimately on his shoulder.

"You coming into my life has changed everything, James. I never used to care about anything like that little fellow. My whole outlook on life is different, and it's all because of you. You're a seeker James, a seeker of all that's good and right in the world. I know that now," she whispered turning to face him. As their eyes met, the brightness of the moon lit up her face and its rays shone deep into her eyes. "I know that I'm a very lucky girl that you happened along. It's like I've been given a second chance with love. Oh... wow! Look... he just jumped closer," she exclaimed.

"Maybe he likes the sound of your voice. I know I do. I think you're beautiful inside and out, but you know what," he said, pushing his hand into the ground beneath them and pulling out a black slippery handful of mud to her surprise. "If you ever get ugly, this is just what you need," he joked as the movement from his hand into the mud, alerted the frog. It croaked, as if giving its blessing, then jumped back into the water. Looked at them once more, and then disappeared into the green water.

"Oh really?" She inquired as they stood back up.

"Oh yes, let me tell you. This the most natural face-mask you could ever get. Fancy giving it a try," he asked as she backed away with a smile.

"You know... I bet we could even bottle it, and sell it. What do you think?" He asked pacing toward her as she slowly backed away.

"Now that wouldn't be fair on the frogs, or me either... so...erm... you keep away from me with that... James. I mean it, James," she offered to his suddenly deaf ears.

"The natural nutrients in this stuff... well. They'll have you looking twenty-one, all over again," he added striding toward her as she turned to run.

"Uh huh," she agreed spinning around and bolting away from his madness.

"So, antioxidant and enzyme rich... the frog droppings and reed pieces are great for exfoliating and removing dead skin," he teased flashing the torch scarily at her feet. "This stuff dates back as far as the fourth millennia B.C don't you know," he explained running after her toward the van.

"Just like you then, Ustinov?" She said increasing her speed.

He captured her panting at her locked door of the van. Dropped his hands to his side and let the mud fall softly to the grass. Then, he threw a passionate kiss on to her lips. "I'll just stick with a little lipstick, then you can always kiss it off."

FORTY-THREE: *Ward Thomas*

"So, back to where it all started, partner. Oh look, there's the barman, I must go and say hello," she said spotting the kindly bartender, still selling his wares in the Skoolhouse as James took a long and hard look at the pool table in the corner.

"Hey fella, how's it hanging?" She asked as he looked up from his cocktail shaker.

"Hello again, Eden," he smiled. "I see you got yourself all hooked up. I'm George, pleased to make your acquaintance Mr..."

"Call me James, and we're hardly hitched, yet," he explained.

"What brings you two down in the big city?" He asked grabbing a whiskey bottle from behind the bar.

"Not that, George. Just a couple of beers will be fine. I have no need to drown my sorrows no more," she whispered watching James's extended attention to pool table in the corner of the room. "We're here to see a band. Ward Thomas. They're in town to bring some of their English flair to the country music sound," she explained watching him pour the first beer.

"Oh really, can't say I've heard of them. English you say?"

"Yep, the Ward Thomas twins. They talk the talk, and walk the walk," she exclaimed shaking her hips, and planting herself down on the same high stool as the last time she was here. Secretly realising how much happier she felt and how everything had changed so much, since she'd sat there.

"Eden, did you say, Ward Thomas?" James interjected.

"Yea, I don't know the name, either. I love my country, but it's hard to keep up with every new talent. I guess I'm just getting old," George said putting the second brimming glass of beer on the bar.

"Yep, I sure did, James," she nodded, slurping down a cold mouthful, and leaving a froth on her ruby red lips.

"I've heard that name...? I'm sure I have," he said searching his brain.

"Of course, you have. Abby told me they we're on the plane with you. But you were apparently fast asleep. There's been a big write-up about them in the papers here. It says they've been sold out on all of their shows. I Imagine tonight won't be any different. I want a T-shirt for bedtime. I think I'll get Page one. For looking after the kids and dogs." she explained to his frown.

"For bedtime?"

"For sleeping, to remember tonight. A little memento of first gig. Oh, never mind mister, pumpkin-head."

"Ah yes, I recall now. Catherine and Lizzie. They lent Abby their phone charger on the plane. I forgot about that."

"Oh, come on, mister-memory. Thanks for the drinks, George," she said climbing off her chair. "Oh, and by the way, you ain't my partner anymore. Now, you're just my weak opponent," she giggled as he watched her making for the pool table and beckoning him to follow as he could feel himself being charmed once again with her beauty and natural way, like the first time. She bent down at the empty table, and threw a dollar into the slot. The balls released without a hint of a glitch as James walked around the table to look her clean in the eye. "I've just noticed... you've got lipstick and eyeliner on, haven't you?" He said feeling stupid that he hadn't noticed when they set out. Her piercing blue eyes seemed to shine the brightest and deepest he'd ever seen.

"I hate the stuff as a rule. But hell, it's nice to make the effort for someone special sometimes. Don't you think?" She asked picking up a cue. "So, mister-enemy, are you set to get slaughtered?" She said smashing the cluster and waking him from his entranced gaze."

Ten minutes later, he was standing in defeat and denial of the sheer beauty that he had holding on to his arm "Are you ok, James? You didn't pot a damn thing? Well, except for the white ball, twice!" She laughed.

"I potted you in the end, didn't I? It was your fault for beguiling me, again."

"Hey, it's your shout then, or would you like to go straight over to the gig, instead. We could have a drink in the bar over there. I imagine we might be queuing for quite a while."

"Ok, let's head over. Is it far?"

"We'll be there in a ten-minutes."

Fifteen minutes later, they we're sat together at the gig bar. With two cold beers, and two Ward Thomas, T-shirts.

"Red or blue?" She asked looking at the cotton emblazoned cloth and the band's name.

"Oh, definitely red. Suits your temper."

"Oh, zip it," she joked grabbing her hair and wildly shaking her head. "I really feel so old around here. Look at all these youngsters," she said gazing around the bar.

"Eden, you look beautiful every night."

Just then, a voice came over the public information system:

#

"Please may I have your attention...?

This is an URGENT call for Mr. James Ustinov. Could Mr. Ustinov Please make his way to any member of staff?

That's Mr. James Ustinov, to any member of staff, ASAP. Thank you."

#

"Oh no.....! What the heck?" She shrieked, almost spitting out her drink as she tightly gripped his arm. "Something's wrong. The kids... something's..."

"Eden calm down," he whispered as a girl nearby automatically screamed at the sound of her shriek.

"There must be a perfectly simple explanation. Come on, just grab your drink and wave goodbye to your seat. Let's head across to the bar," he said looking at the humongous, three deep nest of people standing there. He spotted a black, suited member of staff walking into the room and diverted him in his direction, whilst keeping a grip on Eden. She walked in his steps as they reached the tall, man who was looking around the bar with a pen between his teeth, and counting numbers on a card.

"Excuse me, I'm Mr. Ustinov. There was an announcement for me?"

The member of staff smiled and looked them both up and down. "I see. And do you have any ID with you, sir?"

"Only my work badge from London," he explained feeling inside his pocket to find his LEAPS pass and give it to the man.

"Yes sir, I do see a likeness, although you have slightly longer hair on that," he smirked as she grabbed at the pass expecting to see some kind of ex-convict picture looking back at her from the card.

"OMG. You, young hippy," she joked.

"I think everything's in order sir, may I ask you both to quickly follow me," he said pulling out his intercom and confirming his find, to an invisible colleague, as Eden looked up at James, still feeling worried inside.

"Eden when you can, lose the beer," he said necking his own and putting the the empty glass on a table as they were led out of the room, through three black doors that could hardly be seen, amongst the black of the rest of the walls. They were marched down a long tight staircase, and up four steps.

"James."

"Yes."

"At least we know it's not the kids!"

"Erm, I think you'll find it is the kids Eden! I'm going to bloody kill, Abby!" He said as the situation began to dawn on them both at last.

"Could you both please hurry, we really haven't got much time before curtain," the staff member inferred at a break-neck pace, as e led them through another door, and then in to a brightly lit corridor, with white open doors. With the words, *storage*, and *props* daubed across them. They finally stopped after reaching the last door on the right, which they could see, had a gold star, bang in the middle. "Here they are. Right, I hope you both enjoy the concert," the staff member said as he knocked on the door three times, smiled and left. They looked at each other in a mixture of nerves and excitement. But the door remained closed. He looked at her, gulped hard and knocked again. The door opened to reveal a large white room, with tables of lights around mirrors. At the end was yet another door with muffled female voices coming from behind. As the door opened, and a tall lady walked toward them. "Good evening, Mr. Ustinov, I take it this is Mrs. Ustinov? It's very nice to meet you both. What a lovely couple you make. I'm Phyllis, the girl's American tour manager."

"I'm not erm, Mrs. Ustinov," Eden said feeling somewhat over announced as if they'd made some kind of terrible mistake.

"Well that isn't the information we've been given."

"Who was that, then?"

"Someone called Abby," she said as they began to smile.

"Well, I guess she might be, soon enough," James explained as Eden strenuously tried to say something, as nothing came out. James looked at her and placed his finger on her chin. Closing her mouth as she resigned herself to give up.

"Yes, I think that might be a little closer to the story we were given. Just give a little knock on the door, but make it really quick. Catherine and Lizzy are on stage in less than ten minutes. It's lucky we found you when we did," she said smiling and walking away.

"OMG," Eden gasped grabbing onto the butterfly hair band she'd wore when she first met him.

He tapped on the door, once more.

The door was opened by one of the twin sisters. "Hello there. Come on in you two, quick, quick, quick. We're just rehearsing a new song... how are you James?" Catherine asked, sounding almost as nervous, as they were feeling.

"I'm okay, erm, Catherine. Sorry, I was asleep on the plane and my memory needed jogging by Abby."

"We know," Lizzie jumped in. "She gave us a call and told us all about the swamp and your work and everything. Then she told us about Jamie and his Mum, which I'm guessing would be you?"

"Yes, that's me, I'm afraid," Eden said bowing her head for no reason.

"She also told us you play a pretty mean, acoustic guitar?"

"She certainly does that alright. And the spoons and an accordion, and the trumpet," he said stopping himself when he felt a somewhat painful kick on his right ankle.

"That's good. Well are you up for doing a little backing for us. We're a guitarist down tonight?" Lizzie asked.

"Oh, I don't know about that," she squirmed.

"Oh, go on Eden, I promised Abby. Do you know *Push for the Stride,* it has easy chords?"

"Erm, A C D E and G, I think," she muttered.

"There you go. We're getting the show filmed tonight. Abby's expecting a signed copy from us by post. You wouldn't want to let her down, now would you?"

"I guess not," she paused "Oh what the hell, it'll be a blast," she replied slightly nervous but flushing with pride inside. The door opened and Phyllis reappeared.

"It's time girls. This member of staff will take you to your new seats on the side balcony. It'll be easier access when you get up on stage."

"We're so glad you agreed, because Abby just told us if you didn't, to just tear you out of the audience, and put you on the spot," Lizzie giggled.

"Right sis, it's time to go. I guess we'll be seeing you out there," Catherine added.

"Thank you both ever so much," Eden and James gushed.

"Our pleasure."

FORTY-FOUR: *Reality bites*

"Morning kids, how is everybody?" She asked giving Abby a steely eyed glance as she walked into Page's spare room."

"Owh! What time is it? Where's dad?" She asked yawning from the bed as she nestled down beside her. "Oh, he's gone into the city to speak to someone about your flights, and get another set of suitcases. He say's you'll kill him if he doesn't. Where's Jamie?"

"That's true, I would. Jamie's in the room next door," she said pushing herself back onto the headboard.

"Anyway, never mind your father, I could kill you for last night."

"Didn't you like my surprise then?"

"Did I like it? Oh Abby, it was amazing, thank you, honey."

"Glad you did. But you do realise I kill you, if you don't come."

"What?"

"And so, will Jamie. Because he wants to go as well."

"Come… go…? Go where…?"

"Back with us to England. You know you'll love it."

"God Abby, you are so force. How can we?" She blushed with shock and surprise.

"How can you… not? You sound just like Dad. Making rubbish excuses all the time. I hope you understand that without you there, he's going to be the biggest pain in the backside. And it'll be me that will get it in the neck. Every single day and every single night, until he's got you back by his side," she replied as maturely as aunt May.

"How can we possibly?"

"Look. Just you listen to me. Do you really think that the whole time you and Dad have been falling all over each other, we haven't noticed a thing? Wrong! We know absolutely everything, so we've decided that the best thing for you…for all of us, is to have you both in one place all the same time. For all of the time. Except for work, of course. Whether that place be here or in England…it really doesn't matter. Just tell me you'll think about it. But make it snappy, because we leave soon. Oh, and listen…" she said grabbing onto her hand. "I won't blame you if you won't, but you know you really should. It makes perfect sense. Now, I'm going to the toilet and for a wash. I'll see you in a minute," she said casually pushing off her bedclothes and shuffling out of the room. Leaving Eden completely overwhelmed and lost for words. As she disappeared, Eden sat on the sofa and looked up at the ceiling, with her head in her hands. Abby walked into the lounge five minutes later. Fully clothed and sat down on the floor, in front of Eden and put her hand on her knee.

"Just treat it as a little holiday. Ring work, and tell them the same. You could even say it's for an operation for Jamie. They'd understand. In fact, I'll do it for you if you like. Once Dad has spoken to Iain and Grace about the guardianship, we can be straight back here, in no time, at all." Eden stayed deathly silent. Looking at the wise young girl. "Ask me a question and I won't tell you no lies. Come on with me, Eden, I'm so hungry." She stood up, then pulled her into the kitchen and closed the door. "That's not the well-known phrase you understand, I just changed it for the purposes of this conversation. Sorry, am I being too technical for you? She explained, pouring them a glass of milk and popping two slices of bread into the toaster, then returning to sit by her side on Pages breakfast bar.

"Yes, you are, Abby. What about all of your friends in England?"

"What about them? Yes, I'll miss them, but I'm only a plane ride away. I'd miss Jamie and you much more. The same goes for him and his friends and you and yours. If Dad and I can adapt, then so can you. Think about it, there's really nothing else to say."

"Do you want me there?" She asked lifting her head from her arms.

"You'll never take the place of my, Mum, but you're getting pretty close to a brilliant second," Abby admitted as Eden burst into tears as she held out her arm. Absolutely astounded at the young girl's firm, and adult outlook to life.

"Do you think your Dad will go for it though?" She asked frantically standing up from her seat and grabbing both Abby's shoulders excitedly.

"Are you crazy.... he'll jump at it. If he doesn't, he will by the time I've finished."

"Oh, my God our passports are back at home. What time is the flight again?"

"We could drive back and get them, we might just make it in time?" Abby said teasing, with a glint in her eye as she walked toward Jamie's rucksack.

"What are we going to tell your Dad? Oh, God. And how the heck am I going to ask him? He won't want to miss his flight?"

"That's true. But we could just use these ones, here," Abby brightened producing the passports from his bag.

"You little," Eden gushed, both horrified and astounded. "I don't believe you Abby! But I don't have any flights booked?"

"Tut, a minor detail. You'll have to come up with an excuse on higher ground than that," she grinned, casually biting into her toast.

"Oh no, the dogs."

"Page is looking after Archie, and she's taking Bailey to your aunt May's for a long visit next week. May hasn't seen Chloe and Aaron for a while anyway. Anything else?" Abby asked, secretly going through her own, concisely-covered checklist in her head.

"Has he been in on this with you all the time?"

"Dad knows nothing at all. But my co-agent and co-conspirator, Jamie has been with me, every step of the way."

"God bless you both. Thank you so much."

FORTY-FIVE: *Wings & rings*

"I can't believe I'm even sat here," she whispered to Jamie, who was sat two rows down.

"I'm glad we are, Mom."

"It wasn't part of my master-plan for you two to be sat apart, though," Abby interrupted.

"Excuse me, miss. Could I possibly change seats, so I can be closer to my sister over there," Jamie pointed Abby out to the stewardess.

"I think that might be possible," she replied. "The gentleman beside her is travelling alone," she explained. "And the one on the other side... is erm... oh just give me a moment, I'll see what I can do young man," she said tailing off, then turning around for another look. "It's quite a long flight, it would be better if you're with your family."

Five minutes later, they were all sat in the same line of seats across the middle six rows of the plane. James was flicking through the project house mail, that he'd picked up on the way down to the gig, the day before.

"Abby, there's a letter from Charles solicitor, here," he whispered. "He's left us the Rolls Royce wedding car."

"That'll come in very handy, very soon. Thanks Charles," she said aloud smiling to herself as James turned his attentions to the red haired, blue eyed woman beside him.

"Are you happy, Eden?"

"Ecstatic, mister, jumbo-jet. With you lot around me, I have the best feeling in my heart."

"Could you be any happier?"

"I doubt it."

"I think you could."

"How's that?"

"Oh, you'll see when we get to England," he replied thinking about the small velvet box, in his top pocket.

To be continued…

#

THE MAYAPPLE PLANT

The use of the Mayapple plant on the back-cover dates back centuries to the very first civilizations. Native Americans used it to treat warts, kill parasitic worms and relieve constipation.

Chinese traditional medicine uses a form of it to treat tumors, snakebites & acne.

Fighting cancer is one of the modern uses of Podophylllm. These uses include; uterine, cervical, colon, breast, testicular, lung and lymphoma. Not bad for a plant classed as a poisonous weed.

ABOUT THE AUTHOR:

The Author lives and works in Thurso, in the Highlands of Scotland with his partner, Maria Tamayo and their dog, Blue.

Other Books:

The Market Lads & Me - A Memoir.
(Hard-boiled adult humor)

BRICK LANE - East-end pub share.
(Communal living craziness)

The Time-Travel Twins.
(Future & Past shenanigans)

Children's Titles

A Birds Tale.

Ace has an Accident!

ZAK and ZARA and the INVISIBILITY BALL

MAGNUS and MOLLY and the FLOATING CHAIRS

WINDY and WENDY Get bendy and FLY!

Let's Talk Food!

Raymond's Rainbow

Stinkerbell. The Farting Fairy and the Toxbox Toys

#

Printed in Great Britain
by Amazon

34482656R00163